PRAISE FOR THE OFF-CAMPUS SERIES

"Elle has masterfully captured the feelings, the romance, and the unbridled sexiness of the New Adult genre with this book! You will swoon for Garrett!"

—Alice Clayton, *New York Times* bestselling author

"*The Deal* reminds me of all the reasons I love romance."

—Jane Litte, *Dear Author*

"And she scores again! This is such a romantic read; laughter, swoons, teary moments, *The Score* has got it all and then some! Elle Kennedy once again delivers a fun and delightfully memorable romance."

—Katy Evans, *New York Times* bestselling author

"I loved this book! Garrett is dreamy. If you love NA, you must read *The Deal!*"

—Monica Murphy, *New York Times* bestselling author

"Romance. The most adorable couple. The banter—omg, the banter. The romance. The friends. The flirtation. The smiles it gave me."

—Mandi Schreiner, *Smexy Books*

"This was one of the best college romances I've read… I laughed, I swooned, I couldn't put it down. Highly recommended!"

—*Aestas Book Blog*

"Absolute 'new adult' angsty romance reading PERFECTION!"

—*Maryse's Book Blog*

ALSO AVAILABLE
FROM ELLE KENNEDY

THE SCORE

OFF-CAMPUS

ELLE KENNEDY

Bloom *books*

Published by Bloom Books, an imprint of Sourcebooks
P.O. Box 4410, Naperville, Illinois 60567-4410
(630) 961-3900
sourcebooks.com

Originally self-published in 2016 by Elle Kennedy Inc. This is an updated, edited version.

Cataloging-in-Publication data is on file with the Library of Congress.

Printed and bound in Canada.
MBP 21

CHAPTER 1

ALLIE

Sean: Can we talk?
Sean: Plz??
Sean: WTF, Allie. After everything we've been thru, I deserve more then that.
Sean: You didn't mean it when you said we were done, right?
Sean: Will you plz fuckin ANSWER me?
Sean: You know what? Fuck this. You wanna keep ignoring me? Fine. Whatever.

There are six text messages waiting for me when I check my phone on the way out of the campus fitness center on Friday night. They're all from Sean, my as-of-last-night ex. And although the emotional progression from pleading to pissed off doesn't go unnoticed, I find myself fixating on his grammatical error.

I deserve more then that.

Then, not *than*. And I doubt autocorrect is to blame because Sean isn't exactly the brightest crayon in the box.

Okay, that's not entirely true. He's whip-smart about some things. Like baseball—seriously, the guy can pull stats out of his ass, even ones dating back to the sixties. But book smarts are not his forte. Stellar boyfriend doesn't quite make his list of strengths either, at least not in recent days.

I never wanted to be one of those girls who breaks up and makes up with the same guy over and over again. I really thought I was stronger than that, but Sean McCall has had a hold on me since freshman year at Briar University. He sucked me in with his preppy good looks and little-boy grin. That gorgeous grin, all crooked and dimpled and full of promises.

I glance at my phone again, my wariness climbing like the ivy on the building behind me. Argh. What does he want to talk about? We said everything we needed to say last night. When I told him I was done before I stormed out of his frat house, I'd meant it.

I *am* done. This is our fourth breakup in three years. I can't keep doing this to myself, this twisted cycle of joy and heartache, especially when the person I'm supposed to be building a future with is determined to hold me back.

Even so, my heart hurts. It's hard to let go of someone who's been such a big part of your life for so long. It's even harder when that person refuses to let *you* go.

Sighing, I hurry down the steps toward the cobblestone path that winds through campus. Usually I take the time to admire the scenery—the gorgeous old buildings, the wrought-iron benches and massive shade trees—but tonight I just want to sprint back to my dorm, pull the covers over my head, and shut out the world. Luckily, I can totally do that because my roommate Hannah is away this weekend, which means she won't be around to lecture me about the emotional perils of wallowing in my misery.

She hadn't done much lecturing last night, though. Nope, what she did was step up to the plate and knock the best-friend-ever role out of the park. The moment I'd walked through the door after leaving Sean, Hannah had been waiting in our common room with a carton of ice cream, a box of Kleenex, and two bottles of red wine, and she'd proceeded to stay up half the night passing me tissues and listening to me babble incoherently.

Breakups *suck*. I feel like such a failure. No, I feel like a quitter. The last piece of advice my mom gave me before she died was to never give up on love. Actually, she'd drilled that into me long before she'd ever gotten sick. I don't know all the details, but it was no secret around my house that my parents' marriage had been on the rocks more than once during their eighteen years together. And they'd powered through it. They'd *worked* at it.

Every time I think about walking out on Sean yesterday, my stomach grows queasy. Maybe I should have fought harder for us. I mean, I know he loves me—

If he loved you, he wouldn't have given you an ultimatum, a gruff voice assures me. *You did the right thing.*

My throat tightens as I recognize the voice in my head. It belongs to my father, who happens to be my biggest champion. In his eyes, I can do no wrong.

It's too bad Sean isn't able to see me through that lens.

My phone buzzes when I'm five minutes from Bristol House, where I share a two-bedroom suite with Hannah.

Shit. Another text from Sean.

And double shit because it says: I'm so sorry for swearing at you, bb. I didn't mean it. I'm just upset. You mean the world to me. I hope you know that.

A second text pops up: Coming over after class. We'll talk.

I halt in my tracks, a jolt of panic spiraling through me. I'm not afraid of Sean, at least not in the physical sense. I know he would never lay a hand on me or fly into a manic rage. But I'm afraid of his ability to sweet-talk me. He's *so* good at it. All he has to do is call me *baby* and flash that adorable smile, and I'm a goner.

Anger, dread, and annoyance war for my attention as I reread his messages. He's bluffing. He wouldn't come over uninvited, would he?

Fuckity *fuck*.

With shaky fingers, I pull up Hannah's number. Two rings later and my best friend's reassuring voice echoes on the line. "Hey, what's up? You okay?"

I can hear soft chatter in the background. A female voice—it's Grace Ivers, Logan's girlfriend. That means that Hannah and her boyfriend, Garrett, have already left for their weekend in Boston. She invited me to go with them, but I turned her down because I hadn't wanted to be the fifth wheel. Two madly in love couples and me? No thank you.

Now I wish I'd accepted the invitation, because I'll be all alone this weekend and Sean wants to *talk*.

"Sean's coming over tonight," I blurt out.

Hannah gasps. "What? *No!* Why would you agree to—"

"I didn't agree to anything! He didn't even ask if it was cool. He just messaged saying he's coming by."

"What the hell?" She sounds as displeased as I feel.

"I know, right?" My panic spills over. "I can't see him, Han. I'm still too raw about this breakup. If he comes over, I might end up taking him back."

"Allie—"

"Do you think if I turn off all the lights and lock the door, he'll assume I'm not home and leave?"

"Knowing Sean? He'll wait outside the door all night." Hannah curses. "You know what? I shouldn't have agreed to go to this Bruins game. I should be home with you. Hold on, I'm telling Garrett to turn the car around—"

"No way," I interrupt. "You are *not* canceling your trip for me. This is your last chance to do something fun."

Hannah's boyfriend is the captain of the Briar hockey team, which means his practice and game schedule will be jam-packed now that the season has started. Which means Hannah won't get to see him as much. I refuse to be the one who ruins a rare weekend of freedom for them.

"I just want advice." I swallow hard. "So please, tell me what to do. Should I ask Tracy if I can crash in her room?"

"No, you don't want to be in Bristol if Sean's wandering the halls. Maybe Megan— No, wait, her new boyfriend is in town this weekend. They'll probably want to be alone." Hannah sounds thoughtful. "What about Stella?"

"She and Justin just moved in together last week. They're not going to want a last-minute houseguest."

"Hold on a sec." There's another long pause. I hear Garrett's muffled voice, but I can't make out what he's saying. Then Hannah is back. "Garrett says you can stay at his place this weekend. Dean and Tuck will both be there, so if Sean figures out where you went and drops by, they'll kick him to the curb." The murmur of voices fills the background again. "You can sleep in Garrett's room," she adds.

Indecision flashes through me. I mean, this is ridiculous. I can't believe I'm considering letting Sean drive me out of my own dorm. But my mind is flooded with images of him pounding on my door. Or worse, pulling a *Say Anything* and standing outside my window with a boombox. Ugh, what if he plays the Peter Gabriel song? I *hate* that song.

"Are you sure it's okay?" I ask.

"Yup. Totally fine. Logan's texting Dean and Tucker right now to let them know. You can head over any time."

Relief trickles through me, along with a pang of guilt. "Put me on speakerphone? I want to talk to Garrett."

"Sure. One sec."

A moment later, Garrett Graham's deep voice comes on the line. "Clean sheets are in the linen closet, and you might want to bring your own pillow. Wellsy thinks mine are too soft."

"They *are* too soft," Hannah protests. "It's like sleeping on a soggy marshmallow."

"It's like sleeping on a fluffy cloud," Garrett corrects. "Trust me,

Allie, my pillows rock. But you should still bring your own, just in case."

I laugh. "Thanks for the heads-up. But are you sure it's cool? I don't want to impose."

"S'all good, sweetheart. Just bat those big blue eyes at Tuck and he'll cook you up a nice dinner. Oh, and Logan's ordering Dean not to hit on you, so you don't have to worry about him perving you out."

Yeah, right. Dean Heyward-Di Laurentis is the biggest flirt on the planet. Every time I see him he's trying to get in my pants. And I can't even feel special about it, because he tries to get in *everyone's* pants.

I'm not worried, though. I know how to handle Dean, and Tucker will serve as a good buffer between me and his horndog roommate.

"I really appreciate this," I tell Garrett. "Seriously. I owe you one."

"Nah."

Hannah speaks up. "Text me when you get there, 'kay? And then turn off your phone so Sean can't harass you."

Did I mention how much I love my bestie?

I hang up feeling immensely better. Maybe it's smart to get out of the dorms for the weekend. I can view it as a nice little retreat, a few days to clear my head and regroup. And as long as Tucker and Dean are around, I won't be tempted to call Sean. We need a clean break this time. No contact whatsoever, at least for a few weeks. Or months. Or years.

Truthfully, I don't know if I'll survive this breakup. I've loved this guy for years. And Sean does have his sweet moments. Like all the times he showed up at my door with soup when I was sick. And when he—

Backslide alert!

Alarm bells wail in my head, alerting me to my stupidity. Nope. Not letting myself backslide. It doesn't matter that he was capable of being sweet—because he was also capable of *not* being sweet, as last night proved.

I square my shoulders and walk faster, determined to stick to the game plan. Sean and I are over. I can't see him or text him or do anything that places myself in his path right now.

Day one of my Sean-free existence has officially commenced.

DEAN

It's Friday night and I'm sprawled on my living room couch, sipping a beer while two blonds—two very hot, very naked blonds—suck each other's tongues in front of me. My life is awesome.

"Best night ever," I drawl. My gaze is glued to the trajectory of Kelly's hands as they glide toward Michelle's perky tits. Kelly squeezes, and I groan. "Would be even better if you ladies brought the party over here."

They break apart breathlessly, laughing as they glance my way. "Give us a reason to," Kelly teases.

I arch a brow, then reach down to grip my rock-hard dick. I give it a slow pump. "This ain't reason enough?"

Michelle is the first to sashay toward me, her tits jiggling and ass swaying as she climbs into my lap and presses her mouth to mine. A second later, Kelly is nestled at my side, her warm, soft lips latching onto my neck. Je-sus. I'm so hard it hurts, but these two goddesses are determined to make me beg for it. They torture me with kisses. Long, drugging kisses and wet, wicked tongues, strategic licks and gentle bites designed to drive me wild.

I'd like to say that this dirty little threesome of ours is a new experience for me, or that the man-whore label my hockey teammates have slapped me with has been an exaggeration. But it's not, and the label is spot-on. I like to fuck. I fuck a lot. So sue me.

I grunt when Kelly's fingers circle my shaft. "Christ. How did I get so lucky?"

"You haven't gotten lucky yet," Michelle says, tossing her long hair over her shoulder. "You don't come until we do, remember?"

She's right—I'd made a promise, and I intend to keep it.

Contrary to what my asshole friends believe about me, sex is all about the woman for me. Or in this case, the *women.* Two beautiful, eager women who are not only into me, but each other.

Hey, heaven? Dean Di Laurentis here. Thanks for letting me visit.

"Well. I guess I should get started, then," I announce, and then I lower Michelle onto the cushion and bring my mouth to her breasts.

I capture a nipple and suck hard, and her hips buck off the couch as she moans. A shadow crosses the corner of my eye. Kelly bends over beside me and licks Michelle's other nipple. Oh sweet Jesus. I groan loud enough to wake the dead.

Kelly peeks up to smile at me. "Figured you could use some help." Then she kisses her way down Michelle's flat stomach toward the juncture of her friend's thighs.

Forget heaven. This is nirvana.

I follow the path Kelly has taken, my lips traveling over tanned skin and sweet curves until I reach the place that makes my mouth water. Kelly's already licking it. Holy hell. I'm not sure I can control myself long enough to get them both off. I'm too close to the edge already.

Ignoring the throbbing down below, I moisten my bottom lip, inch my mouth toward Michelle's pussy, and...the goddamn doorbell rings.

Fucking hell. I crane my neck toward the entertainment center. The digital clock on display reads 8:30. I try to remember if I told any of the guys they could come over tonight, but I haven't spoken to anyone but my roommates today, and they're all AWOL. Garrett and Logan left for Boston an hour ago with their girls, and Tucker's taking some chick to the movies tonight.

"Hold that thought." I lick Michelle's thigh in a teasing stroke, then rise from the couch and search for my boxers.

Once my cock is tucked away, I hurry down the hall to answer the door. When I see who's standing on the stoop, I narrow my eyes.

"Bad timing, baby doll," I tell Hannah's best friend. "Your girl's already gone. Come back on Sunday." I move to close the door. Yup, I'm a rude SOB.

Unfortunately, the blond on the doorstep wedges one black snow boot between the door and its frame. "Don't be an ass, Dean. You know I'm spending the weekend."

My eyebrows soar up. "Um, what?" I take a closer look at her, and that's when I notice the overstuffed backpack hanging off her shoulder. And the pink carry-on suitcase by her feet.

Allie Hayes heaves a huge sigh. "Logan texted you all about it. Now let me in. I'm cold."

I tilt my head. Then I not so gently kick her foot out of the way. "Wait here. I'll be right back."

"Are you *kidding* me—"

The door closes on her outraged exclamation.

Battling annoyance, I dart back to the living room, where Michelle and Kelly don't even notice my reappearance—they're too busy making out. It takes almost a minute to find my phone, and when I finally grab it off the floor, I discover that Hannah's friend wasn't messing with me.

There are five unread messages on the screen, which is what happens when you're the meat in a hot girl sandwich. Threesomes trump checking your phone. That's a no-brainer.

Logan: Hey, bro, Wellsy's friend Allie is crashing at our place this weekend.
Logan: Keep your dick in your pants. G and I aren't in the mood to beat you senseless if you try something. Wellsy might be in the mood for violence, tho. So: dick = pants = don't bother our guest.
Hannah: Allie's staying with you guys til Sunday. She's in a vulnerable place right now. Don't take advantage of her or else I'll be unhappy. And you don't want to make me unhappy, do you?

I snicker. Hannah, diplomatic as always. I quickly scan the last two messages.

Garrett: Allie's gonna crash in my room.
Garrett: Your dick can stay in your room.

Jeez, what is everybody's fascination with my dick?

And could their timing be any worse? My rueful gaze shifts back to the couch. Kelly's fingers are exactly where I wish mine were right now.

I clear my throat and both girls glance over. Michelle's expression is hazy from the extra special attention her friend is giving her.

"I really hate to do this, but you ladies need to go," I tell them.

Two pairs of eyes widen. "Excuse me?" Kelly blurts out.

"I've got an unexpected houseguest waiting outside," I grumble. "Which means this house just became a PG zone."

Michelle snickers. "Since when do you care if anyone sees you fucking?"

True. Usually I don't give a damn if there's anyone around. Most times I prefer it. But I can't expose my debauchery to Hannah's friend. Or to Hannah and Grace, for that matter. The boys, who cares. They know the drill. But I know Garrett and Logan wouldn't be cool with me corrupting their girlfriends. The moment they entered committed-relationship territory, my former wingmen turned into prudes. It's sad, really.

"This guest is a delicate flower," I say dryly. "She'd probably faint if she saw the three of us together."

"I would not." Allie's annoyed voice comes from the doorway.

I'm equally annoyed. Chick just walks into the house like she owns it? Nuh-uh.

I scowl at her. "I told you to wait outside."

"And I told you I was cold," she shoots back. And she seems to have no issue with the fact that there are two naked girls ten feet away.

My guests study Allie as if she's a splotch of bacteria under their microscopes. Then they wrinkle their noses and dismiss her from their sights as if she's, well, nothing but a splotch of bacteria under their microscopes. Chicks tend to get competitive when I'm around, but obviously these ones don't view Allie as competition.

Not sure I blame them. She's wearing a puffy black jacket, boots, and mittens, and her blond hair is sticking out from the bottom of a red knit hat. It's the first week of November—there's no snow on the ground, barely a chill in the air, and nothing to warrant bundling up. Unless you're a crazy person. Which I'm starting to suspect Allie Hayes might be, because the girl brazenly waltzes into the living room and flops down in the armchair opposite the couch.

As she unzips her coat, she spares a glance at my guests, then turns back to me. "Why don't you move this little party upstairs? I'll stay down here and watch a movie or something."

"Or you can go to Garrett's room and watch a movie up there," I say pointedly. But truthfully, it doesn't matter. She's already killed the mood, and I don't feel comfortable fooling around with two chicks when it's just me and Hannah's best friend in the house.

Sighing, I turn to the girls. "Rain check?"

Neither of them puts up much of a fight. Apparently Miss Allie didn't just *kill* the mood; she scorched the fuckin' earth and covered it with salt to prevent horniness from ever growing back.

Allie barely pays attention to the girls getting dressed. She's too busy removing a thousand layers of winter clothing and draping them over the side of the armchair. When she's done, she looks substantially tinier in black leggings and an oversize striped top, and she wastes no time making herself comfortable on the big plush chair.

I walk Kelly and Michelle to the door, where each one practically chews my face off before telling me they're holding me to that rain check. By the time they're gone, my lips are swollen and my cock is hard again.

I return to the living room with a frown that refuses to quit. "Did you enjoy that?" I demand.

"Enjoy what?"

"Cockblocking me."

Allie laughs. "Is there any reason you couldn't have taken Blond and Blonder upstairs? You didn't have to kick them out on my account."

"You really think I could screw around knowing you're sitting downstairs?"

That gets me another laugh. "You screw around in *public*. All the time. Why do you care if I'm in the house?" She looks thoughtful. "Unless going up to your room is the issue. Hannah said you always fool around in the living room. What's the deal with that? Do you have bedbugs or something?"

I grit my teeth. "No."

"Then why don't you want to do your naked stuff up there?"

"Because—" I halt, the scowl returning to my face. "It's none of your business. Why are you here, anyway? Did Bristol House catch fire?"

"I'm in hiding." She says it as if I'm supposed to understand that. Then she glances around the living room. "Where's Tucker? Garrett said he'd be here."

"He's out."

She sticks out her bottom lip. "Well, that sucks. He totally would've watched a movie with me. But I guess you'll have to do."

"You cockblock me and now you expect us to hang out?"

"Trust me, you're the last person I want to hang out with, but I'm in crisis mode right now and you're the only one here. You *have* to keep me company, Dean. Otherwise I'll do something really stupid and my whole life will be ruined."

I seem to remember Hannah telling me Allie is a drama major. Yeah. Sounds about right.

"Please?"

Her pleading expression doesn't let up. And I've always been a sucker for big blue eyes. Especially when they belong to cute blonds with great racks.

"You win," I relent. "I'll keep you company, okay?"

She lights up. "What movie should we watch?"

A groan lodges in my throat. My Friday night went from hot threesome sex to babysitting my best friend's girlfriend's best friend.

Oh, and I'm still rock hard thanks to Kelly and Michelle's goodbye kisses.

Fucking wonderful.

CHAPTER 2

ALLIE

My self-control rests in the hands of Dean Heyward-Di Laurentis, a man known for zero self-control. Ergo, I'm in trouble. Big fucking trouble.

I won't do it, though. I won't call Sean. Doesn't matter that twenty minutes ago he sent me a picture of the two of us from our Mexico trip last year. He'd used one of those framing apps to draw a big red heart around our faces.

It had been a really good trip...

I push the memory aside and grab the remote control off the coffee table. "Do you have Netflix linked to your TV?" I glance back at Dean, who still looks aggravated by my presence.

And either I'm imagining it or he has an erection. But I'm nice enough not to tease him about it, because in his defense, he was five seconds away from having sex with two girls before I showed up.

My gaze travels over his bare chest. I cannot tell a lie—his chest is absolutely spectacular. The guy's *ripped*. Tall and lean, with perfectly sculpted muscles. And he's rocking some scruff—sexy blond bristles that shadow his perfectly chiseled jaw. It really is a shame. Someone this douchey shouldn't be allowed to look this good.

"Yeah. Go ahead and pick something to watch," he answers. "I'm just popping upstairs to jerk it and then I'll join you."

"Okay, I think I'm in the mood for— Wait, what?"

But he's already gone, leaving me gaping at the empty doorway. He's popping upstairs to do *what*? He was joking, right?

Despite my better judgment, I picture it. Dean up in his room. One hand wrapped around his dick, the other hand…cupping his balls? Clutching the sheets? Or maybe he's standing up and gripping the side of his desk, his features drawn as he bites his bottom lip…

And *why* am I trying to solve the mystery of how this guy masturbates?

Shaking myself out of it, I click the remote until I find Netflix, then start browsing the latest movie titles.

Less than five minutes later, Dean saunters back into the room. Thankfully he put on some pants. Except he ditched his boxers in the process, which I know because his sweatpants are riding so low on his hips I can almost see…places I have no interest in seeing.

His chest is still bare, and there's a slight flush to his cheeks.

"Did you seriously jerk off just now?" I demand.

He nods as if it's no biggie. "What, you think I can sit through a whole movie with blue balls?"

I gawk at him. "So you can't have sex with anyone while I'm in the house, but you can go upstairs and do *that*?"

A wolfish grin stretches his mouth. "I could've done it down here, but then you would've been too tempted to take over for me. I was trying to be nice."

It's hard not to roll my eyes. So I don't bother fighting the urge. "Trust me, I would have kept my hands to myself."

"With my cock right there in the open? No way. You wouldn't be able to help yourself." He arches a brow. "I have a great cock."

"Uh-huh. I'm sure you do."

"You don't believe me? I can show you a picture." He reaches for the phone on the coffee table. Then he stops and grabs the waistband of his sweatpants instead. "Actually, I can show you the real thing if you want."

"I don't want. In the slightest." I gesture to the TV. "I picked that one. Have you seen it?"

Dean grimaces at the movie poster on the screen. "For chrissake, *that's* what you chose? There're like three new horror movies we could watch. Or Jason Statham's entire filmography."

"No horror movies," I say firmly. "I don't like to be scared."

"Fine. So let's do an action movie."

"I don't like violence."

His cheeks hollow in frustration. "Baby doll, I am not watching a movie about"—he squints at the screen—"'a woman's life-changing journey after being diagnosed with a terminal illness.' No fucking way."

"It's supposed to be really good," I protest. "It won an Oscar!"

"You know what else won an Oscar? *Silence of the Lambs. Jaws. The Exorcist.*" He sounds smug. "And they're all horror movies."

"We can argue about this all night, but I'm not watching anything with blood or sharks or explosions. Deal with it."

Dean's teeth are visibly clenched. Then his jaw relaxes and he releases a heavy breath. "Fine. If I have to suffer through this crap movie, I'm smoking a joint first."

"Whatever gets you through it, sweetie."

He walks toward the doorway, grumbling something under his breath.

"Wait," I call after him. I quickly fish my phone out of my jacket pocket. "Can you take this with you? I might give in to texting temptation if I'm left alone with it."

He gives me a weird look. "Who you trying not to text?"

"My ex. We broke up last night and he won't stop messaging me."

There's a pause. "You know what? You're coming with me."

I barely have time to blink before Dean crosses the room and tugs me off the chair. When my feet connect with the hardwood floor, I lose my balance and stumble right into his massive chest, my nose bumping one defined pec.

I quickly steady myself, armed with a glare. "I was comfy, you ass."

He ignores me, half leading, half dragging me to the kitchen. Since he didn't even let me grab my jacket, I start shivering the second we step through the back door.

Dean's bare chest gleams under the patio light. He doesn't seem bothered by the cold, but his nipples pucker slightly in the chilly night air.

"Ugh. You even have perfect nipples," I gripe.

His lips twitch. "Do you wanna touch 'em?"

"Ew. Never. I'm just commenting that they're frickin' perfect. Like, totally proportioned to your chest."

He peers down at his pecs and considers for a moment. "Yeah. I *am* perfect. I need to remind myself of that more often."

I snort. "Right. Because you're not already conceited enough."

"I'm confident," he corrects.

"Conceited."

"*Confident.*" He pops open the small tin box he grabbed from the kitchen, and I scowl when he extracts a neatly rolled joint and a Zippo.

"Why am I out here?" I grumble. "I don't want to smoke weed."

"Sure you do." He lights up and takes a deep drag, then speaks through the escaping cloud of smoke. "You're acting all jittery and weird. Trust me, you need this."

"This is peer pressure, you know."

He holds out the joint, one eyebrow raised. "Come on, baby," he coaxes in a singsong voice. "Just one toke. All the cool kids are doing it."

I can't help but laugh. "Fuck off."

"Suit yourself." He exhales again, and the scent of marijuana surrounds me.

I can't remember the last time I got high. I don't do it often, but honestly? If any night merits some weed-induced serenity, it's this one.

"Oh, fine. Give it to me." I stick out my hand before I can second-guess myself.

Dean is beaming as he passes it over. "That's my girl. But don't tell Wellsy. She'll kick my ass if she thinks I'm corrupting her best friend."

I wrap my lips around the joint and draw the smoke into my lungs, trying not to laugh at the genuine apprehension on Dean's face. He's probably right to be afraid of Hannah. Girl's got a sharp tongue and she isn't afraid to use it. That's why I love her.

We spend the next couple minutes passing the joint back and forth in silence like a couple of hooligans loitering behind a gas station. This is the first time we've spent any time alone together, and it feels weird hanging out in the backyard with a shirtless Dean Di Laurentis. If I'm being honest, I've never known what to make of the guy. He's cocky, flirtatious...

Superficial.

I feel like an ass for thinking it, but I can't deny that's what comes to mind whenever I see Dean. Hannah told me he's filthy rich, and it totally shows. Not in the pompous, watch-me-roll-around-in-my-money-vault sense, but in the way he struts around like the world is his oyster. I have a feeling he's never experienced a second of hardship in his life. Looking at him, you just *know* this guy gets whatever he wants, whenever he wants it.

Huh. And apparently marijuana makes me both philosophical *and* judgmental.

"So you got dumped?" he finally asks, watching me take another hit.

I blow smoke right in his face. "I did not get dumped. I'm the one who ended it."

"The same guy you've been with forever? The frat guy? Stan?"

"Sean. And yeah, we've been dating on and off since freshman year."

"Jesus. That's way too long to be screwing the same person. Was the sex really boring?"

"Why is everything with you always about sex?" I pass the joint back. "And FYI—the sex was fine."

"Fine?" He snickers. "Wow, what a ringing endorsement."

I'm already feeling the effects of the weed, my head light and my body relaxed, which is probably the only reason I keep talking. Normally, I wouldn't dream of confiding in this guy.

"I guess it wasn't the best by the end," I admit. "But maybe that's because we've pretty much been fighting since the summer."

"But this isn't the first breakup, right? Why'd you keep going back to him?"

"Because I love him." I correct myself. "*Loved* him." God, I don't even know anymore. "The first couple times we broke up, it wasn't because either of us did anything wrong. I thought we were getting too serious, too fast. It was freshman year, and it seemed like we should be sowing our wild oats and all that crap."

"Sowing oats is fun," he agrees solemnly. "One time I sowed this really hot oat who poured maple syrup all over my dick and then licked it off."

"Ew." I roll my eyes. "And actually, the oat sowing sucked. I went out with a few guys and they were all total sleazebags. It made me realize how good I had it with Sean."

Dean blows another cloud of smoke. "Okay. But then you guys broke up again."

"Yeah." The memory evokes a rush of aggravation. "That time it was because he got insanely controlling. One of his frat brothers hit on me at a party, and Sean decided that nobody was ever allowed to look at me again. He started telling me how to dress, texting all the time asking where I was and who I was with. It was suffocating."

It's Dean's turn to roll his eyes. "Says the chick who got back together with him afterward."

"He promised it would be different. And it was. He stopped being clingy, and he was *so* good to me after that."

Dean seems unconvinced, but I don't care. I don't regret taking Sean back. After two and a half years with the guy, I knew we had something worth fighting for.

"Which brings us to breakup number four." Dean slants his head curiously. "What happened?"

Discomfort squeezes my chest. "I told you. We were fighting a lot."

"About what?"

The words spill out before I can stop them. Damn it. Did he lace this weed with truth serum or something? "Mostly about graduation and what we're going to do after college. My plan was always to move to LA and focus on my acting career."

Or New York… But I don't mention that to Dean. I still haven't made any decisions, and Dean is the last person I want to discuss deep, life-changing career moves with. The guy's about as deep as a puddle.

"Sean was okay with it when we first started dating, but this summer he suddenly decided he doesn't want me to go into acting. Actually, he doesn't want me to work at all." I frown. "He got it into his head that he's going to work at his dad's insurance firm in Vermont and I'm going to be the happy homemaker who has dinner waiting for him when he gets home."

Dean shrugs. "Nothing wrong with being a homemaker."

"Of course not, but I don't want to be a homemaker," I say in frustration. "I've spent almost four years working my ass off to earn this drama degree. I want to *use* it. I want to be an actress, and I can't be with someone who doesn't support me. He—" I stop, biting my lip.

"He what?"

"Nothing. Forget it." I snatch the joint from his hand and inhale deeply. Too deeply, because I start coughing like crazy on the exhale. My eyes water for a moment, and when my vision clears, I find serious green eyes watching me carefully.

"What did he do?" Dean demands in a low voice. "And how bad of a beatdown does he deserve? Me and Garrett can handle our own in a fight, but if you want some bone-crushing, we can unleash Logan on him."

"Nobody is crushing anybody's bones, dumbass. Sean didn't do anything terrible, and I don't need you to beat him up. The only thing I want you to do is take this stupid phone." I shove my cell phone in Dean's hand. "Keep it away from me this weekend, okay? Only give it back if my dad calls. Or Hannah and Stella. And Meg and— You know what? I'll check it a few times a day under your supervision. That way you can slap me if I try to text Sean."

Dean looks intrigued. "So I'm…what, your relationship sponsor? I'm the one who makes sure you don't fall off the wagon?"

"Yep. Congratulations, you finally get to do something worthwhile with your time," I say sarcastically.

He tips his head. "What do I get in return?"

"The satisfaction of knowing you're helping someone other than yourself?"

"Nah. How about a BJ? I'll do it for a BJ."

I give him the finger. "You wish."

"Fine, an HJ."

"Don't be a dick. Please. I have no willpower when it comes to Sean."

As if on cue, the phone buzzes in Dean's hand, and my first instinct is to try to grab it. He swiftly takes a step back, then glances at the screen. "It's Sean." His mouth quivers in amusement. "He misses the taste of your lips."

My heart does a painful flip. "Another rule: You're not allowed to tell me what he says."

"You're giving me a lot of responsibility here, baby doll. I don't like responsibility."

Shocker. "You can handle this, *baby doll*. I have faith in you."

Dean takes one final drag of the joint, then snuffs it out in the ashtray and heads for the sliding glass door. God, even the way he walks is arrogant. And he looks good doing it. My gaze unwittingly rests on his taut ass and the way his sweatpants cling to it. Yep, I'm checking out his ass. I mean, it's a spectacular ass, and I'm a *woman*—how could I not?

"You're going about this the wrong way, you know. The best way to get over someone is to hook up with someone else. ASAP."

His words jolt me out of my butt ogling. "I'm not ready to be with anyone else yet."

"Sure you are. Seriously, just find yourself a rebound." Dean whips up his arm. "I volunteer as tribute."

A laugh flies out. "Dream on."

But in the back of my mind, I'm considering the suggestion. A rebound isn't a terrible idea, actually. It's like falling off a horse— people always advise you to immediately get back on, right? Maybe that's what I should do, hop right back in the saddle. If anything, it'll be a good distraction from the ache in my heart.

I definitely won't be doing it with Dean, though. Nope, I'd rather find a saddle that hasn't already been ridden by every girl at Briar.

"We'll put a pin in it," he decides.

"If by that you mean sticking a pin in this stupid idea balloon and deflating it, then sure, let's put a pin in it."

Dean stops at the door and turns, his green eyes doing a seductive sweep from my head down to my toes. "Actually, the more I think about it, the more I like the idea of rebounding you." His gaze lingers on my chest. "I like the idea *a lot.*"

I stifle a groan. "Garrett promised that you wouldn't hit on me this weekend."

"G knows better than to make promises on my behalf," Dean answers with a grin. Then he beckons me. "So are we watching this movie or what?"

I follow him inside. My mind feels foggy from the weed, but in a good way, and when Dean stops in the hall to hike up the sweatpants that are about to fall off his trim hips, for some reason I start giggling as if it's the funniest thing I've ever seen.

My humor fades when we settle on the couch, because Dean flops down directly beside me, slings one muscular arm around my shoulders, and tugs me close. As if it's totally normal.

I frown at him. "Why is your arm around me?"

His expression is all innocence. "This is how I watch movies."

"Really? So you put your arm around Garrett when you watch movies with him?"

"Absolutely. And if he's nice to me, sometimes I slide my hand down his pants." Dean's other hand skims down to the waistband of my leggings. "Be nice to me, and I promise I'll be even nicer in return."

"Ha. Not happening." I shove his hand away, but not before a spark of heat ignites between my legs. His bare chest is glorious, and it's taunting me, begging my fingers to stroke all those roped muscles. And he smells really good. Like the ocean. No, like coconut. I'm feeling way too loopy to pinpoint the scent, but not loopy enough that I don't register how my pussy is still tingling like crazy.

Oh, for crying out loud. My sex life must have really gone to the shitter if I'm getting all tingly in the presence of Dean Di Laurentis.

"What else do we have to do?" he counters.

I point to the TV. "Watch a movie."

"I'd rather be watching you." He waggles his eyebrows. "You know, when you're shouting my name while I make you come."

This time there aren't any tingles. Just a lot of laughter that pours out of my mouth in uncontrollable waves.

"Jesus. You're really bad for a man's ego." He looks insulted.

I suck in a gulp of air between giggles. Yep, I'm high and relaxed and in possession of no filters whatsoever, which means I can make fun of Dean all I want and blame the weed later. "I'm sorry, but you're too fucking much sometimes." I can't stop laughing. "Do girls really fall for these lines?"

He makes an unflattering noise under his breath. "Put on the damn movie already."

"Gladly." I click the remote and shift all the way to the other side of the couch, leaving three feet of distance between us.

To Dean's credit, he doesn't say a word for nearly thirty minutes. His gaze stays focused on the screen, but from the corner of my eye, I don't miss all the fidgeting he's doing. Tapping his long fingers on his thighs. Raking a hand through his hair. Heaving a sigh as we watch the main character prepare an omelet in real time.

When she sits at the counter and starts eating the omelet—in *real time*—Dean erupts like a dormant volcano.

"This movie blows!" He groans. Loudly. "There. I said it. This goddamn movie goddamn *blows*."

"I think it's good." I'm lying. Enduring this film is the equivalent of watching paint dry. Not even the pot we just smoked can make this experience even the slightest bit enjoyable, but I don't want to admit that I'd made the wrong choice. You can't give a guy like Dean the win. Ever. He'll lord it over me until the end of time.

"There's no way you like this movie," he challenges.

"I do," I insist.

He stares me down for several seconds, but my acting skills come in handy, allowing me to convey pure innocence.

"Well, I don't. This is a whole new level of brutal."

I offer a helpful suggestion. "Why don't you go upstairs and jerk off again?"

Shit. Wrong thing to say. His green eyes instantly take on a seductive glint.

With a lazy grin, he leans toward me and drawls, "How about you do it for me?"

This guy is incorrigible. "Are we back to this? Do you *ever* take no for an answer?"

"I'm not familiar with that word. Nobody's ever said it to me before." He moves closer again, resting his palm on the cushion between us and giving the fabric a slow stroke. "Come on, let's make this party more interesting. We're home alone… We're both good-looking…"

I snicker.

"It'll be fun. Sex is always fun."

"Pass."

"Okay, no sex. How about just oral?"

I pretend to think it over. "Am I giving or receiving?"

"Receiving. And then giving. Because that's how it goes." He smiles broadly. "You know, the circle of life and all that."

I can't help but laugh. Say what you want about this guy, but at least he's entertaining. "Pass," I say again.

"Wanna make out?" he asks hopefully.

"Nope."

"I'm a really good kisser…" He leaves that hanging as if to entice me.

"Ha. That just means you're not. Every time a guy says he's a good kisser, he sucks."

"Yeah? You got any empirical evidence to back that up?"

"Of course." I really don't. And Dean knows the word *empirical*? Wow, maybe there is more than air inside that pretty head of his.

He looks ready to argue with me, but we're interrupted by a loud burst of music from his phone. I scowl when I recognize the tune.

Men. They can't take one second to put the toilet seat down, but they have the time to program the ESPN theme song as their ringtone?

Dean's expression brightens when he sees who's calling. He answers without delay. "Maxwell! What's shaking?" He listens, then shoots me a hopeful look. "Wanna go to a party?"

I shake my head.

The person on the other end of the line is forced to endure Dean's overly dramatic sigh. "Sorry, man. I can't. I'm babysitting—"

I smack him on the arm.

"—and she doesn't want to go," he finishes as he glares at me. He pauses again. "No, she's fully grown."

What?

"I'm babysitting an adult, dude. G's girlfriend's friend." Dean rambles on as if I'm not even in the room. "We're watching this movie about a lady with cancer and it sucks... Well yeah, cancer sucks in general. I mean, all my sympathies for people who have it, but this movie is god-awful. Yeah... No, game's on Tuesday... Truth... Yeah, definitely. We can hit up Malone's. Later, bro."

He hangs up and turns to scowl at me. "I could be at a party right now."

"Nobody's forcing you to hang out with me," I point out.

"I'm *trying* to be nice to you, on account of your poor broken heart and all. But is there any gratitude on your part? Nope. You won't even kiss me."

I lean in and pat him on the shoulder. "Aw, honey pie. I'm sure any girl in your phone's contact list would be happy to come over and stick her tongue in your mouth. I, on the other hand, have standards."

"What, I'm not good enough for you?" He lifts his eyebrows. "I'll have you know, your friend Wellsy loved kissing me."

I snort. "Oh, you mean that peck she gave you so Garrett wouldn't know how much she liked kissing *him*? Yeah, I know all about it, sweetie. That was a desperation kiss." Though it still boggles my mind that Hannah actually kissed this guy. Dean is *so* not her type.

Then again, I never thought hockey superstar Garrett Graham was her type either, and look at them now. Soul mates.

"That wasn't a desperation kiss," Dean argues.

"Uh-huh. Keep telling yourself that."

He looks at the screen. The main character is preparing food again. Dinner, this time, and there are far too many unnecessary close-ups of the potatoes she's peeling. She eats a lot in this movie.

"God, just kill me already." He leans back and runs both his hands through his hair until it's tousled to shit. "I can't watch another second of this."

Me neither, but I made this bed and now I'm forced to lie in it.

"You know what?" he announces. "Forget the weed. Only one thing is gonna make this piece-of-shit movie tolerable."

"Yeah, what's that?"

Rather than answer, he hops off the couch and disappears into the kitchen. Wary, I listen to the sounds of cupboards opening and closing, glasses clinking together, and then he's back, holding a bottle in one hand and two shot glasses in the other.

Dean flashes a grin and says, "Tequila."

CHAPTER 3

ALLIE

Someone is pounding my head with a mallet. Like one of those comically huge mallets you see cartoon characters whacking each other with. It's horrible. It's loud.

Oh God. I'm so hungover.

Even the barely audible groan that escapes my lips is enough to bring a shock of agony to my temples. And the act of shifting in bed evokes a wave of nausea that tightens my throat and makes my eyes water. I breathe through it. Inhale. Exhale. I just need to control the queasiness long enough to make it to the bathroom so I don't hurl all over Garrett Graham's clean sheets—

I'm not in Garrett's bed.

The realization hits me at the same time I register the sound of breathing. Not the shallow, I-drank-too-much-tequila breaths that are leaving my throat, but the soft, even breathing of the guy beside me.

This time when I groan, it comes from deep in my soul.

The memories come crashing back in vivid Technicolor. The terrible movie. The tequila shots. The…rest.

I slept with Dean last night.

Twice.

My heart beats faster as I stare up at the ceiling. I'm in Dean's

room. There's an empty condom wrapper on the end table. And…
yep, I'm naked.

Maybe it was a bad dream, a voice in my head tries to assure me.

I draw another deep breath and find the courage to turn my
head. What I encounter seizes my lungs again.

A very naked Dean is stretched out on his stomach. His bare ass
taunts me, not just with its sheer perfection, but because of the red
scratches on his tight butt cheeks.

My nails left those scratches. I lift a weak hand and notice the
fingernail on my index finger is broken. I *broke a nail* while clawing
at Dean's ass. That must have happened downstairs—I remember
him being on top the first time on the couch. The purplish hickey
on his left shoulder had happened up here, during our second round
when *I* was on top.

*"I want to see this mysterious bedroom of yours. I want to be the first
one to christen it."*

My own words buzz around in my already muddled brain. As it
turned out, I'm not the first girl he's brought up to his room. He'd
told me so himself. And that wasn't all he'd revealed. Yep, I am now
in possession of the nugget of knowledge Hannah has been trying to
get her hands on for more than a year—why Dean prefers to screw
everywhere but his bedroom.

Unfortunately, the knowledge doesn't end there. I know what
Dean looks like naked. I know how it feels to have him thrusting
inside me. I know the sounds he makes when he's coming.

I know too much.

My head pounds harder.

Fuck.

Fuckity fuck fuck *fuck*.

What the hell have I done? I've never had casual sex before. My
sex roster features a total of three guys—two in high school, one in
college, and all of them were serious boyfriends.

My gaze strays back to Dean's long, muscular body. Why did

I let this happen? I can handle my liquor just fine. I wasn't black-out drunk last night. I wasn't slurring or stumbling or acting like an idiot. I knew exactly what I was doing when I made the first move and kissed Dean.

I made the first move.

What is the matter with me?

Okay. Okay. Not the end of the world. I massage my scream-ing temples with the pads of my fingers and force myself to ignore the sleeping man beside me. It's fine. It was just a one-night stand. Nobody died. I might regret it—desperately—but regrets are for sissies, as my dad likes to say. Learn from your mistakes and move on.

That's what I need to do. Move on. No, just *move*. As in, sneak out of this bed, take a long shower, and pretend that last night never happened.

Armed with a plan, I gingerly slide out from under the sheet that's haphazardly thrown over my lower body. The mattress squeaks and I freeze, my panicky gaze darting toward Dean.

He's still dead to the world.

Okay. I take another breath and ease my legs over the side of the bed. When my feet hit the floor, Dean stirs. He releases a half moan, half breath. Then he rolls over and *oh my God*, I can see his dick.

Heat floods my cheeks as I stare at his package. Even flaccid, it's impressive. He was right—he does have a great cock.

And unless my memory is failing me, I believe I vocally praised the glory of that cock many, many times last night.

My face grows hotter as I remember everything I said to him. Everything I did to him.

A silent groan rises in my throat. All right, enough reminiscing. I need to get the hell out of this bedroom. No, first I need to find my phone.

I scan the room until I spot Dean's sweatpants. He'd slipped them on after our romp on the couch, and I'm pretty sure my phone is in his pocket.

My own clothes are nowhere to be found—last I saw them, they were in a pile on the living room floor. Which only brings more panic, because that means Tucker must have seen them when he got home last night. Shit. And he had to have heard us, because God knows I wasn't using my indoor voice when Dean's tongue was between my—

Nope, not thinking about it.

I fish around in his pockets for my phone. Yes. It's here. Thank God.

I type in my passcode. Guilt slams into me from all directions when I see the unread messages from Sean.

God. If he only knew what I'd been doing when he was sending me all these heartfelt text messages. Not that I owe him any explanations. We're broken up. We're going to stay broken up. But I still feel awful knowing I slept with someone else while Sean was at home, desperately trying to win me back.

Not just any guy either. I slept with *Dean*. Dean, the guy who was about to have a threesome before I showed up. Dean, the guy who fucks anyone with a pulse. Dean, the guy who—

"Hand it over, baby doll."

His voice startles a squeak out of me. My head swivels toward the bed, where Dean is sliding up into a sitting position, running one hand through his sleep-messy hair. He doesn't look or sound groggy at all. His green eyes are alert, and his naked body is…transforming.

I feel myself blushing at the sight of his quickly hardening dick, so I drop my gaze to my bare feet. "Would you please cover yourself up?"

"That's not what you said last night…"

His mocking tone grates. "We are not discussing last night. Ever."

He looks even more amused. "Oh, relax. It was just sex." He makes no move to pull the sheet over his lower body. Instead, he stretches both arms high over his head, drawing my attention to his flexing muscles. And his wrists. He has red marks around his wrists…

Because I tied him to the bed last night.

Sweet mother of Moses.

When he catches where my gaze has gone, the corners of his mouth quirk up. "Granted, it was a lot kinkier than I thought it would be," he continues with a wink. "But I ain't complaining."

Kill me. Just kill me.

As another rush of humiliation crashes over me, I grab the nearest item of clothing I can find—a black V-neck T-shirt—and throw it over my head. A familiar smell clouds my senses. Something spicy and masculine. It's the same scent I breathed in last night when my lips were traveling over Dean's bare chest. When my face was buried in his neck as I sucked on his skin like it was candy. And yep, there's another hickey on his throat. I really went to town on this guy.

"We are not talking about it," I say through clenched teeth. "It happened, it was fine, and it will never be mentioned again."

"It was *fine*?" Smirking, Dean drags a hand down his chest, his long fingers resting right above the head of his thick erection. "It was more than fine and you know it."

"Would you please, please get dressed?" I beg.

"Can't. You're wearing my shirt." He arches a brow. "Why don't you take it off and toss it this way?"

Fat chance. This guy is never laying eyes on my naked body again.

Since I refuse to give up the shirt, I do the next best thing and turn my back to him to go through my phone. I ignore Sean's texts and skip to the ones from my friends. One from Hannah checking how my night was, and one from Megan asking me to brunch.

I quickly text Meg back with a resounding YES and ask her to pick me up from Garrett's. Just as the gray bubble that indicates she's typing a response appears, the phone is snatched from my hand.

"Hey!" I'm startled to find Dean behind me. Jeez. The guy moves like a ninja.

"I'm in charge of this, remember?" He's mocking me again, keeping the phone out of my reach. "As your sponsor, I must advise you to ignore"—he glances at the screen—"these nine text messages from your ex. No good will come out of reading them."

He's right about that. But after what happened between us last night, there's no way Dean is going to be my relationship sponsor.

"It's fine," I mumble. "I don't need your help."

He echoes his earlier taunt. "Not what you said last night. Your phone stays with me this weekend, Allie-Cat. No arguments."

Allie-Cat? Oh help me Rhonda. He's given me a pet name.

"I'm meeting a friend," I say tightly. "So I need my phone, okay? Besides, your sponsor duties are officially done. I'm going back to the dorms after brunch."

He frowns. "No, you're staying the weekend."

"Not anymore."

I attempt to grab my phone from him. He moves it aside again. "Is this because we fucked last night?"

My cheeks are scorching. "What part of *never mention it again* didn't you understand?"

"This is bullshit. You can't leave just because you and I got wasted and screwed around a couple times. You're totally overreacting."

I take a deep breath. "Can we please not talk about it?"

"Babe, do you think I enjoy talking about this stuff? I'd rather roll around in broken glass than deal with this whole morning-after shit. If you were any other girl, I'd say forget it, but you're Wellsy's best friend, so that means we've gotta talk about it." He curses suddenly. "Oh shit. Wellsy is going to kill me."

Oh shit is right. I'll definitely be on the receiving end of a stern lecture from Hannah if she finds out I slept with Dean. Maybe in a few days, or a week—or a decade—I'll be able to tell her what happened last night, but right now, I want to forget all about it. Which means keeping my best friend in the dark for as long as I can.

"She's not going to kill you, because we're not going to tell her," I say firmly. "Seriously, this has to stay between us."

"Agreed."

"And you're not allowed to bring it up ever again. As far as I'm concerned, it didn't happen."

He gives me a cocky grin. "Don't kid yourself, baby doll. You won't be able to stop thinking about me now that you've had a taste of this." To punctuate that, he grips his semi-hard dick and gives it a slow stroke.

A jolt of heat spirals down to my core.

Argh. Stupid Dean and his stupid awesome dick.

"I've already forgotten all about it," I lie. But in my head, more memories crop up, making me want to scream in frustration.

"I like you like this…"

"Ha. So you admit it—you do *like me," he drawls.*

I smile at his immobilized wrists. "I said I like you like this." *My mouth slowly descends toward his erect cock. "Completely at my mercy…"*

Sweet lord. My cheeks are on fire again. Sean wasn't always on board with my adventurous nature when it came to sex. I was the one who had to coax and plead with him to try whatever kinky new idea sparked my interest.

Dean hadn't even batted an eye at our sexual exploits.

"Do you need me to remind you how good it was?" He tilts his head mockingly, his hand still on his dick.

"No, I need you to be a fucking grown-up," I burst out. I'm losing patience with him, and I'm too angry with myself to control my temper. "I'm hungover and I'm really embarrassed and you're making it worse by throwing last night in my face, okay?"

His expression falters. "Shit." He clears his throat and lets go of his dick, then hastily picks up his sweatpants. "I'm sorry. I didn't mean to make you uncomfortable." He yanks the pants on. "And you have no reason to feel embarrassed. We're both adults. We had fun and made each other come a bunch of times. No biggie, okay? But if you really don't want me to bring it up again, I won't."

I draw a shaky breath. "Thank you."

Dean studies my face. "Are we cool?"

I manage a nod. My head is still throbbing, but it's not the hangover that's making me feel weak and wobbly right now. It's the fact that I did something so out of character for me. It's the horrible knowledge that I slept with someone else a measly twenty-four hours after I broke up with Sean. That's not *me*, damn it.

"Are you sure?" he presses.

I force myself to speak. "We're cool, Dean." My phone buzzes and I see a text from Meg saying she's five minutes away. "I need to get dressed. Megan will be here soon." I bite my lip when something occurs to me. "Crap. My clothes are downstairs. Tucker…"

As I trail off, Dean wanders over to the window and peeks behind the curtains. "He's not here—Logan's truck is gone. Guess he didn't come home last night."

Relief hits me, but also a burst of annoyance. Because where was Tucker yesterday when I needed him? If he'd been home, I probably wouldn't have ended up in bed with Dean. Or maybe instead, I would've ended up in bed with Tucker, who happens to be the hottest ginger I've ever met. He's also far quieter than his roommates and doesn't talk about himself much, but from what I can glean, he's smart, well-spoken, and definitely easy on the eyes.

In hindsight, Tuck would have been a *fantastic* rebound candidate.

"I'm going to run down and get my clothes," I mutter awkwardly.

He calls out after me. "What are you going to tell Wellsy about bailing mid-weekend? You know she'll ask questions."

Damn it. He's right. "I'll tell her I decided to put on my big girl pants and deal with my breakup at home."

I'm halfway to the door when his voice stops me again. "Allie."

"Yeah?" I turn around.

His green eyes flicker unhappily. "Are you sure you're okay?"

Nope, I'm not sure at all. "I'm fine," I lie, then duck out of the bedroom.

As far as walks of shame go, this one isn't so bad because at least there's nobody around to witness it.

CHAPTER 4

DEAN

I'VE ALWAYS BEEN POPULAR. NO MATTER HOW FAR BACK I GO IN my memory bank, I always see myself surrounded by friends. And girls. Lots and lots of girls. The giggling ones in grade school who slipped me *Do you like me???* notes when the teacher was facing the blackboard. The ones in high school who'd fight for my attention and line up to make out with me on the lacrosse field after hours.

And college, don't get me started on college. I thought I knew the meaning of *chick magnet* before I came to Briar, but these past three years have exceeded even my own expectations about my desirability. The older I get, the more the ladies dig me.

So yeah, I'm not surprised that Allie threw herself at me last night. It was an inevitability the moment she informed me I have "perfect nipples."

But the sheer disgust on her face this morning when we woke up in bed together? That's a new one.

"Fuckin' Corsen wouldn't be able to stop a puck if it was moving two miles an hour in a straight path toward him."

My teammate's grumbled complaint draws me from my thoughts and makes me stifle a groan. My boy Hunter doesn't seem to understand bar etiquette. You don't go to bars to gripe and moan about a hockey game. You go to bars to score. Period.

But the kid's only eighteen. He'll wise up one day.

"Dude, the game was two days ago," I tell the freshman. "Get over it."

I scan the bar for Tucker, but my roommate hasn't shown up yet. It's mostly the hockey crowd that fills up the bar tonight. Several of my teammates, tons of fans, and a parade of scantily clad puck bunnies. More than a few appreciative female gazes flit in our direction, but Hunter doesn't seem to notice a single one.

His features are tight, and he's barely touched his drink. "This is your fault, you know." Accusation rings in his tone. "I didn't even want to play this year, but you just *had* to talk me into it. I could have ended my career as the star forward on the number one ranked prep school team in the country. And now I'm the nobody left wing on a team that's going down the shitter."

I sip my beer. "Anyone ever tell you you're a sore loser?"

"Oh fuck off. Like *you* enjoy losing."

"Of course I don't. But I also know that winning isn't everything. Oh, and by the way? Glass houses, throwing stones, et cetera et cetera."

"What the hell is that supposed to mean?"

"It means that instead of blaming Corsen for letting in three goals, you should be concentrating on the fact that you didn't score a single one. This ain't prep school, Superstar. College D-men aren't as easy to deke out."

Harsh, but true. And Hunter Davenport needs to hear it. Coach has been going easy on Hunter in practice, because other than Garrett, he's the only forward on the roster who's capable of greatness. But unlike Garrett, Hunter has one major weakness: overconfidence. The kid thinks he's the next Sidney Crosby.

"You're saying I'm not good enough to play at this level?" Rather than anger, Hunter's expression conveys distress, which only highlights his major *strength*: he's always striving to get better.

"I'm saying you need work. You made some amateur mistakes the other night. Like when Fitzy was in trouble after that power play? You went to bail him out—that's not your job, bro. You don't skate into another winger's corner. You've gotta trust your center to help the other guy out."

Hunter takes a hasty sip of beer.

"And you suck at reading plays sometimes. When Eastwood's D-man made that sweet pass that led to a breakaway? You should've anticipated who he was going to pass to, but you totally misread him."

"I was watching the puck the whole time," he protests.

"Forget the puck. Watch the *player*, dude. Pay attention to who he's looking at, where his teammates are moving. Read who he's targeting and then intercept that pass."

Hunter goes quiet. When he speaks again, he sounds grudgingly impressed. "You know a lot about this stuff, huh?"

I shrug. I know I have a reputation for not being as serious about hockey as my teammates, and maybe there's some truth to that, but that doesn't mean I don't understand the mechanics and nuances of the game.

Hockey has been a part of my life for as long as I can remember. I grew up playing it. Lacrosse too, but that was mostly a way to pass time in the spring until hockey started up again. Both my dad and older brother played hockey at Harvard. I could've too, but I chose Briar instead. I'm always following in their footsteps, and I guess I just wanted to be different or some shit.

Don't get me wrong, I don't play hockey only because they did. I love the game. It just doesn't give me the same thrill that Garrett and Logan seem to experience every time they're on the ice.

Truthfully, I have more fun during practice. I enjoy the drills and the scrimmages, the opportunity to get better and help my teammates get better. I'm not interested in going pro after I graduate, which pleases my family to no end, because Heyward-Di Laurentises don't become professional athletes. They become lawyers. Next fall I'll be attending Harvard Law like every other member of my family. I'm cool with that, and I have no doubt I'll be good at it. The Di Laurentis charm I inherited from my dad pretty much guarantees I'll be winning over judges left and right.

"What else am I doing wrong?" Hunter sounds more curious than pissed.

I grin at him. "Tell you what, how about some one-on-one sessions this week? I'll see if Coach will sign off on extra ice time."

"Seriously? I would really appreciate that, actually. Thanks—"

I interrupt him. "But only if you agree to quit talking about hockey for the rest of the night." I gesture to the packed bar. "Look around. It's a hot girl banquet in here. Pick the one you like and feast, idiot."

Hunter laughs, but his dark eyes gleam as he takes in the view. Several chicks respond to his attention with DTF smiles, but rather than wave them over, he glances at me—or rather, at my neck—and snorts. "Actually, maybe you should introduce me to the wildcat you hooked up with last night. Ms. Hickey seems like fun."

I stiffen. No way am I letting this kid anywhere near Allie. He might be young, but he's well on his way to becoming an even bigger player than I am.

Then again, maybe it's Hunter I should be worrying about. After last night's performance, Allie Hayes proved that she's fully capable of leaving her mark on a man. Jesus. That girl can *fuck*.

Damn, and now my dick is semi-hard. It's been doing that all day, chubbing out every time I think about Allie. It was the hottest hookup I've had in a long while. Hell, my wrists are still sore from being tied to the bed, but it's the kind of sore that just makes me want to do it again.

Tapping the same ass more than once isn't usually my style, but right now my dick is aching to bury itself in Allie's naughty pussy again.

"Sorry, Superstar. Not happening," I tell him. "Find your own wildcat."

"Fine." Grinning, he gives the room another scan. "Oh yeah. I think I know who I'm going home with tonight."

I follow his gaze to the long wooden counter, where a tall brunette has her back turned to us as she leans forward to order a drink. She's in a short black skirt and high heels, with long brown hair falling down her back in waves. The male bartender is damn near drooling, his hungry eyes peering down her shirt, which tells me she must have a great rack. All I can see is her ass, though, and it's pretty fantastic.

Normally I'd be all over the brunette, but I'm not in the mood to score tonight. My mind keeps drifting back to Allie. And Allie's pussy. And her tits. Man, her tits were incredible. A perfect handful, with pale-pink nipples that went harder than icicles when I sucked on them.

I sigh and do some strategic rearranging in my crotchal region. I've gotta quit thinking about last night, for chrissake. God knows Allie is doing her best to forget it.

"What do you think?" Hunter asks me.

I shift my gaze away from the brunette. "She might be a little out of your league."

"I'm a hockey player. Nobody's out of my league."

"Truth." I chuckle. That was the first thing I taught Hunter when I took him under my wing at the start of the season. But even so, the brunette has the sexiest body I've ever seen. A woman like that can have anyone in this bar, and I'm not sure freshman Hunter makes the cut, even if he is wearing a Briar hockey jacket.

Across the room, the chick we're admiring suddenly turns around. Just like that, my appreciation fizzles into disgust. "Oh hell no. Stay away from that one, kid. She's toxic."

"She doesn't look toxic to me," Hunter drawls.

Naive bastard. Luckily, I know better. Sabrina James is undeniably gorgeous, but I'd pour hot wax on my balls before I'd hook up with her. Well, before I'd hook up with her *again*.

Yup. Been there, done that, got the T-shirt.

Someone jostles me from behind, and I turn to find Tucker approaching. His black-and-silver jacket is soaking wet, and so is his hair.

"Je-sus. It's coming down hard out there." He does a full-body shake like a dog who's just scampered out of a lake.

"Hey, Fido, go dry off somewhere else," I order as cold droplets splash my face and hit me in the eye.

Hunter doesn't even notice that Tucker is dripping water all over our shoes. He's too busy ogling Sabrina.

Tuck follows the freshman's gaze. "Nice," he remarks, then turns to grin at me. "I take it you already called dibs?"

I blanch. "Not a chance. That's Sabrina, bro. She already busts my balls in class on a daily basis. I don't need her busting them outside of school."

Sabrina and I are both poli-sci majors on the pre-law path, so we share way too many classes for my peace of mind. We both applied to Harvard Law too, which I'm not particularly happy about. The thought of spending three more years sitting in the same lecture halls as her doesn't sound at all appealing.

"Wait, that's Sabrina?" Tucker says in surprise. "I see her around campus all the time, but I didn't realize she's the one you're always bitching about."

"One and the same."

His southern drawl rears up. "Damn shame. She sure is fine to look at."

"What's the deal with you two?" Hunter pipes up. "She your ex?"

I recoil again. "Fuck no."

"So I won't be breaking the bro code if I make a move?"

"You want to make a move? Go nuts. But I'm warning you, that bitch will eat you alive."

Sabrina's head turns sharply toward us. She probably has some kind of internal radar that goes off every time someone calls her a bitch. I bet it goes off a lot.

As our gazes lock, she smirks at me, then flips up her middle finger before turning to talk to her friend.

Hunter groans. "Well, there goes that. She won't give me the time of day now that she saw me with you. What'd you do to her, anyway?"

"Absolutely nothing," I say darkly.

"Bullshit. A chick doesn't murder a guy with her eyes like that unless he screwed up bad. Did you hook up with her?"

Tucker snorts. "What do you think, kid? I mean, *look* at her."

"Looks can be deceiving," I mutter.

My roommate cocks his head in challenge. "So you didn't sleep with her?"

A sigh slides out. "No, I did. But it was a long time ago. I'm pretty sure hookups have expiration dates. Like after three years have gone by, it doesn't count anymore."

The guys laugh. "Let me guess," Tucker says. "You didn't call her afterward."

"No," I admit. "But in my defense, it's hard to call a chick when one, she doesn't give you her number, and two, when you don't remember it happened."

Hunter's jaw falls open. "How could you not remember *that*?" He's damn near salivating as he checks out Sabrina again.

"We were both wasted. Trust me, she didn't remember much either."

"So that's why she hates you?" Hunter presses.

I wave a hand. "Nah. The beef started over something else. Which I'm not going to fucking talk about right now, because Jesus Christ, it's Saturday night and we should be partying."

Tucker chuckles. "I'm gonna grab a beer. You guys need a refill?"

"I'm good," Hunter says.

As Tuck heads for the counter, I pull out my phone and check the time. It's nine thirty. I scroll through my contacts while Hunter starts talking hockey to me again. I think I still have Allie's number from when she was planning Hannah's birthday this spring. She'd sent about a hundred mass texts outlining every mundane detail of the party.

Yup, it's still in my phone. I saved her contact info as *Wellsy's Blond Friend*. I should probably change that to *Bondage Girl*.

I type a quick message.

Me: You make it back to the dorm ok?

It's a dumb question, because she left our place this morning, so of course she made it back. Still, I'm surprised when she answers right away.

Her: Yep. Here now.
Me: Shitty weather tonight. Prolly good ur staying in.

She doesn't respond to that. I stare at the screen in frustration, then wonder why I care. I'm the king of casual hookups. I rarely ever want a repeat performance after I've slept with a girl, and if there's one girl I shouldn't sleep with again, it's Allie.

Not too many things in this world make it on my Scared Shitless list, but Garrett's girlfriend is solidly positioned in the top three. Wellsy won't be happy if she finds out I slept with her best friend, and if Wellsy's not happy, Garrett's not happy, which means I'll have to deal with G tsking at me all disappointed-like. Logan will follow his lead, and then Grace will jump on the Dean-is-an-ass bandwagon, and the next thing I know, I'll be taking shit from all directions. That's reason enough not to go there, but my sexed-up body is being a stubborn asshole.

I want her again.

One more time wouldn't hurt, right? Shit, or maybe twice? I'm not entirely sure how many times it will take to get her out of my system. All I know is that every time I think about her, my dick gets impossibly hard.

Beside me, Hunter has transferred his attention to a group of girls at a nearby table, and I can't help but be proud when one measly nod from him causes the trio to saunter over to us. My boy's got game.

"Which one of you is going to buy us a round?" one of them teases. She's tall and blond and rocking a minidress that stops mid-thigh.

As Hunter opens his mouth to respond, all the lights in the bar flicker ominously.

I frown and glance over at Tucker, who's just rejoined the group. "Is it the Apocalypse out there or something?"

"It's coming down pretty hard," he admits.

The lights stop flickering. I take that as my cue to bail, because if we're dealing with a potential power outage, I'd rather be home when it happens instead of on the road. Besides, for all my talk about partying, I'm really not feeling the bar tonight.

"Hey, I'm heading out." I clap a hand over my roommate's shoulder. "See you back at home." I don't miss the disappointed pouts on the girls' faces, but I'm confident they'll forget all about me once Hunter and Tuck turn up the charm.

I exit the bar a minute later and realize Tuck wasn't kidding. In the ten seconds it takes me to get to my car, I'm soaked to the bone, dripping water all over the Beemer's leather interior. The bolts of lightning streaking across the sky are so bright, they make the act of flicking on my headlights almost redundant. I could probably just let those blinding white flashes light the way home.

I fish out my phone again.

Me: Weather's worse than I thought. Keep a flashlight near you in case power goes out.

Oh, for chrissake. I sound like I'm writing a shitty survival guide. Why am I even texting her?

Allie responds with Thx for the tip, then follows it up with Srsly, stop worrying about me. I'm reading on the couch. Under a blanket. Snug as a bug in a mug.

Me: In a rug.
Her: ??
Me: Snug as a bug in a RUG. That's how you say it.

There's five whole seconds of radio silence, and then my phone rings in my hand. I'm grinning as I answer the call.

"Why would the bug be in a rug?" she demands.

I snort. "Why would it be in a mug?"

"Because that's a cozy place for it to be! If it's in a rug, someone might step on it."

"If it's in a mug, someone might *drink* it."

"Are we writing a bad Dr. Seuss book right now?"

Laughter bubbles in my throat. "Sure fucking sounds like it."

"Well, either way, I think my phrasing is better."

I'm momentarily distracted by the rain hammering against the windshield. It's falling harder now, and a second later, all the lights in the parking lot go out.

I curse softly as darkness surrounds my car. "Shit. Malone's just lost power," I tell Allie. "Make sure you stay inside, okay? And don't go wandering around the halls of Bristol House if the power goes out."

"What, you think a serial killer is going to sneak into the dorm and hunt me down?" She's quiet for a beat. "Even if that happened, I'd probably be able to take him."

I snicker. "Uh-huh. Sure."

"Hey, I'm *fierce*," she insists. "My dad and I took part in a really intensive father-daughter self-defense program when I was fourteen."

"Father-daughter self-defense? Is that even a thing?"

"No, but we made it one. He traveled a lot when I was growing up, so whenever he was home he would come up with creative ways for us to bond. But since he's Mr. Macho Man, we were only allowed to do boy things. Like fishing or riding dirt bikes or learning how to beat each other up. Anyway, I'm hanging up now. I want to finish reading this play." She pauses. "Drive safe."

"Wait," I blurt out before she can end the call.

"What is it?"

I stare at the rain that's sliding down the windshield. Wondering what the hell is wrong with me.

Then I lick my suddenly dry lips and say, "I want to fuck you again."

I can hear her breath hitch over the extension.

My body tightens in anticipation. I think about the sweet curve of her ass filling my palms. The way her nipples puckered when I flicked my tongue over them. The tight grip of her pussy squeezing my cock.

A silent groan shudders through my chest. Fuck me. I'm lusting hard for this chick. And now I'm holding my breath, waiting for her to answer.

After a long pause, her annoyed voice says, "Goodbye, Dean."

I growl in frustration when the line goes dead.

CHAPTER 5

ALLIE

M<small>Y HEART IS POUNDING AS</small> I <small>HANG UP ON</small> D<small>EAN.</small> I <small>HADN'T EXPECTED</small> him to say that. At all.

"I want to fuck you again."

Well, of course he does. I'm amazing in bed.

But there's no way I'm sleeping with the guy again, not after I spent the entire day feeling like Hester fricking Prynne. Only, the self-judgment I've been hitting myself with is far more scathing than anything that poor woman ever got from those Puritans.

God, I'm not cut out for casual sex. I feel…defiled. Except that's ridiculous, because if anyone was defiled last night, it was Dean. Not only did I seduce him, but I tied him up and rode him like he was my own personal amusement park ride.

I'm such a slut.

You're not a slut.

Okay, maybe I'm not. Maybe I'm just a twenty-two-year-old woman who had some no-strings fun for once in her life.

The only problem is—I like the strings. Sex and relationships go hand in hand for me. I'm all about the snuggling and inside jokes and talking late into the night. I'm a card-carrying member of Team Boyfriend, and after last night, I can honestly say that Team

One-Night Stand sucks balls. The sex was incredible, but the shame it left me with isn't worth the orgasms.

Sighing, I toss my phone on the couch cushion and pick up the script I'd been reading before Dean interrupted. The student-written play will be my final performance at Briar. I'm one of two female leads, and even though the material is a tad melodramatic for my tastes, I'm looking forward to rehearsals. Ever since my theater debut in Boston this summer, I've been itching to perform in front of a live audience again.

Which is just another contributing factor to the stress I've been under. I'm at a crossroads in my career, and I have no idea which path to take, damn it.

When I started college, I asked my agent to concentrate on only finding summer projects for me. It would have been too tempting to drop out of school if a juicy role came along, and I wanted my degree. Now that I'm graduating, all bets are off. Pilot season kicks off around January, and Ira has already sent me dozens of scripts for sitcoms and *Glee*-style dramedies, along with several rom-com screenplays that normally I'd be salivating over.

I always thought I was destined for comedic roles. I caught the acting bug when I was still in middle school, and all the bit parts I landed over the years were light and fluffy, highlighting my comedic timing and girl-next-door persona. I dreamed about being a rom-com queen. The next Sandra Bullock or Kate Hudson or Emma Stone.

Until this summer, when a casting call went out for a super-serious, super-depressing play directed by Brett Carson, an Oscar-winning director and a fricking legend. Somehow my agent made it possible for me to read for Carson, and to my total astonishment I actually got the part—the heroin-addicted younger sister of the lead actress. The show only had a two-month run, but it was a huge success. Since then, I've received a ton of offers to read for more dramatic roles, both on stage and for television.

And someone told me Carson is developing another project for the stage, off-off Broadway this time…

Shit. Why am I so tempted to veer off the course I set for myself? Considering dramatic roles is one thing, but *theater*?

Hollywood means more money. More recognition. Oscars and Golden Globes and Rodeo Drive shopping sprees.

I stare at the stack of scripts on the coffee table. If I get hired for one of these pilots Ira sent over and the show gets picked up? Or if I snag a role in one of these films? I could actually break out in the business. So why am I fantasizing about stage acting?

I'm still lost in thought when my phone rings. I check the screen, and for a second I think it's Dean calling, until I do a double take and realize it's an *S*, not a *D*. Huh. My ex-boyfriend and my one-night stand literally have the same name with one letter replaced. I wonder if that means something…

Sean's calling you, you idiot.

Yeah, that's probably the more pressing issue at the moment.

My chest fills with anxiety. I shouldn't pick up. I really, really shouldn't pick up.

I pick up.

"Are you okay?" are the first words I hear.

Sean sounds so frantic that I'm quick to reassure him. "I'm fine. Why wouldn't I be?"

"I came by after class yesterday and you weren't home. And I texted you all night."

"I know." I gulp. "I spent the night at a friend's. I…" Another gulp. "I told you I didn't want to see you."

"I was hoping you'd change your mind." There's no mistaking the sheer torment in his voice. "Fuck, baby. I miss you. I know it's only been a couple days, but I miss you so much."

My heart cracks in two.

"I messed up, okay? I see that now. I shouldn't have given you an ultimatum, and I definitely shouldn't have said your acting career isn't going anywhere. I was upset and lashing out at you, and you didn't deserve that. When I came to your opening night in Boston this summer, I was blown away. Seriously. You're so talented, baby. I'm an ass for saying all that shit to you. I didn't mean it."

He's practically pleading with me now, and another piece of my heart splinters off. "Sean—"

"You're the most important person in my life," he interrupts, his voice thick with emotion. "You mean the world to me, and I want to fucking strangle myself for driving you away. Please, baby, give me another chance."

"Sean—"

"I *know* I can fix this. Just give me a chance to—"

"*Sean!*"

He stops. "Babe?" he says uncertainly.

My throat goes impossibly tight, almost like it's trying to prevent me from saying my next words. But the guilt is eating me alive. I can't just sit here and listen to him beg, not when I'm feeling this way. I swallow again and force my vocal cords to cooperate.

"I slept with someone last night."

Deafening silence greets my ears. It seems to drag on forever, and with each second that ticks by, my stomach churns harder.

"Did you hear me?" I whisper.

There's a choked noise. "Yeah…I heard you."

We both fall silent. Pain and guilt continue to stab my insides. I involuntarily flash back to the day I met Sean. It was during freshman orientation, and I remember thinking he was the cutest boy I'd ever seen with his floppy brown hair that he's since cropped, twinkling hazel eyes, and the cutest butt on the planet. Being the outspoken weirdo that I am, I commented on the cuteness of said butt, and his cheeks had turned redder than his Red Sox T-shirt.

We had dinner in one of the meal halls that night.

A week after that, we were a couple.

And now, three years later, we're broken up, and I've just

confessed to having sex with someone else. Where the hell had we gone wrong?

"Who?"

The strangled question startles me. "W-what?"

"Who was it?" Sean says flatly.

Discomfort tightens my chest. "It doesn't matter who it was. I won't be seeing him again. It was…" I take a breath. "It was a stupid mistake. But I thought you should know."

He doesn't answer.

"Sean?"

A ragged breath echoes through the line. "Thanks for telling me," he mutters.

Then he hangs up.

It takes a while before I move the phone away from my ear. My hand shakes uncontrollably as I rake it through my hair.

God. That was…brutal. A part of me wonders why I even told him. It's not like I cheated on him. I didn't have to tell him. In fact, I could have spared him the pain he must be feeling right now if I'd simply kept my mouth shut. But I've always been honest with Sean, and some stupid, guilty part of me insisted he deserved to know.

An anguished groan flies out of my mouth. My heart hurts again. The guilt is even worse now, a tight, crushing knot in my stomach.

Rather than pick up my script, I grab my phone instead and shove in my earbuds. Then I yank the blanket up to my neck and put Miley Cyrus's "Wrecking Ball" on repeat because it pretty much sums up how I feel right now.

Wrecked.

DEAN

"AWW, LOOK AT HIM, G. HE'S SO PRECIOUS WHEN HE'S SLEEPING."

"Like an angel."

"A really slutty angel."

"Wait—do angels even get laid? And if so, are heaven orgasms a million times better than earth orgasms? I bet yes."

"Uh, doy. Where do you think rainbows come from? Whenever you see a rainbow, that means an angel just came."

"Ah. Makes sense. Sort of like how whenever a bell rings, an angel gets its wings."

"Exactly like that."

I crank one eye open and direct it toward the doorway. "I can hear you, you know."

My annoyed voice puts an end to the most bizarre conversation I've ever heard. "Oh good, you're up," Logan says.

"Of course I'm up," I grumble, rubbing my eyes. "How am I supposed to sleep when you two fuckers are standing at the foot of my bed talking about angels blowing their loads?"

Garrett snickers. "Like I'm the first one to ever wonder about that."

"Trust me, you are. When'd you guys get back?"

Logan props one massive shoulder against my doorframe. "About an hour ago. Gracie needed to be back early because she has a show to produce tonight."

I nod. Logan's girlfriend works as a producer at the campus radio station. Which reminds me… "You planning on calling in and professing your love again?" I ask mockingly.

He sighs. "You're never gonna let me forget that, are you?"

"Nope." Though I wish someone had recorded that radio segment so I could pull some quotes from it and torture him with them. After screwing up and nearly losing Grace last weekend, Logan had won her back by calling the advice show she produces and saying the sappiest shit imaginable. I worry about him sometimes.

I toss the covers aside and slide out of bed buck-ass naked. My roommates continue to lurk in the doorway.

I find a pair of clean boxers and tug them on. "I swear to God, if you tell me you've been watching me sleep for the last hour like a bunch of creepers, I'm calling the cops."

"Coach called," Garrett tells me. "He said he's been trying your phone all morning but you weren't picking up. He wants you at the arena in an hour."

"Why?" I ask warily.

Garrett shrugs. "Fuck if I know. Maybe he found out you got wasted this weekend—I assume you got wasted, right?—and wants to ream you out."

"How would he even know? It's not like he's got people tailing us."

"Dude, Coach is like that spy master from *Game of Thrones*. His sources are endless."

Shit. Hopefully I'm not in store for one of Coach Jensen's long-winded lectures about keeping my nose clean. We're not allowed to drink or dabble in drugs during the season, but that doesn't stop any of us from getting plastered or smoking the occasional joint. Still, I've never failed a piss test or tarnished the team's good name with my partying, so I'm not sure why Coach is constantly on my case about it.

"Hannah still here?" I ask Garrett as I hunt down some pants.

"Nah, she went home. She's having a girl day with Allie."

I'm glad my back is turned, because the moment he says Allie's name, my dick actually goes half-mast. Wonderful. I'm turned on by the sound of her *name* now?

"You didn't do anything stupid when she was here, did you?" Garrett's tone is lined with suspicion.

I fucked her twice. So…yes?

I bite my tongue and throw on a T-shirt, followed by a navy-blue Briar hoodie. "I was a perfect gentleman."

Logan snorts. "Well, that's a first."

"Fuck you very much. I happen to be skilled in the art of gentlemanry."

"That's not an art. Or a word." Logan rolls his eyes and disappears from the room, but Garrett stays behind.

He studies my face for so long I shift in discomfort. "What?" I mutter.

"Nothing," he says, but he still wears a suspicious expression as he ducks out of my bedroom.

When I pop into the bathroom to brush my teeth, I realize that the purple hickey on my neck is still very, very noticeable. Had Garrett seen it?

But so what if he had? Anyone could've sucked on my neck this weekend. There's no reason for him to suspect it was Allie.

Goddamn Allie. I told her I wanted her again, and she'd *hung up* on me. That doesn't happen to me—ever. I'm Dean Di Laurentis, for fuck's sake. I can snap my fingers and a dozen chicks appear, begging to ride my dick. Last time I was at the campus coffeehouse, the hot barista handed me a free coffee and then offered to suck me off in the stock room.

So what the hell is Allie's problem? I spent way too much time last night wondering if she's playing hard to get. I mean, it's not like she hadn't enjoyed the sex. I've never been with anyone who showered my dick with so much glowing praise.

"Oh my gosh, I want to marry your cock!"

"Best. Dick. Ever."

"Dean, you're making me come…"

Her throaty cries run through my head on a perverted, boner-inducing loop, and I grip the towel rack with one hand as a groan slips out. The toothbrush in my mouth falls into the sink. My cock tents in my pants and nudges the porcelain, needing to make contact with something, anything.

I wonder if Coach would be pissed if I was late to meet him because I was jerking off.

Probably.

THIRTY MINUTES LATER, I SWIPE MY STUDENT ID IN THE KEYPAD at the hockey facility, sipping on the coffee I grabbed on the way here. The wide corridor is deserted, and my sneakers squeak on the shiny floors as I head to the back of the building. I walk past the row of classrooms and the screening room, bypass the kitchen and weight rooms, then duck through the massive equipment area.

Our facility is state of the art. There are half a dozen big cozy offices that Chad Jensen could've parked his ass in, but for some reason he chose this modest office tucked away near the laundry room.

I knock on the door, only opening it when I hear Coach's gruff "Get in here." The last player who waltzed in without knocking got a tongue-lashing that the rest of us could hear all the way from the showers. I like to think Coach uses the office to jack off and that's why he insists on privacy. Logan hypothesizes that he has a secret office family that's only allowed to venture out in the wee hours of the night.

Logan is an idiot.

"Hey, Coach. You wanted to see me—" I halt when I realize we're not alone.

I'm not caught off guard often. I'm a go-with-the-flow kinda guy, which means it takes a helluva lot to shock or surprise me.

Right now, the only flow I'm going with is the rush of anxiety that travels through my blood and seeps into my bones.

Frank O'Shea rises from the visitor's chair and flicks his cool gaze over me. I haven't seen him since my senior year of high school, but he looks exactly the same. Dark buzz cut, stocky body, severe mouth.

"Di Laurentis," he says with a curt nod.

I nod back. "Coach O'Shea."

Jensen glances between us, then gets right down to business. "Dean, Frank's coming on board as our new defensive coordinator. He filled me in about your history at Greenwich Prep." Coach pauses. "I decided it would be prudent if you two aired out your issues before practice tomorrow."

I can only imagine what O'Shea had to say about our "history." Whatever it was, I'm positive it was both inaccurate and in no way favorable toward me, because O'Shea's version of the story is so skewed it makes the stories in the *National Enquirer* seem like well-researched academic papers.

Coach Jensen steps to the door. "I'll leave you to it."

Goddamn it, he's leaving us alone? Woulda been nice to have a witness around in case O'Shea tries something. After all, this is the man who clocked one of his own players in the empty parking lot of a high school. I was eighteen at the time. I didn't report it because I understood why he'd done it, but that doesn't mean I've forgotten about it. Or forgiven him for it.

O'Shea doesn't speak until the door latches firmly behind Coach. "So. Are we going to have a problem here?"

I set my jaw. "You tell me." I force myself to add, "*Sir.*"

His dark eyes flash. "I see you're still the same insolent smartass you were when I coached you."

"With all due respect, sir, I've been in this office for all of five seconds. I don't think you can make that judgment." My tone is polite, but inside I'm seething. I loathe this man, which is so fucking ironic because I used to worship him.

"There isn't a problem on my end," he says as if I hadn't even spoken. "The past is in the past. I'm willing to wipe the slate clean if that makes for a more conducive training environment."

How generous of him.

"All I ask in return is that you treat me with respect and listen to me when we're on the ice. I won't tolerate any insubordination." His mouth pinches in a frown. "And I won't condone any shenanigans. Jensen said you have quite the reputation as a party boy. Which doesn't surprise me"—he makes an unflattering noise—"but if you want to keep your roster slot, I expect you to be on your best behavior. No booze, no drugs, no brawling. Understood?"

I jerk my head in assent.

"As for our former issues, they will not be discussed." O'Shea levels me with another cold glare. "Not between us, and not among you and your teammates. The past is in the past," he repeats.

I shove my hands in my pockets. "Can I go now?"

"Not yet." He moves toward the desk and picks up a thin folder. Either I'm imagining it, or there's a smug gleam in his eyes. "Two more things. And rest assured, Coach Jensen is in complete agreement about this."

Uneasiness tickles my stomach.

"First, we're moving you to the second line with Brodowski—"

"What?" I balk.

O'Shea holds up his hand. "Let me finish."

I slam my mouth shut, fighting to control my rising temper. I'm no longer seething. I'm fucking enraged.

There isn't a problem on his end, my ass. I've always played on the first line with Logan. We're the two best defensemen on the roster. A dynamic duo, for chrissake. Brodowski is a junior who needs so much work I'm surprised he's still on the team.

"Jensen trusts me to work with this defense and make decisions as I see fit," my old coach barks at me. "The second line is weak. Kelvin and Brodowski aren't gelling, and each of them will benefit from being paired up with players of your and John Logan's caliber."

"Did Coach happen to mention that he tried this already during pre-season?" I can't help but say, snidely enough to make him frown. "I was paired up with Kelvin for the St. Anthony's game. It was a disaster."

"Well, you won't be with Kelvin this time, will you?" he counters in an equally snide tone. "I'm putting you with Brodowski. And the decision is final—I'm doing what's best for the team."

Bullshit. He's doing this to punish me, and we both know it.

"What's the second thing?"

He blinks. "Pardon me?"

"You said there were two things." It's a struggle to keep my voice calm. "You're rearranging the lines—that's number one. What's number two?"

He slants his head as if trying to decide if I'm being disrespectful again. Dude doesn't even know how badly I want to slam my fist in his jaw right now. It's taking all my willpower not to.

O'Shea flips open the folder and extracts a single piece of paper. The satisfied gleam returns as he passes it to me.

I scan the page. It's a photocopy of what looks like a practice and game schedule, but it's not for our team. "What's this?" I mutter.

"Starting this week, you'll generously be volunteering your time to the Hastings Hurricanes—"

"The what?"

"The Hastings Hurricanes. That's the hockey team at Hastings Elementary. Middle school league, seventh and eighth graders. Briar has a community outreach program in which our student athletes volunteer to coach or act as assistant coaches with local sports teams. The senior who's been working with the Hurricanes—she's the left wing for the Briar's ladies team. She came down with mono, so we need to replace her. Jensen and I think you'd be the perfect candidate to take over."

I try to mask my horror. I don't think I'm successful, because O'Shea is openly smirking at me now.

"It's two afternoon practices a week, and game day is Friday at six. I went ahead and peeked at your class schedule and it doesn't interfere with the Hurricanes' schedule. So we're all set." He tips his head. "Unless you have an objection…?"

Damn right I do. I don't want to spend three days a week coaching a bunch of middle-schoolers. This is my senior year, for chrissake. My course workload is massive. And I'm already practicing six days a week with my own team and playing my own games, which doesn't leave a lot of downtime.

But if I object to this, O'Shea will no doubt make my life miserable. Same way he did back in high school.

"Nope, it sounds like fun." I force the words out and resist from giving him the finger.

He nods in approval. "Well, look at that. Maybe you *have*

changed. The Dean Di Laurentis I knew only cared about one person—himself."

The jab stings more than it should. Sure, I can be a selfish bastard at times, but I hadn't done anything wrong back then, damn it. Miranda and I had been on the same page...until suddenly we weren't.

But I guess it doesn't matter who was in the wrong, does it? Because it's pretty fucking clear that Frank O'Shea is never going to forgive me for what went down between me and his daughter.

CHAPTER 6

DEAN

FIRST THING I DO AFTER I STALK OUT OF THE ARENA IS CALL MY older brother. It's Sunday, so I try his cell first, though there's a good chance he's at the office. Nick works long hours at the firm, including most weekends. I think he's trying to impress our dad with his dedication to the law, and honestly, I think it's working.

The cheerful voice that slides into my ear, however, doesn't belong to Nick.

"Dicky! Yay! I haven't spoken to you in ages!"

The nickname never made me cringe when we were kids, but now that we're adults, it's fucking mortifying. As far as I'm concerned, once my little sister learned how to pronounce *Dean*, our folks should've ordered her to kick Dicky to the curb. Then again, ordering Summer to do anything pretty much ensures she'll do the opposite. My sister is a stubborn brat.

"Why are you answering Nick's cell?" I ask suspiciously.

"Because I saw your name and wanted to talk to you first. You never call me anymore."

I can envision the pout she's no doubt sporting, and it brings a smile to my lips. "You never call me either," I point out.

Summer goes quiet for a second. Then she heaves a colossal sigh. "You're right. I don't. I've been a terrible sister."

"Nah, you're probably just as busy as I am." I head down the cobblestone path toward the back of the training center, making my way to the parking lot.

"I have been pretty busy," she relents.

I hear a loud snort over the extension. "What was that?" I ask.

"Nothing. Just Nicky being an ass. He's been driving me nuts all weekend. Has he always been this uptight, or did it happen once he became a *lawyer*?"

She says *lawyer* as if it's a dirty word. Though to Summer, it probably is. My sister had declared at the age of twelve that law is "hella boring," and eight years later her stance remains the same. She only agreed to attend an Ivy League college to placate our parents, but last we spoke, she told me she wants to go into interior design after she graduates.

"Compared to you, everyone is uptight," I tell my sister. "Which isn't to say I approve of all the batshit crazy things you do."

Summer is two years younger than me, but she gives me a run for my money when it comes to grabbing life by the horns and seizing the day and all that crap. I'm surprised our parents haven't disowned her yet.

A thought suddenly occurs to me. "Why are you in Manhattan? Shouldn't you be at school?"

"I felt like visiting my big brother."

Her tone is way too innocent for my liking. "Bullshit."

"It's true," Summer protests. "I wanted to see Nicky. And I want to see *you* too, so don't be surprised if I show up on your doorstep sometime soon." She pauses. "Actually, I'm thinking of transferring to Briar."

An alarm goes off inside me. "Why? I thought you were happy at Brown."

"I am. But…uh…yeah." Summer sighs again. "I'm on probation."

I halt midstep. "What did you do?" I demand.

"What makes you think I did something?" There's a sniff over the line.

"Save your Little Miss Innocent act for the parentals." I snicker. "Not that it works on them anymore either. Now tell me what happened."

"Let's just say there was an incident at the sorority house. Togas were involved."

I choke down a laugh. "Can you be more specific?"

"Nope."

I groan in exasperation. "Summer—"

"I'll tell you all about it when I see you," she chirps. "Nicky wants to talk to you now."

"Summer—"

She's already gone. My brother's deep voice comes on the line half a second later. "Hey," he says.

"What'd she do?" I ask him.

Nick gives a hearty laugh. "Oh no, I'm not spoiling it for you. All I'm going to say is, classic Summer."

Fucking hell. I'm not sure I even want to know anymore. "Do Mom and Dad know?"

"Yup. They're not thrilled about it, but it's not like she got kicked out. It's just two months of probation and twenty hours of community service."

The last bit distracts me from Summer's woes. "Speaking of community service…" I quickly fill him in about O'Shea's new gig at Briar.

"Shit," Nick says when I'm done. "Did he mention Miranda?"

"No, but it's obvious he still blames me for everything that happened." Bitterness clogs my throat. "A part of me is tempted to track her down and talk some sense into her, maybe ask her to speak to her dad."

"She didn't bother doing that back then," Nick points out. "Why do you think she'd do it now?"

Good point. "I know, but…" I reach my car and jam my finger

on the key fob to unlock the door. I'm still on edge from O'Shea's unexpected reappearance in my life, and I just want to get the hell away from the arena. "Whatever," I say darkly. "I guess it's stupid of me to think Miranda would want to help me. I'm the monster who broke her heart, remember?"

"You want my advice? Just keep your head down. Show up for practice, do what O'Shea says, and don't start any shit. Spring will be here before you know it, and then you'll graduate and never have to see that bastard again."

"You're right," I concede. "It's not worth stressing over. I'll be out of here soon enough, right?"

"Yup. But let me know if he gives you any trouble, okay? I'll try to come up with a good reason to sic a lawsuit on him."

I chuckle. "You don't practice civil law."

"For you, baby brother, I'll make an exception."

I'm in a far better mood after we hang up. My friends like to mock me about being a rich kid from Connecticut. I'm sure they think my parents are snobs and my siblings are spoiled, but truth be told, my family is awesome.

Both my parents are high-powered attorneys, but they're the most down-to-earth people you'll ever meet. Don't get me wrong, my siblings and I definitely had a ton of perks growing up. We had a nanny and housekeeper. We went to private schools and got a cushy weekly allowance. But we also had to do chores and finish all our homework before we ever saw a dime. If our grades slipped, we'd be grounded in a heartbeat. And if we tried pulling that gimme-whatever-I-want-because-we've-got-oodles-of-money crap, we were punished for it. The one and only time I demanded money from my dad, he turned around and donated my entire college fund to a charity for underprivileged kids. Then he made me clerk at his firm for the whole summer to earn it all back.

"What'd Coach want?" Garrett asks when I stride into the living room fifteen minutes later.

"To introduce me to the new defensive coordinator." I flop down in the armchair and glance at the flat screen. G and Logan are battling each other in a game of *Ice Pro*, and judging by the score, Logan is getting his ass handed to him.

"We have a new defensive coordinator?" Logan instantly pauses the game. "And why did you need a private introduction?"

I choose my words carefully. "His name's Frank O'Shea. He was my high school coach, so Jensen figured we'd want to catch up before O'Shea is officially introduced to the team."

Logan furrows his brow. "Okay. But why is he just coming in now? Season's already started. Seems weird to bring in a DC after we've already played our first game."

"And lost," Garrett mutters.

"Still just one game," Logan insists. "It's not like we're in such bad shape that we need a new coach to turn shit around. This feels like a panic move on Coach's part." Frowning, he turns to me again. "What's he like? Good guy?"

He's the devil. "He's decent," I lie, then change the subject. "Where's Tuck?"

"Not sure. Don't think he came home last night." Logan unpauses the game and refocuses his attention on the screen.

I wrinkle my forehead. Tucker hadn't spent Friday night at home either. I wonder if he's seeing someone new, because he doesn't usually stay out two nights in a row.

Since my roommates are distracted by the video game, I go upstairs and force myself to catch up on the course readings I'd fallen behind on. I spend the rest of the day alternating between reading and napping, only going downstairs to steal a few slices of the pizza Garrett and Logan order in the evening. I don't know why I'm feeling so antisocial. Maybe I'm still edgy about O'Shea showing up at Briar. Or maybe it's because every time I closed my eyes for a nap today, I pictured Allie's sexy mouth wrapped around my dick. Her smooth, golden curves pressed up against me. Her tits filling my palms.

Why can't I get this girl out of my mind? Yes, the sex was phenomenal. Yes, I find her attractive. But phenomenal sex and attractive girls aren't exactly an anomaly in my life.

Get over it, I order my dick when it yet again hardens at the thought of Allie.

It twitches in response. Taunting me.

"Goddamn it," I growl. Then I fumble on the bed for my phone and bring up the number I'd dialed last night.

Allie picks up after four rings, her wary voice sliding into my ear. "Hey. What's up?"

I let out a ragged breath. "I want to fuck you again."

"Is this a thing now? You're going to call me every night and say that?"

"Maybe?" Shit. I'm cranky and horny and as confused as she is. "Say yes, baby doll. Just say yes and put me out of my misery."

"I already told you, it was a one-time thing. I'm not into casual sex. We had fun, sure, but— Shit, I've gotta go. Call one of your puck bunnies and I'm sure they'll take care of you, okay?"

For the second time in two days, she hangs up on me.

ALLIE

"Who was that?"

I jump nearly two feet in the air at the sound of Hannah's voice. I disconnected the call when I heard her footsteps in the hall, but I hadn't expected her to appear in my doorway this fast.

"Uh, it was no one." Brilliant answer.

She raises one dark eyebrow. "No one?"

"Telemarketer," I amend. "Which is the equivalent of no one."

She grumbles in annoyance as she heads for my bed. "How do they even get our cell phone numbers? When I signed up with my phone provider, they had this whole section in their policy about how they'll never, ever give my number to a third party. Well, I call bullshit, because guess what? I get daily calls from airlines and clothing stores and all these companies telling me about their awesome sales and saying I won some bogus prize. Oh my God, and the worst one? This stupid cruise ship promotion that starts the call with an automated foghorn! It's *awful*."

Hannah's tangent lasts for several minutes, and I'm grateful for it because it means she's too riled up to figure out I lied to her. And she's so caught up in her rant that she doesn't notice when I discreetly check the text message that pops up on my phone.

Dean: You really need to stop hanging up on me.

I text back, You really need to stop propositioning me. I know I'm a great lay, but get over it already.

Him: I can't. Trust me, I've tried.
Me: Try harder.
Him: C'mon, baby doll. Just one more time. Think of how good it will be...

Of course it'll be good. He's a sex champion. But that doesn't change the fact that I'm not comfortable with casual sex.

Me: Go away. I'm running lines w/ Hannah.
Him: Text me when ur done and I'll sneak into your dorm. Wellsy won't even know I'm there.

I'm startled to feel a sharp ache between my legs. The idea of Dean sneaking in and fucking me while Hannah sleeps obliviously in the next room is a turn-on I didn't expect.

I ignore the unwelcome response and type, Good night, Dean.

Then I turn to Hannah and say, "Are we done bashing telemarketers? Because this script isn't going to read itself, babe."

"Sorry. I can't help it—I hear the word 'telemarketer' and I turn into a ball of rage." She sits cross-legged on the center of my bed and catches the script I toss at her.

I remain standing. The opening scene requires my character to pace, and I want to get a feel for how talking while marching back and forth will affect my breath control.

Hannah thumbs through the intro pages. "All right. Who am I? Jeannette or Caroline?"

"Caroline. Her defining traits are petty and insensitive."

My best friend grins widely. "So I get to play the bitch? Nice."

Honestly, I wish I were playing the bitch. My character is a young widow who lost her husband in Afghanistan, which is the more emotionally draining role. Thanks to this breakup with Sean, my emotion well is dangerously close to depleted, and I'm scared I won't be able to tap into it and do this role justice.

My fear isn't off base. We're only five pages in and I'm already drained, so I call for a quick break.

"Wow," Hannah remarks as she skims the next few scenes. "This play is intense. Everyone in the audience is going to be bawling the entire time."

I collapse next to her and stretch out on my back. "I'm going to be bawling the entire time." Literally, because my character weeps in every other scene.

Hannah falls back on her elbows and a comfortable silence falls between us. I like it, because I don't have this with many people. Even with Megan and Stella, who I consider close friends, one of us is always trying to fill the silence with conversation. I think it takes a certain level of trust to sit next to someone and not feel the pressing urge to babble away.

My dad once told me that the way a person responds to silence reveals a lot about them. I always figured he was talking out of his ass, because Dad has a habit of coming up with insightful-sounding adages and insisting there's wisdom in them, when half the time I know he's bullshitting me.

But right now, I see the truth in his words. When I think of the silences I've shared with my other friends, I realize they really are incredibly telling.

Meg breaks a silence with jokes, doing her damndest to fill the lull with laughter. For as long as I've known her, she's resorted to humor whenever shit gets too serious for her.

Stella fills the silence by barraging you with questions about your life. For as long as I've known her, she's avoided discussing herself if she could help it. I guess that's why it surprised me when she started dating Justin Kohl, the football player Hannah had a crush on before she fell for Garrett. Stella has openly admitted more than once that she's afraid of intimacy.

The thought of Justin has me turning toward Hannah. "Hey, did Garrett ever own up to being wrong about Justin?"

She wrinkles her forehead. "Where did that come from?"

I grin. "Sorry. I was just thinking about Stella, and it reminded me of how Garrett was convinced that Justin had sinister motives. Didn't he insist that Justin was a slimeball?"

"Yep." She sits up with a laugh. "We actually talked about it a while back. I accused him of being subconsciously jealous of Justin."

"Ha. I bet he loved that."

"It's the only thing that makes sense, though. Justin is one of the nicest guys I've ever met. But Garrett insists he just misread him."

"Well, either way, I'm glad Justin turned out to be a good guy. Stella deserves to be happy." I hear the wistful note in my voice and hope Hannah doesn't pick up on it.

She does. "You deserve to be happy too. You know that, right?"

"I know." I swallow the lump that rises in my throat.

Her green eyes take on a hesitant light. "Allie...do you regret breaking up with Sean?"

The lump gets bigger. It makes it hard to breathe, especially when I remember the agony in Sean's voice when he'd asked me who I slept with.

"No," I say finally. "I know it was the right decision. We wanted completely different things for our future, and it wasn't something we could compromise on, not without one of us resenting the other."

Hannah looks pensive. "Do you think you're ready to start dating again?"

I shudder out a breath. "Nope, not even close." But God, what I *would* like is a distraction. I'm tired of being sad. I'm tired of wondering how Sean is doing and fighting the urge to call him. I might not want to get back together, but I hate knowing that I hurt someone I care about. I have this terrible habit of wanting to make everyone happy, even if it means sacrificing my own happiness. My dad insists it's an admirable quality, but sometimes I wish I were more selfish.

I guess I was selfish on Friday night, though. My rebound sex with Dean was all about satisfying my own base urges, and as guilty and embarrassed as I felt afterward, I can't deny it was hella satisfying.

Shit. Maybe Dean's right. Maybe we *should* hook up again.

"Maybe I need a fling," I say aloud, just to test out the idea.

Hannah's response is swift and scolding. "You tried that, remember? After you and Sean broke up the first couple times. You hated it."

It's true. I did hate it. "But I didn't actually sleep with anyone," I point out. "All I did was go on a bunch of crappy dates and make out with a few jerks. Maybe that was my mistake—actually *dating* those guys. Maybe this time I should pick a hot dude and bang his brains out for a few weeks. Just sex, no expectations."

She snorts. "Good luck with that. We both know you can't even make out with a guy without hearing relationship bells in your head."

Also true.

And why am I even contemplating this? If this is how Hannah responds to me broaching the subject of a fling, I can just imagine what she'd say if I admitted I'm considering a fling with *Dean*. The guy is a player to the extreme. Not only is he not relationship material, but I doubt he could even commit to a fling. I can't see him being exclusive to me, which is absolutely nonnegotiable, because there's no way I'm sleeping with someone who's also sleeping with other people.

Yeah…I need to nip this Dean idea in the bud. I don't know why he's so eager to jump into bed with me again, but I'm confident he'll get over it eventually. The guy has the attention span of a fruit fly, and the affection-giving habits of a puppy, offering his sexual devotion to whoever happens to be holding the treat. By which I mean the vagina.

As I return to my senses, I change the subject. "Hey, what are you doing for Thanksgiving?"

"Garrett and I are going to my aunt and uncle's place in Philly. My parents are flying in and meeting us there."

"Nice. Sounds like fun."

"You'll be in Brooklyn, right?"

I nod. I spend every holiday in Brooklyn with my dad. I always look forward to seeing him, but this year I'm a tad worried because the last time we spoke, he insisted on cooking Thanksgiving dinner himself.

Usually I'd be cheering over that announcement, because Dad happens to be the best cook on the planet. But since he was diagnosed with multiple sclerosis five years ago, I've been doing my best to make sure he doesn't push himself. The only reason I turned down a free ride to UCLA's drama program was so I could remain within driving distance of him. The man is so damn stubborn, insisting he doesn't need help and that he can manage on his own, but I hadn't felt comfortable moving to the opposite end of the country once his remission periods became few and far between.

Now I'm even more relieved I stayed on the East Coast, because Dad's condition has gotten progressively worse this past year.

Like most people who suffer from the disease, he was initially diagnosed with relapsing-remitting MS, but now it's transitioned into the secondary-progressive type, which means his relapses are more frequent and more severe than they used to be. When I visited him over the summer, I was shocked by the change in him. Suddenly he was having trouble walking, when before it was the occasional loss of balance and mild numbness in his limbs. He had two attacks of vertigo when I was there, and when I pressed him, he admitted that the pain was getting worse and he was experiencing the occasional vision problems.

All this? Fucking terrifies me. I already lost my mom to cancer when I was thirteen. Dad is all I have left. I refuse to lose him too, even if it means chaining him to his recliner in our Brooklyn brownstone and forcing him to watch football while I cook dinner in his stead.

"Okay, break time is over." Once again I need a distraction from my bleak thoughts. Groaning, I sit up and open the script to where we left off. "Caroline is about to yell at Jeannette again."

Hannah tucks a strand of dark hair behind her ear. "For the record? If you ever lost your husband, I would never call you a crybaby and tell you to 'get over it.'" Her expression grows serious. "In other words, you can keep moping about Sean for as long as you need to. I promise I won't judge you for it."

Emotion wells up in my throat, but I manage to squeeze out two words. "Thank you."

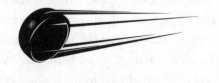

CHAPTER 7

DEAN

FOR ALL HIS BULLSHIT ABOUT THE PAST STAYING IN THE PAST, IT'S painfully evident that my former coach is pushing a Make Dean's Life Miserable agenda. The first practice with our new defensive coordinator runs an hour late—but only for the defensemen. While everyone else heads to the locker room to shower, change, and go home, O'Shea forces the D-men to stay behind for extra skating drills after announcing that we're the sorriest excuse for hockey players he's ever seen.

When he finally dismisses us, my teammates and I skate off the ice, cursing and grumbling the entire time. We're all dripping with sweat, steam is rolling out of our helmets, and our mood is foul as we strip off our gear in the now-deserted locker room.

"Decent guy, huh?" Logan says sarcastically, echoing the description I'd offered yesterday.

"He was just showing us his dick is bigger than ours," I mutter. "It's probably his way of trying to earn our respect."

No, it's his way of punishing me for hurting his daughter, but I keep that delightful tidbit to myself. Not because O'Shea ordered me not to discuss it with my teammates, but because I'd rather not think about all the shit that happened with Miranda.

Ironically, my relationship with Miranda O'Shea didn't just impact my high school life, but also my college one. Miranda is the reason I now spell out my intentions—or lack thereof—before every single hookup. Granted, I thought I'd spelled everything out back then too, but clearly I hadn't articulated it as well as I should have. These days, I make sure women know exactly where we stand before their heads can fill up with fantasies about happily ever after.

"You doing anything for dinner?" Logan asks as we hit the showers. "Grace is grabbing Chinese food in town and meeting me at the house. I think she's bringing enough grub for everyone."

"Ah, thanks for the invite, but I'm having drinks with Maxwell. Not sure when I'll be home."

The conversation ends as we step into our respective stalls. I've barely finished soaping my balls when Logan shuts off his water. Jeez. Dude just showered like someone had offered him a million bucks if he could lather up and rinse off in less than thirty seconds.

"Later," he calls as he slaps a towel around his waist and ducks out of the shower area.

I know he's eager to see Grace, and for some reason that brings a strange flutter to my chest. It's not quite jealousy. Not quite resentment. Disappointment, maybe?

I get it. My best friends are in love. They'd rather cuddle and make kissy faces at their women than hang out with the boys, and I'm not pissed at them for it, not in the slightest. Thing is, this feels like the beginning of the end for us.

After my older brother graduated from Harvard, he lost touch with his college friends within months. Teammates he once would've laid down his life for? Hardly speaks to them now. Friends from law school? They exchange one email a month, tops.

I understand that friends drift apart after college. People get married. They move away. They make new friends and develop other interests. But I hate the idea of not having Garrett or Logan or Tuck in my life. I also hate this cynical part of my brain that points out the inevitability of that outcome.

I'll be in law school next year. I won't have time to sleep let alone see my friends. Garrett will most likely be living in another city, playing in the NHL. Logan too, if it works out with the Providence Bruins, the farm team that has already stated their interest in signing him after he graduates. It's only a matter of time before he's called up to the pros and moving away too. And who knows what Tucker plans to do after college. He might move back to Texas, for all I know.

Fuck. Why am I feeling so philosophical tonight? Maybe it's because I haven't had sex in three days. Sadly, that's a long time for me, and my balls don't like it. I blame Allie, of course.

"Dean!"

A familiar voice calls out to me as I leave the team facility. I spot Kelly sashaying up the path toward me, looking like she stepped off the pages of a New England clothing catalog. A thick red scarf winds around her neck, and she's rocking a pair of brown leather boots and a long gray peacoat. Her blond hair is up in a messy knot, with long strands framing her face.

She's hot as fuck, but truthfully, I haven't thought about her or Michelle since I slept with Allie. Still, I don't feel guilty that I haven't called or texted her, and Kelly doesn't scold me for it as she greets me with a warm hug. Like I said, chicks know where I stand these days. And ironically, when Kelly and Michelle approached me at Malone's, they'd given me the no-strings speech before I could even open my mouth. They'd straight up told me they only wanted my dick, and I was happy to oblige.

"Did you have a good weekend?" she asks.

I shrug. "Could've been better." If a certain someone didn't keep turning me down.

"Aw, that's no good." She smiles. "I have something that will cheer you up, though. My best friend from high school is in town. I told her all about you, and she'd love to meet you. She's staying with me and Michelle…"

There is no way to misinterpret the invitation. "Ah. Well…" I'm not sure how to respond to that.

"Oh, and Michelle's down too…" Kelly winks at me. "Everyone always says three is the magic number, but I'm thinking four is even better."

I wait for my dick to respond. Fuck, I *order* it to respond. A semi, a ball tingle, a twitch. *Anything*, damn it. But there's nothing stirring south of the equator. It's like my equipment just stopped working.

Come on, Little Dean, help me out, I plead silently. *We're talking fourgy here.*

Still flaccid. Apparently Little Dean isn't going to cooperate unless I give him what he wants. And what he wants, unfortunately, is not Kelly, Michelle, and Kelly's best friend.

It's Allie Hayes.

"That sounds…amazing. Really. But I have to pass. I'm having drinks with a buddy tonight," I say ruefully.

"Anyone I know?"

"Uh, maybe. Beau Maxwell. He's—"

"The quarterback of our football team," she finishes. A seductive glint lights her eyes. "Invite him along. Five can be just as fun as four…"

Oh sweet baby Jesus.

I want to be turned on. I *pray* for it to happen. But Little Dean ain't having it.

As frustration forms a knot in my gut, I mumble another excuse, ask for a rain check, and then stomp toward my car, cursing my dick the entire time.

TWENTY MINUTES LATER, I SLIDE INTO THE BACK BOOTH AT Malone's. "Sorry I'm late," I tell Beau. "Practice lasted an extra hour."

Briar's starting quarterback shrugs his big shoulders. "No

worries. I just got here a couple minutes ago." To my relief, the glass of dark ale in front of him has barely been sipped.

As I shrug out of my hockey jacket and toss it beside me on the bench seat, a cute brunette waitress wanders over to take my order.

"So whatcha been up to?" Beau asks after she leaves. "I haven't seen you since midterms ended."

"I know, man. Our practice schedule has been brutal. We lost every pre-season game and Coach Jensen is shitting a brick."

"Fuck, I hear ya. Deluca is shitting bricks too," he admits, referring to his head coach. "We have no chance of making the playoffs. Hell, I'll be surprised if we even play in a bowl game." His face is gloomier than I've ever seen it, but there's not much I can offer in terms of reassurance.

The football team already has three losses under their belt. One or two, maybe they could've come back from. But three pretty much torpedoes their chances of ranking this season.

Beau's blue eyes darken as he takes a long swig of beer and chugs nearly half the pint glass. I feel his frustration. I know what it's like to be an above average player on a below average team. Granted, the hockey season just started and pre-season games don't count for standings, but our ineffective game play and clumsy practices don't bode well for the upcoming season.

On the other hand, we're three-time national champions, so it's not like I'll be crying in my pillow every night if we don't make it to the playoffs this year. Hell, maybe we're due for a bad season. Could be the hockey gods' way of keeping us humble.

Beau's situation is different, though. Briar recruited him out of high school and he blew everyone away during his freshman year. The coaches actually benched their senior quarterback and named Beau as the starter. He led the team to an undefeated season and took them all the way to the championship game. They lost, sure, but Briar going to the playoffs after more than a decade of being shut out had been a major achievement.

The following year, shit fell apart. Nearly all the star players on the team either graduated or declared early for the draft, leaving Beau with a weak offensive line and an even weaker receiving corps. The team has been racking up losses ever since, which is disheartening in general, but even more so because Beau happens to be an incredibly talented quarterback. Unfortunately for him, he doesn't have the necessary weapons around him that it takes to win.

"You had the opportunity to transfer in sophomore year," I remind him. "LSU all but sucked your dick to lure you down there."

He scowls. "And, what, abandon my team? What kind of asshole does that?"

An asshole who wants to play for the NFL, I want to say, but I bite back the remark. Thanks to the football team's recent performances, the chances of Beau going high in the draft—or getting drafted at all—are pretty slim. But I suppose his loyalty to Briar is admirable. It definitely speaks to his character, that's for sure.

"Subject change," Beau orders. "Now, before I start crying in my Sam Adams."

As if on cue, the waitress returns to deliver my Coors Light. I'd asked for a bottle instead of a pint glass, and she makes an elaborate show of popping off the cap and passing me the longneck, bending low so I have a perfect view of her cleavage.

"You boys let me know if you need anything else," she coos. "I'm only a holler away."

We both check out her ass when she turns around. I don't even feel pervy about it, because she's pretty much inviting our appreciative glances by shaking that round bottom and swaying her hips as she walks. Her short black shirt reminds me of the other fine ass I saw this weekend. An ass that Beau, despite my numerous vocal warnings, is very familiar with.

"I saw Sabrina at Malone's on Friday," I tell him.

He shifts his gaze away from the waitress. "Yeah?"

I nod. "You still seeing her?" And by seeing, I mean no-strings banging, because Beau and I are kindred spirits. He doesn't do relationships either.

"Nah. It fizzled out," he admits. "She's too busy."

"Busy doing what?" As far as I know, Sabrina doesn't even have a job.

"No clue. She lives in Boston, so I guess the commute has something to do with it. But it got to the point where she was only coming to see me once, maybe twice a month? And she disappears on the weekends, just...*poof*, disappears." He shrugs. "I figured she was playing hard to get, but now I legit think she's leading a double life." He pauses. "You think she's CIA?"

I consider it. "No conscience, black heart...yeah, makes sense."

He snickers. "Aw, fuck off. She's a cool chick, even if she is impossible to read."

"If by 'cool chick' you mean 'judgmental bitch,' then sure." It's my turn to change the subject. "Hey, so Justin came by last week, and he said there's this freshman wideout on the team who might amount to something?"

Beau nods. "Johnson. He's fast, but he still has issues with securing the ball."

We chat about our respective teams again for the next ten minutes. I might play hockey while Beau is Mr. Football, but we're fans of each other's sports, so the conversation flows smoothly between us. After we've ordered a second round of beers, the subject shifts back to chicks, as I glumly relay to Beau the offer Kelly had made back at the arena.

"What the fuck, man? You turned down an *orgy*? An orgy I was invited to?" He shakes his head at me. "Are you coming down with the flu or something?"

I run my fingers along the neck of the beer bottle. "Nah. Just wasn't feeling it."

"You weren't feeling an orgy." Disbelief drips from his tone. "Who the hell are you and what have you done with my man Dean?"

I groan. "I don't know. I'm screwed, dude. I hooked up with someone the other night, and now I can't get her out of my head."

"You're shitting me."

"Nope. God-awful truth."

Beau continues to gape at me.

"You think I *like* this?" I say defensively. "Trust me, I don't need this headache in my life." I swallow a mouthful of beer. "Hey. You know *Twilight*?"

He blinks. "Excuse me?"

"*Twilight*. The vampire book."

His wary eyes study my face. "What about it?"

"Okay, so you know how Bella's blood is extra special? Like how it gives Edward a raging boner every time he's around her?"

"Are you fucking with me right now?"

I ignore that. "Do you think it happens in real life? Pheromones and all that crap. Is it a bullshit theory some horndog dreamed up so he could justify why he's attracted to his mother or some shit? Or is there actually a biological reason why we're drawn to certain people? Like goddamn *Twilight*. Edward wants her on a biological level, right?"

"Are you seriously dissecting *Twilight* right now?"

God, I am. This is what Allie has reduced me to. A sad, pathetic loser who goes to a bar and forces his friend to participate in a *Twilight* book club.

"I don't know whether to make fun of you or refer you to a shrink," Beau says solemnly. "I've never met a dude who's actually read that book."

"I haven't read it. My sister was obsessed with those books when they came out. She used to follow me around the house and offer me recaps against my will."

"Uh-huh. Sure. Blame it on your sister." Beau laughs before going serious again. "Okay, so you're horny for this chick. Why don't you just nail her again?"

"Because she doesn't want to hook up again," I reply through clenched teeth.

"Impossible. Everyone wants to hook up with you."

"I know, right?" I lift the bottle to my lips. "So what should I do?"

Beau offers a shrug. "Get over it. Go out with someone else."

He gestures around the bar. "This place is full of women who'd sell their firstborn to go home with you. Pick one and sex this other chick right out of your head."

"My dick won't let me," I mutter.

Beau snickers. "Can you repeat that, please?"

"My dick is being difficult," I explain irritably. "I tried to jerk off to porn last night, and swear to God, damn thing wouldn't get hard. Then I thought of All—this girl"—I correct myself, because I promised Allie I wouldn't tell anyone about our night together—"and *bam*"—I snap my fingers—"hard as a rock."

Beau eyes me thoughtfully. "You know, I don't think we're dealing with a Bella's-magical-blood situation here."

"No?"

"No. I think you've imprinted on this girl's pussy."

A choked cough sounds from behind me, and I turn in time to see our waitress walking by. Her cheeks are red, lips twitching as if she's trying not to bust a gut.

I turn back to Beau. "What do you mean?"

"I mean you're facing a Jacob quandary. You imprinted on her pussy, and now it's the only pussy you can think about. You exist solely for *this* pussy. Like Jacob and that weird mutant baby."

"You fucking asshole. You've totally read those books."

"Nuh-uh," Beau protests. He gives a sheepish grin. "I've seen the movies."

I decide to save my taunting for later because there are more pressing matters to focus on. "So what's the cure, Dr. Maxwell? Go on a fuck spree and hope I unimprint? Or keep working the charm and hope I wear her down?"

My buddy snorts loudly. "How would I know?" He raises his pint glass. "I'm drunk, dude. Nobody should ever listen to me when I'm drunk." He drains his glass and signals the waitress for another. "Hell, nobody should listen to me when I'm *sober*."

CHAPTER 8

DEAN

THE SECOND GAME OF THE SEASON IS AN UNMITIGATED DISASTER. No. Scratch that. It's a goddamn bloodbath.

Nobody says a word as we file into the locker room, the humiliation of the loss creeping behind us like a puddle of tar. We may as well have yanked our pants down, stuck our bare asses in the air, and cheerfully asked the other team for a spanking. We fucking handed them the win. No, we handed them a *shutout*.

As I whip off my jersey, I mentally replay every second of the game. Every mistake we made out there tonight is burned into my mind like a cattle brand. Losing sucks. Losing at home sucks harder.

Damn, there are going to be a lot of disappointed fans at Malone's tonight. I'm not looking forward to seeing them, and I know my teammates are equally upset. None more so than Hunter, who hurriedly strips out of his uniform as if it's covered with fire ants.

"You got some nice shots on goal tonight," I tell him, and it's the truth. Our scoreless game wasn't for lack of trying. We played hard. The other team just played harder.

"Would've been nicer if one of them went in," he mutters.

I stifle a sigh. "Their goalie was on point tonight. Even G couldn't get one past him."

Garrett takes that moment to lumber up to his locker, and he's quick to reassure the frowning freshman. "Don't sweat it, kid. There's plenty more hockey to be played this season. We'll bounce back."

"Yeah. Sure." Hunter is unconvinced. We don't get the chance to offer more encouragement, because Coach Jensen strides into the locker room, tailed by Frank O'Shea.

Coach wastes no time delivering one of his brief, post-game speeches. As usual, it sounds like he's talking in point form.

"We lost. It feels shitty. Don't let it get to you. Just means we work harder during practice and bring it harder for the next game." He nods at everyone, then stalks out the door.

I'd think he was pissed at us, if not for the fact that his victory speeches more or less go the same way: *We won. It feels great. Don't let it go to your head. We work just as hard during practice and we win more games.* If any of our freshman players are expecting Coach to deliver epic motivational speeches à la Kurt Russell in *Miracle*, they're in for a grave disappointment.

O'Shea lingers in the room. My shoulders instinctively tense when he trudges toward me, but he surprises me by saying, "Good coverage in the defensive zone tonight. That was a solid block in the second."

"Thanks." I'm still suspicious of the unexpected compliment, but he's already moved on to praise Logan for successfully killing the power play in the third period.

I toss my gear in one of the huge laundry bins, then head for the showers and wash the stench of failure off my body. I hate losing, but I don't allow myself more than ten minutes to dwell on it. My father taught me that trick when I was eight years old, after a particularly demoralizing loss on the lacrosse field.

"You have ten minutes," he told me. "Ten minutes to think about what you did wrong and how bad you feel right now. Are you ready?"

He'd actually clicked a button on his watch and timed me, and for those ten minutes I brooded and sulked and wallowed in humiliation. I remembered the errors I'd made on the field and corrected them in my head. I imagined punching every player on the opposing team square in the mouth. And then Dad told me my time was up.

"There. It's over now," he said. "Now you look forward and figure out how you're going to get better."

I fucking love my dad.

By the time I'm out of the shower, the bitterness of tonight's loss has faded, tucked away in my internal filing cabinet in a folder labeled Shitty Stuff.

I think Garrett uses the same filing system, because he's damn near chipper as we meet up with Hannah in the parking lot. He pulls her into his arms and smacks a kiss on her lips. "Hey, babe."

"Hey." She snuggles closer to him. "It's getting so cold! I wouldn't be surprised if it started snowing right now."

She's not wrong. It's freezing out, and every breath we take floats out in a visible white cloud.

"Bar or home?" Logan asks, joining us at our cars.

"Bar," Garrett says. "Don't feel like having anyone over tonight. You?"

After a game, we either hit Malone's or invite our teammates and friends over to the house, but it's obvious none of us feel like playing hosts tonight.

"Bar," Logan echoes, and I nod in agreement.

"Are we waiting for Tucker?" I search the lot, but I don't see our roommate anywhere. "And what about Grace?"

"Tuck already left with Fitzy," Logan answers. "And Grace isn't coming tonight. She's at the station."

Feigning nonchalance, I glance at Hannah. "What about your other half?"

"I'm right here," Garrett says smugly.

"I mean her other other half." I grin at Hannah. "The little blond drama queen you hang out with?"

"She didn't feel like going out tonight. She's too busy moping."

"Moping about what?" But I already know the answer to that. The ex-boyfriend, obvs.

Hannah confirms my thoughts. "Sean. He called her this morning, and I don't know what he said to her, but she got really quiet afterward and she's been mopey ever since. I would've stayed home tonight, but I didn't want to miss the game."

Garrett leans down to kiss her cold-reddened cheek. "I'm glad you didn't. We appreciate your support, babe."

"I'm so bummed you guys lost," she says, but I'm more concerned about the idea of Allie sulking all alone in the dorm. She's probably ovaries-deep in a carton of Ben & Jerry's right now while Mumford & Sons plays in the background.

"Are you sure you shouldn't go home and braid her hair or something?" I ask Hannah. "That's what chicks do for moral support, right?"

"Yes, Dean. That's exactly what we do. Hair braiding, followed by naked pillow fights and then kissing practice."

"Can I come?" Logan and I blurt out in unison.

"You wish. And no, I'm not going home yet. I texted Allie during the third period and she insists she's fine. She's drinking margaritas and watching this awful show. Like, I'm talking *really* awful. Wild horses couldn't drag me back there tonight."

"What show?" Garrett asks curiously.

"The worst thing to ever happen to television" is all she says, and everyone laughs.

Logan taps the hood of my Beemer. "Are we ready to go?"

I hesitate. "Actually, do you mind riding with G and Wellsy? I need to make a few stops first. I'll meet you guys there."

"Sure," he says easily. He moves away from my car and toward Garrett's Jeep.

I slide into the driver's seat and start the engine, but I wait until the Jeep disappears from the lot before I pull out of my parking space. I have only one stop to make, and it's not one I want any of my friends knowing about.

ALLIE

WHEN I HEAR THE KNOCK, MY FIRST THOUGHT IS THAT SEAN IS AT the door. Then I pray he isn't, because after the bizarre and upsetting conversation we had this morning, I'm not ready to see him.

"I forgive you."

He'd blurted out those three words the second I answered the phone. I, in turn, had to fight from spitting out something nasty in response, because forgiveness implies that I'd done something wrong by sleeping with someone else, and that wasn't the case. I hadn't cheated on him. I hadn't lied to him. Sure, having sex with Dean so soon after my breakup with Sean isn't something I'm proud of, but I'm not the first girl to jump into rebound sex and I certainly won't be the last.

Still, despite the resentment his "forgiveness" had triggered, a part of me was relieved to hear it. God knows I've been feeling guilty about my night with Dean, so maybe absolution is exactly what I was seeking when I confessed my sin to Sean the other night.

That doesn't mean I'm ready for a face-to-face with him, though. He'd asked if we could meet up for coffee, claiming he had more he needed to say but didn't want to do it over the phone. I told him I'd think about it. Now, as another knock pounds on the door, I really hope he didn't decide to force the issue.

I brace myself for a confrontation and open the door. But it's not Sean. It's Dean.

"Hey there, baby doll." He flashes a grin and barrels his way inside. "Wellsy said you were sulking, so I stopped by to turn your frown upside down."

"I'm not sulking," I grumble.

"Even better. Saves me from having to do any work." He unzips his jacket and tosses it on the arm of the couch. Then he strips off his sweater, leaving him in nothing but faded blue jeans.

I stare at him in disbelief. "Did you really just take off your shirt?"

"Yeah. I don't like shirts."

He doesn't like shirts.

This guy… Goddamn it, I don't even know what I think of him.

He turns toward the sofa, and the way his tight butt moves beneath the snug denim reminds me of how firm it felt when I squeezed it. Then he lowers his long body on the sofa cushions, which causes the denim to stretch over his package, and now I'm reminded of the way my mouth had watered when Dean's cock was filling it.

"Oh yeah, suck it, baby. Suck it like you own it."

The raspy command echoes in my mind. My lips start to tingle, because damn it, I *had* sucked it. I'd sucked it like it was a lollipop and an ice-cream cone and every other delicious treat imaginable, all rolled up in one hard cock.

Crap, I think I might be blushing, which is confirmed when Dean winks at me. Does he know I'm thinking about blowing him?

What am I even saying? Of course he does. A guy like Dean probably assumes that everyone, at all times, is thinking about blowing him.

He stretches one arm along the back of the couch and beckons me with the other. "You sitting or what?"

"I'll stand, thanks."

"Aw, come on. I don't bite."

"Yes you do."

Those green eyes twinkle. "You're right. I do."

He looks way too comfortable sitting there on my couch. A blond Adonis with his golden chest and sculpted muscles and perfectly chiseled face. If the hockey thing doesn't work out for him, he ought to consider going into modeling. Dean Di Laurentis oozes sexuality. He could slap his face on a laxative label and every woman in the world would be praying for constipation just to have an excuse to buy it.

"Seriously, Allie-Cat, sit down. You're starting to make me feel unwelcome."

"You *aren't* welcome," I sputter. "I was having a perfectly nice evening until you showed up."

He looks hurt, but I don't know if it's genuine or if he's putting it on. I suspect it's the latter. "You really don't like me, huh?"

Guilt pricks at me. Crap. Maybe it *is* genuine. "It's not that. I do like you. But I wasn't kidding when I said I'm not into casual sex, okay? Every time I think about what we did this weekend, I feel—"

"Horny?" he supplies.

Yes. "Slutty."

I don't expect the flare of irritation I glimpse in his eyes. "You want some advice, babe? Erase that word from your vocabulary."

I suddenly feel guilty again, but I'm not sure why. Very reluctantly, I join him on the couch, making sure to keep some distance between us.

"I mean it," he continues. "Stop slut-shaming yourself. And fuck the word 'slut.' People should be able to have sex whenever they want, however many times they want, with however many partners they choose, and not get some shitty label slapped on them."

He's right, but… "The label is there whether we like it or not," I point out.

"Yeah, and it was created by prudes and judgmental assholes and jealous pricks who wish they were getting laid on the regular but aren't." Dean shakes his head. "You need to stop thinking there's something wrong with what we did. We had fun. We were safe. We didn't hurt anyone. It's nobody's business what you or anyone else does in the privacy of their bedrooms, all right?"

Oddly enough, his words succeed in easing some of the shame that's been trapped inside me since Friday night. But not all of it. "I told Sean," I confess.

Dean frowns.

"Not about you," I add hastily. "I just told him I had sex with someone else."

"Why the hell would you do that?"

"I don't know." I moan. "I felt like I owed him the truth, but that's crazy, right? I mean, we're broken up." Another moan slips out, this one more anguished than the first. "But we were together for so long. I'm so used to telling him everything."

Dean absently rubs the cushion behind my head. The movement directs my gaze to his biceps, the delicious flex of muscle honed from years of physical activity. "Be honest," he finally says. "Do you want to get back together with the guy?"

I slowly shake my head.

"You sure about that?"

"I'm sure." I think about the nonstop arguments Sean and I had since the summer, and I feel even more confident in my decision to end it. All those spiteful comments he'd hurled my way…mocking me about my dreams…giving me ultimatums for the future…

Sean might have forgiven me for what I did after our breakup, but suddenly I'm not sure I've forgiven *him* for what he did before it.

"We weren't right for each other anymore." I swallow the pain in my throat. "If it was possible to stay in college forever, then yes, Sean and I would probably be together. But it's time to grow up, and we want completely different things for the future. Or at least I think we do. This breakup is screwing with my head. I don't even know what to think anymore."

"That's your problem. You think too much."

I can't help but laugh. "Gee, is that your advice? Stop thinking?"

"Stop obsessing." Dean shrugs. "You broke up with the guy for a reason—a damn good reason, if you ask me—and now you've gotta follow through on it. Quit talking to him and quit second-guessing yourself."

"You're right," I say grudgingly.

"Of course I am. I'm always right." With an arrogant smile, he moves closer and rests one big hand on my knee. "Okay, so here's our plan for tonight. First we'll bone down to take the edge off. Then we'll order a pizza and replenish our energy, and after that, round two. Sound good?"

Exasperation rises inside me. Every time I think there's more to Dean than simply being a sex-obsessed horndog, he goes and proves me wrong. Or actually, he proves me *right*.

"Have you considered seeing a psychiatrist about your delusions?" I ask politely. "Because, sweetie, there's no chance in hell of us boning tonight."

"Fine. How about we go down on each other instead?"

"How about you leave?"

"Counter offer—I stay and we dry hump."

God, this guy is incorrigible. "Counter offer—you can stay, but you're not allowed to talk."

He counters with "I stay, I'm allowed to talk, but I won't hit on you."

I think it over. "You stay, you can't hit on me, and you have to watch my show without a single complaint."

A broad grin stretches across his face. "I accept your terms, madam."

CHAPTER 9

ALLIE

"So what are we watching?" Mr. I Don't Like Shirts glances at the television screen. It's paused to the opening credits of the episode I was about to play before Dean showed up.

"*Solange*," I answer.

He wrinkles his nose. "What's *Solange?*"

"It's a French soap opera I'm watching so I can learn to speak the language."

Dean snickers. "You know there's a French Department at this college, right? Classes you can take?"

"Yeah, where all you do is conjugate verbs and learn how to ask for directions and where the bathroom is. I'm all about immersion. If I hear people talking in French for long enough, I'll pick it up a lot faster."

He raises his eyebrows. "How's it going so far?"

"Not great"—he snickers again—"but I'm only on season one," I protest. "I'm sure after a few more seasons, I'll be fluent."

Dean looks at the screen, then back at me. I can tell he's debating whether he made a grave error by coming over tonight. But he surprises me by saying, "All right. Catch me up. What's this show about?"

"Are you being serious right now?"

"As a heart attack."

"Really?" I beam at him, because this is the first time anyone has offered to watch this show with me. My friends refuse to, though to Hannah's credit, she did manage to sit through the pilot. Afterward, she informed me that she'd rather have crows peck at her eyes than watch the next episode. Honestly, I don't blame her. It's not a good show. I know this. But what started off as a language exercise ended with me getting totally hooked. It's like crack to me now.

"Okay, so that's Solange." I press Play, and a gorgeous redhead with massive boobs and a teeny waist appears on the screen.

"Ah," he says. "The titular character."

"You only used that word because it has 'tit' in it."

"Obvs. Tits are great."

I sigh. "Anyway, Solange is dating Sebastian—"

"Sebastian, huh? That's my middle name." He pauses. "Well, one of them," he amends.

My brow furrows. "How many middle names do you have?"

"Two. My full name's Dean Sebastian Kendrick Heyward-Di Laurentis."

I shake my head in dismay. "What is wrong with your parents? Why would they give you so many names? Did they *want* you to get made fun of in school?"

That makes him chuckle. "Trust me, it's nothing compared to some of the dudes at my prep school. This one guy I played lacrosse with had six middle names."

"So you're saying it's a rich person thing? Cram as many unnecessary syllables on your kid's birth certificate?"

"Nah, it's usually done to acknowledge the grandparents or some other wealthy relative." He shrugs. "Sebastian is my grandfather on my dad's side. Kendrick is on my mom's."

I guess that makes sense. But man, his full name is a total mouthful.

As something catches my eye, I quickly point at the screen. "See that guy lurking in the corner? The one with the mustache? That's Antoine. He's stalking Solange."

Dean gives a mock gasp. "The plot thickens!"

I give him the finger. "*But*, in the last episode, we found out the reason he's stalking her, and it's not because he wants to jiggle down."

"Jiggle down?"

"You know, fuck her."

"Right." His lips twitch like he's trying hard not to laugh. "So why's he creeping on her then?"

"Because her mother *paid* him to." I lower my voice, then feel like an idiot, because it's not like Solange can fucking hear me. "Ooh, and get this. Last episode there was another huge twist. Solange's colleague from the modeling agency— Oh, there she is." On the screen, a stunning blond enters the restaurant and sashays her way to Solange's table. "That's her mother," I inform Dean. "Solange's mother is pretending to be her colleague!"

He frowns. "How does that work? They're the same age."

"Nope," I say smugly. "This is where the cosmetic company comes in."

Dean looks utterly lost. "What cosmetic company?"

"*Beauté éternelle*. I looked it up, and it stands for Eternal Beauty. Solange's family owns it. Oh, and her father and uncle are big-time plastic surgeons. Anyway, Solange thinks her mother ran off when she was a kid. Well, her mother *did* run off, actually. But after the dad died, Marie-Thérèse came back to the French Riviera and black-mailed the uncle into doing plastic surgery on her, so now she looks like a totally different person. Solange has no idea that she's spent the last six months working with her mother."

"Allie." Dean leans forward and fixes me with an eerily somber stare. "This show is fucking stupid."

"I know," I say sheepishly. "But it's addictive. Trust me, one episode of this crap and you'll be hooked."

"Sorry, baby doll, but I can pretty much guarantee that's not gonna happen."

DEAN

It happened.

God help me, I'm into this show.

I came over tonight with the single-minded purpose of working the charm and convincing Allie to get naked with me again. Instead, I'm sipping on a margarita, I've just watched two hours' worth of a French soap opera, and now I'm texting Logan to let him know I won't make it to Malone's. Because…God help me…I want to know what happens next.

Marie-Thérèse and Antoine hooked up in the last episode, which ended with a crazed Marie-Thérèse holding a letter opener to his throat—when there was no previous indication that she had any sort of beef with Antoine. Or hell, maybe there was and we just didn't pick up on it because *we don't fucking speak French.*

"I still don't get why she has a grudge against Solange," I admit as Allie hovers over the coffee table to top off our margaritas. The wide neckline of her shirt shifts to one side, providing me with a view of one bare shoulder and the swell of her left boob.

I'm about to comment on how the sexy view is much appreciated, then think better of it. I promised I wouldn't hit on her tonight, and if I break that promise she might kick me out before I find out why Marie-Thérèse tried to kill Antoine.

Allie flops down beside me, and I give myself a mental high-five because she didn't leave a foot of distance between us this time. We're inches apart now, which tells me she's starting to warm up to me.

"I'm not sure either. I haven't figured out the whole backstory yet. I think it has something to do with Solange's father loving his daughter more than his wife," Allie muses. "There were some flashbacks in the earlier episodes that heavily implied he wanted to jiggle down with his daughter."

"Kinky."

She snickers.

We go quiet as the next episode picks up exactly where it left off. Antoine manages to subdue Marie-Thérèse, and the two proceed to argue for ten minutes. Don't ask me about what, because it's in French, but I do notice that the same word—*héritier*—keeps popping up over and over again during their fight.

"Okay, we need to look up that word," I say in aggravation. "I think it's important."

Allie grabs her cell phone and swipes her finger on the screen. I peek over her shoulder as she pulls up a translation app. "How do you think you spell it?" she asks.

We get the spelling wrong three times before we finally land on a translation that makes sense: *heir.*

"Oh!" she exclaims. "They're talking about the father's will."

"Shit, that's totally it. She's pissed off that Solange inherited all those shares of *Beauté éternelle.*"

We high-five at having figured it out, and in the moment our palms meet, pure clarity slices into me and I'm able to grasp precisely what my life has become.

With a growl, I snatch the remote control and hit Stop.

"Hey, it's not over yet," she objects.

"Allie." I draw a steady breath. "We need to stop now. Before my balls disappear altogether and my man card is revoked."

One blond eyebrow flicks up. "Who has the power to revoke it?"

"I don't know. The Man Council. The Stonemasons. Jason Statham. Take your pick."

"So you're too much of a manly man to watch a French soap opera?"

"Yes." I chug the rest of my margarita, but the salty flavor is another reminder of how low I've sunk. "Jesus Christ. And I'm drinking *margaritas*. You're bad for my rep, baby doll." I shoot her a warning look. "Nobody can ever know about this."

"Ha. I'm going to post it all over the internet. Guess what, folks—Dean Sebastian Kendrick Heyward-Di Laurentis is over at my place right now watching soaps and drinking girly drinks." She sticks her tongue out at me. "You'll never get laid again."

She's right about that. "Can you at least add that the night ended with a blow job?" I grumble. "Because then everyone will be like 'Oh, he suffered through all that so he could get his pole waxed.'"

"Your pole waxed? That's *such* a gross description." But her eyes are bright and she's laughing as she says it.

Christ, she's so pretty. And sexy...so goddamn sexy. I wonder why I never noticed it before, but I guess it's because every time I saw her prior to Friday night, she was glued to her boyfriend's side.

The moment I think about Allie's ex, her phone buzzes. Speak of the devil.

"What does he want now?" I have trouble hiding my irritation, but she's too distracted by the text message to notice.

She tilts the screen toward me, and my annoyance grows. So can we meet up for coffee? it says. I really need to talk to you.

"Say no," I advise.

Her teeth dig into her bottom lip. "It's...hard."

"You have no problem saying no to *me*."

"I didn't date you for three years," she points out.

I gently take the phone from her hand and set it on the table. "Okay. You ready for some real talk?"

She nods shakily.

"Sean is going to keep texting you. He's going to keep emailing and calling and doing everything in his power to win you back. You want to know why? Because you're smart and funny and smoking hot, and he knows he's a total idiot for letting you go."

Surprise fills her eyes.

"He's going to keep at it. Which means you need to learn to ignore it." I study her face. "That is, if you're serious about moving on."

She nods again, resolute this time. "I am."

"Then move the fuck on, babe. You can't run to your friend's boyfriend's house or hide out in the dorm every night. Tell the guy you don't want to talk to him, and then go out and find yourself some distractions. I can help you, if you want."

"Let me guess," she says dryly. "You volunteer as sexual tribute?"

"Nope. For once, I'm not talking about sex."

"What do you suggest, then?"

I grin. "I think you need to live the Life of Dean."

"Huh. Okay. So I should throw on some hockey pads, let a bunch of behemoths smash me into the boards every night, and reward myself with a never-ending string of casual sexual encounters. Got it."

I lean in and tug a strand of her hair. "Don't be an ass."

"My apologies." She smiles. "Please, tell me more about the Life of Dean."

My hand travels across her smooth cheek to grasp her chin. "Look at me, Allie-Cat. Does it look like I have many problems? Are you ever going to find me moping in my room or stressing out about trivial bullshit?"

"No," she says slowly.

"I'm an overall happy person, right?"

Her suspicious gaze locks with mine. "Yes. But how is that even possible? Nobody is happy *all* the time."

"It's absolutely possible." I rub my thumb over her lower lip. Her lips are so fucking soft. I'm dying to kiss them again. "You want to know my secret?"

"Mmm?" She sounds distracted. I stroke her lips again, and I'm gratified when her breath hitches.

"I do what I want, when I want it. And I don't give a shit what other people think about me."

That gets her attention. "Sounds nice, being able to do what you want all the time. Sadly, that's not how life works."

"You make life work for *you*, babe." My fingers travel down her slender throat, skimming over her pulse point. "What do you want, Allie? Tell me one thing you've been dying to do but haven't gotten around to doing."

Her forehead furrows as she thinks it over. "Well. I've been wanting to start a new cleanse, but I keep putting it off."

"I have no idea what that means."

"I go on these juice cleanses a couple times a year," she explains. "It sucks, because you're stuck on a liquid diet for two whole weeks, but you feel *so* much better afterward."

"You're a fucking weirdo. Pick something else. Something *normal*."

She pauses, deep in thought again, and then her expression brightens. "I've always wanted to learn how to salsa dance."

Fuck. That's such a chick thing to say. "Then do it," I tell her.

She chews on her lip again. "I don't know… I mentioned it to Sean once, but he didn't want to take lessons with me and I was too embarrassed to go alone. I looked into it and found out that if you show up alone, they pair you up with a random partner."

"So what? It's an opportunity to make some new friends." I shrug. "I think you should sign up."

"Are you offering to take salsa dancing lessons with me?" Her expression is hopeful.

I snort. "No way. I only do what *I* want, remember? And I do not want to salsa dance. But I think *you* should."

"Maybe I will," she says thoughtfully.

"That's the spirit." I give her chin a teasing pinch. "Stick with me, kid, and your entire life will change for the better. That's the Di Laurentis guarantee."

Allie heaves out a sigh.

"What?" I demand.

"I can't decide if you're being sincere or if you're trying to get in my pants again."

I waggle my eyebrows. "Who says it can't be both?" When that gets me another sigh, my voice becomes gruff. "I'm being sincere."

"Wow. I think you actually mean that."

For some reason, her careful scrutiny has me shifting uneasily. And I'm suddenly wholly aware of the fact that I'm not wearing a shirt. She is too, because those big blue eyes drift lower, focusing on my abs before she wrenches her gaze away. The air between us seems to crackle. Allie's pupils are dilated, and there's no mistaking the rapid flutter of her pulse in the center of her throat.

I know arousal when I see it. Little Dean knows it too, and he promptly thickens behind my zipper.

"Allie…" My voice comes out hoarse.

She's off the couch before I can blink. "Annnd it's time for you to go."

She sounds overly cheerful, and I can tell she's struggling to control the same waves of desire that are practically swallowing me whole.

When I remain seated, she frowns deeply. "Shirt up and go home, Dean."

"Allie." Slowly, I rise to my feet. My mouth is full of gravel as I say, "I want—"

She whips up her hand. "Don't you dare finish that sentence. I mean it, it's time to go."

I want to ask her how long she's going to keep fighting this, but since I know it'll only piss her off further, I keep my mouth shut and do what the lady asked—I leave.

On the drive home, I resign myself to another night of getting up close and personal with my right hand.

CHAPTER 10

DEAN

THE NEXT DAY, I HAVE THE MISFORTUNE OF LEAVING THE International Relations lecture hall at the same time as Sabrina. I tense up, waiting for the inevitable bitchy barb.

"You looked a little lost in there, Richie. Was Professor Burke not speaking slowly enough for you?"

Yep, there it is.

I roll my eyes. "Right, because I'm dumb. Good one." I don't bother asking her not to call me *Richie*. I can't stop her from doing it any more than I can stop Summer from ditching my old childhood nickname. Sabrina decided I was a stupid, spoiled Richie-Rich type from the moment we met.

Of course, that didn't stop her from banging me, now did it?

"So which poor freshman will be writing your paper for you?" she asks sweetly. "You have a whole slew of them on speed dial, right? I assume one of them wrote the LSATs for you too."

I halt at the top step of the front entrance. I tolerate her taunts because they're not worth defending myself against, but every now and then I have to draw the line. "It just kills you that I scored two points higher than you, huh?" When her nostrils flare, I know I've hit my mark.

She recovers quickly. "Again, probably because you paid someone else to take the test for you."

"Keep telling yourself that, sweetheart. Whatever helps you sleep at night, right?"

Sabrina tosses her long dark hair over her shoulder. "I sleep just fine, thank you. Knowing I've actually *earned* my grades leads to a very restful existence. You should try it sometime."

This time *she* hits her mark. A frown tightens my mouth, but I don't take the bait because that's exactly what she wants me to do. She's been holding this bullshit over my head since sophomore year, and I'm damn tired of it.

"Enjoy the rest of your day, Sabrina." With a shrug of indifference, I make my way down the steps and wonder if she plans on keeping this feud going when we're at law school next year. I fucking hope not. The hostility she dishes out is getting old, not to mention annoying.

Speaking of annoying, I'm supposed to be at Hastings Elementary in twenty minutes for my first practice with the rugrat team. Go Hurricanes.

As I make the ten-minute drive into town, I curse O'Shea for forcing this volunteer gig on me and ponder the authenticity of voodoo dolls. Eventually I decide it doesn't matter if they're real or not. It'd still be fun to poke needles into a teeny doll version of Frank O'Shea. Once it starts falling apart from all the holes, I can use the head as a stress ball.

At a red light, I shoot a quick text to my teammate Fitzy: Hey, do you know how to make a voodoo doll?

His response doesn't come until I reach the small arena across the street from the school.

Him: I'd think you were fucking with me, but the question is stupid enough to feel legit. No idea. Can prolly use any old doll? Challenge will be finding a spellcaster to link it to your target.

Me: That makes sense.

Him: Does it??

Me: It implies magic, hexes, etc. I don't think any doll would work. Otherwise every doll is a v-doll, right?

Him: Right.

Me: Anyway. Thx. Thought you might know.

Him: Why the fuck would *I* know?

Me: Ur into all those fantasy role-play games. You know magic.

Him: I'm not Harry Potter, ffs.

Me: HP is a nerd. Ur a nerd. Ergo, ur a boy wizard.

He sends a middle-finger emoji, then says, Bday beers at Malone's tonight. You still down?

Me: Yup.

Him: C you ltr.

I tuck my phone in my jacket pocket and hop out of the car. At least I have something to look forward to after this. Celebratory beers for Fitzy's twenty-first birthday will be my reward for spending the afternoon coaching children against my will.

The rink is empty when I stride through the double doors. The cold air greets me like an old friend and I breathe it in, shifting my duffel to my other shoulder and making my way to the home team bench, where a tall man in a red sweater and scuffed black hockey skates is peering at a clipboard. The whistle around his neck tells me he's the coach of the Hurricanes.

"Di Laurentis?" When I nod, he extends a hand. "Doug Ellis. Nice to meet you, kid. I watched your Frozen Four game on TV in April. You played well."

"Thanks." I gesture to the deserted ice. I'm ten minutes early, just like O'Shea ordered me to be. "Where're the kids?"

"Locker room. They should be out soon." He sets the clipboard on the ledge that spans the bench. "Chad fill you in on what's expected of you?"

"Nope." Despite what O'Shea told me, I don't think Coach Jensen has any idea I've been recruited to work with the Hurricanes.

"Well, it's not all that complicated. We start each practice with thirty minutes of drills, then do a thirty-minute scrimmage split up into three ten-minute periods. The boys work their asses off. Good kids, the lot of them. Talented, smart, eager to sharpen their skills and get better."

"That's good to hear."

"They loved Kayla—" At my blank expression, he says, "Your predecessor." Right, the chick who'd come down with mono. "Anyway, she worked mostly with the offense. Did a terrific job, but I'll be honest, I'm glad to have a D-man on board. A few of the boys have trouble manning the defensive zone. I'd like for you to work closely with them."

We chat for a few minutes about my duties, and then he delivers a few warnings about not dropping f-bombs around the kids and not manhandling them in any way.

"Got it—keep it PG and don't touch 'em. Anything else?" I ask.

"Nah. You'll figure out the rest as you go along."

All in all, Ellis seems like a decent man, and when the kids thunder out of the locker room and greet him like he's Jesus Christ brought back to life, my opinion of him climbs higher. He told me he's the school gym teacher but that even if he lost his job, he'd never walk away from this team. Or the eighth grade girls' volleyball team, which he apparently also coaches.

I drop onto the bench and quickly kick off my Timberlands, replacing them with the Bauers I stowed in my duffel. Then I hop the ledge and skate toward Ellis and the kids. Half of them are wearing red practice jerseys; the other half are in black. Ellis introduces me to the team, who ooh and aah when he informs them of my multiple

Frozen Four wins. By the time we set up the first skating drill, every kid on the ice is begging for one-on-one attention from me.

I'm not gonna lie—I have a blast from the word *go*. The boys' passion for the game reminds me of when I was a kid, how excited I was to put on a pair of skates and tear down the ice. Their enthusiasm is downright contagious.

When Ellis blows his whistle to signal it's time for the scrimmage, I find I'm genuinely disappointed that the drills are over. I'd been giving tips to a seventh grader named Robbie during the last shooting drill, and the wrist shot he'd floated past the goalie had been a beauty. I want to see him do it again, but now it's time for the boys to take the skills they just learned and apply them to the scrimmage.

Ellis and I serve as both refs and coaches, calling out penalties and offering advice when needed. The thirty-minute game ends way too fast for my liking. I could stay out there forever, but Ellis signals the end of the scrimmage and gestures for everyone to skate forward.

There's a strange clench in my chest as he addresses each boy, one at a time, to tell them one thing they did right at practice today. Face after face lights up at his compliments, and by the time Ellis is done I think I might be in love with him.

Damn, he's a great coach.

After that, we follow the kids to the locker room and help them put away their equipment in the proper cubbies. They're a loud, boisterous group, laughing and joking and chirping one another as they change into their street clothes. The hallway outside the door is littered with vending machines and parents waiting for their sons. Robbie, however, stays behind. He's changed out of his practice uniform, but I'm troubled to see him lacing up his skates again and tucking the bottoms of his jeans into them.

"Whatcha doing, kid?"

He looks surprised to find me standing there. "Oh." He flushes. "I get an extra thirty minutes to skate." A defensive note creeps in. "Coach knows."

Since I know better than to take a thirteen-year-old's word at face value, I duck out to track down Ellis, who's in the equipment room securing sticks on the long rack against the wall.

"What's this about Robbie staying behind to skate?"

Ellis glances toward the doorway. "Oh. Yes, it's fine. I'm heading out there in a sec to supervise him. Tell him not to step on the ice until I get there."

I can't hide my frown. "Why does he get extra ice time?"

"His mother doesn't get off work until four thirty on Tuesdays and Thursdays, and the family lives in Munsen, so the school bus isn't an option." Ellis makes an annoyed sound. "Some bullshit about town boundaries and the Hastings buses being unable to 'service' other townships. Robbie's mother managed to get him enrolled here because he's an asset to our hockey program, but apparently the school district doesn't think it's important to provide safe transportation home to the kids who live out of the district."

"So Robbie hangs around the arena until his mom shows up?"

Ellis nods. "I arranged it with Julia at the start of the season. I stick around after practice, watch him and his sister until she gets here."

Did I mention how much I love this man?

"I'll stick around too," I offer. "I was teaching Robbie the art of wrist shots before the drill ended. Wouldn't mind finishing up the lesson."

His expression is a combination of surprise and respect. "I bet he'd love that. Thanks, kid."

When I reenter the rink, Robbie is skating lazy circles along the boards. His dirty-blond hair ruffles behind him, and I decide he might need a lesson about hair too—as in, trim the shit out of it before it reaches mullet status, or wave goodbye to any chance of getting laid.

I'm walking down the concrete aisle when a high-pitched voice startles me to a stop.

"Who are you?"

I turn to see a tiny elfin creature sitting at the halfway point in the bleachers. Well, it's a girl, but holy hell, she might as well be a character from a Pixar movie. Huge blue eyes take up her entire face, her hair is so fair it's nearly white, and her mouth is a tiny pink rosebud.

"Who are *you*?" I call back, one eyebrow arched.

"I asked you first."

Fighting a smile, I climb the steps until I reach her row. A glance at the rink reveals that Robbie is having fun skating aimlessly. Ellis is at the boards keeping an eye on him, so I plop down in the seat next to the cartoon elf and say, "I'm Dean. The new assistant coach of the Hurricanes."

Those big eyes study my face, as if she's trying to decide if I'm lying. "I'm Dakota," she finally says. She points a skinny finger at the ice. "That's my brother."

"Ah. You're Robbie's little sister."

"Who says I'm the little one?" she challenges. "Maybe I'm his big sister."

"Kid, I'd be surprised if you're not still in diapers."

"I do not wear diapers!" Her cheeks redden. "I'm *ten*," she says haughtily.

I gasp. "Holy sh—sugar. You're practically an old lady, then."

That makes her giggle. "I am not. How old are *you*?"

"Twenty-two."

Her jaw falls open. "*That's* old."

"I know, right? I should probably start planning my funeral. Who do you think I should leave my fortune to in my will—the chick from the *Hunger Games* or the one from *Divergent*?"

"They're not real people," she says frankly.

I feign innocence. "Are you sure? I swear I saw Katniss walking down the street the other day."

"You're lying."

"Yup, you caught me." I gesture to the pink spiral notebook in her lap. "Whatcha doing?"

Her bottom lip sticks out. "Homework. Mrs. Klein said to write a whole page about what I'm thankful for on this Thanksgiving."

"Mrs. Klein sounds like a monster."

Dakota giggles. "Naw, she's okay. She ordered pizza for the *whole class* one time. It was after we got the highest scores on the literary test."

"Literacy," I correct.

She waves her hand. "Whatever."

A grin springs free. "All right, let's stop wasting time." I flip her little notebook to a fresh page. "It's time to figure out what you're thankful for."

Pleasure lights up her face. "You're going to help me with my homework?"

"Sure, why not? We've got twenty more minutes to kill until your mom gets here. What else are we gonna do?"

ALLIE

I'M IN THE PASSENGER SEAT OF MEGAN'S CAR WHEN DEAN TEXTS me. I'm not surprised to see his name on my phone. I've been expecting another "I want to fuck you" from him all day, so it was only a matter of time before it happened. But tonight he throws me a curveball.

> Him: A bunch of us r at Malone's tonight for Fitzy's bday. Join us if you feel like it.

Megan glances over from the driver's side. "Who's texting you? And please don't say Sean."

"No, it's not Sean. It's one of Garrett's friends," I answer vaguely. "A bunch of the hockey guys are at Malone's for someone's birthday. He says we're welcome to join them."

"Is Hannah there?"

I shake my head. "She's at rehearsal tonight." Like me, Hannah is also busy preparing for one of her final projects. As a music major, she's required to perform an original song for the department's winter showcase.

I guess Megan doesn't think it's odd that I'm getting invited to hockey gatherings without Hannah, because she doesn't comment on it. Instead, she says, "Let's do it."

"Are you serious?" After more than thirty minutes debating a dozen options for our girls' night out, we finally decided to grab a late bite at the diner in Hastings. Malone's is the only bar in town, so obviously that suggestion had come up early in the conversation, but Meg had been the one to veto it. "I thought you didn't want to deal with the whole bar scene tonight."

She pushes her red bangs out of her eyes. "Changed my mind. I think I'm in the mood to be surrounded by cute boys."

"Really?" I say in surprise. "What about the new boyfriend? Is there trouble in paradise already?" Megan has been so cagey about this new guy she's dating, but I assumed they were doing okay. Normally she's a huge chatterbox when it comes to her love life, but not this time. All I know about him is that he lives in Boston and she only sees him on the weekends.

"No, we're fine." She pauses. "Well, not really." Another pause. "It's complicated."

"You know, if you actually told me something about him instead of being Ms. Secretive, I might be able to offer some advice..."

Her green eyes stay focused on the road. Even if she wasn't driving, I know she'd still be avoiding my gaze.

"Okay. Spill. What's wrong with him?"

"Nothing's wrong with him."

"Bullshit. There has to be, otherwise you wouldn't be hiding him from all of us. So what is it? Does he like to set barns on fire in his spare time? Does he kill squirrels and make little hats out of their fur? Does he have a weird mole that takes up his whole face? Does he—"

"Thirty seven," she interrupts. "He's thirty-seven."

My eyebrows shoot up. "Oh. Wow. That's…"

Old, I want to say, but I've always believed in the *age is nothin'* *but a number* philosophy. Or at least I *want* to be that open-minded. I mean, I think it's hella creepy when a sixty-year-old man dates an eighteen-year-old girl. But thirty-seven isn't exactly geezer status. It's only fifteen years older than me and Meg.

"See? This is why I didn't tell you guys." Accusation colors her tone. "I knew you'd be all judgy."

I hold up both hands in surrender. "I'm not judging. You surprised me, that's all."

Her pretty features relax.

"Tell me more about Mr. Thirty-Seven," I urge. "I promise there's no judgment on my end."

She grudgingly provides a few more details. "His name's Trevor. He's a pediatric surgeon at Boston General."

Okay, I'm impressed.

"He's divorced, and he has a five-year-old daughter."

Hmm. Not so impressed anymore. "And you're cool with that?" I ask carefully. "You're only twenty-two, hon. Are you ready to be someone's stepmother?"

"That's the problem," she moans. "I wasn't even thinking that far ahead. Trevor and I met online. We were chatting all through September, but we didn't meet in person until a month ago. He's sweet. Smart, gorgeous, easy to talk to. But we're still in the early stages of the relationship, you know? More casual than serious." She taps her polished nails against the steering wheel. "When I saw him last weekend, he said he wants me to meet his daughter."

Eek.

"Eek," I say out loud.

"I know, right? So now I'm second-guessing the whole relation-ship. Meeting his kid is a huge deal. What if she hates me? Or worse, what if she *loves* me, and then me and her dad break up and this poor kid ends up traumatized?"

"She won't fall in love with you after one meeting," I assure her. "But I agree—this *is* a huge deal."

Meg stops her little red Toyota at the intersection one block from Hastings's main stretch. "I don't know... I told him I'd let him know on Friday when I see him, but I'm super confused. I have no idea what to do." She goes quiet for a second, then lets out a heavy breath. "If we go to Malone's, can you DD on the way home? I might want something stronger than soda."

"No prob." I wasn't planning on drinking tonight, anyway. I have rehearsal at 7:00 a.m., and a pounding hangover will make it hard for me to cry on command. In the opening scene alone, my character wails like a newborn three times. "Should we go to another bar, though?" I ask hopefully. "Maybe the one in Munsen?"

"Why would we do that?"

I shrug. "The hockey crowd can get kinda rowdy."

"I could use a little rowdy," she admits. "Trevor is great, but he's not much into partying anymore. He's in bed by ten o'clock every night. Even on weekends." Her bottom lip sticks out. "Maybe that's another reason I should end it, huh?"

"Look, I'd never dream of telling you what to do," I say gently. "And I'm not saying you should break up with someone just because their party days are behind them. But you're in your senior year of college, hon. You shouldn't be going to bed at ten if you don't want to. You should enjoy this last year of freedom, in this weird place where you're an adult but not an adult, know what I mean? Save the early bedtimes for next year when you become a card-carrying member of the real world."

A pensive look crosses her expression. I can tell she's absorbing the advice, and I hope she reaches a decision that makes her happy. God knows I've been dealing with tough decisions lately too. Breaking up with Sean. Figuring out where I want to take my acting career.

Walking into a bar to willingly spend time with the guy I had a one-night stand with...

Shit, what *am* I doing coming to the bar? Nothing good can be gained from seeing Dean tonight. Worse case, he'll accidentally let something slip, and everyone will know that we hooked up. Best case, he'll flirt shamelessly with me and just be plain annoying.

Since Malone's is the only alcohol game in town, it's the go-to place for both locals and Briar students every day of the week. If you show up after nine, you're looking at standing room only. Meg and I waltz in at ten thirty, and it's like stepping into a sauna crammed with hundreds of sweaty bodies. The main room is jam-packed. I can barely see the counter because too many bodies are swarming in front of it, and the row of booths in the raised sections on either side of the main area are all occupied.

"I want to order a drink!" Megan shouts over the music. Some rock song I don't recognize is blasting from the speakers. If Garrett Graham were here, he could probably tell me the name of the song, who's singing it, and what year it was released. Hannah's boyfriend has a hard-on for classic rock. I wouldn't be surprised to find out he makes Hannah play Lynyrd Skynyrd role-playing games in bed.

We're about to head for the bar when a familiar voice rises above the music. "Allie-Cat! Over here!"

I shift my head to see Dean waving at me from a large booth to my right. I don't know how he spotted me in the throng of people. I hadn't even texted him to say I was coming, so he's either got exceptional Spidey senses or he's been monitoring the door like a creeper.

Megan and I link arms to avoid getting separated and make our way through the sea of bodies. I inhale a gust of perfume from a platinum blond in a short skirt. I manage to survive the perfume assault only to breathe in a cloud of something more potent from the guy beside her. My eyes start to water, and I almost turn around to tell him to go easy on the Axe body spray before he kills someone.

"Look, Fitzy, *girls!*" Dean announces when Megan and I reach the booth. He rapidly addresses the other guys. "Quick, make room for them before they disappear."

Laughter breaks out, and I notice most of the players are grinning at one guy in particular, who I've seen before at some of the hockey parties Hannah dragged me to. I think his name is Colin, but I usually hear him being referred to as either Fitz or Fitzy. He's a big guy with messy brown hair, dark scruff on his face, and what looks like a tattoo peeking from the collar of his shirt. I suspect he's definitely rocking a chest tat, because I've seen him in a T-shirt, and I remember him having full sleeves on both arms.

The boys shuffle around to accommodate us. Megan slides in next to a guy with a buzz cut. He introduces himself as Hollis. I squeeze in between Tucker, who's engrossed on his phone, and Pierre, one of the French Canadians on the team. He greets me with a smile, and a pair of adorable dimples pop out. Rounding out the group are two players I've never met. In his heavy accent, Pierre introduces them as Wilkes and Ekberg.

Dean, who is across from me on the other side of Hollis, winks when our eyes lock. "You made it. Didn't think you would."

"We were in the neighborhood," I say lightly.

"Glad you were, because this was becoming a total sausage fest. Seriously, the birthday boy didn't invite a single chick tonight."

"Fitzy is allergic to women," Hollis says helpfully.

The birthday boy—or man, rather, because there's nothing boyish about this guy—rolls his eyes. "I didn't realize that wanting to celebrate my birthday with the guys was such a crime."

"Did you even stop to consider the implications?" Dean shoots back. "What about the time-honored birthday blow job? Did ya think of that? Or do you expect one of *us* to do it?"

"I'm sure Pierre's down," Hollis pipes up. When the French Canadian gives him the finger, he smiles sweetly. "What? I thought that's what you guys did up in Quebec, no? Blow your buddies while whispering sweet French nothings to them?"

Pierre snorts. "You're from San Francisco. I'm pretty sure that's the blow-your-buddies capital of the world."

A round of smack talk ensues, which is cut short when a frazzled waitress comes to take our order. Meg orders a vodka cranberry. I ask for a glass of water.

"Water?" Dean mocks after the waitress dashes off. "You sure you don't want anything else, baby doll? Maybe…hmm…how about tequila? I always pegged you for a tequila girl."

I narrow my eyes at him. Fortunately, nobody else puts much stock in the comment. Why would they? It's not like any of them know that tequila is the reason I wound up in bed with Dean. The only person who knows is Dean, who promised to keep his mouth shut about it.

But…the teeny smirk on his face is making me antsy.

Why do I get the feeling he's about to spill the beans?

CHAPTER 11

ALLIE

I'M STILL GLARING AT DEAN WHEN MY PHONE VIBRATES IN MY PURSE. I absently fish it out and my breath catches when I see the message.

Him: Remember when I took that tequila shot off your tits?

I look up to find Dean blinking innocently at me. But I can see his arm moving under the table. Sure enough, a follow-up message appears.

Him: When I poured it all over your nipples and licked up every drop? Mmm. Getting hard just thinking about it.

Argh. I can't believe he's sexting me in the bar. During his friend's birthday hang.

I grit my teeth and text him back.

Me: Cherish the memory, sweetie. Cuz it's never happening again.

Him: You saying you didn't like it when I was sucking on those sexy nipples?

The nipples in question tighten into hard peaks. I know the padding of my bra hides the traitorous response, but the way Dean's smug gaze drops to my breasts tells me he knows.

I draw a breath and answer, Meh. It was all right.

His smile widens. "Nah," he says in response to something Wilkes just asked. "I'm not worried. Yale's goalie has nothing against G's slapshot." I guess they're talking about their game against Yale on Saturday, but I'm too busy watching the subtle movement of Dean's arm. He's typing something else.

> Him: Hmm. I see. What about when I licked your pussy? Just all right too?

I ignore the sharp clench between my legs and scowl at him.

"Allie," Megan says in exasperation.

"Sorry. What?"

"I was asking about your play. Rehearsals started this week, didn't they? How's it going?"

"Pretty good," I answer in an absent tone. I can't tell if Dean is typing something else. I hope not. "The guy who's playing my dead husband is fun to work with. How's yours going?"

"Shitty."

"Aw, I'm sorry, hon." I know Meg isn't happy with the playwright she'd been paired with, and I don't blame her, because he happens to be the most pompous asshole in the drama department. Everything he writes is pretentious and brimming with over-the-top angst. He thinks he's the reincarnation of Arthur Miller.

"'Slade' likes to rewrite entire scenes during rehearsal." She puts quotation marks around his name, which makes Fitzy chuckle.

"I don't think you know how to use air quotes," he informs her.

"No, I do. 'Slade' isn't his real name. It's actually Joshua Sandeski." She snorts derisively. "This ass is so full of himself I'm surprised he doesn't poop out little brown replicas of his smug face."

The guys hoot at the disgusting image she's painted.

"First day of classes, we all had to sit around in a circle and introduce ourselves to our fellow actors." She glances at me. "Remember that?"

"Oh, I remember," I say dryly.

"Anyway," she tells Fitzy, "this jerk stands up and says, 'I'm Joshua Sandeski, but I go by Slade. Refer to me as anything else and I will not respond.' And he wasn't kidding. Any time the teacher slipped up and called him Sandeski, he would flat-out ignore her."

"That's the douchiest thing I've ever heard," Dean remarks.

Shit, his arm is moving again.

"I think it's ballsy," Hollis disagrees. "You know what? Fuck it. I'm pulling a Slade and giving myself a solo name. From now on, you guys can only refer to me as Thunder."

I discreetly peek at the latest message, and my breath hitches.

Him: My dick is so hard right now. I'm dying to be inside you.

I don't indulge him this time. If I don't respond, he'll eventually stop, right?

Wrong.

The messages keep popping up, each one filthier than the last.

Him: Gonna take it slow next time. Savor every single second.
Him: So fucking slow, baby. Just slide in and out of your tight pussy...
Him: Until you're begging for more.

I grab my glass and choke down some water. I'm aware of Dean's soft chuckle, audible even with the music blasting in the bar.

Him: I won't give you what you want, tho. I'll keep feeding you my cock, inch by inch.

Him: And then I'll take it away again.
Him: Every time you beg me to pound into you, I'll go even slower.
Him: Gonna torment that sweet pussy all nite, baby.
Him: All. Fucking. Night.

I shoot to my feet like someone lit a fire under my ass. "I need to use the ladies' room," I blurt out.

Ignoring the broad grin stretching Dean's infuriatingly sexy mouth, I dart away from the booth as fast as my high-heeled boots can carry me.

Fuckity *fuck*. I'm so turned on my thighs are actually sticking together, and I'm worried there might be a wet spot on the back of my jeans. To make matters worse, Megan hadn't even made a dent in her drink, which means we won't be leaving anytime soon. Which means I need to collect my composure and extinguish every spark of desire that's burning like jet fuel through my blood.

I hope to God that Dean quits sexting me when I get back.

If he doesn't, there's a good chance I might orgasm at the table.

HE KEEPS SEXTING.

I keep ignoring him.

Our battle of wills lasts for more than an hour, and I can't say I'm not impressed by his persistence. Not to mention the sheer amount of dirty words he has in his vocabulary.

When I notice Dean visibly squirming on his side of the booth, I flash him a cheeky grin and finally text him back.

Me: Ur just torturing yourself, honey pie. Better stop before the blue balls set in.

I punctuate that with two emojis that seem fitting for the situation—a pair of blue circles.

Dean sighs and rises to his feet, but not before he does some strategic rearranging down below. I think I'm the only one who sees him do it, and my smile grows impossibly wider.

"I'm going to change up these tunes," he tells the group. "Whoever keeps putting on Aerosmith rock ballads is bumming the hell outta me."

As he walks off, my eyes betray me by homing in on his backside. His black pants hug his taut buttocks like a glove, which makes me wonder, are cargo pants usually that tight? I didn't think they were. Maybe Dean has a tailor on retainer who makes him special cargo pants that show off his ass? That seems like something he would do, vain bastard that he is.

Either way, his ass is yummy. Damn it, *everything* about him is yummy. I can't help but admire the way his broad shoulders fill out his long-sleeve Under Armour shirt or how his blond hair is the perfect amount of tousled. Then I lose him in the crowd, and I feel a flicker of relief because now that he's out of sight, I have some time to get my raging hormones under control. The respite is brief, though. When he returns to the booth, he's still as gorgeous as ever and I'm still a horny bundle of nerves.

He resettles in his seat just as the current song ends and the opening strains of Dean's selection blare out of the speakers.

It's Cheap Trick's "I Want You to Want Me."

I can't stop a burst of laughter, which earns me a strange look from Fitzy. "Did I miss the punchline?" he asks.

"Nope. Sometimes I just laugh for no reason," I say flippantly. "I'm weird like that."

Megan pipes up. "It's true. She is."

I swallow another laugh and avoid Dean's eyes as his song continues to play. I'm not surprised when my phone vibrates.

Him: I could've gone with something a lil more subtle. But why play games? I'm goddamn aching for you, Allie.

Shit, he called me Allie. He means business.

I lift my head, and the intensity burning in his gaze makes my heart stutter, then propels it into a hard gallop. Dean is already insanely attractive to begin with, but when he's turned on? He's absolutely spectacular.

With his smoky green eyes at half-mast, lips parted slightly, strong throat working as he swallows, I can almost believe he *is* aching. That he's truly in physical pain from wanting me so bad. But this is Dean, for crying out loud. He probably springs a boner if a light breeze floats over his crotch. Seriously, just bump into him and you get him hard. The guy is obsessed with sex, and half the girls at this school can attest to that, because half the girls at this school have slept with him.

Sure, it's flattering to be on the receiving end of all that heady sexual energy. What woman doesn't like feeling desirable? But I'd be an idiot if I believed even for a second that I'm the *only* woman Dean Di Laurentis is flashing those bedroom eyes at. Nope, I'm nothing more than another notch on Dean's exorbitantly long belt.

The reminder spurs me to my feet. "I'm really not feeling Cheap Trick tonight," I say sweetly. "Think I'll switch it up again."

My purposeful stride takes me to the jukebox across the room. It's not one of those old-school ones, but a modern jukebox with a touchscreen and slots for both cash and credit. I feed a dollar bill into the machine and study my options. Jeez. Nearly every song that's ever been written is available on this thing.

I grin when one artist in particular jumps out at me. I scroll through her discography, select the title I'm searching for, and add it to the queue. The sidebar on the screen reveals there's one other song ahead of mine, a Kesha track that sends a horde of college-age patrons to the dance floor. Which really just means they start dancing wherever they're standing, because the area in front of the karaoke stage that usually serves as the dance floor has been taken over by a cluster of hipsters who are all engrossed by their cell phones.

"Nice pick," Tucker calls out to me. He's been phone-obsessed tonight too, so I'm surprised that he's suddenly being social.

"Not mine," I call back.

"What'd you choose, then?" Dean asks suspiciously.

"You'll find out soon enough, my pretty."

Three minutes later, the intro comes on, and a chorus of female whoops rings out through the bar.

Dean glares at me.

My song choice? Pink's "U and UR Hand."

"Hell yeah!" Megan slams her glass down and hops to her feet, sticking out her hand to me. "We're dancing."

I don't have time to object, because she's already dragging me into the crowd. Well then. I guess we're dancing.

As the bass line thuds beneath our heels, we throw our arms up in the air, shimmy our hips, and rock the fuck out. Meg's red hair whips past my face as she spins around. I do a spin too, because it gives me the opportunity to sneak a peek at Dean. He wears a resigned look, but there's also a flicker of amusement there.

When we get to the part of the song where Pink—who is a goddess, by the way. A *goddess!*—says "buh-bye" to the creep she's singing to, I shoot Dean a saccharine smile and flutter my fingers in his direction.

The tip of his tongue touches his bottom lip as a slow grin curves his mouth. He gives a little wave in response. *Well played*, I can practically hear him drawling.

Meg and I keep dancing, and our twosome draws more and more attention, and more and more participants. Suddenly we're surrounded by other girls who are digging the song as hard as we are. It's pretty much an anthem for any woman who's ever had to deal with a slimy jerk hitting on her at a bar, or plying her with drinks in the hopes of getting laid, or just plain annoying her when she's trying to hang with her gal pals.

A tiny Asian girl with multiple facial piercings and spiky pink hair bumps her hips to mine, and then we're dancing back-to-back, smacking our butts together as we share a moment of female camaraderie. I'm laughing and breathless from how much fun I'm having, and this time when I seek Dean out, he doesn't look amused anymore.

Oh crap.

He's aroused again.

His sultry eyes track every move I make. By the time the song ends, I'm burning up. Not from sweat or exertion, but from Dean's gaze raking over me like flames licking through a hayfield.

Once Meg and I return to the booth, I chug the rest of my water, then lift my hair up to fan my hot neck with one hand. My phone sits on the tabletop, and I instinctively tense when the screen lights up. A quick glance at Dean reveals he's got his hand under the table again.

I bite my lip and stare at my phone.

Don't read it, I order myself.

I read it.

Him: Next time you put on a show like that for me, you better fucking be naked.

CHAPTER 12

ALLIE

MEGAN AND I GET BACK TO CAMPUS A LITTLE AFTER MIDNIGHT. My two-bedroom suite is shrouded in shadows when I creep inside. There's no light spilling out from Hannah's door, which tells me she's already gone to bed.

Making an effort to be quiet, I gather up my toiletries and duck out to use the bathroom we share with the six other girls on this floor. Ten minutes later, I tiptoe around my bedroom and change into my pj's, then shut off the light and crawl under the covers.

I've never had any trouble falling asleep—I'm usually out cold the moment my head hits the pillow.

Tonight, sleep eludes me. Dean's sexts left me hot and bothered, and I spend the next hour tossing and turning in an attempt to get comfortable. But I'm *not* comfortable. My boobs are achy and my pussy is throbbing. Every time I roll over, my nipples scrape the mattress and the innocent friction makes them ache even harder.

This is Dean's fault. Why did he have to text me all those dirty, dirty things?

A groan slides out. I roll over again, this time onto my side. Normally I like to sleep with a part of the blanket tucked between my thighs. Right now, having something jammed down there is an

THE SCORE **123**

excruciating tease, and my hips involuntarily start rocking against the comforter.

"God*damn* it." My tortured voice echoes in the darkness. I roll onto my back and prop one knee up, because obviously I won't be getting any sleep until I take care of business.

"U and UR Hand" is proving to be a prophetic song choice.

I grit my teeth and stick my hand down my plaid pajama bottoms. Unfortunately, I'm not one of those women who can rub her clit a few times and presto! Orgasm! Nope, I need a story, a delicious fantasy to take me over the edge. In recent days, my fantasies have featured my go-to celebrity crush: the perfection that is Ryan Gosling. So it's Ryan I turn to now, in my grave hour of need.

The fantasy always starts differently. I'm at a bar and we get our flirt on. I'm in a hotel room and there's a mix-up that forces us to share a bed. I'm jogging on the beach in Malibu and look who I run into!

But it always ends the same—with the Gos screwing me silly.

I opt for the hotel room, since it allows for a plethora of Choose-Your-Own-Sexual-Adventure scenarios. Tonight, I'm sleeping naked because the air-conditioning is on the fritz. I suppose I could just sleep naked without giving myself an excuse to do it, but I like my fantasies to be somewhat consistent with my real life, and since I'm not a naked sleeper in real life, broken air conditioner it is.

Okay, where was I? I rub my index finger over my clit as I picture myself lying on a king-size bed. I'm drifting off to sleep when I hear a *beep*. Someone swiped a key card in the door. I'm outraged! Did the concierge decide to send the housekeeper up in the middle of the night? Who could possibly be walking into my— Well, look at that. It's Ryan Gosling. He saunters into the room, bare-chested for some reason. His jeans ride so low I can see the glorious man-vee of his naked hips.

He's surprised to find me there, and we quickly determine there's been a double-booking error. Then we have a five-minute conversation about our lives, in which he reveals that Eva Mendes broke up with him.

Yes, there's both dialogue *and* small talk in my sexual fantasies.

Eventually, I climb out of bed and— Oh no! The sheet covering my naked body falls to the carpet. Ryan's blue eyes widen with appreciation. His cock visibly hardens beneath his zipper.

He licks his lips and steps closer.

I teasingly glide my fingers down the valley of my breasts. His eyes burn like liquid sapphires.

No, like emeralds. Because his eyes are green now. Why are they green?

In the darkness of my dorm room, I release a low, irritated curse. For *fuck's* sake.

Why is Dean crashing my fantasy?

My finger stills over my clit. Okay, well, this is just rude. Ryan and I were about to jiggle down. Dean is not allowed to ruin that for me.

I squeeze my eyelids shut and transport myself back to the fantasy. But I'm no longer in the hotel and Ryan is no longer with me. I'm at a hockey arena with Dean, and we're making out on the ice.

Stifling another groan, I shake myself out of the scene and once again order my hand to stop moving. Where on God's green planet is this fantasy going? Ice is *cold*. Who wants to freeze to death when they're getting it on? And why is Dean kissing his way down my naked body? His practice is scheduled to start any minute. The entire team is going to walk out and catch us—

"I like the idea of getting caught."

The groan escapes before I can corral it. Dean's raspy confession isn't part of the fantasy—it's one hundred percent real life.

The night I'd asked him why he doesn't have sex in his bedroom, his eyes had gone heavy-lidded, pure molten sex dripping from his voice as he'd drawled, "I like the idea of getting caught."

Yep, Dean Di Laurentis gets off on the thought of someone catching him in the act.

And did he end the confession there? Of course not, because

that would mean he *hasn't* made it his mission in life to sexually torment me. Nope, he'd followed the first part with "And once I get caught, I like being watched."

I'm lusting over an exhibitionist. Hell, maybe I'm an exhibitionist too, because rather than stop the fantasy, I let it play out.

"You better come fast, baby." Dean's breath tickles my inner thigh. "Otherwise my teammates are gonna walk out of that locker room and see my face buried in your pussy."

My breathing quickens. I squeeze one breast, lightly toying with my nipple. My other hand strokes my clit in tight little circles. Oh God. I'm so wet. And my clit is swollen with desire. I can practically feel Dean's tongue swirling over it.

"Oh, you like that idea, don't you?" The pad of his finger grazes my opening. "Look how wet you are."

He pushes his finger inside me.

No, I'm pushing my own finger inside me. My breasts have been abandoned and now I've got both hands between my legs. Rubbing my clit with one, fingering myself with the other as I melt into the mattress and imagine Dean going down on me.

"Gonna fuck you right here on the ice, Allie."

My toes curl. The pressure in my core is unbearable.

In the fantasy, Dean rises to his knees. His chest gleams under the bright lights in the arena. His cock is long and proud. He wraps his fist around the base and leans forward, bringing it closer and closer to where I want it most.

And then we hear it. Footsteps. Voices. Laughter. The players are coming out of the chute. Dean smiles wickedly. Then he plunges that hard dick inside me—

And I come so hard I forget how to breathe. I lie on my bed, gasping, trembling. Stars flash behind my closed eyelids as the orgasm crashes through me in hot, pulsing waves.

Oh my *God*.

That was... It was... I don't even have the words to describe it.

And the sad part? The orgasm that just ripped me to shreds wasn't half as powerful as the ones Dean gave me in person.

I'm still shaking from the aftershocks as I fumble in the dark until my hand lands on the box of tissues atop my nightstand. I pull a couple out and use them to wipe between my legs. I can't remember the last time I got this wet during a solo session.

Think of how much wetter you'll be if you fuck me again...

Argh. I can practically hear Dean taunting me. Enticing me...

I take a breath. Okay. I'm a pragmatic person. And I aced that Argumentative Logic course I took in freshman year. So maybe I need to rationalize this out.

Premise I: Dean Di Laurentis is a phenomenal lay.
Premise II: He wants to have sex with me again.
Premise III: The idea of having sex with him turns me on.
Conclusion: I should have sex with Dean.

All right, that one was easy enough. Now comes the complicated part.

Premise I: Casual sex makes me uncomfortable.
Premise II: I just got out of a long-term relationship and am not ready for another one.
Premise III: Even if I was, I wouldn't want a relationship with man-whore Dean.
Conclusion: Um...?

I try another one:

Premise I: I don't want a relationship with Dean.
Premise II: He doesn't want a relationship with me.
Conclusion: We should have casual sex.

Another no-brainer, but it still doesn't solve the Casual Sex conundrum. Really, though, if I stop to think about it, the only person dishing out any judgment here is me. Will a fling with Dean make me a slut? He certainly doesn't think so. Neither would my friends, although I certainly don't plan on telling them about it if I choose to fling Dean. Which raises the question, why do I want to keep it a secret?

I chew on the inside of my cheek as I ponder that. The answer continues to stump me, but the idea of everyone knowing I'm screwing around with Dean still brings a rush of discomfort. Fine. It'll have to remain a secret. Maybe tomorrow I can give some more thought as to why I feel that way.

Well...shit. Have I actually reached a decision?

I'm already grabbing my phone, so...yeah, I guess I have.

I tap Dean's name and enter one word in the message box: Okay.

You've got to give the man credit—he knows exactly what I mean, because he types back When?

Me: Tmrw nite? Hannah's staying at your place. You can come here. 8?

Him: Kiddie game starts at 6. Won't be free til 9.

Me: Kiddie game?

Him: Don't worry about it. Tell you tmrw.

Him: What changed your mind?

What changed my mind... Insanity maybe? An unhealthy obsession with sex? His awesome dick?

Me: Decided it was time to live the Life of Dean.

Him: Took you long enough. So. 9 o'clock work for you?

I hesitate.

Me: Yes.

God, what am I doing? Maybe I *have* gone insane.

There's a long delay before his next message appears. A border-line-hysterical laugh pops out of my mouth after I read it.

Him: I'll bring the rope.

CHAPTER 13

ALLIE

I MET MY AGENT, IRA GOLDSTEIN, THROUGH A FRIEND OF MY DAD'S. He's been representing me since I was twelve years old, and the very first gig he booked for me was a cereal commercial. I had only one line, which I still remember to this day:

> *"How could something THIS TASTY be SO GOOD for you? YUM!"*

I'm pretty sure my dad still has a DVD copy of the commercial somewhere in our brownstone. I hope it's locked up in his gun safe, because lordy, I never want that mortifying tape ever leaking.

Ira splits his time between the agency's Manhattan and Los Angeles offices, so most of our interactions take place over the phone. Today he's calling from LA.

"How's my girl doing this morning?" he asks in the booming, jovial voice I've grown to love.

"This afternoon," I correct. Rehearsal just finished, and I balance my phone on my shoulder as I button up my coat on the way out of the auditorium. "It's two o'clock on the East Coast."

"Ah, right. Fucking time zones. They're liable to make me senile. I never know where I am or what time it is."

I laugh.

"You get a chance to read the Fox pilot I couriered over?" Ira is a no-nonsense, business-minded person, which I appreciate. He's also a shark, but agents are supposed to be sharks, and I still adore him even when he's trying to sell me on projects that I know he's only chosen for the money.

"I skimmed it. It looked like it had potential."

"Well, give it another read and don't skim this time. I spoke to one of the producers last night. They're really keen on having you come in to read for the part."

"Remind me which part? Bonnie? Or was it Sarah?"

"Hold on. Let me check." Papers shuffle over the extension. He's back a few seconds later. "Bonnie."

I swallow my disappointment. Damn it. I was hoping it would be Sarah. The pilot is for a thirty-minute comedy about three girls who hated one another in high school but are forced to room together in college. It follows them as they navigate their freshman year, learning about love and life and friendship while getting into many a pickle. It was described to Ira and me as an ensemble cast, but a well-known television actress has already committed to the role of Zoey, so clearly they plan for her to be the star.

The other two roles are up for grabs, but I would've preferred reading for Sarah, the prude who needs to learn how to let her hair down. I could've had some fun with that.

Bonnie, on the other hand, is the airhead of the trio. She's got some funny lines, but she's dumber than a bag of rocks. Her flaky personality and one-digit IQ are enough to set women's lib back a thousand years.

But maybe I'm worrying for nothing. Maybe the writers have a meaty arc planned for Bonnie. It doesn't make sense to have three female leads but only develop two of them, right?

"It's the perfect role for you, sweetheart," Ira raves. "You can play the cute ditzy type in your sleep."

Yes. I can. But I'm not sure I want to. Every role I've ever had has been the cute ditzy type. It would be nice to broaden my horizons, stretch my acting muscles a bit.

Except...this is *network television*, for crying out loud. I have a chance to costar in a pilot that, going by the buzz already surrounding it, will undoubtedly be picked up for a full season.

"I'll give it another read tonight," I promise. Then I try to conjure up some enthusiasm about potentially playing Bonnie, but I'm not feeling even an iota of *wheeeee!*

Come to think of it, it's been a while since I've read anything that's triggered my *wheeeee!* meter. The last project I was excited about was the play I did for Brett Carson this summer.

"Casting starts in February," Ira tells me.

I furrow my brow. "That's almost three months from now. Why did they cast the part of Zoey so early?"

"They wanted to lock down Kate Ashby before another network could poach her. The producers are wrapping up the final season of their other show, and then they'll be ready to get the ball rolling on this project. They want you to fly out on February 6."

My stomach drops. "I can't. *Widow* opens on the eighth. We have dress rehearsals that week."

"*Widow?*"

"The play I'm doing at school."

Ira sighs. "Any chance they'll let you skip dress rehearsals?"

"Not a one."

"Shit."

Silence ensues. Ira does that a lot, falling deep in thought for minutes at a time. I think he forgets we're on the phone and not in the same room.

"Ira?" I prompt.

"Sorry, sweetheart. Thinking..." After another long pause, his brisk voice returns. "All right, let me get Virgil's assistant on the line. I'll see what we can do."

He disconnects the call without saying goodbye, which is another bad habit of his. He insists he doesn't have time for "that crap."

Ten minutes later, I walk up the path to Bristol House and swipe my ID at the entrance. I probably won't hear back from Ira today, and a part of me hopes the producers come back and say, *Tough shit. If she can't read on the day we want her to read, we'll give the role to someone else.*

Which is a crazy thing to hope for, because, again: Network. Television.

What is wrong with me?

Many things, apparently, because not only am I considering skipping an audition that could launch my career, I'm also planning on having sex with Dean Di Laurentis tonight.

Yep, our sex date is still on like Donkey Kong. I haven't changed my mind. In fact, I'm…God have mercy on my soul…anticipating it. I'm even bailing on my workout today to prepare for it.

After wolfing down a grilled cheese sandwich for lunch, I call a cab to drive me to the salon in Hastings.

Tanya, my mani/pedi/wax guru, is ready and waiting when I stroll through the door. I decided long ago that she's a sadist, because she's alarmingly gung-ho about torturing my nether regions. We get the Brazilian out of the way first, because I don't like having the idea of Hot Wax Torture hanging over my head during my manicure.

Once I'm bare as a baby's bottom, Tanya rubs soothing oil over the sensitive area and ducks out of the room while I slip my undies and leggings back on. It usually takes a few hours before the redness down below subsides, but Dean's not coming over until nine, so I'll have plenty of downstairs recovery time and then I'll be good to go.

I leave the wax room and join Tanya at her manicure station. An hour later, I waltz out of the salon rocking fire-engine-red nail and toe polish, because I think Dean will get a kick out of seeing my bright-red nails scraping his washboard abs. I'd asked Tanya to make them shorter and rounder this time, so I don't scratch the shit out of him again.

On the cab ride back to the dorm, I try to figure out whether I'm excited or disappointed in myself. I still can't believe I caved in to Dean's potent masculinity, but I can't deny I'm eager to reacquaint myself with his magical penis.

Unless…what if it's lost its appeal? I mean, how many times can you really rub a genie's lamp before its magical powers run out? Or does a genie's lamp hold an infinite number of wishes?

Deep thoughts with Allison Jane Hayes, folks.

Huh. Maybe *that* should be my television show.

BY THE TIME NINE O'CLOCK CREEPS UP, I'M READY TO, AS WILL Smith so aptly phrased it, get jiggy with it.

I've undergone a beautification process from head to toe. I'm waxed, polished, scrubbed, and lotioned, and I even flat ironed my hair after blow-drying instead of leaving it at its natural state of kinda wavy.

It feels like a waste to go through so much trouble beauty-wise and then not wear a little black dress or some sexy lingerie, but I figure Horndog Dean is going to rip my clothes off the second he gets here, so I'm in yoga pants and a tank top. No bra (because, again, what's the point?), but I am wearing panties because I don't like going commando unless I'm feeling scandalous. Sometimes I'd do it when Sean and I were going to a fancy restaurant. It drove him crazy knowing I wasn't wearing anything underneath my—

You're not allowed to think about Sean when you're minutes away from sleeping with another guy!

Too late. Sean's in my head now. I still haven't agreed to meet him in person, but I know I should probably give him an answer one of these days before he resorts to the bulldozer approach. He does that a lot.

Case in point: showing up at my dorm uninvited.

Which drove me to flee to the safety of Garrett's house.

Which drove me into Dean's bed.

Seems like there's a morality tale in there somewhere, a nugget of wisdom that Sean would benefit from acquiring. *Push your ex-girlfriend too hard and she sleeps with a man-whore.*

Or maybe it's better if he skips that particular lesson. Besides, it's an unfair indictment on my part, because it wasn't Sean's fault I slept with Dean. It was my decision to do it.

And now I'm making the decision to do it again.

Dean is five minutes late. I fidget impatiently on the couch while I wait for him, unable to concentrate on the episode of *Solange* that's playing on the TV. I haven't watched the show since the night Dean was over, and I'm startled to realize it's not as much fun without him. I kind of enjoyed his running commentary and how every five minutes or so he'd pause the show to announce, "Allie-Cat, I have no fucking idea what's going on!"

It was...cute.

Oh brother. Did I really just use the word *cute* in conjunction with Dean? I jot down a mental note to never say that out loud. He'd probably accuse me of having a crush on him.

Footsteps thump in the hall, causing anticipation to rise in my chest. My heart does a silly, unwelcome flip when two knocks thud against my door. It's a manly-sounding *thump-thuuuump*, and when I swing the door open, Dean is standing in front of me. He's wearing faded jeans with a rip in one knee, a hunter-green cable knit sweater beneath his Briar jacket, and a black wool hat.

"Hey." I'm suddenly feeling awkward about this whole situation.

"Hey." He tugs off his hat as he strides inside. I notice his hair is wet, as if he's just come out of the shower. His gaze travels to the television. "Oh shit, what did I miss? Did Marie-Thérèse manage to find a copy of Claude's will?"

"I don't know. I started the episode about three minutes before you showed up."

"'Kay, well, if you watch any more without me, shoot me a text to let me know what happens." He tosses his hat and coat on the couch.

I swiftly pick them up. "Nope, these are coming with us. Boots too," I add, gesturing to the black Timberlands he's in the process of removing.

"Where are we taking them?"

"My room. I don't want there to be any evidence of your presence in this room in case you forget something. This is a covert operation."

"Whatever you say, Mrs. Bond."

In my bedroom, I drop his stuff on the desk chair. Then shit gets awkward again, because Dean is standing there. Five feet away. Smirking at me.

"What?" I mutter defensively.

He shrugs. "Nothing." But he still doesn't make a single move toward me.

"You're just going to stand there? Come here and do something, damn it."

The corners of his mouth quirk up. "Do what?"

I'm even more frazzled. "I don't know. Kiss me. Take my shirt off. Anything."

Dean crosses his arms over his broad chest. "Nuh-uh. If you want me, come and get me."

Aggravation climbs up my spine. "So we're playing games now?"

"Nah, no games." He lifts one dark-blond eyebrow. "But I'm still not convinced this isn't some sort of trickery on your part."

"What, you think I invited you over so I could fuck with you?" I offer a saucy smile. "Sweetie, I invited you over so I could fuck you. Period."

He chuckles, and the deep, husky sound goes straight to my core. Oh, screw it. If he needs me to make the first move, I'll make the first move. It's not like we both don't want the same thing.

Without a word, I bridge the distance and sweep my palm over his cheek.

Dean gives a slight intake of breath. His face is completely clean-shaven, and I find myself longing for some stubble. I liked the way it felt against my skin last time.

But unlike last time, I'm stone-cold sober tonight. There's no way I can use alcohol as an excuse for what I'm doing right now.

I glide my hand over the back of his scalp and slide my fingers through his damp hair. As our eyes lock, I tug his head down and our lips meet in a featherlight kiss. No tongue. No urgency. It's an exploratory hey-how-are-ya between our mouths, before I pull back to look at him.

Sweet Lord. His gaze contains so much raw, palpable heat it startles a gasp out of me. The next thing I know, Dean's mouth crashes over mine again, and there's nothing exploratory about *this* kiss.

It's pure hunger.

His tongue thrusts into my mouth in a deep, punishing stroke. I hear myself moan, but Dean swallows the desperate sound with another greedy kiss, his warm hands clamping on my hips as he kisses me until I'm breathless.

My heart is pounding. Holy hell, I'm insanely turned on. So is he—I feel the proof of it when he grips my ass and yanks me against him, grinding our lower bodies together.

"You get me so fucking hard," he growls.

He rotates his hips, bending slightly so his shaft lines up in the cradle of my thighs. Then he rocks forward and his erection rubs over my clit, triggering a shockwave of pleasure that sizzles along my spine.

"Naked," I choke out. "Now."

With another chuckle, he ignores the frantic request and kisses me again. His lips are as greedy as before, utterly dominating, and just when I think this frenetic, passionate make-out session couldn't possibly get any hotter, Dean abruptly slows it down. His tongue tickles my bottom lip. His perfect teeth give it a tiny nip. Then he buries his face in my neck and lavishes it with soft, open-mouthed kisses that leave shivers in their wake.

Since he doesn't seem to be in any hurry to get naked, I take matters into my own hands. I capture the hem of his sweater and draw the heavy material upward. I get it up to his collarbone, and he lifts his head to help with the rest of the way. The moment his sweater comes off, I eagerly sweep my palms over his warm, bare flesh.

He makes a husky noise and threads his fingers through my hair, watching me with lust-filled eyes as I caress his chest.

This guy is *built*. I damn near purr with happiness as I explore the hard planes of his chest. I trace each sculpted pec with my index finger, then target one flat nipple and press down on it. He jerks, his breathing going heavier. I trail that same finger down the line of dark-blond hair leading to his waistband, then flatten my palm and stroke the defined ridge of his abs.

Dean's lips find my neck again. With deft fingers, he works the material of my shirt up and eases it over my head.

He sucks in a breath. "No bra?"

"Seemed redundant."

Pleasure ignites inside of me when he cups my breasts. He sweeps his thumbs over my nipples and groans softly. "You don't know how badly I've wanted to play with these tits again."

My head lolls to the side, and he takes advantage and licks a path from my neck to my ear. He sucks lightly on the lobe, and I sag against his warm chest, losing myself in sensation. Dean continues to tease my nipples but uses only the pads of his fingers. He's barely making contact, and my nipples tighten painfully every time his fingertips ghost over them.

"Perfect handful." He squeezes both breasts, his thumbs dancing along the underside of each one. "And these nipples. Jesus Christ, baby."

He dips his head, and I cry out when he flicks his tongue over my right nipple. After all that tortuous non-attention, the firm, purposeful lick he gives me is like an electric shock through my body.

"Hell yeah," he groans. "I could suck on these sweet little nipples all night long."

And then he follows through. At least with the sucking part. He closes his lips around the hard bud and draws it into his hot, wet mouth.

"Oh fuck." I gasp.

"Feel good?" His breath tickles my breasts as he kisses his way to my other nipple.

"Mm-hmm."

"Is it making you wet?"

I mumble something unintelligible, because he's licking playful circles around my nipple and I no longer remember how to create words with my mouth.

"What was that?" he teases.

More gibberish comes out. "Mmrrmblergh."

Dean laughs. "Okay, then. I guess I'll have to find out for myself." He hooks both hands under my waistband and tugs my leggings and panties off. After I kick them away, he wastes no time bringing his hand between my legs.

I don't expect it when he slides two fingers inside me. "Oh my God," I moan. The wave of pleasure nearly knocks me off my feet.

"Jesus. You *are* wet. Dripping wet, baby." A growl leaves his mouth. His eyes are feral, glittering. "If I don't lick this pussy right this second, I'm going to lose my mind."

I expect him to push me onto the bed. He surprises me by backing me up against the door. He sinks to his knees and wrenches my legs apart, and I shiver when I see him peering up at me, lust darkening his gaze. He licks his lips and I almost come on the spot.

Dean smiles wickedly when he sees my expression. "You want my mouth on you? My tongue?"

I manage a jerky nod.

When his mouth nears my core, I make a strangled sound.

When his tongue finds my clit, someone else makes a sound.

It's not me, and it's not Dean, and as Hannah's cheerful voice echoes in the hallway, the two of us freeze in place. Me on my feet, Dean on his knees, as if we're performing a perverted tableau for a live audience.

"Hey!" Hannah calls out. "I just came back to grab my sheet music. I forgot to bring it with me to Garrett's."

Dean's head tilts up, but his lips are still centimeters from my pussy. Panic flutters through me when Hannah's footsteps get ominously close to my bedroom door.

"Allie?"

I press my lips together. If I say nothing, maybe she'll assume I went out.

But no. There's no way she can't see the light under my door. And she had to have noticed my coat, shoes, and purse out in our common area.

"Allie?" She raps on the door.

I look helplessly at Dean. The evil gleam in his eyes has me narrowing my own. I don't know what he's planning, but I— Oh God. He drags the tip of his tongue over my clit, and now my eyes are widening in horror, because I'm pretty sure I just moaned.

"I can hear you in there," Hannah accuses.

Yep, I moaned.

I clear the gravel from my throat. "Uh, yeah, I'm here. Sorry, I was…"

Dean peppers kisses up and down my slit. I forget how to talk again.

"I… Oh gosh," I squeeze out. "I didn't hear you before."

There's a pause. A long, worrisome pause.

"Allie…" Hannah trails off, coughs, then keeps going. "Am I interrupting you while you're, um…riding the solo train to Orgasmville?"

Dean's shoulders begin to shake uncontrollably. His muffled laughter vibrates against my clit, and the resulting effect rivals the good vibrations of every sex toy in my nightstand.

A hoarse "*Yes!*" is wrenched from my throat. It's meant for Dean, but Hannah, of course, doesn't know that.

"Shit," she blurts out. "I'm sorry! Leaving now! I swear!"

Her hurried footsteps retreat down the hall. I hear her moving around in the common room. Then the front door shuts.

My heart is still racing as I lower my gaze to Dean.

"I thought she'd never leave," he rasps.

CHAPTER 14

DEAN

Allie comes faster than I expect. My tongue barely touches her clit before she's trembling and moaning and rocking against my mouth. I guess the idea of almost getting caught is as big a turn-on for her as it is for me.

Damn, I wish I'd gotten her off when Hannah was still behind the door. That would've been so fucking hot. A dirty little secret just for us. But this is good too, Allie riding my face like she's a jockey and I'm her championship racehorse.

Scratch that, it's more than good. My dick is an iron spike trying to chisel its way out of my jeans, and each time her inner muscles bear down on the two fingers I've got lodged inside her, I feel an answering jolt in my balls. When her body finally relaxes, I give her clit one last teasing lick, then hop to my feet.

"You okay there?" I grin at her hazy expression.

"I'm great." She sounds sleepy and sated, but she snaps to attention when I reach for my zipper.

I let my pants drop to the floor. I'm not wearing boxers because—what was it she said before?—it's redundant. When my cock springs free, I grip it in my right hand and give it a much-needed stroke. Christ, I'm painfully hard.

I eat up the sight of her naked body. She's shorter than the chicks I usually go for, but I'm okay with that. And she's somehow slender and curvy at the same time. I take in every appetizing detail, from her perky tits to her smooth, pale skin to the pink paradise between her legs.

I was almost expecting to be let down in some way, that my week's worth of lusting for this girl had exaggerated her appeal. It hadn't. Thank God she changed her mind, because I want her as badly as I did before.

My gaze travels back to her face, resting on her sexy mouth for a moment, then drops back to her completely bare mound.

I groan in frustration.

"What's wrong?" she asks huskily.

"I'm trying to decide what I want more—those pretty lips wrapped around my cock, or your tight pussy squeezing the hell out of it." I slowly pump my erection as I consider the two equally tempting options. "Give me your mouth."

Her blue eyes narrow. "What if I don't want to?"

I squeeze my swollen tip before sliding my fist down to the base, wagging my full length at her. "Don't act like you didn't like sucking on this the other night."

When she doesn't answer, I step forward and press my naked body against hers. She shivers. I take her hand, wrap it around my shaft, and she shivers harder.

I dip my head to whisper in her ear. "Please, baby, I've been such a good boy… I've waited a whole week for this. Don't I deserve a reward for my patience?" I rub the side of her neck with my lips. "I've been"—I kiss her jaw—"such"—I kiss my way up to her mouth—"a good boy."

Allie makes a breathy noise and moves her hand along my shaft. Then she sinks to her knees without a word. My dick twitches in excitement. She parts her lips. Licks them. Licks them again. I can't take my eyes off her mouth. I want it on me, but the ache in my balls warns me that the second there's any kind of suction on my cock, it won't be long before I explode.

One flick of the tongue. That's all Allie is able to do before I'm yanking her to her feet. "No, not happening," I grind out. "I'm gonna come too fast."

Outrage flashes in her eyes. "Oh my God. You're such a mouth-tease!"

"Don't care. I want your pussy. Get on the bed."

I half expect her to argue with me, because she seems to get off on that, but she's surprisingly obedient. In a heartbeat, she's stretched out on the mattress, opening her legs enticingly.

Fuck me. Her pussy lips are glistening. I can still taste her on my tongue, and now I'm trying to decide whether to go down on her a second time, because holy hell, I want another taste. Little Dean both loves and hates the idea, cautioning that if my mouth so much as touches her again, I'm going to come sans stimulation all over her goddamn sheets. And where's the fun in that?

Drawing a breath, I settle on my knees in front of her and ease forward so I'm cradled by the softness of her thighs. Allie reaches out a hand and grips my shaft, and I almost shoot right then. I hadn't noticed her nails before—they're bright red. Downright sinful as she scrapes them along my length. She rubs the little slit that's leaking moisture, and I shudder, pushing my cockhead toward her opening.

"Condom," she reminds me.

Shit. I can't believe I almost forgot to suit up. Usually it's second nature to me, like throwing on my pads before I hit the ice.

I fling my arm over the side of the bed and feel around on the floor until my fingers collide with my pants. I fish out the condom I'd tucked in my pocket.

A moment later, I'm between her legs again. I watch her face as I fist my cock and guide it closer. The tip nudges her, demanding entrance. She visibly trembles. With her cheeks flushed and her blond hair fanned out behind her, she paints the sexiest picture I've ever seen.

We both sigh happily when I sink into her tight sheath. Fuck, I love sex. I don't care if men and women were created by God or evolution or little green Martians. I'm just eternally grateful that someone gave us dicks and pussies and a fun way to use them.

I bend down to brush my lips over Allie's, which changes the angle slightly, pushing me deeper inside her. A shudder of pleasure overtakes me. Centers me. I pull my hips back, then ease back in. Slowly. Deliberately.

Allie's breathing gets choppier. "Stop teasing me."

"You think this is teasing?" I splay my palm on her flat belly, my thumb lightly grazing her clit.

When she arches her hips, I move my hand away and she wails in disappointment. I chuckle. "*That* would be teasing."

"Oh my God. I hate you. Touch me," she orders. "Touch me and fuck me and make me come again."

I narrow my eyes. "You weren't this bossy last time. Or was I too drunk to remember it?"

Allie sits up in an impressive show of flexibility and loops her arms around my neck. She's in my lap now, grinding down on my dick. "I was bossier. But that's because you needed a lot more instruction."

"Bullshit. You were panting in orgasm the second I touched you."

"How do you know I wasn't faking?" she taunts, and then she rocks her hips and we both groan.

I still her by clasping her waist. "Were you?" I'm suddenly reminded of Logan's confession that Grace faked an orgasm the first time they hooked up. I'd ragged him mercilessly about it. Now I'm horrified that Allie might have done the same thing. She is a drama major, after all...

She says, "No, I wasn't faking" and relief courses through me. She grudgingly adds, "You're really good in bed."

"I'm *great* in bed," I correct, then give an upward thrust that makes her gasp in delight.

"Do that again," she begs.

"Do it for me." I fall onto my back so she's astride me and reach up to tweak one puckered nipple. "Ride me until I shoot."

Her mouth curves in a wicked smile. Oh yeah, she likes that idea. Bracing her hands on my abs, she raises herself up, then sinks down on me before I can blink. There's a hot blond riding my dick and I'm in heaven. Her perky tits sway as she moves over me, and when her hair falls onto her forehead, she pushes the golden strands away and keeps her gaze fixed on mine. Undulating. Grinding. Driving me crazy.

"Touch me." Her don't-mess-with-me expression prompts me to bring my hand to where we're joined and obediently rub her clit with my thumb.

Pleasure floods her eyes, but the orders don't stop there. "Slower." Her breathing quickens. "Do it in little circles. No, not that much pressure. Softer… Oh my gosh, yeah, like that."

I ain't gonna lie—I appreciate how blunt she is about telling me exactly what she needs. After all, she knows her own body a helluva lot better than I do. But I'm a quick learner. It isn't long before her words become moans and she starts fucking my cock in earnest.

She's lying on top of me now, her lips so close to my ear that every sexy noise she makes goes straight to my balls. My hips snap up, over and over again, as our bodies slap together and our mouths meet in a sloppy kiss.

I'm still kissing her when she starts to come. She bites down on my lower lip and gives a low cry, and the mind-blowing sensation of her pussy spasming around me triggers my own release. I go off like a rocket, pleasure blurring my vision and clouding my brain. I'm surprised the condom doesn't burst from the massive load I just poured into it.

"What the…?" As I float down from the high, I register a coppery flavor in my mouth. I touch my lip. My fingertips come back stained with blood. Jesus. Allie had bitten me hard enough to draw blood. I choke out a laugh.

She lifts her head at the strangled sound. Her hair is a tangled mess, her eyelids so heavy they're nearly shut. "What...?" Alarm fills her face. "Oh no! You're bleeding!"

I laugh even harder. I'm so frickin' glad I didn't abandon my pursuit of her. This chick who claws and bites and fucks with total abandon. I've never had this much fun in my life.

"It's nothing," I assure her.

She clearly disagrees, sliding off me and reaching for the night-stand. She comes back with a tissue and presses it to my lip. "I'm sorry. Does it hurt?"

"Not in the slightest," I answer cheerfully. I take the tissue from her hand and toss it over the side of the bed. Then I rearrange my body so my head is on the pillow instead of the mattress and tug her toward me.

Allie nestles all that naked goodness beside me and rests her head on my shoulder. "Endless supply of wishes," she mumbles.

"Huh?"

"Your dick." She sighs. "It's the gift that keeps on giving."

"Damn right it is. I told you I've got a great cock."

I grin up at the ceiling and stroke her side boob. We lie there in silence for a bit, both of us still catching our breath. Eventually she murmurs, "So what's this kiddie game you mentioned?"

It takes a second to figure out what she's talking about. "Oh. The Hurricanes. My new defensive coordinator is forcing me to volunteer at the elementary school, so I'm helping out as assistant coach of the hockey team."

"That sounds like fun."

"I can't believe I'm saying this, but...it is. Fun, I mean."

And tonight's game was a lot more exciting than I'd anticipated. The Hurricanes faced off with the team that's leading their division, and every kid on the ice tonight played at a level that impressed me. Oh, and the winning goal was a wrist shot courtesy of Robbie Olsen. Damned if my chest didn't overflow with pride.

"I volunteered at a drama camp every summer when I was in high school," Allie tells me. "I always had a blast, and I was so bummed when the camp shut down. They held it at this old theater in Brooklyn, but the area was rezoned, so the city tore it down and now it's a computer store." She sits abruptly. "Oh crap. I forgot to do something."

Her body drapes over my chest as she leans toward the nightstand. I can't resist capturing one nipple in my mouth and suckling on it. The tight bud feels so fucking good on my tongue. I suck harder, and Allie shivers before batting my head away. "Hold that thought. I don't want to forget this again."

She grabs her phone, and I see her pulling up a reminder app. She types something. From my vantage point, it appears to be "train ticket."

"Train ticket?"

"Yes, Mr. Nosy." She sets the phone down. "I'm reminding myself to book my ticket to New York. I need to do it way in advance this time because it gets really busy on Thanksgiving. Last year I ended up having to take a later train that didn't get in until four in the morning."

"You spending Thanksgiving with your parents?"

She stretches out beside me again. "Just my dad." She pauses. "My mom passed away."

"Ah, I'm sorry to hear that." I stroke my palm along her bare arm. Then I note how weird it is to be lying in bed with her, just talking. But I'm still limp from our trip to the bone zone. The Jaws of Life couldn't pry me off this bed right now. "Are you close with your dad?" I ask.

Her head lightly bumps my shoulder as she nods. "Very close. He's the best man I've ever known."

"What does he do?" I'm not sure why I'm asking all these questions. It's not a habit of mine to try to get to know the chicks I'm sleeping with. But Allie is different. She's Wellsy's best friend, for starters. And it doesn't feel right to wham-bam-thank-you-ma'am her.

"He was a scout for the Bruins," she reveals.

"No shit?" I'm highly impressed. "He must know his hockey, then. Did he play?"

"In college. He was drafted by the Kings, but he tore his ACL during training camp so his career kind of ended before it even began. I think he was relieved, though. He always says he was better at finding the talent than being the talent."

"Still, that's a tough job," I point out. "He must have been traveling all the frickin' time."

"He was. That part sucked, how often he was away. But Mom and I coped. After she died, Dad would take me with him when he could, but most of the time I stayed with my aunt in Queens."

"Is he retired now?"

She stiffens slightly. "Yeah. He is." Another pause. "So what are you doing for Thanksgiving? Where are you from again? Connecticut?"

"Yup. Greenwich. And Manhattan. My family split our time between the two, but I went to high school in Connecticut."

"Prep school," she corrects.

I tweak her hair. "Still considered high school."

"Sure, but I bet you got a ton more perks there than I did at Washington Public in Brooklyn. You spoiled brat." I can hear in her voice that she's teasing. "And you didn't answer what you're doing for the holiday."

"I'm not sure yet," I admit. "Timing wise, I'm kinda screwed. We play Harvard two days after Thanksgiving."

"So? Greenwich isn't that far from here. Neither is Manhattan. You can hop a train or flight to either and still be back in time for the game."

"My family won't be in Greenwich or Manhattan. They'll be at the house in St. Bart's."

Allie sits up again, her mouth agape. Then she starts to laugh. "Well, la-di-da." In the next breath, she affects a flawless British accent. "Why, yes, dear boy, my family does indeed own a home in St. Bart's. *Fah*tha is an avid sailor, and Mutha simply *adores* sipping mimosas on our private beach."

I poke her in the side. "You're just jealous."

"Of course I am. You have a house in St. Bart's. That's badass." Her expression is thoughtful. "Your parents are lawyers, right?"

I nod.

"I didn't realize lawyers made tropical-island-beach-house kind of money."

"It depends on the lawyer. My dad is one of the top criminal defense attorneys in the country, so yeah, he's doing all right," I say wryly. "And Mom specializes in real estate law, which is also pretty lucrative. But they both came from money too."

"Let me guess. Grandpas Sebastian and Kendrick were oil barons?"

For some reason, I'm stupidly pleased that she remembered my middle names. "Nope, there's no oil in our family. Grandpa Seb owned a shipping company. Well, he still owns it, but a board of directors runs it now. And Gramps Kendrick was a real estate developer."

"Like Donald Trump before he got involved in politics?"

"Pretty much. Did you ever go into Manhattan when you lived in Brooklyn?" I frown as something occurs to me. "Hey, how come you don't have the Brooklyn accent?"

"Neither of my parents was originally from New York, so maybe that's why? Dad's from Ohio. Mom grew up in California. I talk like them, I guess. Anyway, of course I've been to Manhattan. Do you think I spent my days hiding under the Brooklyn Bridge like a troll?"

I snicker. "Ever spend any time on the Upper East Side?"

"Sure. I had a friend who lived—" Her eyes widen. "Holy shit. Heyward Plaza. I *just* put that together."

The awe on her face makes me grin.

"You own the Heyward Plaza Hotel?" Allie exclaims.

"Me personally? No. But I suppose I might inherit it one day. My mom's side of the family, the Heywards, owns real estate all over the globe. Hotels mostly, but we've got this cool condominium in Abu Dhabi that's basically made entirely of glass. It's—"

"Okay, you need to stop talking now because you're making me want to punch you. I honestly didn't realize you were *this* rich. I'm not sure if it's a turn-on or a ladyboner-killer."

"Turn-on," I say instantly. "Everything about me turns you on, remember?"

She snorts. "Uh-huh. If you say so."

I flash a cocky grin and start pointing at various parts of my body. "My face? Turn-on. Chest? Turn-on. I'd roll over and show you my ass, but we both know the answer will be 'turn-on' so I'll skip that one. Dick? *Turn* the fuck *on*. And then we get to the non-physical awesomeness that is Dean."

"Speaking in the third person? Not a turn-on."

I ignore the jab. "I'm adorable, first off. My sense of humor is stellar—obvs."

"Obvs," she echoes dryly.

"I'm extraordinarily skilled in the art of conversation."

She nods. "When it's about yourself, of course."

"Of course." I pretend to think it over some more. "Oh, and I'm a mind reader. No lie. I always know what the other person is thinking."

"Yeah? What am I thinking right now?" Allie challenges.

"That you want me to shut up and fuck you again."

She shakes her head in dismay. "Goddamn it. That's actually what I was thinking."

I smirk at her and tap my forehead. "Told ya. Mind reader."

"Congratulations." She sighs. "How many condoms did you bring?"

"One."

"Underachiever. Stick your hand in that drawer. Should be a few in there."

I open the nightstand drawer, which—well, lookee here—contains more than just rubbers. My hand emerges with a seven-inch silicone vibrator in a comical shade of pink.

"Aw, who's this little fella?" I wave the dildo up and down, and it's flexible enough that it flops around like a real dick.

Allie snatches it from my hand. "*Little?* You better take that back or else you'll give Winston a complex."

"*Winston?* Are you kidding me?"

"Oh, come on, you're telling me he doesn't look like a Winston?"

I study the pink sex toy. For something that's shaped like a cock, it's actually ridiculously girly. And Winston is a girly name if I've ever heard one. "Huh. I guess he does."

She nods earnestly. "I have a talent for picking suitable dick names."

I promptly scowl at her. "Don't get any ideas about naming mine, you hear me?"

"Why? Are you scared I'll come up with something better than what you've already got?" Her tone is pure sweetness.

"Who says I named my dick?"

Allie slants her head in challenge. "Are you saying you didn't?"

I shrug in response.

"Ha! I knew it! What's his name?"

My scowl deepens.

"Come on, tell me," she begs. "I promise I won't make fun of you."

After a five-second internal debate, I capitulate. "It's Little Dean."

That makes her howl in laughter. "Oh my God. Of course it is. You are *such* a dork."

I pinch her thigh in retaliation, but she only laughs harder, so I shut her up by rolling her over and slamming my mouth down on hers. She immediately parts her lips to grant my tongue access, and soon we're making out and rubbing up against each other like cats in heat.

I ease my mouth away and rasp, "Feel like tying me up again?"

"Nope. I've got something else in mind."

"Damn, but I was really excited about it."

"Stop complaining, sweetie. Trust me, you're going to like this."

It's her turn to roll me over, and I groan as she starts kissing her way down my body. A moment later, her warm mouth engulfs my cock, and...yeah...Little Dean sure ain't complaining.

CHAPTER 15

DEAN

Saturday night's game against Yale starts off promising.

After Garrett scores an early goal, we successfully manage to keep Yale out of our zone for most of the first period. Well, except for when Brodowski foolishly gets out of position and hands Yale's center and right wing a breakaway.

Thanks to that bonehead move, I'm faced with an odd man rush and it's pure blind luck that Yale doesn't get a goal out of it—the shot smacks off the pipe. I dive toward the puck and snap off a quick pass to Hunter. Our forwards blessedly fly past the center line into Yale territory, while I do my damnedest not to strangle Brodowski as we whiz toward the bench for a line change.

I squirt water through my face guard and spit it at my feet. Sweat pours down my face from the exertion it took to singlehand-edly defend our zone.

Beside me, Brodowski is properly shamefaced. "I messed up the coverage," he mutters to me.

I grit my teeth and say, "Happens to the best of us." Because that's what you're supposed to say when you're part of a team. We don't play the blame game here at Briar.

But if anyone is to blame for that breakaway? It's Brodowski, sure as shit.

"What happened to your lip?" he asks, studying the thin red cut splitting my bottom lip.

"Sex," I grunt in response.

On my other side, Tucker snickers. He'd asked me the same thing this morning, and I'd given him the same nonanswer.

On the other side of Tucker, one of our freshman wingers looks highly impressed. "You're my idol, dude," he calls out.

The first line's shift lasts for the rest of the period, and we hit the locker room with a lead of 1–0. For the first time in weeks, morale is high.

The second period starts off exactly like the first. Another early goal, this time courtesy of Fitzy. We're leading 2–0 now, and Yale is feeling the pressure. As a result, they come at us hard, playing aggressively and taking shot after shot at goal. Patrick Corsen, our goaltender, is nowhere near as talented as our old goalie Simms, who graduated last year. He also has a bad habit of skating too far from the crease, so when the opposing winger connects with a centering pass from his D-man, Corsen isn't in position to stop the puck.

But it's all right. We're still in the lead. For…oh, about another thirty seconds. I'm hopping out for my shift when the same winger who'd just scored does an impressive wraparound and flicks another shot past Corsen. The fucker scores again. Two goals in less than a minute, and just like that, our lead becomes a tie.

The rest of the second is scoreless.

In the third, everything falls apart for us. I can't even count all the things that go wrong—it's one bullshit error after the other.

Logan takes a two-minute penalty for slashing. Yale scores on the power play.

2–3.

Wilkes lands in the sin bin for hooking. Yale scores on the power play.

2–4.

Corsen is faked out by a winger, who moves as if he's shooting low, then snaps the puck high. It flies into the net, top left corner. Yale scores, and this time we weren't even short-handed.

2–5.

Hunter slaps in a one-timer.

3–5.

I take a brainless tripping penalty. Yale scores on the power play.

3–6.

The final buzzer sounds, and we've lost our third game of the season. Fun times.

O'SHEA PULLS ME ASIDE BEFORE I CAN BOARD THE BUS. HE ALREADY yelled at me and Logan in the locker room for taking foolish penalties that resulted in two goals for the other team, and I sincerely hope he's not gearing up to do it again. I'm in a foul mood and my brain-to-mouth filters aren't working at full capacity right now. If O'Shea pushes my buttons, I don't know that I can control my temper.

"What is it, Coach?" I ask as politely as possible.

His dark eyes flick over me, and then he reaches into his pocket and pulls out a BlackBerry. Which momentarily distracts me, because I can't remember the last time I saw a BlackBerry. Doesn't pretty much everyone have a smartphone these days?

"Anything you'd like to tell me?" O'Shea says coolly.

I am literally drawing a blank. "Um…about what?"

His jaw ticks. Without a word, he hands me the phone.

There's a slight queasiness in my gut as I glance at the screen. It's open to an Instagram account I don't recognize, but the photo in question features a slew of familiar faces, including my own. I'm not sure who took it, but it was obviously some chick who was at Malone's on Thursday night, because the hashtags below the image are #HockeyHotties and #SexyBriarBoys.

I'll be honest—I'm not really seeing the problem here. The picture shows the guys and me clinking our shot glasses together in cheers. We'd ordered the round of shots before switching to pitchers of beer. And sure, we're drinking, but none of us are minors, and it's not like we'd gotten caught with our pants down, hanging brain. We're just sitting in a booth, for chrissake.

"Still have nothing to say?"

I raise my gaze to O'Shea's. "This was taken on Thursday night. We were celebrating Fitzy's birthday."

"I can see that. And exactly how much celebrating did you do?"

"If you're asking if we got sloppy drunk, the answer is no."

That doesn't appease him. "Do you remember what I told you in Jensen's office the other day? I said no boozing, no drugs, and no brawling."

"We weren't 'boozing,' sir. We just had a few drinks."

"Are you aware of Briar's policy regarding drug and alcohol restrictions for student athletes? If not, I'd be happy to provide you with a copy of it."

"Oh, come on, Coach, you can't expect us not to drink. We're in college, for fu—Pete's sake. And we're all over twenty-one."

"Watch your tone, Di Laurentis," he snaps. "And yes, the other coaches and I *do* expect that of you. As long as you play hockey for this school, you're to follow the rules set out by your coaches and the NCAA and conduct yourself accordingly."

"Sir…" I take a calming breath. But I don't feel calm. I'm pissed about tonight's loss and not in the mood to get chewed out for having a couple goddamn drinks. "My teammates and I conducted ourselves *superbly* the night in question. So rest assured, you have nothing to worry about."

"Don't get smart with me, son. We have a serious problem here—"

"No, we don't," I cut in. "I think you're overreacting. We went to a bar and had a few beers. It's what we do, okay? But hey, if this is something you're truly concerned about, maybe you should run it by Coach Jensen and see what *he* says." My mouth twists in a sneer. "He's the head coach of this team, right? Shouldn't he be the one to handle this 'serious problem'?"

I regret the words the moment they exit my mouth, but goddamn it, I've had it up to here with this man.

Predictably, O'Shea doesn't take kindly to having his authority challenged. "Chad has given me free rein over the defensemen, and it would serve you well to remember that," he spits out. "When it comes to the defense, *I* handle any issues that arise. And this, Mr. Di Laurentis, is an issue. You will not indulge in alcohol or drugs of any kind while you're a member of this team, you hear me?"

For chrissake. I'm done with this shit.

"You got it, Coach. Can I get on the bus now?"

Anger reddens his face. "You want to join your teammates on the bus? Then you'd better take some fucking responsibility for your actions. Acknowledge that you did something wrong."

I'm seconds away from losing it. My hands ball into fists, but by some miracle, I manage to stop myself from hitting him. "Out of curiosity, are you planning on delivering this same lecture to everyone else in that picture? Or am I just special?"

"I plan on talking to all of them, don't you worry. I chose to speak to you first because I was already aware of your history with alcohol abuse." He lifts one eyebrow, and holy fucking shit, I almost let my fist fly.

My history with alcohol abuse?

Fuck that. And fuck *him*.

He knows damn well I don't have a problem with alcohol. He's just being a spiteful ass and trying to find new ways to punish me for what happened with Miranda. But this? Referencing the one time I drank too much—when I was a goddamn *teenager*—and using it to imply I'm a drunk?

I'm. So. Done. With. This. Shit.

"Thank you for your concern," I say pleasantly. "It's much appreciated. Really." Then I leave him standing on the pavement and stalk toward the bus.

Fortunately, he doesn't stop me.

I'm still fighting to gather the scattered pieces of my composure as I slide into my usual seat next to Tucker, who shoots me a quizzical look. "What was that about?"

"Absolutely nothing." I fish my earbuds out of my pocket and pop them in. If Tuck considers that rude, he doesn't say anything—he just lowers his gaze to his phone, and a few minutes later, we're on the road.

The rock track that comes up on my iPhone only riles me up more, so I pull up the playlist Wellsy made for me this summer and try to calm down to the sounds of smooth jazz and easy crooning. Nope. Not working either. I switch off the iPhone and listen to the low chatter of my teammates instead.

Logan and Fitzy are babbling about a first-shooter video game that Fitzy is reviewing for the college blog. Hollis is trying to convince someone to meet him at his dorm—"I'll make it worth your while, baby"—which means he's either on the phone, or he and his seatmate just came out to the entire bus. Corsen and *his* seatmate are arguing about who the hottest actress on *Game of Thrones* is: the chick who plays Daenerys or the broad who plays Cersei.

"You're both wrong," Garrett calls out. "Melisandre is the hottest. Hands down."

"The red witch? No way. She gave birth to a gross shadow creature. That pussy's tainted, dude."

"Spoiler alert!" Wilkes says irritably. "I was planning on starting season one this weekend!"

"Don't bother," Fitzy advises. "The show sucks. Read the books instead."

"I swear to God, if you tell us to 'read the books' one more time,

I'm going to strangle you," Corsen announces. "I mean it. I'll straight up strangle you, Colin."

Our resident nerd shrugs. "Can't help it if the books are better."

I don't join in, but secretly I agree with Fitz. The books *are* better. Though I doubt anyone will believe me if I said I read 'em. With the exception of my roommates, most of my teammates don't take me seriously. I'm pretty sure they think I'm only attending Harvard Law because my rich parents bought my way in. Doesn't bother me, if I'm being honest. I get a kick out of it when people underestimate my intelligence. Half the time I willingly play into the dumb blond stereotype, just for funsies.

As the chatter continues, I tune everyone out and reach for my phone. I don't know what compels me to open the Facebook app and search her name. I'm on autopilot, barely aware of what I'm doing until the search results pop up.

There are dozens of Miranda O'Sheas on Facebook, but none of them are the one I'm looking for.

I do another search, this time with her name and the words *Duke University*. I have no idea if she even goes there, but it seems like a good place to start. When we were dating, all Miranda ever talked about was how much she wanted to get into Duke.

This time her profile appears on the screen.

I study the small thumbnail pic. She hasn't changed in four years. She still has the same round face, the same unruly dark curls, the same brown eyes.

To my dismay, her profile is private. I can't see anything except her profile pic and cover photo, which is a generic beach landscape. I stare at the little green button at the top of the page.

Add friend.

I don't know what possesses me to click it. But I do.

With the friend request sent, I turn off the app and put my phone away. Tucker isn't on his anymore either. He's leaning back against the headrest with his eyes closed, and I decide to follow his lead. We've got two more hours until we reach Boston, then another hour to Hastings. Might as well get some sleep and try to forget tonight's disastrous game.

The nap does the trick. I wake up feeling centered and relaxed, and when I peer out the window and wait for the next road sign to appear, I discover we're only a half hour from campus.

In the seat beside me, Tucker is also awake, typing on his phone again.

"Dude, are you dating someone?" I can't stop myself from asking. I've barely seen Tucker lately, and we live in the same house.

"No," he says dismissively.

"You sure about that?"

"I think I would know if I was dating someone." But there's an odd note in his voice, which I can't for the life of me decipher.

"Where've you been, then? You're never home anymore."

Tucker shrugs. "I go to class. Study at the library. Chill in my room." He pauses. "I crashed at a friend's place in Boston a few times."

"What friend?"

Before he can answer, my phone rings, and I swear he looks relieved. I make a note to cross-examine him again later. It'll be good practice for law school.

I pick up when I see Beau's name and give him the usual greeting. "Maxwell. What's shaking?"

"Hey. How was the game?" Loud music blasts in the background, but I can hear him loud and clear.

"Shitty."

"Yeah. I read the recap on the college sports blog. You got your asses kicked."

"Why'd you even ask how it went if you already knew the answer?"

"I was being polite."

I have to snicker.

"Anyway, party at my place tonight. I know it's late, but I'm still extending an invite. Figured you might need something to help take your mind off the beating you got from Yale."

I consider it, but only briefly. "Nah. Thanks, but I'm not in the mood." A tired breath slips out. "It's been a crap night."

"All the more reason for you to come out. It's a hot girl smorgasbord in here. And you know women—they can't resist a mopey, brooding man. Tell them how sad you are about losing your game, and they'll be begging you to let them make you feel better." He pauses. "Wait. Unless you're still dealing with…ah, equipment malfunctions?"

"Nope. We're all better now."

"Nice! Does that mean Bella finally threw you another bone?"

"Bella?" I say blankly.

"Yeah, you know, the chick you imprinted on."

I chuckle. "Right. Yeah, she did." I keep my response vague, because Tucker is right there and he's not allowed to know about Allie and me. And…shit. I guess that means I'm not allowed to harass him for being so secretive lately, what with this pot/kettle situation we're in.

"Good, then you're all fixed. Now come over and put that newly functioning dong to good use."

"Nah," I say again. "I'm really not feeling it." But I am feeling something else, because as usual, the mere thought of Allie gets me hard. "We'll connect sometime this week. Go out for beers or something."

"Sounds good. Later, bro."

The second we hang up, I open a new text box. It'll be nearly 1:00 a.m. by the time I get home. That's absolutely booty call territory, but it's Saturday night and Allie doesn't have classes tomorrow, so I figure I'm safe.

Me: You + me = wild animal sex tonight?

She responds right away. Good, she's still up.

Her: You = tempting — me = already in bed ÷ sleep.

Me: Why the division sign??

Her: I don't know. I was trying to answer in math. Bottom line: I'm in bed.

Me: Perfect. That's right where I want you to be. I'll be there in 45.

Her: You can't. Hannah's home.

Me: We'll be very, very quiet. She won't even know I'm there.

There's a short delay, and even before her answer appears, I know it's going to be a no.

Her: Don't want to risk it. Let's wait for a nite we can be alone.

Me: You have no sense of adventure.

Her: You have no patience.

Me: Not when it comes to you.

Her: We had sex 3 times last nite! I'm sure that'll tide you over til we see each other again.

Me: And when will that be?

Her: Tomorrow nite maybe? I'll let you know.

Me: Fine.

Me: BTW—totally gonna think of you when I'm jerking off tonight.

Her: That's cool. I just fingered myself and pretended it was you.

I groan out loud.

Tucker swivels his head toward me. He looks at my face, then my phone, then rolls his eyes. "Seriously, man? You're sexting right beside me? Get a room."

I *wish* I could get a room. Allie's room, to be exact. But clearly that's not in the cards tonight. And now, thanks to that little cocktease, I get to spend the rest of the bus ride with a stiffy.

CHAPTER 16

DEAN

"Do you have a girlfriend?" Dakota skips around the equipment room like a tiny pixie while I stack helmets on the shelf in front of me.

Since the boys' locker room isn't exclusive to the hockey team—it's also the one used by every other male student at Hastings Elementary—that means all the hockey gear needs to be stored in this equipment room. As assistant coach, it's my job to put it all away.

"Well, do you?" she demands when I take longer than two seconds to respond.

I glance at her over my shoulder. "No, I don't. And shouldn't you be doing your homework right now?" Not that I mind her company. Dakota is highly entertaining.

She hops up onto the closed lid of a large storage container and sits cross-legged. "Don't have any homework today." Twirling the end of her blond ponytail, she chews loudly on her gum, blows a big pink bubble, then says, "Why not?"

"Why not what?" I shove the last helmet on the shelf and turn toward her.

"Why don't you have a girlfriend?"

"Because I don't."

"Have you *ever* had a girlfriend?"

"Sure. I've had lots." Well, not since I started college, but I don't tell Dakota that. It probably isn't appropriate to reveal to a ten-year-old girl that I've been single for the last few years because I was busy screwing my way through Briar.

Speaking of screwing, if I don't get some action soon, I swear to God my balls will explode. I didn't end up seeing Allie on Sunday, and she wasn't able to meet up yesterday either. She's been busy with rehearsals and mentioned something about needing to make an audition tape, but I'm starting to wonder if she's dodging me. She'd better not be, because I'm not ready for this…fling? Sure, fling. I'm not ready for this fling to end.

"You know my brother Robbie?" Dakota asks in a hushed voice.

I snicker loudly. "No, kid, I don't know Robbie. I just coach his team."

A sheepish flush blooms on her cheeks. "Oops. Right. That was a stupid question."

"Ya think?"

Giggling, she says, "Anyway, you can't tell *anyone*, but Robbie has a girlfriend!"

I raise my eyebrows. "Yeah? And how do you know that? Are you spying on your big brother?"

"No, he told me, dum-dum. Robbie tells me everything. Her name is Lacey and she's in *eighth grade*." Dakota shakes her head in amazement. "That's a whole grade higher than him."

I stifle the laughter threatening to spill over. "Landed himself an older woman, huh? Good for Robbie."

Dakota lowers her voice to a whisper and proceeds to tell me every single detail about her brother's eighth-grade girlfriend. I listen obligingly, all the while trying to pinpoint exactly when it was that hanging out with middle-schoolers became the highlight of my days.

Don't get me wrong, the time I've spent at Briar has been awesome. My hockey team won three national championships, and academically I've always been at the top of my class. The only course I had trouble with was an incomprehensible politics class in sophomore year, which I finished with a B+. But I don't like to think about that grade, because it's tangled up with a lot of other bullshit I'd rather forget. Despite that, I can't deny I've had a successful academic career. I knocked the LSATs out of the park. I got into Harvard Law on my own merit instead of relying on my family name.

But I don't remember ever being excited about my courses. I didn't jump for joy when my LSAT scores came back. And I'm certainly not doing cartwheels at the thought of going to Harvard.

It was always assumed that I'd go the law school route. It's not something my folks pushed me into, but I can't pretend it's something I'm passionate about. Not like my brother, who lives and breathes the law. He loves his job at the firm, says that every time he steps into a courtroom, he feels alive. It's the same way Garrett and Logan feel about playing hockey.

Me? I've never had that feeling before. Loving something so hard that it buzzes through my blood and makes my entire body come to life.

Or at least I hadn't felt that way before Friday night, when I witnessed the Hurricanes utterly dominate the division leader. And then again today, when I set up a passing horseshoe drill and watched every boy on the ice absolutely kill it.

"Dean, you're not *listening*!"

Dakota's aggravated voice jerks me from my thoughts. "Sorry, kid. I spaced out. What were you saying?"

"Nothing," she mutters.

She's obviously upset about being ignored, which tells me she must have said something important. I drag a metal chair toward her, twist it around, and straddle it, resting my forearms on the backrest. "Talk to me."

Her bottom lip sticks out in a pout. "I was asking you a question."

"Okay, then ask it again. I promise to listen this time."

"Will you"—the rest flies out in a hurried rush—"*teachmehowtoskate?*"

"Can you slow that down?" I ask with a smile.

"Teach me how to skate," she repeats.

I furrow my brow. "You don't know how to skate?"

Dakota slowly shakes her head.

"Why the he—heck not?" I'm aghast. Who lives in New England and doesn't know how to skate? That's just blasphemy.

"My mom only had enough money to send one of us to skating lessons, and Robbie's older so he got to go. And he's gonna be a famous hockey player one day, so he needs to know how to skate."

Although Dakota's tone is defensive, I don't miss the note of hurt beneath the surface. My heart does a painful little somersault. My siblings and I never had these kinds of problems growing up. Our family had plenty of money, which means we didn't have to make any sacrifices. Summer got her ballet lessons and swimming certificates. Nick and I got our skating lessons and hockey camps and all the equipment we ever needed.

I hadn't lied to Allie the other week—the Life of Dean is pretty fucking sweet. I've always gotten whatever I wanted.

Now, seeing Dakota's upset face, I feel like a spoiled, ungrateful brat.

"I guess that means you don't own skates?" I say slowly.

She gives another shake of the head.

"What size are your feet?"

"I dunno. Small?"

I chuckle. "Let me see one of your shoes."

She quickly pulls off a neon-pink sneaker and holds it out for me.

After I check the size tag, I hand the shoe back and wander over to the large metal cabinet that holds the boys' skates. Most of them are far too big for her, but after some rifling and digging around, I find a pair of Bauers on the bottom shelf that might fit her.

I hold up the scuffed black skates. "Try these on."

Horror fills her big blue eyes. "But those are boy skates! I want *girl* skates."

Another laugh tickles my throat. When her expression collapses, I sigh instead. "Okay. Don't worry, kid. I'll see what I can do, okay?" I tuck the evil boy Bauers back in the cabinet and firmly shut the door before she bursts into tears or something.

Coach Ellis chooses that moment to poke his head in the room. "Your mother's here," he tells Dakota.

I'm afraid he'll notice her stricken face and have me arrested for upsetting a minor or something, but when I glance back at Dakota, she's all smiles.

"Bye, Dean!" She hops off the crate and darts out the door.

Ellis grins at me. "Sweet kid, huh?"

I follow him out of the equipment room and we spend a couple minutes discussing what we want the boys to work on next practice. Once we wrap up, I leave the arena and check my phone on the way to my car. There's a text from Garrett saying he's crashing at Bristol House with Hannah tonight but that he left his Jeep at home, so he'll need a ride back from practice tomorrow.

When I stride into our kitchen ten minutes later, I find a note from Tucker on the fridge, informing us he's spending the night at a friend's. His mysterious non-girlfriend, I suppose.

And then? The trifecta. Logan wanders in to grab a bottle of water and says he won't be home till late.

"Where're you going?" I ask as I rummage around in the fridge.

"Boston. Grace's dad got us tickets for this orchestra thing. Neither of us really want to go, but she says he'll be hurt if we don't."

I grin over my shoulder. "So you're spending your evening listening to classical music?"

"Yup," he says glumly. "But there's an intermission, so Grace promised we could fool around in the coatroom during it."

"Sounds like a good tradeoff."

"I know, right?"

Logan leaves a couple minutes later, and my in-dire-need-of-sex libido springs to life at the thought of having the house to myself tonight. I don't waste any time contacting Allie, who must be as horny as I am, because she answers right away.

> Her: YES! 3 days of stress = coming over right after my workout. Gimme a couple hours, tho.
> Me: Favor to ask.
> Her: ?
> Me: Bring Winston.

The request earns me a laughing emoji and a winky face, which could either mean "That's hilarious but *no*" or "That's hilarious and yes I will." I hope for the latter.

I FLIP THROUGH A *SPORTS ILLUSTRATED* AT THE KITCHEN COUNTER while I scarf down my dinner, which consists of leftover chicken and broccoli. The team nutritionist emails us a weekly list of suggested meal plans, but Tucker, our resident chef, seems to think the word "suggested" means "mandatory" because he refuses to keep any junk food in the house. Since he's the only one who remembers to go grocery shopping and the only one who actually enjoys cooking, this is the healthiest house on the fucking planet.

After dinner, I shower, shave, and do a little bit of manscaping, because I'm nice like that. Then I settle at my desk to start my International Relations paper, which I'm still working on when Allie rings the doorbell. I save the file, close the laptop, and go downstairs to let her in.

She's on the phone when I swing open the door. She mouths *Sorry* and holds up one finger to indicate she'll be a minute.

"Want dinner?" I murmur as she enters the front hall. "We've got leftovers."

Allie covers the mouthpiece for a second. "Thanks, I already ate." She lifts her hand. "No, I'm still here, Ira. And yes, I sent you the tape. I don't get why you needed it this fast, if they're not making any casting decisions until February."

We head upstairs, and I let her walk ahead of me so I can admire her ass. When we reach the second-floor landing, I can't help but ease in behind her, rubbing my aching groin against her bottom as I bend my head to kiss her neck.

She shivers and swats me away. "I don't know," she says into the phone. "I'm still on the fence about this role." She pauses. "Yes, I read what they asked me to read. My friend Megan read Zoey's part off-camera."

I notice that she keeps rubbing her lower back. Every time her palm touches a certain spot, her expression grows pained. Or maybe she's just annoyed with whatever this Ira dude is saying to her.

"I overnighted it to you at the campus shipping center, so you should get it tomorrow afternoon." She presses her hand to her tailbone, massaging absently. "If you think I need to redo it, I will. But I did the best I could with what they gave me... Yes... *Yes*, Ira... We'll talk tomorrow."

She hangs up and turns toward me. "My agent is driving me nuts," she announces.

I hadn't even known she had an agent, so I'm notably impressed. "How come?"

"He wants me to audition for this Fox pilot, but I'm not able to fly to LA for the casting session so I had to send an audition tape instead. Now he's all worried that my 'natural charm' won't show through on camera. Which is fricking stupid, because that's what television acting *is*—conveying emotion *on camera*."

I frown when I notice she's still clutching her back. "What's wrong?"

"I don't know," she moans. "I think I pulled something at the gym. I've been super stressed about this play I'm doing, and I worked myself too hard tonight. My back is killing me."

"Want me to rub it for you?"

"God yes. Please?"

I'm about to instruct her to lie on the bed, but then I have a better idea. "Get naked," I order. "I'll be right back."

After years of playing sports, I'm no stranger to aches and pains. Tight muscles, sore ribs, busted knees…I've had it all, and I discovered a long time ago that nothing loosens me up more than a good soak. Since a visit to the team facility's whirlpool or steam room isn't an option, I do the next best thing by running a scalding hot bath.

As the water level rises, I rummage in the cabinet under the sink to see if there are any bath salts or oils I can dump in there. I find a bottle of bubble bath, which I assume belongs to Grace because Hannah has the luxury of using Garrett's private bathroom. G, that greedy bastard, pulled rank on us and used the team captain card to claim the master bedroom when we moved into this house.

Logan, Tuck, and I are forced to share the one in the hall, and it shows. The shelves are overflowing with dude products, the towels are forever on the floor, and the wastebasket contains an alarming amount of condom wrappers.

Sighing, I start collecting the discarded towels. Logan left a pair of khakis on the rack, but I just drape the damp towels over the pants, then grab two clean ones from the linen closet and set them on the closed toilet lid.

I return to the bedroom to find a very naked Allie sitting on the edge of the bed. My body responds, hardening at the sight of all that smooth, bare skin. Her nipples are pointed in salute. Fuck, I want to suck on them.

A grin breaks out when I notice what she's holding. "You actually brought him?"

"You texted when I was still at the dorm, so I decided to grant you your favor." She menacingly waves the dildo at me. "But if you want me to shove Winston up your butt, it's not happening."

I choke out a laugh. "Don't worry. I'd prefer it if my butt stayed Winston-free."

"Good." She lovingly strokes the pink phallus. "Don't get me wrong—I'll totally shove whatever you want up there. Just not Winston. He's special to me."

Wait, what?

"Hold up. *That's* your issue? You're willing to peg me if I ask you to, but only as long as we don't use your precious Winston?"

"Of course I'd peg you if you asked me to." She says this as if it's the most normal thing on the planet. "Why would I ever deny you all that prostate pleasure? It's like telling a woman you won't touch her clit."

"As a man who has never experimented with his prostate, I can't comment on the strength of that comparison."

Her jaw drops. "Never? Really? Okay, we're definitely going to have to change that."

"Pass." I tug her to her feet, enjoying the sight of her bare tits swaying. "Come on, I've got something that will make your sore back feel better."

I lead her to the bathroom, and her face lights up when she sees the bubble bath I'd prepared. "Oh my gosh. This is awesome."

Taking the vibrator out of her hand, I nudge her toward the tub. "Get in. But make sure to leave some room for me."

"Ooh, we're bathing together? Kinky." She delicately dips one foot in the water, then moans loud enough to wake up my dick. Not that he was asleep. He's always on high alert when this girl is around. "Nice and hot," she purrs.

I second that.

I set Winston on the edge of the tub, then strip out of my T-shirt and sweats. The water sloshes as Allie slides forward so I can get in behind her.

The steam rising around us smells like the strawberry flavor of the bubble bath. I make a contented noise, drawing her slippery, naked body against my chest. My legs are too long for this damn tub, so I have to prop my knees up, but I don't care, because Allie's round ass is pressed up against my cock and I'm perfectly willing to deal with some leg cramps if it means keeping her in this position.

"Okay, back to our butt talk. Are you really not the least bit curious to know what it feels like?"

I glide my hands down to her tailbone and start kneading her smooth, wet flesh. "Not in the slightest."

"Ooh, that feels great… Keep doing that…" She moans again as she sags into my touch. "What about a finger? Let me stick one finger up there and see what happens."

I snort. "I appreciate the offer, but no."

"Would you feel better if a guy did it to you? Because, sweetie, I have a few gay friends who would kill to get their hands on your ass."

This time I give her a "*Hell* no."

"I never took you for a homophobe," she taunts.

"I'm not."

"Liar."

"I'm not. Seriously, I don't care if you're gay or straight or bi or whatever other category you fall under. I'm just not interested in bottoming for some dude. Dicks don't do it for me."

"How do you know?" she challenges. "What if you hook up with a guy and end up loving it?"

"Trust me, I won't."

"How can you be sure unless you try it?" I shrug, which summons a squeal from her. "Oh my God, you *have* tried it!" Water splashes over the edge of the tub as she twists around so we're face-to-face. "Who was he? What did he look like? What did you guys do? Tell me everything!"

"There's nothing to tell."

"Bullshit." She runs one hand over the tiny white bubbles

clinging to my pecs. "I'll make you a deal. If you tell me about your gay experience"—she pauses enticingly—"I'll tell you about my lesbian one."

Just like that, I'm harder than steel. "Deal," I say instantly.

Her laughter bounces off the shower tiles. "Men. You're so easy to manipulate."

"Of course we are. It's our fatal flaw—we're ruled by our cocks." I skim my hands up her soapy stomach to cup her tits. I keep catching tantalizing glimpses of her nipples peeking through the white suds, and I can't help but seek them out with my fingers. When I pinch the rigid peaks, Allie makes a throaty sound and closes her eyes.

"Nuh-uh," I chide, dropping my hands. "You can't dangle a lesbian encounter in front of me and then not follow through."

"Oh, right. I forgot." She shrugs dismissively, which causes droplets to fly off the ends of her hair. "I made out with a girlfriend of mine in junior year of high school. We got drunk at a party and decided to try it." Another shrug. "It was all right."

"Just kissing?"

"Yep."

"And it was only 'all right?'" I grumble. "Well damn. That's disappointing."

"Gee, I'm so sorry my experience doesn't live up to your pervy standards. But that's what happened. Okay, your turn. When did *you* go gay?"

"Also happened in high school," I confess. "A buddy and I were on a double date and the girls dared us to kiss. We said we'd do it only if *they* kissed. Didn't think they'd call our bluff, but nope, they actually started making out like porn stars. So Jason and I couldn't back out."

"Did you like it?"

"It wasn't awful, but it didn't get me hard."

"Was there tongue?"

"Yup."

"A lot of tongue?"

"I don't know. A normal amount."

She looks as dissatisfied by my tale as I was with hers. "And it didn't go any further than that? You didn't touch the tips of your dicks and pretend you were sword fighting?"

I laugh hard enough to make all the water in the tub eddy like a river rapid. "No, but now I kinda wish we did. That sounds like a blast," I choke out between chortles. "*Dick swords.*"

Allie goes into hysterics too, but the way she's shuddering with laughter causes her soapy thighs to slide up and down my crotch, which swiftly transforms my amusement into pure arousal.

She's still laughing when I capture her mouth in a hungry kiss. But not for long. Soon she's gasping against my lips, locking her hands at the nape of my neck as her tongue tangles with mine.

I clasp her hips and ease her forward until my shaft is lined up with her pussy. She whimpers when I glide my length along her wet flesh, rubbing my cockhead over her clit.

"Dean…"

Her breathy whisper barely registers. I'm too distracted by her warm, slippery pussy and the soft tits I'm now squeezing in my palms.

"Dean."

"Mmm?"

"Did you hear that?"

I suddenly notice she's gone stiff, and her head is slanting toward the closed door. I still the slow movement of my hips and listen carefully, but the house is silent. "I don't hear anyth—"

Oh shit. Wait. I do hear it. The unmistakable sounds of someone thumping up the stairs.

And then:

"Bro, you will *never* believe what happened!"

Before I can blink, Allie is out of the tub, her naked, dripping-wet body diving behind the door half a second before Logan throws it open.

CHAPTER 17

DEAN

"We drove all the goddamn way to goddamn Boston, only to realize I left my goddamn wallet at home. So we had to get back in the truck and drive all the way home, and now—"

Logan skids to a stop, cartoon-character style. I'm surprised his head doesn't spin and his eyeballs don't bug out.

"Um." His gaze bounces around the bathroom like a rubber ball.

He looks at the towel rack, where his cargo pants are hanging.

He looks at the bathtub, where I'm lounging like Cleo-fucking-patra.

He looks at the bubbles surrounding my body like a fluffy white cloud.

And then he looks at Winston.

"Dude," I blurt out. "It's *not* what it looks like."

"Nope, nope, nope, I don't want to know!" Logan throws his hands in the air and starts backing toward the door as if he accidentally walked into a lion's den. He halts. Snatches his pants off the rack. Continues backing away. His eyes once again focus on the pink dildo two inches from my hand.

I try again. "I promise you, it's not—"

"I don't want to know."

He lunges out the door and slams it shut. I hear his footsteps thump toward the stairs. Then they thump back to the bathroom.

"Hey, listen, I'm gonna stay with Gracie tonight. That way you can...uh...finish up whatever it is you're...uh...doing."

Fucking hell.

I wait until I hear the front door shut before I address Allie. "You *hid* behind the door? *Really?*"

She steps forward sheepishly. "I'm sorry."

"You can shove your sorries in a sack, baby doll. You realize what you've done, right?" I glare at her. "You've officially allowed my best friend to believe I like to shove dildos up my ass."

"Aw, that's not true. If anything, Logan is enlightened now. We opened his mind to the delightful possibilities of anal play."

"Get in here," I order.

Allie quickly lowers herself in the water and kneels in front of me. "I *am* sorry, you know. I probably should've told him I was in here." She tucks a strand of wet hair behind her ear. "I just...I like the idea of keeping this a secret. You know what will happen if everyone finds out we're screwing around. They'll get all up in our business and turn this fling into something bigger than it is."

She's right. That's the nature of the social beast, and I was trying to avoid the same thing. But goddamn it, Logan is never going to let me live this down. Taking a bubble bath with a pink dildo? Allie has doomed me to a fate as the punchline of a never-ending joke.

"Let me make it up to you," she begs. "I'm sure we can find *some* way to get Logan off your mind..." Her soapy fingers encircle my cock, which rapidly hardens in her hand. "See? You're already forgetting."

I groan when she gives me a firm stroke. "Nope, I'm still mad at you."

"What'll it take for you to be unmad at me?"

"Your mouth, for starters."

She considers it, her gaze tracking the motion of her own hand beneath the water. "Normally I'd say yes, but I don't think I can hold my breath for that long. And I'm pretty sure I'll drown if I try to suck you off with my head underwater."

Chuckling, I rise to my feet and brace one palm on the tiled wall. Suds slide down my chest and cling to my wet skin. "How about now?"

"*This* I can work with." She scoots closer so her face is a scant inch from my jutting erection. Then she licks her lips, and it's the hottest thing I've ever seen.

No. Correction—watching her wrap those lips around me is the hottest thing I've ever seen.

She sucks gently, her tongue curling around my tip as if she's sampling a delicious treat. Her soft moan hums through my body, triggering a jolt of pleasure.

I reach down and trace my finger along the perfect O formed by her lips as they stretch tight around me. "You have no idea how gorgeous you look right now."

Her blue eyes lock with mine. I shudder when her mouth welcomes me in, hot and wet and eager. With each slow suck, she takes me in deeper and deeper, until I'm damn near poking the back of her throat. Jesus. I want to pump into her mouth, hard, but I know if I increase the tempo, I'll shoot way too fast.

"You"—her breath tickles my engorged tip—"are so"—she licks the underside, and I tremble with need—"suckable."

A laugh wheezes out. "And what makes me 'suckable'?"

"This." She squeezes my shaft. "This gorgeous dick. Big, but not too big." Her fingers wrap around me tighter. "Thick, but not too thick. It's perfect."

"Is there such a thing as too *anything* when we're talking dicks?"

Laughing huskily, she swallows me up again, and I no longer remember what we're talking about, because Allie Hayes is too damn good at giving head.

She cups my sac as she works me with her mouth, licking and

swirling and basically driving me out of my goddamn mind. Every square inch of skin starts to buzz. The growing pleasure makes my knees wobble.

Keeping one hand on the wall, I thread the other through Allie's damp hair until my palm is cupping her scalp. "You gonna let me come in your mouth, baby?"

She hasn't yet. The last blow job she gave me ended with her jacking me through the climax. But I've been dying to shoot in her mouth, feel her throat working to swallow every drop.

Allie peers up seductively. My balls go tight to my body, heavy with need. When she gives a slight nod, I'm a goner. The release sears into my body and spurts out of my cock. A hoarse groan breaks free as she sucks me dry.

It takes almost a full minute to recover. Once my breathing steadies and my vision clears, I drop into the water again, nudging her backward. Allie squeaks when I lift her up on the small porcelain ledge. It's about a foot and a half wide, offering plenty of room for her to sit.

"My turn," I mutter.

Her eyes smolder as I part her legs and stroke her inner thighs. The skin there is baby-soft, silky beneath my fingers. I'm about to lower my head and feast when I remember something.

With a wicked grin, I slide backward in the tub and reach for Winston.

Allie's breath hitches.

"Let's see if Winston gets you off as good as Little Dean, shall we?" I drag the tip of the sex toy over her clit, chuckling when she widens her legs even farther apart. I love her shamelessness, how she's up for anything and completely unapologetic about it. Just like me.

I tease her for a while, gliding the toy up and down her slit until she's bumping her hips forward, visibly agitated. Aroused. Then I spread her apart with my fingers and ease the head of the pink toy toward her opening.

We both watch as I feed it inside her. I was trying to go slow, but she's so wet that the toy's entire length slips in without resistance. I draw it out, leaving only the tip there, then plunge it in again.

Allie moans.

I do too, because yet again I've been proven wrong. Watching the dildo tunnel in and out of her? *That's* the hottest thing I've ever seen.

"How do you feel?" I murmur.

"Full," she murmurs back.

With the toy still wedged inside her, I bend down and press my tongue to her clit. I lick it softly and start moving my hand, the lazy drag of my tongue matching the lazy thrust of the toy. Allie clutches my hair and squirms on the ledge. The movement of her legs splashes water in my face. I don't care. I capture her clit between my lips and suckle it, while Winston continues to do his job down south.

The noises escaping her throat get breathier, faster. I suck harder and shift the toy so it's hitting her at an angle, and that gets me a delighted "*Oh my God.*"

I smile against her hot flesh as she convulses. I love making this girl come. She always reacts like she's just received an unexpected gift, like she truly didn't expect this big shiny present but hoo boy she's more than happy to tear open the wrapping.

Her body sags on a blissful cry, and then her eyelids flutter open. "I love Winston."

I gently pull out the toy. But I'm not gentle in the way I scowl at her. "You know he's not real, right?"

"I think I'm reconsidering sharing. Let me put him inside you just one time and I bet you'll be singing a different tune."

We drip water all over the bath mat and tiles as we get out of the tub. When I bend over to drain it, Allie smacks my butt and says, "Stop tempting Winston."

I snicker, then turn around to grab her a towel.

In my room, Allie sets the toy on my dresser and starts to dry off.

"I really am sorry, by the way." She sighs. "Logan is going to torture you about what he saw, huh?"

"Big-time." When guilt floods her expression, I sigh too. "Don't worry, it's fine. I'll tell him someone was hiding behind the door because she was embarrassed."

Allie looks alarmed.

"I won't say it was you."

My reassurance has the opposite effect. Her eyes darken with displeasure. "So you're going to tell him you had a random girl over?"

"Would you *rather* I said it was you?"

"No. But…" She bites her lip and says nothing.

I've been with a lot of women. I *know* women. And when they clam up like this? They're not just working one thought over in their brains. Nope, they're constructing a complicated web of scenarios and what-ifs, each thread layering over another, thickening and twisting until suddenly they're mad about something that never even occurred to you.

I stifle another sigh. "Spit it out, Allie-Cat."

"Are you sleeping with anyone else?"

That catches me off guard. "No. Of course not." Once again, the reassurance falls on deaf ears. She's even warier now. "I'm not," I say firmly.

She studies my face as if she's playing Where's Waldo, except she's hunting for a lie instead of a weirdo in a hat. Then she lets out a breath. "We probably should've had this conversation before we had sex again. The whole are we or aren't we exclusive."

I suppose she's right, though it's not a discussion I have often. Everyone I hook up with already knows it's not exclusive. On both sides, because it's not like they're staying true to me either. I fucked a cute sophomore a few months ago who openly admitted she'd just come from a date with someone else.

With Allie, I just assumed it was exclusive. I wouldn't dream of playing games with Wellsy's best friend.

"We're exclusive," I tell her.

"You seriously haven't been with anyone else?" She doesn't even try to hide her surprise, and I don't know if I should be insulted.

"Not since the first time you and I were together."

She nods. "And you're cool with that?"

"Are you?"

Another nod. "I want it to be exclusive. I mean, I understand that this is a fling, but I don't feel comfortable with the idea of you sleeping with anyone else. Same goes for me—I won't do it either."

"Okay," I say easily.

Allie remains unconvinced. "You're being too agreeable about this."

"Would you prefer I throw a tantrum and demand to fuck other people?"

"No, but…" And there she goes, biting her bottom lip again. "You're saying you're perfectly content to just be with me for as long as this lasts? What if I get busy again like I was these past couple days? You won't go out and jiggle down with someone else?"

I was good with this talk up until this point. Now I'm annoyed. "What, you don't think I can keep my pants zipped for a couple measly days?"

"We didn't see each other for three days, Dean, and you wouldn't stop whining about how hard up you've been."

"Just because I like having sex on the reg doesn't mean I'm crawling the bars every second of the day looking to get my nut off."

"Okay. Sorry," she says ruefully. "But I had to ask." She fidgets with the bottom of her towel. "Look…do me a favor, all right? If someone hits on you when you're out and you're dying to sleep with them, or if you just feel like, um, taking another lover…will you shoot me a text saying 'fling over' or something?"

"I will," I promise her.

But honestly, I don't envision that ever happening. I haven't thought about anyone else since Allie bulldozed her way into my bed that first night. Which is disconcerting. I figured that if we hooked up enough times, I'd eventually get her out of my system, but this girl turns me on something fierce. Even now, in the midst of an awkward conversation about "taking other lovers," my body is primed for a second round.

I'm starting to wonder if I'll ever get her out of my system.

ALLIE

I WENT ON MY FIRST CASTING CALL WHEN I WAS TWELVE. I WAS super pumped about it, and although I didn't get the part, I still had a blast reading for the casting director, who was the loveliest woman I'd ever met. She gave me valuable feedback I still remember to this day and advised me to keep at it because she saw "something" in me.

It wasn't too long after that when I realized the audition process isn't always kittens and rainbows. Doesn't matter if you're reading for commercial gigs or day player jobs or juicier roles—you're bound to face this particular hurdle at least once: the difficult acting partner.

Yep, there's one of those at every audition. The person who tries to sabotage you even though you're reading for different parts. Or out-act you because *they* need to look better. Or behave like an unprofessional ass and forget all their lines, making you look bad in the process. Or sometimes they're just jerks and you'd rather boil every inch of skin off than be in the same room as them, let alone read a scene together.

I've encountered all types of scene partners over the years, and the best advice I ever got about how to handle it came from Jack Emery, the acting coach at the drama camp where I volunteered.

He told me to use the negative energy.

You can't control how the other actor is going to behave. You can't force them to remember their lines or force yourself to make nice with someone who, frankly, doesn't deserve the energy it takes for you to fake a smile. Jack instructed me to take that negative energy and channel it into my own performance. Sure, the advice doesn't necessarily apply when you're reading for a cereal commercial and you're supposed to be happy-go-lucky, all smiles as you shovel sugar into your mouth.

But it absolutely helps if your characters have a combative relationship. In that case, it's easy to use the anger or irritation or just plain hatred and bring it to the performance.

Which is what I'm desperately trying to do at Thursday night's rehearsal with the senior who's playing my sister.

I've had classes with Mallory Richardson in the past, but this is the first time we've acted together onstage. Last week, we had our scripts on hand because it was the start of rehearsals.

This week, our student director wants us to perform sans script. Not the whole play, but a couple of script-free scenes to jumpstart the memorization process. I'm fine with that, because I've memorized half the play already.

Mallory? She can hardly string together a full sentence.

"Face it, Jeannette, you're weak," Mallory says flatly. "Why do you think Bobby left? Because he couldn't—" She stops. "*Line!*" she calls to the front row, where our director and two student producers are seated.

There's no mistaking Steven's frustration. I don't blame him. This past hour, I've heard Mallory shout "*Line!*" so many times that the word has lost all meaning.

"'He couldn't stomach your sniveling,'" Steven supplies, his baritone voice carrying through the cavernous room. "'You're pathetic. You—'"

Mallory interrupts. "Thanks, I know the rest. I tripped up on the sniveling part."

Steven signals for us to start again.

"Face it, Jeannette, you're weak. Why do you think Bobby left? Because he couldn't stomach your sniveling. You're pathetic. You fall apart... *Line!*"

I resist the urge to lunge across the stage and tackle her to the ground. Maybe scream the words into her ear at top volume so they sink into her lazy brain.

Steven rattles off the next line.

We start again.

"I'm tired of being the one who has to hold your hand and wipe your tears and—"

"Bobby is *dead*!" I roar, staggering toward her. "If I want to cry about it, I'm damn well allowed to! And nobody asked you to hold my hand. I didn't ask you to come here, Caroline."

"I'm here because…"

I wait for it.

"*Line!*"

And on and on it goes.

Line!

Line!

Line!

We have the auditorium until ten thirty, which leaves us another hour to rehearse. Normally Steven makes use of every available second. Tonight, he's clearly had enough. He stands up and announces that rehearsal is over.

I'm surprised it took him this long.

"We'll regroup tomorrow," he says. "We've got the space from noon till three, so we can cover a lot more ground then. Read over the scenes a few more times, Mal. You really need to nail down your lines."

"I'm so sorry, Steve," Mallory moans. At least she has the decency to look embarrassed. "I didn't get a chance to study the scene last night. I was preparing a monologue for Nigel's class." She sighs loudly. "I'm swamped right now."

Welcome to college, I want to say, because come on, does she think she's the only one with a heavy workload?

I'm taking a screenwriting course that requires me to write two scenes a week. My film theory prof assigns so many readings my eyes are starting to cross. For my audition workshop, we're expected to prepare monologues every week; the seminar is designed to help student actors get comfortable and build confidence for the audition process, but apparently it's too "easy" to let us use existing material to fake-audition with.

Needless to say, I'm equally swamped, but you don't see *me* making excuses. Nope, I still find time to memorize a few measly pages of dialogue.

I'm happy that rehearsal is over, though. I'm too close to throttling Mallory, who doesn't even say goodbye as she leaves the stage.

"We'll do better tomorrow," I assure Steven. I feel awful that we let him down today, because I know how serious he is about directing.

The first time we met, I teased him that he should be in front of the camera and not behind it. Seriously, the guy is gorgeous. Dark skin, flawless features, mesmerizing eyes. He reminds me of Idris Elba minus the sexy British accent. But Steven isn't interested in being an actor. He once told me that his goal is to win a Best Director Oscar by the time he's forty.

"You're not the one who needs to get better," Steven replies. "You're doing a terrific job."

I tuck the compliment in my proverbial back pocket and exit the stage through the wings, digging into my bag as I walk. I find my phone, and my heart flips when I see a missed call from Ira. I'd called him last night for an update about the Carson play that I'm dying to audition for. I'm not certain it's even happening or if it was just a rumor buzzing around Broadway, so I asked Ira to look into it.

I check the time. It's nine thirty, so that means six thirty on the west coast. I know he's still in LA because he texted earlier that he was "doing lunch" with the producer of the Fox pilot. I don't know if I'm happy or disappointed that the producers let me send in a screen test. Luckily, I probably won't hear back from them anytime soon, since they aren't officially casting until February.

"Hey, Ira," I say when he picks up. "It's Allie. I wanted to check if you had any news about the Brett Carson play."

"Actually, I do."

Then why didn't you call me back yesterday?

"The production process has definitely started. I know one of the producers, so I reached out to her." He pauses. "It's not good news."

My heart drops to the pit of my stomach. "Oh. What did she say?"

"It's an all-male cast. Bold move, huh?"

Very bold. Not to mention devastating. I suddenly find myself desperately wishing for a penis.

"Unfortunately, that means there isn't a role in it for you—" No kidding. I'm penis-less! "But I told Nancy you're interested in working with Brett again. She promised to pass that along, so who knows? Maybe he'll give you a ring when he has something else brewing."

That cheers me up. A little. I'm still mega-bummed by the news.

I send Dean a message on my way out of the building.

Me: Such a crappy day! Might vent to you later. How was the game?

He doesn't message back. Granted, it's only been three seconds, but he's usually pretty quick to reply.

Five minutes into my walk to Bristol House, and there's still no answer. His game would be over by now. Hannah said it started at six. It's nearly ten.

Five more minutes pass. I'm almost at the dorm. Why isn't he answering?

It's been ten minutes, crazy pants. Relax.

Instead of relaxing, I grow even more distressed because something troubling has just dawned on me.

I didn't contact Dean because I wanted sex.

I wanted to vent about my day.

Oh shit. Hannah is absolutely right—the word "casual" doesn't exist in my vocabulary. I had a crappy rehearsal, and my first instinct was to reach out to the guy I'm sleeping with and tell him all about it. Have him listen to me and comfort me and tell me it's all going to be okay.

Repeat after yourself, Allison Jane. He. Is. Not. Your. Boyfriend.

"He is not my boyfriend," I say firmly.

"What?" A tall guy in a parka slows his gait and glances over at me.

I jerk in surprise. "Oh, I wasn't talking to you."

His gaze rests on my ear, and I realize he's searching for a Bluetooth. When he doesn't find one, he gives me a strange look and keeps walking.

"Talking to yourself doesn't make you a crazy person," I call out after him. Well, unless you're the homeless guy I used to see around Brooklyn, who would scream about government conspiracies and how aliens are stealing our brain cells via our phones.

Then again, who's to say Lou isn't perfectly sane? Maybe aliens *are* doing that. I can't prove otherwise.

I trudge the rest of the way home and let myself into the darkened suite. Hannah isn't home yet. I know she went to the hockey game tonight, so I give her a call to find out what she's up to now.

"Hey!" Wherever she is, it's loud. I hear a cacophony of voices in the background and a pounding bass line that thuds in my ear. "I'm at the bar. You want to join us?"

I put on a casual voice. "Who's there? Garrett and the guys?" *And Dean?*

I stop myself before the question pops out. Damn it, I'm acting like a girlfriend again. An incredibly nauseating girlfriend to boot, the kind who checks up on her man when he isn't with her.

"Yup. Most of the team is here. We won tonight, so everyone's celebrating." Another wave of music swells over the line. "Garrett keeps trying to challenge me to a shot contest."

"What are the others up to?" I ask with feigned nonchalance. "Logan…Tuck…Dean…?"

I hate myself right now. I really, really do.

"Tuck isn't here. Logan's playing pool. And some girl is trying to eat Dean's face off."

My entire body goes cold.

Um…excuse me?

"Anyway, I can barely hear you," Hannah says. "Text me if you're coming."

My hand trembles as I put down the phone. Dean is at the bar making out with someone else?

Two days after we talked about being exclusive?

Oh *hell* no.

CHAPTER 18

ALLIE

MY MOTHER WAS A BEAUTIFUL WOMAN. I'M NOT SAYING THIS because I'm her daughter and therefore saw her through rose-colored lenses. I'm saying it because it's true—Eva Hayes was a beautiful, stunning, exquisite woman. She modeled when she was in her twenties, and though she wasn't tall enough for runway work, she was a high commodity in the print market. I still have every catalog and magazine spread she ever did in a scrapbook I keep on my bookshelf.

I inherited her blond hair and blue eyes, but my features aren't flawless like hers. Mom had one of those classically beautiful faces that would make men, women, and children stop and stare whenever she walked by.

Me, I'm more cute than beautiful.

But I've learned that the right makeup and the right clothes can transform any girl from *cute* to *sex bomb*.

I don't know what my plan is. Dean and I aren't dating, first off. And since I don't want anyone to know we're fooling around, I can't storm into Malone's and dump a pitcher of beer over his head.

What I *can* do is show him exactly what he's giving up.

I won't lie—it hurts that he didn't give me advance warning

like he'd promised. And it definitely stings that he's with someone else tonight when I would've been happy to keep flinging with him. But I knew going into this who I was getting involved with. Dean Heyward-Di Laurentis sleeps around. The End.

My ego, however, refuses to stand for this, which is why thirty minutes later I find myself sliding out the backseat of a taxi and stepping onto the curb in front of Malone's.

My peacoat keeps me toasty as I linger near the door debating my plan of action. A couple of college guys pop out of the bar, and I'm gratified when both of them stop to check me out. Ha. And their appreciative gazes are based solely on my makeup and fuck-me-silly updo. They'd probably be salivating if they saw what was underneath my coat.

I reach for my phone. Here, I tell Hannah. Where r you?

Her: Pool table.

Taking a breath, I walk inside and make my way through the crowd. The music vibrates in the floor beneath my heels as I pass the booths on the left and head toward the archway where the main room opens onto the game room.

There are half a dozen more booths and tall standing tables in this section of the bar. I instantly spot my best friend. She's talking to Logan and Hollis, while Garrett circles one of the green-felt tables with a pool cue in his hand. Holding a beer bottle, Fitzy is watching Garrett line up a shot, his own cue resting on the wall beside him.

I finally catch a glimpse of Dean. He's almost hidden from view in the corner, talking to a curvy brunette in skinny jeans and a low-cut sweater.

Nice sweater, sweetie, but I can beat that.

I unbutton my coat, slip it off, and tuck it under my arm. Then I square my shoulders and saunter up to the pool table.

A wolf whistle slices through the music, courtesy of Logan.

"Je-sus," he marvels at me. "You look bangin'." His blue eyes twinkle. "What's the occasion?"

I smile demurely. "Just felt like looking pretty."

Hannah snorts. "Babe, you look more than pretty. I think every dude in this bar just sprung a boner."

I shrug. I only care about one boner in particular. I wonder if Little Dean has noticed me yet.

"So you won the game, huh?" I say to Logan.

"Damn right we did."

"Nice. You guys are back on track, then." I know Big Dean was upset about their three-game losing streak.

"Yeah, don't get ahead of yourself. We were up against a Division II team. And even then we barely squeaked out the W."

"Yo, Logan!" Garrett shouts. "Think I can make this shot?"

"'Scuse me, ladies. My supreme billiards skills and best friend services are required." He wanders off.

Hannah leans in closer. "So. Does this mean you're ready to dip your toe in the dating pool again?" Grinning, she gestures to my outfit, which, if I'm being honest, doesn't really say "I want to date."

It says DTF.

My royal-blue bandage dress stops at about mid-thigh. I wore a push-up bra, so my cleavage is out to there. My smoky eye shadow makes my eyes look huge. My five-inch stilettos make my legs look impossibly long. Sure, they nearly froze off during the walk from the cab to the bar, but the quest for hotness sometimes requires a sacrifice. That's Beauty 101.

"Nah, I'm just testing the waters."

Her smile widens. "Well, consider this test aced. I'd do you."

I tense abruptly, feeling Dean approach before he even sidles up to me. "Looking good, baby doll," he says lightly.

But I hear the edge in his voice, and his displeasure is unmistakable. Which is preposterous because what does *he* have to be peeved about? I'm not the one who was making out with someone else.

"Thanks. Who's your friend?" I ask in the sweetest voice I can muster.

His expression goes blank. "Huh?"

I nod toward the brunette, who's inspecting us with visible suspicion. I can't believe Dean has the gall to act like he doesn't know her. I *just* saw them talking.

"Oh," he answers. "Polly? Paula? I didn't catch her name."

Of course he didn't.

"Penelope," Hannah supplies. "I sat next to her during the game. She's a *massive* Dean fan. Talked my ear off about you the whole time." My best friend smirks. "I finally had to interrupt and tell her you don't live up to the hype."

I second that.

"Bullshit. I'm better than the hype." Even as he protests, he sounds distracted. I can feel him staring at me.

"I'm going to get a drink." I push away from the table.

"Great idea," Dean says in an overly cheerful voice. "I could use one too."

I clench my teeth as he follows me. It's damn hard to run in these heels, so I settle for a speed-walk and hope I lose him in the crowd.

God, it was a stupid idea to come out tonight. I don't know what I was expecting, but it wasn't this. If anything, I'm even tenser and angrier than I was before.

A squeak flies out of my mouth when I'm suddenly tugged backward.

Dean's lips brush my ear as he growls, "If you came here to tease me, it's working."

My jaw stiffens. I spin around and level him with a glare. "Contrary to what you believe, the world doesn't revolve around you." Except he's right. That *is* why I came, and now I feel totally and utterly foolish, because I'm not the kind of girl who plays games.

I should have stayed home. Rehearsal had left me in a bad mood, and then I let the thought of Dean with someone else turn me into a character from a bad rom-com. Dressing up like a harlot to get some undeserving guy's attention? Who *am* I?

My self-disgust spurs me to keep walking. I approach the counter, where the throng of men there parts for me like the Red Sea. I guess that's one benefit of looking like sex on stilettos.

I order a Cosmo, because why not? I might as well live up to the image I've created. I brought a little black clutch with me, but when I open it to get some money, three different hands brandishing twenty-dollar bills fly up in the air.

"I got this—"

"It's on me—"

"Let me buy you a drink—"

Dean rumbles out an annoyed sound. The next thing I know, he's yanking out his own twenty and shoving it at the bartender. "On *me*," he says sharply. He glares at my other suitors, who all avert their gazes.

"Are you going to pee on me now to mark your territory?" I hiss at him.

His eyes flash. "I don't know—should I? What the hell is going on here, Allie?"

"Nothing." I take the drink the bartender hands me and swiftly duck away from the counter.

Dean stays hot on my heels, so I walk faster, and then we're with our friends again and I breathe in relief. Good. Now he can't pester me for answers anymore.

Penelope immediately rushes over, and my spine stiffens when she latches her talons onto Dean's bare forearm. The black T-shirt he's wearing stretches across his perfect chest and shows off his perfect arms. The same arms that were pinning me down the other night when he was moving inside me.

I swallow a mouthful of my drink and try to pay attention to Hannah. She's talking about her showcase rehearsals and how happy she is that the faculty is letting her sing an original composition instead of pairing her up with a songwriting major.

"I'm thinking of sending out some demos to labels," she admits.

"Really?" She mentioned a few months ago that she might want to focus more on songwriting than performing, but I hadn't realized it was a serious consideration on her part.

"Yeah." She toys with a strand of dark hair, which draws my attention to the neon-green clip holding it back. It's the only splash of color in her all-black getup. "I love composing. I mean, I also love being onstage, but Dexter and I were fooling around on the piano at rehearsal last night, and when he sang one of the songs I was working on, it was…"

I tune her out. I'm an awful friend, I know, but I can't help it. I'm far too distracted by the evil vulture that's pecking at Dean like he's a juicy carcass. Running her manicured fingers up and down his arm. Stroking his biceps. Leaning in to whisper something in his ear.

In his defense, he doesn't appear to notice that Penelope is glued to his side. His gaze is fixed on me, and it's growing cloudier by the second.

I sip my drink and spend the next hour making an effort to be social. But I'm just getting increasingly angry—at *myself*.

I inadvertently cast Dean in a role that he shouldn't be playing. He's *not* my boyfriend. I shouldn't be texting him after I have a bad day. I shouldn't be upset that he didn't text back or that he's talking to another girl.

Though, again, in his defense, he doesn't seem the least bit interested in Penelope. Every time I sneak a peek at them, he's on his phone and not paying her a lick of attention.

My clutch keeps buzzing, which tells me he's most likely texting me. But my phone stays in my purse because I'm too busy dealing with the realization that apparently I'm helpless without a boyfriend.

I'm…co-dependent? Is that the right word? And is that why I

kept getting back together with Sean? Because I can't be alone? I had a boyfriend the entire time I was in high school too...

Okay. I might be making a mountain out of a molehill right now. Just because I've always had a boyfriend doesn't mean I've got issues, right? I like having a boyfriend. I like holding hands and kissing and snuggling and telling each other about our days. That doesn't mean I *need* one at all times.

Maybe I just suck at flings. I'm sure plenty of other women have problems separating emotions from sex.

Still, this is all very disheartening. I decide it's time to go. I'm not paying attention to a word anyone is saying, and now I kind of want to go home and Google *codependency* to see if I can self-diagnose myself.

I do want to pee first, though, so I excuse myself and walk toward the restrooms. I don't bother turning around to see if Dean is following me, because I know he is. I caught a glimpse of him in my periphery, disentangling himself from Penelope the moment I moved away from the table.

To my frustration, the line for the ladies' room is unacceptably long. Nope, I'm not waiting thirty minutes to use the toilet. I don't have to go *that* bad. But I know if I turn around, I'll probably bump into Dean.

I keep walking straight ahead toward the emergency exit. I've used it before, so I don't expect an alarm to go off, and it doesn't. Cold air hits my bare arms and legs when I step into the alley behind Malone's. I hurriedly put on my coat just as the door flies open and Dean emerges.

"Go away," I tell him.

His nostrils flare. "No."

"Fine, then stay out here. I'm going home." I fumble with the clasp of my clutch. I need to call a cab and tell Hannah I'm leaving. Dean snatches the purse from my hand, summoning an irritated expletive. "Can I please have my purse back?" I demand.

"No. Not until you tell me why you're pissed at me."

I don't answer.

"Stop acting like a brat and fucking talk to me," he orders.

"Why don't you go find Penelope?" I suggest. "I'm sure she'd be happy to talk to you. If you're lucky, she might even stick her tongue down your throat again."

He's momentarily startled. Then he starts to laugh. "You're jealous of Penelope?"

"I'm not jealous," I answer coolly. "I just don't appreciate being lied to."

Dean's jaw falls open. "When did I lie to you?"

My cheeks heat up. Damn it. Damn *him*. And damn *me* for giving him the power to make me feel so...so... God, I don't even know what I'm feeling right now.

"You promised to let me know if you were going to hook up with someone else," I accuse.

"I didn't hook up with her."

"Hannah said you were kissing her."

"No, *she* was kissing *me*. Or trying to, at least. I told her I wasn't interested."

"You did?" Some of my indignation falters, but I force myself not to soften. It doesn't matter what Dean did or didn't do. I still allowed this fling to veer in a direction I'm not comfortable with, and now it's time to get back on the right path.

"Yes, I did," he retorts, "because contrary to what *you* believe, I'm a man of my word. I told you I wouldn't screw around with anyone else."

"Fine. I believe you." I swallow. "Can I go now?" I try to grab my purse, but he keeps it out of my reach.

"You're still pissed," he says flatly.

"I'm not."

"Don't bullshit a bullshitter, baby doll," he snaps.

"Are you saying your she-kissed-me story is bullshit?" I snap back.

"No, what I'm saying is—" He spits out a frazzled curse. Then exhales slowly. "I'm saying you're not leaving until you tell me what's wrong. And FYI? If anyone should be pissed right now, it's me."

My jaw drops. "How so?"

"I've been getting shit for two days thanks to your Houdini act in the bathtub," Dean says darkly. "I found a bottle of lube under my pillow last night with a note from Garrett saying 'For your ass.' Logan bought a carton of pink lemonade and keeps giving me a thumbs-up every time he drinks a glass. Grace can't look me in the eye without giggling. And now I'm getting shit from you, and you won't even do me the courtesy of telling me why?"

"I'm… I'm… Argh, I'm *done* with this." The words burst out before I can stop them. "We're not flinging anymore, okay? It's done."

Dean's shoulders set in a severe line. "Why?"

"Because I said so."

"And *I* don't get a say in it?"

"No."

"Bullshit," he says again. "You can't just call it off without giving me a good reason."

A powerless feeling rises in my throat, because I *don't* have a good reason.

I had a bad day and you were the first person I called.

That sounds insane if I say it out loud. But I know myself. I can feel myself falling into the boyfriend bear trap, and I need to step out of it before the damn thing snaps shut and mangles my poor helpless heart.

"Are you telling me you're not attracted to me anymore? Is that it?"

"No, that's not it. You know I am. But—"

"But nothing." He edges closer, and my breath gets trapped in my lungs. His eyes are on fire, his chiseled features twisted in a feral look. I've never seen Dean angry before. It's hot as hell. "How about we recap what happened tonight? How does that sound?"

Before I can blink, I'm against the brick wall, and his mouth is inches from mine. We're half-hidden between a stack of milk crates and a dumpster that is blessedly empty. Not that it matters, because even if it were overflowing with garbage, I still wouldn't be able to smell anything other than Dean's spicy, masculine scent. Every time I inhale, the addictive fragrance makes my brain foggier and foggier.

"You heard I was at the bar with another chick, and you got jealous. How am I doing so far?"

I clench my jaw.

"Then you freaked out because you got jealous, right? Am I still nailing this?" When I don't answer, he locks my chin in his hand. "What's going on in that gorgeous head of yours? You think this means you're going to fall for me? That because you want me all to yourself, it means we're on the track to marriage and babies?"

His mocking tone grates. "Don't be an ass."

He ignores me. "Well, it doesn't mean anything, baby doll. So you were jealous. Big deal. Do you know how fucking jealous *I* am right now? Do you think I like seeing every guy in the bar drooling over your tits and shoving their hands in their pockets to rearrange the stiffies you gave them showing up in that getup? I want to rip their eyes out just for looking at you."

My surprised gaze rises to his.

"No lie," he tells me. "But do you see *me* freaking out about it? No, because it doesn't mean a damn thing. Only that we're not done turning each other on."

He thrusts one big thigh between both of mine, grinding against me so I can feel his erection.

"I still turn you on, don't I?"

The hard ridge pressing into my belly distracts me from replying. I can feel my panties dampening. God, I'm ridiculously wet. And my nipples are suddenly incredibly sensitive, aching wildly as they pucker against the lace of my bra.

"It's okay. You don't have to answer. I know I still do." His lips brush over my ear, eliciting a flurry of shivers. "If I slide my hand under that dress right now, we both know what I'll find. That your pussy is wetter than it's ever been."

I can't breathe. Because there's no air. Dean is stealing it all with his filthy taunts. And his hands are pushing my coat off my shoulders. I'm frozen in place, too fascinated by the intensity simmering in his eyes. He lets the coat drop to the dirty pavement, then eases the hem of my dress up and cups his palm over my core. The resulting flash of pleasure is what snaps me out of my trance.

We're in public, damn it, but Dean doesn't seem to care. And even though it's cold outside, his fingers are surprisingly warm as they dip under the crotch of my panties.

Chuckling, he rubs the wetness pooled there. "Yeah. That's what I thought."

He's mocking me again, and my indignation returns in full force. "Get over yourself," I mutter. "I'd be wet if any guy was rubbing up against me."

"Bull. Fucking. Shit." His thumb brushes my clit. I almost fall over. "It's me. You want *me*." He pushes one finger inside and my inner muscles betray me by tightening around it. "And as long as this hungry pussy keeps dripping for *me*, we're not fucking done."

Oh God. He's fingering me in earnest now. The pleasure is unbearable, centered between my legs, pulsing in my veins. It's all I can concentrate on.

"Dean…" Somehow I remember how to talk. "Anyone can walk outside right now."

"Good. Let them. Let them see what a bad girl you are."

I moan so loud it's embarrassing. Dean adds another finger and works both inside me, curling them until they hit a spot that brings white dots to my vision. I rock against his hand, no longer putting up a protest, but greedily taking what he's giving me.

"Should we give them a real show? Should I take you right here against the wall?"

My vision comes back into focus. His eyes are blazing with

unadulterated lust. His free hand hovers over his zipper. He tips his head, waiting for me to respond.

I don't know what spell he's cast over me. I should push his hand away. Tell him to keep his pants zipped and stop being a jerk. We're in *public*. Someone really might see us.

So why is my heart pounding even harder?

And why am I dipping my head in a nod?

Approval flashes in his eyes, along with a dose of pure need. His fingers slide out of my core, and then he spins me around so I'm facing the wall.

I tense when muffled voices drift toward us from the street beyond the alley. What if we get caught? What if we get caught by a *cop*? People go to jail for this, right?

Dean's hot breath fans over my neck as he lifts my dress up to my waist. The chill in the air raises goose bumps on the backs of my thighs.

I should stop this. Probably. Maybe. But I don't.

I hear the sound of plastic tearing, clothes rustling, and then his erection slides between my ass cheeks. It moves lower and lower until the tip nudges my opening.

"You better come fast," Dean whispers in my ear. "I'm so hot for you I won't last more than a couple strokes."

I don't know if I'll last more than a couple *seconds*. My clit is swollen to the point of agony. So are my breasts. I've never had a quickie outside a bar before, and everything about this moment is different and thrilling and terrifying. The added element of danger, the risk of someone catching us, has turned my body into a live wire just waiting for one spark to ignite it.

And that spark comes in the form of one deep thrust from Dean.

My cry of climax is cut short when he claps a hand over my mouth. For someone who just taunted me about putting on a show, he's suddenly cautious of our surroundings.

I, on the other hand, can't even remember what continent we're on. The orgasm races through me and leaves me breathless. I bear down on Dean's shaft with every uncontrollable shudder, and he gives a barely audible groan and buries his head between my neck and shoulder as he pumps into me from behind.

He wasn't kidding. He comes so fast I don't know whether to be impressed or tease him about it. He drives into me one last time and trembles wildly, his hands clamped tight on my hips.

I'm trembling too, but I don't know if it's from the orgasmic aftershocks or the frigid breeze on my bare butt.

When loud voices break the silence, I jump away from Dean and shove my dress down to my thighs. A peek behind the dumpster reveals shadowy figures ambling along the sidewalk. Not a single head turns toward the alley.

I pick up my coat and hurriedly put it on as Dean tucks his still-hard cock into his pants. He flicks the condom in the dumpster and gives me a wary look.

"What?" My voice doesn't sound like my voice. It's lower. Throatier.

His gaze rakes over me from head to toe before locking with mine. "We're not done," he says gruffly.

I bite the inside of my cheek and say, "I know."

CHAPTER 19

ALLIE

ACCORDING TO HOMELESS LOU IN BROOKLYN, WHENEVER YOU GET a déjà vu, it's simply a glitch that happens when aliens attempt to access your memories. I guess that's what the little green men are up to now, because holy hell, déjà vu city.

Friday night starts out the same way it did two weeks ago. I leave the fitness center with my gym bag in one hand and my phone in the other. There are three unread messages from Sean waiting for me.

I read them and groan. He really, *really* needs to talk to me. Crap.

Somehow I've successfully managed to avoid seeing him for two weeks. Sex with Dean has served as a great distraction, but tonight I don't have that luxury. Dean is still at the rink for the Hurricanes game and he has plans with his friend Beau afterward.

I need to decide what to do about Sean. Do I want to talk to him? Is there a point? I'm starting to think our previous breakups didn't stick because we tried to remain friends afterward. That's just a bad idea all around. You can't be friends with an ex, at least not right away. Megan insists that a six-month no-contact period is required before you can even consider it.

Not that Megan is a relationship expert. Last I talked to her, she was still seeing the thirty-seven-year-old doctor but keeps making up excuses for why she can't meet his daughter. If she can't communicate with him about her fears and concerns, how is that a recipe for a healthy relationship?

But I should be focusing on my own love life right now. Well, *ex* love life, because I don't love Sean McCall anymore. It's scary how quickly it took for my feelings to fade.

My mother used to say that time heals all wounds. That's definitely true. The year after she died, just picturing her face would trigger a rush of gut-wrenching pain. Now when I think about her, it still hurts, but in a duller, bittersweet way. I miss her, but I don't feel the urge to curl up in a ball and cry the day away.

But that's grief. I thought love would take longer to fade, which makes me wonder if maybe the process had begun long before Sean and I broke up. Maybe I fell out of love with him earlier and hadn't realized it.

And maybe coffee isn't a terrible idea. I guess I can use it as an opportunity to gauge how my heart responds in his presence.

I'm still debating as I walk up the stairs to the dorm. Bristol House only has four floors, so there's no elevator, just four flights I have to climb while carting my gym bag.

I exit the stairwell into the hall and freeze when I spot Sean sitting in front of my door.

Once again, he's taken the decision out of my hands.

His head is bent over his phone, but it snaps up at the sound of my footsteps. Then he's on his feet, walking toward me.

My heart *does* respond, but not in the way I expected. Sean looks exactly the same—dark hair sticking out the sides of a backward Red Sox cap, deep brown eyes, clean-shaven face. Shouldn't the sight of the boy I spent three years with make my heart ache?

But all I feel is annoyance.

"Don't be mad," he blurts out instead of saying hello. He's obviously picked up on my displeasure. "I know I shouldn't have shown up unannounced."

"Then why did you?"

"Because you're not answering any of my texts." He shakes his head angrily. "We were together almost four years, Allie. You can't even spare five minutes to talk to me?"

"I didn't have anything to say." I unlock my door and dump my bag in the hall. When Sean tries to follow me inside, I frown and grip the edge of the door to deny him entrance.

He scowls. "What, I'm not allowed to come in now?"

"There's no reason for you to come in. Say whatever you need to say, Sean."

"I'm not doing it out in the hall where the entire floor can hear me."

I draw a deep breath. I don't know why I'm being so harsh right now. Maybe because seeing him just reminds me of the fight that led to our breakup. All the unfair, insensitive, cruel words he'd hurled my way.

I force myself to exhale. I'm probably being extra snippy because this evening's rehearsal sucked again. My breakneck pace on the treadmill hadn't helped either.

"Look, I desperately need a shower, so why don't I meet you at the Coffee Hut in thirty minutes? We can talk there."

I can tell he's still upset I won't let him in, but he nods. "Fine. I could use a caffeine fix, I guess."

I nod back. "I'll be there soon." Then I close the door and lean against it for a few seconds. Shit, I don't think I want to have this conversation, whatever it is.

I wish Hannah were here so I could get her advice on how to handle this, but she's at rehearsal. With her showcase coming up, I doubt I'll be seeing much of her until the performance is out of her hair.

In the shower, I remind myself that I broke up with Sean for a reason. Well, many reasons. We wanted different things for the future. I wasn't happy. He was angry all the time.

Bottom line, it was too much heartache and not enough reward. I like to think my mom would agree with me on that. Yes, she'd urged me to work hard at relationships, and yes, relationships do require effort, but they shouldn't be hostile, right?

I can't imagine what Sean could possibly say that would make me reconsider.

SEAN HAS SNAGGED US A TABLE IN THE BACK OF THE BUSY COFFEE shop, half-hidden behind a huge ceramic planter with a fake fern fanning out of it. I don't quite understand the decor of this place. There are way too many plants. Are they going for a jungle theme? Eh, I don't care. I love the way it smells like freshly ground coffee beans, and I'm grateful for the privacy.

Sean slides a tall foam cup closer to me. "I got you coffee." He smiles wryly. "Vanilla latte with an extra shot of espresso."

This time, my heart does react accordingly, clenching hard. Of course he knows my coffee order. He knows everything about me, and vice versa. I don't need to peek in his cup to know he's drinking a medium roast, one cream, no sugar. And that the paper bag on the table contains a blueberry muffin, which is the only type of muffin he eats. When we were together, I forced him to try every muffin and pastry behind the counter, but he insisted that blueberry is the only flavor that "enchants" his taste buds.

Fuck. Now I'm just sad.

"How've you been?" he asks quietly.

Oh no, we're starting off with small talk? I wrap both hands around my cup to stop from fidgeting. "All right. You?"

"Not the greatest, but…" He shrugs.

I notice he looks tired. Is he not getting enough sleep? I bite back the question before it slips out. We're not together anymore. His sleeping habits are no longer my concern.

"I miss you," he mumbles.

I hastily sip my coffee. I don't say it back, because the truth is…I *don't* miss him. Right after we broke up, sure, of course I did. But since then, I've had other things on my mind. The play. Dean…

When I don't respond, he continues with a dejected look. "I've been doing a lot of thinking since you ended it. A lot of soul-searching."

I finally find my voice. "That's good. I'm glad."

"I was thinking back to the last six months, and I realized how badly I screwed up. I was such an ass to you, Allie." His expression is earnest. "But now I know *why*."

My throat tightens. "Why?"

"Because I was scared."

Aw shit. There's vulnerability swimming in his eyes. I battle the overwhelming urge to reach across the table and squeeze his hand.

It's not my job to take care of him anymore.

"You've had your entire future planned out since you were twelve. You knew exactly what you wanted to do, and that's so fucking rare. Not a lot of people can say that." His tone grows rueful. "I sure as hell can't. I didn't grow up dreaming about working for my dad's insurance company. But it's a guaranteed job, and not a lot of people have *that*, especially coming out of college, but it's not like I've been chomping at the bit to go back to Vermont."

"You sure made it sound like you were," I point out.

"Because it's the only option I have." He sounds frustrated. "I was trying to get myself excited about it. And…honestly, picturing you there with me made the idea of going home more bearable. An easier pill to swallow, I guess. But it wasn't fair to you. I had no right to insist that you sacrifice the future you want just so I could feel better about the future I'm stuck with."

I'm dumbfounded. Sean hadn't given any indication that he didn't want to be in Vermont, but I suppose that's yet another sign of the communication breakdown between us.

"You told me on our very first date that you planned on moving to LA after graduation. You *kept* telling me that, up until the moment we broke up." He shakes his head, shame-faced. "But this summer I decided not to hear it anymore. I convinced myself that I was the most important thing in your life and you'd go wherever you had to in order to be with me."

"That's not a fair expectation to have of anyone," I say softly. "You can't *order* someone to put your happiness ahead of their own."

"I know, and I was wrong to give you an ultimatum. I told you, I've been doing a lot of thinking." He takes a breath. "I came to a few conclusions."

My stomach drops when he sticks one hand in his jacket pocket. Oh dear God. *Please* don't let him pull out a velvet jeweler's box.

Is it crazy that I almost wish he's going for a gun? That he plans on holding everyone hostage until I agree to get back together with him? For some screwed up reason, I think I'm better equipped to handle that than a proposal.

But his hand emerges with a narrow envelope. He sets it on the tabletop.

"What's that?" I stare at the envelope as if it contains poison.

"Open it," he urges.

Fuckity fuck.

"Please."

The sincerity in his tone causes me to cave. I pick up the envelope. It's not sealed, but the flap is tucked in so I use my fingernail to pry it out. I peek inside and see a single sheet of paper, which I extract and unfold as I fight my growing trepidation.

Shock hits me first. Followed by suspicion. Followed by deep distress, because…what the heck am I supposed to say to *this*?

I'm staring at a confirmation receipt for two airline tickets to Los Angeles, California. The flight departs the day after graduation.

I bite my lip and lift my gaze to Sean's.

"You and me, baby," he says fervently. "This is what I should've done in the first place. It was stupid to try and force you to move to Vermont. What I needed to do was swallow my pride and move to *LA*. With you."

Oh God. Why did I insist on meeting in public? Public is *bad*.

Public means everyone is about to witness Sean's agony and humiliation when I say—

"No."

Uncertainty passes over his face. "What?"

"You're not coming to LA with me."

Sean's mouth opens. Then closes. Then opens again. I give him a moment to digest what I just said. Unfortunately, it's the same moment my phone buzzes. I dig around in my purse and...wonderful, a text from Dean.

Him: Game's done. Hurricanes rocked it like a hurricane. Beau can't meet up til later. Quickie?

God, I wish.

Me: Can't. In the middle of something brutal over here.

"Why not?" Sean finally asks.

"Because..." I'm distracted.

Him: Everything ok?
Me: Yeah. Having coffee with Sean.

There's an interminably long delay.

Sean is still waiting for me to answer. I'm waiting for Dean to answer. I realize I probably shouldn't have said anything to Dean, but I'd been typing on autopilot.

He comes back with: WTF?

Me: I know *sigh* I'll explain everything later, k?

There's no response after that, and Sean is looking increasingly irritated. "Who are you texting?" he demands.

"Hannah," I lie.

The worst part about dating someone for as long as I dated Sean? They *always* know when you're lying.

"Bullshit." Anger infuses his eyes, dark and fierce. "Is it that guy? The one you slept with?"

"No, it's not." This time I don't care if he sees through the lie. "And even if it was, it's none of your business. We're broken up." I take a breath. "And that's the reason you can't come to LA with me."

Sean's mouth flattens. His face and neck take on a deep flush. Even the tips of his ears are red. "You don't mean that."

"Yes, I do. I'm sorry. I just think…it's time we moved on from each other."

"Move on from each other, or move on to other people?" His snotty tone raises my hackles. "Like this guy whose name you won't tell me?"

I could be a jerk and toss out another "it's none of your business." I could also philosophize and give him the whole "if you love someone, let them go" spiel.

I do neither. I simply slide the tickets toward him and say, "I'm sorry. I hope you're able to get a refund for these. And I really hope you figure out what your passion is, whether it's working for your dad or doing something else." Damn it, I'm choking up. "I really do want the best for you, Sean. I want you to be happy."

He doesn't answer. He sits there. Stone-faced.

I scrape my chair back. My hands shake as I put on my coat. I don't bother telling him we can still be friends, because I know he doesn't want to hear that right now. Besides, I'm not about to make any promises I might be unable to keep.

"Bye, Sean," I say softly.

TWENTY-FOUR HOURS AFTER MY HEARTBREAKING ENCOUNTER with my ex-boyfriend, it becomes glaringly obvious that Dean is giving me the silent treatment.

I texted him after I left the coffeehouse, asking if he still wanted to meet up.

No answer.

I texted again later to ask if he went out with Beau.

No answer.

I texted to say good night.

No answer.

I texted to say good morning.

No answer.

Now, as I sit on my bed, home alone on a Saturday night, I'm finding it hard to cut Dean any slack. Last night, I was fully willing to take responsibility. Of course Dean had assumed the worst when he found out I was with Sean, and I don't blame him for getting pissy about it. A few hours of sulking is a perfectly reasonable reaction to thinking I might've gotten back together with my ex.

But twenty-four hours? That's bullshit. If Dean is mad at me, fine, let him be mad. If he's done with me, fine, I guess he's done. At least have the balls to *tell* me. Ignoring someone until they get the "hint" is downright insulting, and I don't have patience for that.

I grab my laptop from the nightstand because I desperately need a distraction right now, and nothing is more distracting than watching adorable videos on YouTube. Hopefully there's a baby giraffe out there that decided to cough, or a baby hippo that felt like splashing around in a pond.

Somehow I end up on Twitter. And gee, look at that. Dean is alive. Now he can't use "I was dead" as an excuse for why he's snubbing me, because a Briar student is live tweeting tonight's home game and just mentioned a "Di Laurentis" goal.

I close the browser and hop off the bed. Maybe I'm a masochist, but seeing Dean's name makes me want to see *Dean*. I want answers, damn it. I want him to look me in the eye and tell me if the fling is over.

It takes me nearly thirty minutes to walk to the arena, which is on the opposite end of Briar's huge campus. At the ticket booth, I flash my student ID to get the discount rate. The student teller says "Standing room only" as she slides a ticket under the glass.

A minute later, I'm in the area reserved for standing patrons. The second period just started.

I peer at the ice trying to remember Dean's jersey number. My mind draws a blank, so instead I scan the names on the back of the black-and-silver jerseys. Dean's surname contains so many letters it should be easy to spot, but nope, I'm not seeing him on the ice. Maybe his line isn't playing right now? But he doesn't seem to be sitting on the home bench either.

Weird.

On a whim, I open Twitter on my phone and search for the profile I was following earlier. Maybe @BriarBryan38 tweeted some updates when I was walking over. I skim the most recent posts until one catches my eye.

My heart promptly lurches to my throat.

Dean was thrown out of the game.

CHAPTER 20

DEAN

I SIT IN THE EMPTY LOCKER ROOM, HEAD DOWN, SHOULDERS hunched. Valiantly trying not to grab the nearest item—which happens to be my helmet—and hurl it at the wall. The knuckles of my right hand are cracked and bleeding thanks to the violent uppercut I unleashed at the St. Anthony's forward, but I press my palms against my thighs and let the blood soak into my hockey pants.

I despise those fuckers from St. Anthony's. Our teams are long-time rivals, so whenever we play each other, tension and smack talk are to be expected. But the hostility has gotten worse over the past two years. And a couple weeks ago, a bunch of St. A's guys had messed with one of Grace's friends, taking away her phone and refusing to let her leave their seedy motel room.

Tonight, I'm the one at fault. There was the usual trash talk in the face-offs, aggressive skating, overly physical hits on both sides. But I was already hot-tempered going into this game, and when that asshole goaded me into taking a swing, I just lost it.

They tossed me out for unsportsmanlike conduct. Yeah right. If the refs heard even half the filth Connelly was spewing about our mothers, they'd throw that fucker out too.

As it stands, I'm the only ousted player. One punch thrown in an already heated game probably won't get me a suspension from the team, but now I'm stuck in the locker room, prohibited from leaving until I get the obligatory tongue-lashing from Coach Jensen.

Or maybe he'll delegate again and let O'Shea deliver the lecture. Lucky me. That would mean *two* lectures from that bastard in the span of twenty-four hours. He'd called me into his office last night when I was driving home from the Hurricanes game. Add to that Allie's admission that she was with her ex, and it's no surprise I ended up getting trashed with Beau.

I swear to God, if Allie got back together with that undeserving ass, I'm going to…what? Lose it again? "Break up" with her? All I've done so far is avoid her, big talker that I am. Truthfully, I'm afraid of what she might say.

Footsteps echo beyond the door. I instantly tense. Wait, it's the wrong door, I realize. Not the one leading out to the ice, but the one that opens to the main hallway.

"Dean?" Allie's voice has my head snapping up.

How the hell did she get back here? We have security guards manning the facility during home games to prevent people from stealing into the locker rooms and messing with the equipment. That actually happened a couple years ago—a rabid fan of our opponents' snuck in and spray-painted *LOSER* on our lockers. I hadn't realized some colleges let in five-year-olds.

There's a soft knock. "Dean, are you in there?"

I answer on a ragged breath. "Yeah."

Allie pokes her blond head in the room. She spots me on the bench and makes a beeline toward me. She's in jeans and a red sweater, with her hair up in a messy bun, and either I'm imagining it or her eyes are rimmed with red. Has she been crying?

"How'd you get past security?" I ask gruffly.

"I told the guard I'm your girlfriend and that I desperately needed to check on my man. There may have been some crocodile tears involved." She grins wryly. "The ability to cry on command really comes in handy sometimes."

"And he bought it?"

"Yep. I'm very convincing. But I did have to show him my Briar ID to prove I wasn't a saboteur." She sits beside me. "Why did you get kicked out of the game?"

I stare straight ahead. "I sucker punched someone. Damn foolish on my part. I deserve to be in here."

"Maybe. But it still sucks." She goes quiet for a moment. I can feel her blue eyes boring into the side of my face. "You're avoiding me."

I glance over. "Just a bit."

"A bit? There aren't *degrees* of avoidance, Dean. You're either avoiding someone or you aren't."

"Not true. Sometimes there're extenuating circumstances. Unexpected variables."

"Like what?"

I shrug. "Doesn't matter."

"It does matter," she corrects, "but we can put a pin in that for the moment." She presses one hand against my cheek, then slides it to my chin to twist my head toward her. Forcing eye contact. "I know you're pissed at me for seeing Sean."

"I'm not pissed. You can see whoever you want." I put on an indifferent tone when inside I'm bristling. "But let me just point out the hypocrisy of that. Weren't we supposed to give each other a heads-up before we hooked up with anyone else?"

"I didn't hook up with him."

"No?"

"No," she says in a firm voice. "And if your silent treatment also has to do with you thinking Sean and I got back together, I can assure you, we did not. He wanted to, but I said no."

I can't explain the gust of relief that slams into my chest. "Good to know," I say lightly, but the knowing gleam in her eyes reveals she is absolutely aware of how pleased I am.

She takes my hand and twines our fingers together. "Sean and I are over. I don't want to be with him, and that's exactly what I told him yesterday."

"Bet he wasn't thrilled to hear it."

"Nope, but it's something he'll need to accept." She rubs her thumb over my tender knuckles. They're not bleeding anymore, but the way she gasps, you'd think my hand had been amputated. "You shouldn't be fighting," she says sternly.

"Hockey players are hot-blooded, babe. We fight sometimes. Not the end of the world."

"What did the jerk say to get you to punch him?"

"I don't even remember," I admit. "It was all a blur, and I was already in a shitty mood to begin with."

Guilt fills her expression. "Because of me?"

"Nah." My fingers tighten through hers. "O'Shea is on my case again because another goddamn picture showed up on Instagram." I chuckle harshly. "I really need to start paying more attention when I'm at Malone's."

"O'Shea is your assistant coach? The one who forced you to volunteer at the middle school?"

"Defensive coordinator, and yes."

"Okay, and what picture are we talking about? Wait, a picture from Malone's? Of *us*?" Her face goes pale.

"No," I assure her. "Me and Penelope, the puck bunny who was chewing on my neck. O'Shea is pissed."

"Why? Are PDAs forbidden?" She quickly adds, "Not that I'm saying you were PDA'ing with her—I know she was the one coming on to you. But for argument's sake, even if you *were* reciprocating, how is that a punishable offense?"

"He wasn't bitching about the PDA. I'm holding a beer in the picture, and O'Shea's got a stick up his ass about us not drinking."

"Um. He realizes he's coaching college players, right? A no-drinking rule is impossible to enforce."

"I know."

"And all you're doing in the picture is holding a *beer*? What the hell? It's not like you got caught snorting lines of coke off her tits."

A smile tickles my lips. "Of course not. If I was going to snort lines off anyone's tits, it would be yours."

"Aw, thanks. That's so romantic." Still stroking my palm with her fingertips, she leans closer and kisses my cheek. "O'Shea is an idiot, sweetie. Don't let him get to you, okay? Especially not to the point where you're so angry you're punching people and getting thrown out of games."

She's right—I need to do a better job of controlling my temper. But Frank O'Shea...fuck. Just the sound of his sharp, condescending voice riles me up.

Allie's lips brush over my jaw in a fleeting kiss. Then she releases my hand, visibly reluctant. "I should probably go before someone sees me in here. The third period will be over soon."

"Did you happen to catch the score before you came back here?"

"I think it was tied."

Shit. Well, hopefully my boys manage to turn the tie into a lead, because I'm sick to death of losing.

And I'm sick of sneaking around, if I'm being honest.

It was exciting at first, sleeping with Allie behind our friends' backs, but I'm not feeling it anymore. When she showed up at Malone's the other night looking like *that*? I wanted to stick my tongue down her throat in front of everyone. It was damn hard pretending to be unaffected by her, and I'm damn tired of furtively texting her for quickies and lying to my friends about where I'm going.

Friends who, by the way, now think I incorporate dildos in my jerk-off routine. When Tucker handed me a plate of bacon and eggs this morning, he innocently asked if my "little pink buddy" would be joining us for breakfast. Garrett almost broke a rib laughing. Poor Grace still can't look at me without blushing.

I know Allie doesn't want our friends to know we're fooling around, but I wish there were a way we could have a little more freedom. Maybe we could book a hotel room for the weekend, just spend two whole days in bed without worrying about—

Inspiration strikes. "Hey, wait." I reach for her hand before she can stand up. "Did you book your train ticket for Thanksgiving yet?"

Allie curses. "No, I didn't. Argh! Why am I so bad at remembering things? I set a reminder!"

"Don't book it."

"Why not?"

"Because I have a better idea." I hesitate. "Why don't I come to New York with you? We can drive up in my car."

She looks startled. "Oh. You…uh…want to spend Thanksgiving together? Um. Well. I'm seeing my dad—"

"I'm not inviting myself to dinner or anything," I cut in. "I figured I'd stay at my place in Manhattan while you're with your dad, and if you're free Thursday or Friday night, you can come over." I waggle my eyebrows. "We'd have the whole place to ourselves."

"Well, that's intriguing," she says slowly. "When do you need to be back at Briar for the game?"

"I'd have to leave Saturday morning. When were you planning on coming back?"

"Saturday morning." A tiny smile lifts her lips. "Timing works out…"

"Does that mean you're down?" I ask hopefully.

"A free ride to New York and wild weekend sex? Of course."

"Good. I have one favor to ask, though."

She tips her head, waiting for me to continue.

My mood, which had been lower than low before, is now as bright as the grin I flash her. "Bring Winston."

AND THAT'S HOW I END UP DRIVING TO NEW YORK WITH ALLIE IN the passenger seat.

The sun has already set by the time we hit the road, because Allie had rehearsal until six, and then it takes her a whole frickin' hour to pack. Me, I bring a backpack. Her? She brings an overstuffed suitcase that barely fits in my trunk.

I had left my hockey bag in there because it literally didn't occur to me that she'd pack so much shit for three short days. Luckily, the parking lot behind Bristol is completely deserted, which means nobody sees us trying to jam the suitcase in the trunk. The campus is eerily silent, almost as if the Rapture sucked everyone up into the sky. Clearly we're not the only ones who decided to head out the day before Thanksgiving.

Hannah and Garrett flew to Philly this morning, and Grace and Logan were gone a few hours later. They're visiting Logan's father in rehab, then hitting up his mother in Boston for the night before coming back to Hastings to spend the holiday with Grace's dad. Tucker was still home when I left, but he's driving to Hollis's place in New Hampshire tomorrow morning. I'm glad, because if he didn't have anywhere to go, the guilt would've suckered me into inviting him to Manhattan.

After Allie and I are finally settled in the front seat, I discover that we have completely different tastes in music. It takes about five minutes of bickering before we reach a compromise—we each get thirty-minute music blocks, during which the other person isn't allowed to complain. The little brat even sets a timer to ensure we abide by the rules. And of course, she announces she's going first.

"Why can't I go first?" I object.

"Because I'm playing the vagina card."

I smirk at her. "Fine. Then I trump it with the penis card."

"That's not how it works." She sounds exasperated.

"Then how *does* it work? Because last I checked, genitals don't decide who gets to listen to their music first."

"Oh yes they do." Allie addresses me like I'm a kindergartner. "See, if you take away my dick privileges, I'll be fine for months.

Years, even. But if I take away your pussy privileges? You'll be utterly lost. Like a drowning man at sea, desperately grabbing for the vagina preserver." She beams. "Therefore, vagina trumps penis."

My smirk fades, because she's right.

As a result, I spend the first thirty minutes of the drive listening to cheesy '80s ballads that all feature the word *love* in their titles.

"I Want to Know What Love Is."

"I Just Called to Say I Love You."

"It Must Have Been Love."

You'd think Allie was not so subtly trying to tell me something, except I'm fairly certain every song from the '80s is about love.

When it's my turn, I pick the filthiest tracks I can find. Ol' Dirty Bastard. Some non-radio-friendly Jay-Z. Cypress Hill. I even throw an Insane Clown Posse song in there.

Allie retaliates by putting on Madonna's greatest hits.

Instead of punishing her, I decide to reward myself and switch from hip-hop to country. Yup, rich boy likes Tim McGraw. So sue me.

We're still on the highway with about two hours left to go when Allie pulls out her phone and starts typing.

Keeping my eyes on the road, I ask, "Who you texting?"

"Dillon…a friend from high school. She goes to college in Florida, but I'm hoping she's coming home for the break. Ooh, and I should check if Fletch is around."

"Fletch?"

"Kyle Fletcher, but I call him Fletch," she says absently. "Ex-boyfriend."

My head swivels toward her. "You're making plans with your ex-boyfriend?"

"Retract those claws, missy. Fletch is still a good friend of mine."

I can't fight my curiosity. "How long were you together?"

"Three years."

I whistle softly. "And then three and a half more with Sean… You're a nester, huh?"

"No I'm not," she protests.

"Babe, that's almost seven years of your life spent in a serious relationship. And you're only twenty-two."

"Twenty-one. I'm a Christmas baby."

"For real? Your birthday's the twenty-fifth?"

"The twenty-fourth. I guess that makes me a Christmas Eve baby. Sorry."

"You better be sorry. How dare you mislead me like that?"

She rolls her eyes. "Anyway, fine. You're right. That *is* a long time." She pauses. "What's your longest relationship?"

"A little over a year." I answer without moving my gaze from the dark highway.

"Really?" she says in surprise. "That's a lot longer than I expected. High school?"

I nod.

"Why'd you break up?"

It's my turn to roll my eyes. "Because we were in high school."

"So? What if she was your soul mate?" Allie challenges. "You don't believe high school sweethearts can make it?"

"Nope. I don't think you're capable of knowing what you want or need from a relationship at that age. When you're in high school, you have no concept of real life. You don't realize how much growing up you still have to do. I'm definitely not the same person now that I was in my teens. Hell, I'm not the same person I was last *semester*."

"Sure you are." She smiles sweetly. "You were a man-whore last semester and you're a man-whore this semester."

"True," I say with a snicker.

Allie drops her phone in the cup holder and shifts around in her seat so she can see me better. "Do you still talk to your high school girlfriend?"

Tension slices into my bones. "No."

"You just lost touch?"

"I guess you can say that." I exhale slowly, hoping to ease the tightness in my chest. "She's the reason Coach O'Shea hates me, actually. Miranda's his daughter."

"Uh-oh. You dated your coach's daughter?" Allie takes on a chiding tone. "Oh, sweetie, that's like rule number one in the dating handbook—never date the kid of your authority figure."

"Do I look like someone who follows the rules?" My answering grin fades rapidly. "I couldn't help it," I admit. "At the time, Miranda was pretty fuckin' awesome. Impossible to resist. She attended Greenwich Prep for free because Frank coached there, so she wasn't a rich kid. She was completely different from the girls I'd always gone to school with. She didn't give a shit about image or being the Queen B, didn't shame other people to make herself feel better. She was down-to-earth. Funny. Hot."

"Well, duh. Dean Heyward-Di Laurentis only bangs hotties."

"I didn't bang her. At least, not right away. It took a long time to get there, but I wasn't in any hurry." I wink. "We had fun doing other stuff."

"So when did you do the deed?"

"A couple months before we broke up." My shoulders stiffen again. I hate thinking about that night.

Allie senses it, because her tone becomes wary. "What happened?"

Fuck, why did I even open this door? "About nine months into the relationship, things got…intense." And why am I even answering the question? "Miranda started talking about us staying together when we went to college, which was never part of the deal."

"Wait—did O'Shea know at this point? That you were dating his daughter?"

"Yeah, he knew. He wasn't thrilled, but he said as long as Miranda was happy, he was happy. Didn't stop him from giving me grief about it, though. I'd pick her up for a date and he'd interrogate me about where we were going, who would be there, when we'd be back. And one time he threatened to shoot my balls off if I didn't treat her with respect."

"My father gave Fletch the same speech when we started dating.

Trust me, it's a dad thing." Allie's laughter dies off. "So Miranda was talking about college…?"

"All the time, and it really fucking worried me because we were on the same page going into the relationship. I didn't want to do the long-distance thing in college. I saw my brother and his ex-girlfriend go through it, same with a few buddies who graduated the year before. They spent their freshman year holding on to something they should've just let go. The phone calls got less frequent, the visits stopped, the jealousy and insecurity set in. Worrying about what the other person was up to, who they might be hooking up with. I didn't want that, and neither did Miranda. She was planning on going to Duke. I was planning on Briar or Harvard. We both agreed that if we were still together by the time graduation rolled around, we would end it."

"But she changed her mind?"

"Yup. It was subtle at first. She'd talk about something we were going to do in the future, I'd remind her it probably wouldn't happen, and she'd laugh it off and say she forgot. But then she got…clingy. She'd call like ten times a day, and suddenly she was paranoid I was cheating on her. I wasn't, by the way—I've never cheated on anyone I made a commitment to."

"So you ended it? No, wait, first you had sex with her."

I hear the accusation in Allie's tone, and I can't deny it hits its mark. "Yeah. I did." My mouth runs dry. I try to swallow. "Miranda was with this other guy for two years before she went out with me. When we started dating, she told me she'd had sex before."

"Oh no," Allie murmurs. "I don't like where this is going."

"We were at a party, and she was acting all clingy again, not letting me talk to anyone, refusing to let go of my hand. She even followed me into the fucking bathroom. I was frustrated and angry, and I started pounding beers because it was the only way to pass the time. She didn't want to leave, but she also wouldn't leave my side. I was actually considering breaking up with her right then, and I guess she sensed it because next thing I know she's dragging me upstairs."

Regret throbs inside me. "I was disgustingly wasted, not to mention seventeen and horny, so I wasn't exactly fighting her off. We had sex. And then afterward, she admitted she was a virgin."

"Shit."

"If I'd known, I would have been more…I don't know, careful? Gentler? I was sloppy drunk and she got a sloppy lay. For her *first* time, Allie. I felt like a total ass the next day, but Miranda wasn't mad. She said she felt closer to me than ever, and after that, it was like DEFCON level clinginess. Suddenly she was planning college visits and saying how we should think about getting engaged, that a stronger commitment would make it easier to stay true to each other." My stomach churns just thinking about it. I hadn't even turned eighteen at that point.

"So like any teenage boy would, you freaked out and ended it."

I nod.

She sighs. "I don't blame you. I'm sure anyone would feel overwhelmed in that situation."

"Maybe. But…Miranda didn't handle the breakup too well," I confess, fighting the nausea clawing at my gut. "Turns out she'd dealt with depression in the past, but she never told me about it. I never would've guessed either, because she was so happy and easygoing all the time. But I found out that's because of the meds she was taking. The meds she *stopped* taking after I ended it."

"Shit," Allie says again.

"She changed completely. She was crying all the time, screaming at me in the halls, calling me in the middle of the night threatening to kill herself. I had no choice but to involve her dad, because I was terrified she might actually commit suicide. Frank pulled her out of school after that, and I haven't seen or heard from her since."

Allie's jaw drops. "Are you serious?"

"Frank wouldn't allow it." The frustration I felt back then rises again now. "He told me Miranda was back on her meds and getting professional help. Oh, and that if I ever tried to contact her again, he would rip my throat out. That didn't stop me from worrying about her. I mean, I still cared about her even though we were broken up, so about a month after she left school, I cornered Coach in the parking lot and demanded to see Miranda." My jaw twitches. "And he punched me in the face."

"Oh my God. Did anyone see him do it?"

"No. It was late, and he was coming out of a staff meeting. Nobody else was around. But yeah, he clocked me good. That's when I found out that Miranda told him we had sex. She also told him I was drunk out of my mind when it happened."

"Well, that's not cool," Allie says angrily.

"None of it was cool. I shouldn't have let her seduce me that night, absolutely." Bitterness clogs my throat. "But she let her father believe I was some drunk asshole who took advantage of her, and that wasn't fair either." I force myself to relax my grip on the steering wheel. "Anyway, that's why O'Shea can't stand the sight of me. He thinks I played the long game with his daughter—spent a year trying to get into her pants and then dumped her once I got what I wanted."

"And you really have no idea how she's doing now? You haven't tried to contact her?"

"I sent her a Facebook friend request a while ago," I admit. "She hasn't accepted it. I think she's doing well, though. Her profile said she goes to Duke."

"I guess it makes sense that O'Shea was so overprotective of her," Allie muses. "It must have been really hard for him, watching his daughter struggle with depression. Watching her get better, and then fall into that dark place again."

Maybe, but I refuse to empathize with that bastard, not when he's trying to make my last year at Briar so damn miserable.

"You make more sense to me too now," she adds.

"How so?" I don't like her thoughtful, probing gaze.

"This is why you're always so upfront about sex, right? You're making sure your hookups are on the same page as you?"

"I'm not misleading anyone ever again, that's for sure. Or taking their agreement at face value. I don't care if it makes me an ass, but I never, ever lie about my intentions. And I never date virgins," I say as an afterthought. "Or freshmen, because they tend to be clingier."

"The Life of Dean sure has a lot of rules."

"Without those rules, there is no Life of Dean."

"I suppose." She pauses. "The virgin thing is tough, though. It's easy for a girl to lie about that. I mean, horseback riding alone has probably broken quite a few hymens."

I bark out a laugh. "Trust me, my virgin radar is infallible these days."

"Oh yeah? How did you know *I* wasn't a virgin?"

"Because Garrett stays at your dorm every other weekend and he heard you and Sean in the bone zone tons of times. He told me you were a screamer."

She gasps. "He did *not* say that."

"He totally did. Face it, babe, you're a loud lay." I chuckle at her stricken expression. "That's not a bad thing. Vocal is good." I think of her throaty moans and breathy *Oh my Gods,* and I'm semi-hard in a nanosecond. "Vocal is *very* good."

"No, it's embarrassing," she mutters. Her cheeks are bright red.

"Hey, I'd way rather be in bed with a loud woman than a quiet one. Silent comers are the *worst.* I slept with this one chick who didn't make a sound the entire time. Seriously, I had no idea if she was even enjoying herself, and then when it was over she turned to me and thanked me for the multiple orgasms."

Allie lets out a hoot. "You're lying."

"I don't lie."

"You…really don't, huh? I'm starting to think you might be the most honest person I've ever met."

"Another requirement in the Life of Dean. Say what you mean, mean what you say."

"And do what you want."

"And do what you want," I echo.

"I think I really like the Life of Dean."

I think I really like you, I almost blurt out.

Fortunately, I manage to tamp down the sentiment, because… what the hell? I like *banging* her. Allie is easy to talk to and fun to fuck—that's all there is to it. And considering how adamant she is about this being nothing more than a fling, I know she agrees wholeheartedly with me on that.

But a couple hours later, when I pull up in front of a three-story brownstone in Brooklyn Heights, Allie throws me a curveball.

"Do you want to come for dinner tomorrow?"

The invitation is alarming and unexpected.

And alarming.

Did I mention alarming?

My unease must be written all over my face, because Allie hurries on. "I won't be insulted if you say no. Honestly, you can say no. I was just imagining you all alone in Manhattan for Thanksgiving while your family is scarfing down a tropical turkey in St. Bart's, and it was such a lonely, depressing picture that I figured I'd extend the invite."

"What…" I clear my throat. "What will you tell your dad?"

She shrugs. "I'll say you're a friend from school who didn't have anywhere else to go. It won't be a big deal, I promise. You guys will talk hockey, I'll cook dinner, we'll watch some football, and there's a forty percent chance we all get food poisoning. Just a regular old Hayes family Thanksgiving."

A laugh flies out. "Sounds like a blast." I consider it. "Okay, I'm in. What time do you want me to show up?"

"Four should be good, but we probably won't eat until five."

I nod.

"Okay. Awesome." She smiles ruefully. "Now help me get my suitcase out of the trunk, will you? I'm pretty sure I'll break my back if I try to lift that thing myself."

CHAPTER 21

DEAN

ALLIE'S FATHER HATES ME ON SIGHT.

I'm sure if I mentioned it to Allie, she'd wave off my concerns and say things like "he's just grumpy" or "oh, that's just how he is with everyone." But she'd be wrong.

Joe Hayes hates me from the moment he opens the door and sees me standing on the stoop. And hoo boy, don't *I* feel overdressed. Allie told me to dress "nice," so I'd chosen a white Tom Ford dress shirt and gray Armani trousers. No suit coat, but my black Ralph Lauren jacket gets an eyebrow flick from Allie's dad, who's in sweat-pants and a flannel shirt.

"You AJ's friend from school?" he barks.

I wrinkle my brow. "AJ?"

"My daughter. Allison Jane?" Mr. Hayes looks annoyed that he has to explain.

"Oh, ah, yes, sir. I know her as Allie, though."

"And you didn't know her nickname?" He makes a derisive sound. "Not much of a friend, are ya?" He mutters "Come in" and turns around stiffly. Stiff in the literal sense, because his gait is visibly labored as he stumbles forward on a slender cane.

Allie warned me that her father has MS. She also advised me

not to bring it up in conversation, saying he doesn't like talking about it and will most likely bite my head off if I mention it. So I don't, but it's clear even with my nonmedical background that he's in pain right now.

I follow Mr. Hayes through a surprisingly large main floor with gleaming hardwood and what looks like the original woodwork and doors from whenever this brownstone was built. Allie and her dad have the two lower floors, which I'm brusquely told contain four bedrooms and three baths. Either the family purchased the apartment before the Brooklyn Heights neighborhood became super exclusive, or pro-hockey scouts make *way* more money than I thought.

He leads me into a spacious living room with a bay window that overlooks a neatly tended garden and patio. "Do you garden?" I ask politely.

Allie's dad scowls at me. "Woman upstairs takes care of the garden."

Okay then.

"Dean. Hey."

Oh thank Christ. Allie pops into the room, and I'm relieved to see she's wearing a knee-length blue dress. Not a fancy one, but nice enough that I no longer feel like I showed up to a potluck in a tuxedo.

"You want anything to drink?" she asks after she greets me with a quick hug.

I glance at the brown leather couch that Mr. Hayes is slowly lowering himself onto. He tucks the cane on the edge of the sofa and snatches a beer from the coffee table. His hand trembles wildly as he raises the bottle to his lips. When he catches me staring, he scowls again.

"Uh…" I gulp. "A beer would be nice."

"Coors or Bud?"

"Bud."

She nods. "Coming right up."

I'm once again left alone in the clutches of Mr. Hayes, whose blue eyes are now glued to the Lions game flashing on the flat-screen TV. I've got about five inches and thirty pounds on the man, but he still fucking terrifies me. I suspect he was a bruiser when he played hockey. He's got that stocky barrel chest. And the surly attitude.

"What are you waiting for, pretty boy? Sit down already."

Pretty boy?

Goddamn it. Why did I show up in Ford and Armani? Allie's dad probably took one look at my expensive getup and decided I was a rich prick.

Very reluctantly, I sit on the other end of the sectional.

Mr. Hayes glances over briefly. "AJ says you play hockey."

"Yes, sir."

"Forward?"

"Defenseman."

"What're your stats so far this season?"

I pause uncertainly. Wait, does he expect me to rattle off actual numbers? Like goals and assists and penalty minutes? I could probably ballpark it, but reciting my own statistics feels pompous.

"They're decent," I say vaguely. "The team's had a rocky start. We won the Frozen Four last season, though."

He nods. "Won it junior year. Boston College."

"Nice. Uh. Congrats." His face is utterly expressionless, so I can't be sure if this is some kind of pissing match. If so, I could probably mention I won it the year before too. But I keep my mouth shut. Luckily, Allie is back with my beer, and I reach for it as if it's a life preserver. "Thanks, babe."

We both freeze the moment the endearment leaves my mouth. Shit. I hope Mr. Hayes didn't hear that.

He's sitting right here. Of course he heard.

I twist off the bottle cap and take a much-needed swig of alcohol.

"So what did I miss?" Allie asks in an overly cheerful voice.

Her father scoffs. "Pretty boy over here was just telling me how he won the Frozen Four."

Fucking hell.

This is going to be a long Thanksgiving.

DINNER IS AWFUL. WELL, NOT THE FOOD—FOR SOMEONE WHO claims to suck at cooking, Allie did a pretty good job with the meal. It's the act of eating said food that I find excruciating. The conversation is brutal. Mr. Hayes seems to be going out of his way to antagonize me. His preferred phrase of the evening is "of course." Except it's spoken in a flat, condescending tone that makes me wish I was spending Thanksgiving in the empty house in Hastings.

When Allie tells him I'm going to law school next fall, he says, "Of course."

When she mentions my family owns a place in Manhattan, he says, "Of course."

When I thank him for having me to dinner, he says, "Of course."

Goddamn. Brutal.

Don't get me wrong, I'm making a genuine effort to be polite. I ask him what it was like to be a pro scout, but all I get is a half-mumbled, one-sentence response. I compliment him on how nice this brownstone is, and he grunts out a "thank you."

Eventually I give up, but Allie is more than happy to fill the awkward silence. As she tells her father about the play she's acting in, her courses, her upcoming auditions, and everything else she has going on, that's the only time Mr. Hayes seems to come to life. It's obvious he loves his daughter deeply, and he hangs on every word she says like she's offering him the secrets to eternal life. He does scowl at her once, though, after he asks if she's still in touch with Sean and she admits they had coffee.

"Never liked that boy," Mr. Hayes mutters. For once, he and I are on the same page.

Allie chews her last bite of gravy-laden mashed potatoes before voicing a protest. "Aw, that's not true. You guys always got along when we came to visit you."

Her father chuckles. Well, look at that, he's actually capable of conveying humor. I never would have guessed.

"He was your boyfriend—I had no choice but to get along with him. Now he's not, so I don't have to pretend to like him anymore."

I cover up a laugh behind my napkin.

"Boy was too needy," Mr. Hayes continues. "I didn't like the way he looked at you."

"How did he look at me?" Allie asks warily.

"Like you were his entire world."

She frowns. "And that's a bad thing?"

"Damn right it is. Nobody should ever be someone else's entire world. That's not healthy, AJ. If your whole life is centered on one thing—one person—whatcha going to be left with if that person goes away? Absolutely nothing." He gruffly reiterates, "Not healthy."

Joe Hayes has a very practical way of looking at things. I'm oddly impressed.

"Well, now you're just making me feel bad for Sean. Let's change the subject. Dean, tell my dad about your last game."

I sigh ruefully. "Really? The one I got thrown out of?"

Her dad harrumphs. "Of course."

The conversation becomes strained again. I'm relieved when it's finally time to clear the table, eagerly standing up to help Allie gather the dishes. There's still half a turkey left in the serving platter, which Mr. Hayes reaches for as he staggers to his feet.

"No, Dad," Allie says in a strict voice. "Go and watch the rest of the game. Dean and I can clean up."

"I'm not an invalid, AJ," he grumbles. "I'm perfectly capable of carrying one plate to the kitchen."

No sooner do the words exit his mouth than the platter wobbles in his hand. Or rather, his hand wobbles and the platter follows suit, abruptly slipping from his grip and smashing to the hardwood.

The ceramic shatters to pieces, sending the slippery turkey careening across the floor. I immediately set down my plates and hurry around the table. Allie does the same, and our heads bump when we both reach for the same broken piece.

"Goddamn it," Mr. Hayes bites out. "I'll take care of the mess."

"*No.*" Her tone isn't strict anymore—it's commanding. She snatches the ceramic shard from my hand and says, "Dean, would you take Dad to the living room and make sure he stays there?"

Her father levels me with a death glare that makes my balls shrivel up, but no way am I facing Allie's wrath right now. Stifling a sigh, I lightly clasp Joe's arm and lead him out of the small dining room.

The scowl stays fixed on his face even after he's settled on the couch. "I could've cleaned it up myself," he informs me.

"I know." I shrug. "But I think we made the right call sneaking out of there. For such a tiny little thing, your daughter sure is terrifying when she's trying to get her way."

His lips curve ever so slightly. Holy shit, did I almost make him smile?

But whatever shred of humor I might have induced disappears before I can blink. Mr. Hayes lowers his voice to a deadly pitch and asks, "What do you want with AJ?"

I shift in confusion. "I don't understand the question."

"I see the way *you* look at her too." His jaw begins to twitch, but I don't know if it's from anger or the disease he's battling. "You like her."

"Of course I do," I say awkwardly. "We're friends."

"Don't feed me that bull. I've been alive a lot longer than you, pretty boy. You think I can't tell when a man is in lust?"

And I thought the dinner conversation was uncomfortable.

"I get it. AJ's a catch. She's smart, pretty like her mom. She's caring—too damn caring sometimes," he admits. "If she loves you, she'll always put your needs ahead of hers." And I know he's talking about his own relationship with Allie now. It's obvious that because of his MS, she puts his needs first, not to mention coddles him more than he likes.

"She needs a man who will take care of *her*." His voice goes soft for a moment, but then it sharpens. "You're not that man, kid. You're incapable of that."

Insult prickles my skin. Who is he to make that sort of judgment?

He notices my frown and chuckles. "I was a hockey scout for more than twenty years. You think you're the first cocky SOB I've met in my life? Cockier, too, because you grew up with money. You already have that entitled sense of importance that comes after a player signs his first seven-figure contract."

I force my hands not to clench into fists. "Just because my family has money doesn't mean I'm a bad person, sir."

"Not saying that." He shrugs. "But guys like you, you know nothing about real-world problems. And if shit does go wrong, you throw a little money at the problem and *poof*—all fixed." Blue eyes, a shade darker than Allie's, sweep over me from head to toe. "You're not what she needs, Dean. You wouldn't step up and be there for her if it came down to it." A pause. "I don't trust you to take care of my daughter."

With that final cutting remark, he shifts his gaze back to the football game.

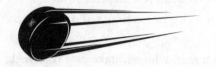

CHAPTER 22

DEAN

Allie calls me at noon the next day with an update about her ETA. "Hey, I'm in a taxi. I'll be there in fifteen or twenty, depending on traffic."

I just stepped out of the shower, so I'm in a towel as I stride past the floor-to-ceiling windows in my bedroom, balancing the phone on my shoulder. "Why didn't you take the train? Woulda been faster."

"I felt like treating myself to a cozy backseat instead of a cramped subway ride."

"Right on."

"Any special instructions for when I get there? What floor are you on?"

I absently enter the walk-in closet and grab a pair of sweatpants off a shelf. "Just tell the concierge who you are and someone will bring you up. The elevator requires a key to get to the penthouse."

She sighs. "You live in the penthouse of the Heyward Plaza Hotel?"

"Yup." I drop the towel on the polished hardwood. "Hey, what do you think—will that make your dad hate me less or hate me more?"

Her laughter tickles my ear. "Oh shut up. He doesn't hate you."

Yeah right. She'd be singing a different tune if she'd heard the shit he said to me in the living room last night.

I don't trust you to take care of my daughter.

Fuck. MS or not, the old man is still delivering blows that sting days later.

I shove the angering exchange out of my mind and say, "I'll see you soon." Then I wander around my room collecting random items of clothing.

The cleaning staff already tidied up the place this morning—they show up twice a week like clockwork, whether or not anyone is staying at the penthouse—but I have a mystifying habit of accumulating a mess even if I've been somewhere for only a couple hours. Our housekeeper Vera calls me the Accidental Slob.

Twenty minutes later, after the front desk buzzes to let me know my visitor has arrived, I head for the elevator that opens directly onto the living room.

Only my prep school friends have visited me here before, and since their homes are equally...luxurious...none of them had ever batted an eye when they came over.

Allie bats an eye.

The second she emerges from the elevator, her jaw is on the marble floor and her eyebrows are higher than the fifteen-foot ceiling.

"Sweet mother of Moses," she breathes. Her awed gaze travels around the parlor, living room, and north-facing terrace before returning to me. "Okay. I *demand* a tour."

I offer a self-deprecating laugh. "It'll be a long tour," I warn her.

"I don't care if it takes five hours. I want to see every inch of this palace, your majesty."

As I show her around the penthouse, I find myself viewing it through her eyes. Every room we enter makes her gawk and gasp and curse in amazement—the walnut-paneled library, the modern chef's kitchen, the gym, the wine cellar... Okay, I guess this place is a *wee* bit over the top.

"Where are the bedrooms?" She looks confused when we wind up back in the living room and stop near the hand-carved mantelpiece of the massive fireplace.

"Oh, that was just the first floor," I say sheepishly.

"This place has *two* floors?"

I mumble, "Three."

"*Three* floors?" She stares at me as if I just stepped off an alien spaceship. "I think I want to punch you right now."

"I think I want to punch myself." I don't like this unwelcome pang of self-consciousness. Or rather, I don't like feeling like I'm the most overindulged prick on the planet.

Allie's father's voice suddenly buzzes through my mind. Disparaging and cold, mocking me about how I know nothing about "real-world problems."

Damn it. Why am I letting that man get under my skin? So what if I grew up with money? I still know the meaning of struggle and hardship and... Fuck, who am I kidding? The Life of Dean is pretty sweet. It always has been. But I can still empathize with people who've been less fortunate than I am. I can still "step up and be there" when someone fucking needs me.

We climb the sweeping marble staircase and she stops to admire one of my mom's favorite abstract paintings. For all the pomp and circumstance of this place, my parents didn't go overboard with the decor. The penthouse has a clean, modern design, and most of the art on the walls is by no means expensive. Mom is all about supporting local artists.

"Is your room on the second floor?" Allie asks.

I shake my head. "Master bedroom is down there." I point to the left. "Guest rooms are there." I point to the right. "You want to see any of those or can we skip this floor?"

"We can skip it." She's already bounding up the stairs again.

I lead her into my bedroom. She admires every inch of the enormous room, from the custom-made oak bed to the built-in bookshelves to the wall of gleaming windows.

"No curtains?" She sounds a bit dazed.

"Automatic shades," I admit. "Remote-control operated."

"Wow." As she wanders around exploring, the sunlight flooding the room catches in her golden hair, which is loose around her shoulders. She studies the endless rows of titles on the bookshelf, then whirls toward me. "Okay. Admit it."

"Admit what?"

She points an accusing finger at me. "You're smart."

I snort loudly. "Of course I'm smart."

"You sure as hell don't act like it." Allie crosses her arms over the front of her loose striped sweater. "In fact, I feel like you go out of your way to make everyone believe you're a dummy. With your 'baby dolls' and foul language and the way you throw 'ain't' into a sentence every so often."

I flash her a grin. "Nope, that's just how I fucking talk, baby doll. Ain't nothing wrong with that."

Her eyes dance with amusement. "Uh-huh. So how come you never talk about law school?"

"What's there to talk about? I'm not in law school yet." I sit on the edge of the bed that I hastily made right before she got here.

"But aren't you excited about it?" she presses.

"Eh. Not really." At her frown, I chuckle softly. "I'm sure I'll be excited when I'm there. I'm a live-in-the-moment kinda guy, remember?" I pat the bedspread, then crook a finger at her. "Get over here already, will ya?"

"Give me one good reason why I should."

I slide my hand into my crotch and cup it. "Little Dean is feeling ignored."

Laughing, Allie climbs into my lap and rests her hands on the back of my neck. She brings her mouth close to mine. "Poor guy. Does he need an afternoon delight?"

"He's dying for it," I murmur. Our lips meet in a kiss at the same time I ease my hands under her shirt. I groan when her bare breasts fill my palms. I frickin' love it when she doesn't wear a bra. Makes it so much easier to lift up her shirt and pop one sweet nipple into my mouth.

"Ohhh," she moans. "That's nice."

"About to get nicer, baby." I work my other hand between our bodies so I'm cupping her over her leggings. "Fuck. We need to get these clothes off."

Allie's gaze darts toward the windows. "Should we close the shades? Where's the remote?"

I'm wholly focused on the delicious task of suckling her nipple, working my tongue over the hard bud.

"Dean," she protests. "We're pretty much in a glass box! What if there's someone with a telescope watching us from one of the other buildings?"

"Then they're going to get a helluva show." I pinch both nipples, and I'm rewarded with a throaty noise.

Her objections die off as I lower her onto the mattress and proceed to peel every stitch of clothing off her body. She pushes my sweats off my hips and I kick them away, and then we're naked and kissing and rolling around on my huge bed until we're both breathless.

"Cool if we save foreplay for later?" I whisper against her neck before dragging my tongue back to her tits again.

"Mm-hmm. Just get inside me already," she whispers back.

I grab a condom and fit myself against her soaked pussy, thanking God and any other deities who care to hear my gratitude that Allie's as turned on as I am. Our sexual compatibility is off the charts. We both hiss out pleasure-laced breaths as I slide home. *Home?* I halt midthrust.

"Don't stop." Allie's husky command makes my balls tighten. I'm developing a Pavlovian response to her catalog of sounds. Breathy moans, raspy sighs, and I'm semi-hard, if not at full mast. Happy noises, laughs, and I'm grinning back. It's...different.

She taps me on the shoulder impatiently. "Need some instruction? Because Little Dean isn't all the way in yet."

I muffle a chuckle against her luscious tits and thrust home.

There. I said it. *Home*. This is sex, for chrissake. I don't need to overthink this. Not with Allie. She wants me balls deep, fucking her mindless, and that's what I want too.

"Oh, he's in, baby. He's in so far and so hard you're going to feel it for days." I jack forward hard enough that it feels like she skitters halfway across the mattress. She braces her hands against the padded headboard and stares at me from under heavy-lidded eyes with a come-and-get-me look.

Yeah, she rocks my world. And I'm going to return the favor.

The walls of her pussy convulse around me, squeezing me in the most erotic hug ever invented. I fight off my orgasm. No way am I coming yet. I want to see those gorgeous eyes rolling back in her head. I want her mouth falling open and her face to take on that totally-lost-in-the-moment glazed expression she gets when she's so into the fucking that I know nothing is in her head but me.

I push her hair back, tangling my fingers in the thick strands and tugging her head so I can kiss her properly. She attacks my tongue, sucking it into her mouth, letting me fuck her with it while I hammer her with my dick.

We're both getting sweaty. Our slippery bodies move against each other in a perfect rhythm, one that makes me dizzy with excitement.

"You feel so good. Like a goddamn dream," I tell her through gritted teeth. The effort not to come is testing my last bit of control.

"Yes. There. Fuck me right *there*," she cries, punctuating her orders with claws in my shoulders. I brace myself, elbow near her head, knee digging into the mattress for leverage, and give her everything I've got. In measured, powerful strokes, I work her into a mindless state of pleasure until she's shaking and screaming her satisfaction into the empty rooms of this penthouse.

She's still trembling when I flip her over and ram into her from behind. My balls slap against her thighs, and the tightness of her pussy from this angle nearly makes my eyes water from the pleasure.

She makes these incredibly sexy sounds that include the words *Dean* and *oh God* and *yes* until it's a strange sort of song, her moans the melody, our bodies banging out the sex beat, our hearts getting mixed up in all of it until *I'm* the mindless one. All my senses are filled with her—her sounds, her smell, her touch. *Her.*

Bare ass pumping into her, I don't care if there's a telescope out there watching. Let them see how much I love being inside this girl.

WE SPEND THE WHOLE DAY IN BED. WELL, NOT JUST IN BED. WE also fuck in my enormous walk-in shower under the spray of four showerheads and multiple body jets.

And I go down on her in the kitchen while she's sprawled on the marble counter.

And she blows me in the game room.

And we sixty-nine in the private sauna.

Did I mention this is the best day ever?

By the time nine o'clock rolls around, I'm legit spent. Drained. There isn't a drop of semen left in my body. Allie Hayes sucked and fucked it all out of me.

"You're a sex fiend," I grumble when I feel her hand stroking my thigh. We just finished eating dinner—burgers and fries delivered by room service and consumed in bed—and now we're lying on my million-thread-count sheets, recovering from the most intense sex marathon I've had in a long time. Or ever.

"I can't help it," Allie protests. She sits up, and I'm floored by how gorgeous she looks right now. Flushed cheeks, tousled hair, hazy eyes. "The Life of Dean gets me all hot and bothered."

My phone rings, and I groan in relief. "Oh thank Jesus. Hopefully whoever this is will save me before you break my dick." Turns out my savior is Beau, and I pick up with my usual "What's shaking, Maxwell?"

"We are," Beau answers cheerfully. "As in, we're shaking our asses on the dance floor tonight."

"Um. Are you asking me to go out dancing with you?" I pause. "And shouldn't you be in Wisconsin with your grandmother right now?"

"Grams bailed on us—went on some seniors' cruise instead of spending the holiday with her family. How dare she, right? That *bitch*." Beau snickers, which I take as an indication that he's joking. If not, I feel bad for his grandmother. "Joanna and I are in the city with our folks. Let's meet up."

"How do you know I'm in the city?" I ask suspiciously. I have a Boston cell number and I hadn't told him I was coming to Manhattan, so there's no reason for him to think I'm here.

"I've got that friend finder app. Shows you where all your friends are at all times."

Awesome. I'm being stalked by one of my best buds.

"We're going to a club in SoHo. You down?"

"Hold on a sec." I cover the mouthpiece and look at Allie. "Feel like going out? Beau and his sister are in town and they're hitting up a nightclub."

Reluctance creases her forehead. "Beau, as in Briar's quarterback?"

I know exactly what she's thinking and I'm quick to squash her fears. "He won't say anything if he sees us together. Seriously. Maxwell knows how to keep his mouth shut."

After a very long beat of hesitation, she finally nods, a tiny smile lifting her lips. "I haven't been to a club in ages."

I lift my hand from the phone. "We're in."

"We?"

"I'm bringing a friend."

"Nice. Meet you there in an hour?"

"Sounds good." I hang up to find Allie in distress. "What's wrong?"

"I didn't bring anything clubby to wear." She chews on her bottom lip. "Can we stop in Brooklyn first so I can change, or is that too much of a hassle?"

"No need," I say, tugging her off the bed. "You can borrow something from my sister. You're about Summer's size."

"Are you sure she won't mind?" Allie frets as I usher her across the hall into my sister's room. "Some girls get super touchy about lending out their clothes."

"Trust me, she won't care."

Allie's face fills with astonishment when we enter Summer's closet. And by closet, I mean the cavernous room that's almost the size of Allie's brownstone.

"How is this a *closet*?" Allie exclaims. She moves forward and squeals. "Oh my God. She's got an entire *wall* of shoes. Now I want to punch your sister."

I chuckle. "I wouldn't try it. Summer plays by schoolyard rules. She'll claw your eyes and rip your hair out."

Allie examines another rack overflowing with hangers. "If I check any of these tags, am I going to see words like 'Prada' and 'Kors' and 'Lagerfeld'?"

"Yup."

"Then please direct me to the cheap section so your sister doesn't kill me if I spill something on her precious Versace."

"Babe, you really need to trust me when I say she won't mind. Or notice, for that matter. Summer left all this stuff behind when she went to Brown," I remind Allie. "Not to mention all the clothes in her closet in Connecticut. Just pick whatever you'd like."

"Okay then. Well, since I probably won't get the chance to wear a Valentino dress ever again—until I get one custom designed for the Oscars"—that gets another laugh from me—"I pick this one." She holds up a black lace minidress with a gaping neckline, then glances at the shoe wall. "And I'll pair it with…ooh, are those Jimmy Choos?"

"And that's my cue to leave," I announce. "Come find me when you're ready."

I leave Allie to fawn over Summer's closet and go to my own room to get dressed. Which takes all of five minutes. I throw on a gray sweater and the same trousers I wore last night, then lie on my bed watching YouTube videos on my phone while I wait for Allie. Somewhere at the twenty-minute mark, she pops into the room in a blur of designer black, grabs a small makeup kit from her purse, and disappears into my bathroom.

"Oh hey!" she calls a few minutes later. Her head pokes out from behind the doorway. "My friend Dillon just texted. She got in last night and she wants to meet up. Her boyfriend's here too. Can I invite them to the club?"

"Sure, go ahead."

My phone buzzes, and I shut off YouTube so I can access my messages.

> Logan: Just found the perfect Xmas present for you in Boston.

A photo promptly appears, summoning a loud groan from my throat. The asshole sent me a pic of a novelty My Little Pony dildo. Damn thing is bright pink, with rainbow sparkles on the handle.

> Logan: And it's rechargeable! You don't have to buy batteries. THAT'S handy!
> Me: Hardy-har-har. You = comedian.

Then I message Grace: Tell your BF to stop being mean to me. She texts back a smiley face. Traitor.

"I'm ready."

My head snaps up, and holy hell, I forget how to breathe for a moment. Man, she should consider ditching acting and becoming a makeup artist, because this girl has the ability to completely transform depending on what she does to her face. Just when I got used to thinking of her as the girl-next-door type, with her subtle makeup and shiny lip glosses, she suddenly showed up at Malone's looking like a wet dream come to life, with big smoky eyes and pouty crimson lips.

Tonight it's a combination of the two—natural with a splash of glamour. Nude lips, shimmery gold eye shadow, and mascara that makes her lashes appear impossibly long.

"How do I look?" She plants a hand on her hip and does a sexy pose.

"Ridiculously fuckable." I hop off the bed and zero in on her, drawing her body toward mine as I bend down to give her a quick kiss. Her scent fills my nostrils. I breathe deeply, trying to identify it. Strawberries? Mangos? Roses? I can't figure it out, but it's goddamn addictive.

"What is it?"

I'm startled to find her frowning at me. "What do you mean?"

Her frown deepens. "You were staring at me."

I was? Shit, I hadn't even realized it. "Sorry, I must have spaced out." I paste on a careless smile, doing my best to ignore the weird flutter in my stomach.

And the funny little shiver racing up my spine.

And the way my chest somehow feels both tight and light at the same time, which is as perplexing as Allie's unnameable scent.

Swallowing, I force myself to ignore the paradox in my chest and follow Allie's sexy ass out the door.

CHAPTER 23

ALLIE

I'm nervous about Beau Maxwell's reaction to me and Dean showing up together, but it turns out to be unnecessary. Beau doesn't even blink when Dean introduces me as "G's GF's BFF." Maybe all the letters Dean threw out confused him? Either way, he just seems thrilled that we came out to the club at all.

Beau's sister, Joanna, is equally overjoyed, throwing her arms around Dean. "Di Laurentis! Oh, thank God you're here. You don't understand how close I've come to killing my idiot brother these past couple days."

"Nah, you don't want to kill me," Beau says with a broad grin. "You love your little brother and you know it."

Joanna gives him the finger, but she's grinning too. She's as attractive as Beau, tall and statuesque with sparkling blue eyes and dark hair cut in a short bob. Dean told me she currently has a small role in a Broadway show, which is the first thing I ask her about as we head inside after going through the line. By which I mean skipping it altogether, because one word in the bouncer's ear from Dean and the velvet rope magically lifts for us.

Inside, the strobe lights are going strong and the music is deafening. Joanna and I need to scream our lungs out in order to continue our conversation. Dean and Beau, who were walking ahead of us, are immediately swallowed up by the frenzied mob.

"We lost the boys," I shout in Joanna's ear.

She shakes her head and points at the spiral staircase to our left. Sure enough, the guys are ascending the metal steps. Dean glances over his shoulder, finds us in the crowd, and gestures for us to follow them.

I discover that the staircase leads to the VIP area. We reach the top in time to hear Dean address the beefy bouncer manning the rope. "Dean Heyward," he shouts. "Tony knows me."

The bouncer touches the tiny Bluetooth tucked in his ear. His lips move, but I can't make out what he's saying. A second later, our little group saunters past yet another velvet rope.

Fortunately, the music isn't as loud up here, so I don't need to shriek like a banshee anymore. "Dean Heyward?" I tease. "Are we not using Di Laurentis anymore?"

He slings his arm around me, and the spicy scent of his aftershave infuses my senses, making me shiver. "Di Laurentis works better at country clubs or charity benefits. The Heyward name opens more doors in Manhattan."

It sure does. Not only do we have access to the VIP lounge, but we're given a spacious table by the wrought-iron railing that overlooks the dance floor. I take out my phone to check if Dillon texted—yep. She and her boyfriend will be here soon. I tell her to come upstairs when they arrive, then refocus on the conversation around me.

Joanna is teasing her brother about someone named Sabrina, but he's insisting the relationship is over, which seems to upset his sister.

"You're such an idiot. Seriously, Beau-Beau, you needed someone like her to keep you in line."

Since Dean still has his arm around me, it's impossible not to feel it when he stiffens. I study the hard set of his profile and lightly squeeze his thigh. "You okay?"

"Ah, don't mind him, sweetheart," Beau says with a chuckle. "He always gets like this when the subject of Sabrina comes up. I think he's still sulking that she snubbed him after they boned down."

I'm not surprised to hear that Dean slept with this girl, whoever she is. What I am surprised about is my complete lack of jealousy.

The same thing happened during our drive to the city. Listening to Dean talk about "silent comers" and past hookups hadn't upset me, not the way it had the night I saw Penelope pawing him at Malone's. But I hadn't felt threatened this time around. Maybe because they were clearly memories for him and not present-day specters that could interfere with whatever we have going on? I'm not entirely sure what the reason is, but I like this odd, unexpected trust I have in him.

In the seat beside me, Dean is rolling his eyes in response to Beau's taunt. "Trust me, I'm happy to be snubbed."

I wait for him to elaborate. When he doesn't, it heightens my curiosity, so I poke him in the side and say, "Spill, sweetie. I want to hear about this blood feud you've got going on." As Hannah can attest, I'm too nosy for my own good.

"So do I," Beau says honestly.

Dean waves it off. "It was just some stupid bullshit in sophomore year. No big deal."

"Obviously it is if it still bothers you two years later," I point out.

Reluctance creases his forehead. "Long story short? I was struggling in a course, but every time I thought I failed a test or wrote a shitty paper, I'd get an A on it. Me being a total moron, I didn't connect it to the fact that I was banging my TA."

Beau snickers. "Love it."

I sigh. "Oh boy."

"I know, it was a stupid move," Dean says penitently. "Anyway, Sabrina and I were paired up on the final project. We each did half the work and it was graded separately. My half was C-material at best and we both knew it, except then our grades came back and I got an A. Sabrina got a B-minus." His jaw tightens. "She was pissed.

She went to the professor to bitch about it, and he ended up reread-ing every paper I turned in and every test I took—all graded by the TA I was screwing. Turned out I should have been failing the class. But I was acing it."

Dean sounds so disgusted it startles me. Before we hooked up, I assumed he was the kind of guy who breezed through life on a free pass because of his looks and money. This story corroborates that. But the anger in his voice reveals something else—he doesn't *want* the free pass.

"I couldn't stomach it," he admits, confirming my suspicions. "I told the prof to give me the F. I was perfectly willing to retake the course over the summer. But the bastard wouldn't fail me."

"Why not?" Joanna speaks up, both indignant and bewildered.

"He knew my father," Dean mutters. "They went to law school together, and he told me he'd look the other way as a favor to my dad. I said no way. We argued for a while, until he finally agreed to lower the grade to a B-plus. It was the 'best he could do.'"

Dean's expression is darker than a storm cloud. "I should've failed that fucking course, but the Di Laurentis name bought me a pass, and Sabrina never lets me forget it. She thinks I'm a rich asshole who gets whatever he wants." His tone grows dismissive again. "Whatever. She can think what she wants. Only matters what I think, right?"

I see right through the careless smile he flashes. It bothers him that people think he's a wealthy playboy who has everything handed to him on a silver platter. And yes, I do recognize that side of him—the Life of Dean is pretty fucking sweet—but I've also seen other facets of his personality this past month.

He's tenacious. Seriously, this guy never, ever gives up when he wants something.

He cares about his friends and teammates. Hell, I didn't see him on Monday and Tuesday this week because he'd requested extra ice time so he could help some guy named Hunter hone his skills.

He owns more books than the public library in Brooklyn, and I can tell from their wear and tear that he's actually read all of them.

He—

"Your purse."

My head lifts up. "What about it?"

Dean gestures to the black clutch on the bench seat between us. "It's vibrating."

I shake myself out of the bizarre Why Dean Is So Great list I was composing and snap open the clutch to find my phone buzzing.

I set down my rum and Coke. "My friends are here. Will you come get them with me? I might need you to talk to the bouncer again."

He gives an exaggerated sigh. "I knew it. You're just using me for my connections."

"Yep," I answer cheerfully.

We head back to the staircase, and I squeal when I spot a familiar face behind the rope.

"They're with us," Dean tells the bouncer.

A moment later, there's a teeny, equally excited brunette hurling herself into my arms. "Oh my God! It's *so* good to see you!" shrieks my best friend from high school. "You don't fucking call me enough!"

I grin and say, "It takes two to tango," and then we're happily hugging again until I notice the shadow looming over us.

Dillon disentangles herself from the embrace and introduces us to her boyfriend. "This is Roy."

Last time we spoke on the phone, she mentioned she was dating a football player. I would've guessed it even if she hadn't told me. At least six seven, with arms as thick as tree trunks and thighs that are bigger than my torso. And either I'm imagining it, or he looks exactly like—

"Dude, anyone ever tell you that you look like a young Samuel L. Jackson?" Dean demands, stealing the words right out of my mouth.

Roy's massive shoulders set in a rigid line. "Ah, I get it. All Black people look the same to you and the only reference you have are celebrities, right?"

My alarmed gaze flies to Dillon, because the menacing glare twisting Roy's features is downright terrifying. And his voice is deeper than the bass line thudding through the club.

"What next?" Roy growls. "Do you think there's something wrong with me dating a white woman? Is that what you're saying?"

Dean is unfazed. "Yeah, you got me, man. I'm a huge racist." He shakes his head incredulously as he continues to stare at Roy. "But for real, it's uncanny. You look *exactly* like him."

I'm seconds away from clapping my hand over Dean's mouth before this behemoth snaps him like a twig, but to my astonishment, Roy's ominous expression dissolves.

"I'm just playing with you, bro. I get it all the time." Roy breaks out in a huge grin. "I won ten grand last summer at a celebrity impersonation contest—first place for my Sam Jackson. I did the speech from *Deep Blue Sea*, right before the shark gets 'im."

"Nice. Great film."

Roy slaps Dean on the arm and says, "You're all right."

Just like that, they're best friends, talking animatedly as they charge ahead.

Dillon sighs and links her arm through mine. "Roy likes to scare people," she apologizes.

I snicker. "Don't worry, Dean doesn't scare easily."

"Dean, huh?" Her eyes light up. "Why didn't you tell me you had a new boyfriend?"

"Because I don't. We're just having some fun. Nothing serious."

"Ha! Yeah right, AJ. With you, it's *always* serious."

Not this time, I want to say, but we've reached the table and the guys' voices drown out our conversation. Beau and Roy are already talking football, and because the latter is so damn enormous, he takes up at least three people's worth of space on the bench-style seat. Dillon slides in beside him, which leaves zero room for me.

Grinning, Dean tugs me into his lap and winds one strong arm around my waist. "You can sit right here, baby doll."

"Aw, thanks, honey pie."

The six of us make such an unlikely group that I suddenly have scenes from *The Breakfast Club* flashing in my mind. Beau the East Coast quarterback. Dean the hockey player. Roy the linebacker from Louisiana. Joanna the Broadway actress. Dillon the finance major. And me, the future star of rom-coms.

Despite that, there's no shortage of conversation. Dillon and I fill each other in on what we've been up to the past few months. Since I started college, I've lost touch with most of my high school friends, but Dillon's friendship is one I was determined to preserve.

As I chat with her, I'm very aware of the fact that Dean is touching me. Constantly. Stroking my shoulder. Grazing my thigh. Nuzzling my neck. At one point he even brushes his lips over my cheek, which summons a loud hoot from Beau.

"Jesus, Bella," he marvels. He's highly amused as he meets my eyes. "What kind of spell did you cast on my man Dean? I've never seen him like this with a chick before."

"My name's Allie," I correct.

That makes him laugh harder.

Dean sighs, then leans in close and murmurs, "Wanna dance?"

"Depends… Are you a good dancer?"

"Every man is a good dancer."

I snort. "The broken toe I got in high school begs to differ."

"Sorry, what I should've said is—every man is *capable* of being a good dancer." His hands lock around my waist as he lifts me to my feet. "There's just one move a man needs to know in order to rock it on the dance floor."

"Yeah? What's the move?" I ask curiously.

Dean twines his fingers through mine as we descend the staircase. "STAG." He has to shout his answer, because the music is louder down here.

I stand on my tiptoes so my mouth is close to his ear. "What's STAG?"

"The only one of Logan's crazy acronyms I live my life by— STAG." His mouth stretches in a broad smile. "Stand There and Grind."

Laughter bubbles out of my throat, turning into a shriek of delight when Dean hauls me into his arms. I wrap my legs around his waist and hold on tight as he carries me to the dance floor. Then he sets me on my feet, presses his delectable body against mine, and proves that STAG really is the only move that matters.

As the sultry, pulse-pounding beat snakes its way into my blood, I toss my hair and shake my hips and run my hands up and down Dean's rippled chest. The strobe light flashes through the dark club, offering tantalizing glimpses of Dean's chiseled features, his hypnotic green eyes, the sensual curve of his mouth.

We dance for hours. Or at least it feels like hours. The others join us on the dance floor, and I can't remember the last time I had this much fun. I dance with Beau, who grabs my ass every chance he gets. I dance with Roy, who has some sick moves for a man mountain. I dance sandwiched between Dillon and Joanna. I dance with Dean, and the erotic grinding of his hips makes me hot and achy and utterly blissful.

Dillon and I sling back two shots at the bar, but I'm not drunk, just deliciously buzzed. Dean seems to be taking it easy too, but the others are definitely on their way to getting plastered. Especially Beau, whose cheeks are flushed and eyes are bright as he vertical-sexes a gorgeous redhead on the dance floor.

Joanna begs off around eleven thirty, saying she has an early rehearsal in the morning. Dillon and Roy follow suit soon after; the moment Dillon starts slurring her speech, Roy proves to be not only a responsible adult but a conscientious boyfriend and promptly whisks her away. Around midnight, after Beau staggers up looking more wasted than ever, Dean decides it's time for us to go too.

"Where's your friend?" I ask Beau, peering past his shoulder in search of the redhead.

"Went home to her husband."

I fight a laugh. Dean, who's pretty much the only thing holding Beau upright at this point, snickers loudly.

We exit the club and step into the frigid night air. Beau is leaning on me now because Dean is at the curb hailing us a taxi. With Joanna gone, I'm worried about Beau getting home safely, so I insist he share a cab with us.

"You should go upstairs with him," I tell Dean. "Make sure he gets all the way to his door."

A cab miraculously appears. I slide in first, followed by Beau, who groans, closes his eyes, and proceeds to pass out with his head on my shoulder.

Dean gets in and rattles off Beau's address to the cabbie. He looks at his sleeping friend, then meets my gaze over Beau's head.

"His parents are home, right?" I say slowly. "Will they freak out if they see him like this?"

"Maybe." Dean sighs. "Beau says they're kinda strict. He went to all-boys Catholic schools his whole life."

I bite my lip. "Maybe we shouldn't take him home, then."

"Probably not." Dean leans forward and taps the driver's seat. "Forget the first address. Just take us to Heyward Plaza, please." He glances back at me. "I'll let him sleep it off in the penthouse."

Fifteen minutes later, we're in the hotel elevator. It's weird, but a few measly hours at the nightclub and somehow I've already forgotten that Dean lives in a fricking palace. I'm once again amazed by my luxurious surroundings, and so is Beau, whose blue eyes widen when he stumbles out of the elevator.

His jaw falls open as he stares at the endless wall of windows that overlook the sparkling city skyline. "Holy shit. I feel like a prince."

"I know, right?" I say to him.

Still shaking his head in astonishment, he staggers toward the huge armchair near the C-shaped leather sectional and collapses on it. Within seconds, he's snoring.

Dean wraps his arms around me from behind and kisses my neck. "Bedtime?" he asks.

I twist around. "I'm not tired," I confess. "Do you feel like watching a movie?"

"Actually, I've got something even better." He waggles his brows enticingly. "Go change into something comfy. I'll get it set up."

Get what set up? And I hope *comfy* actually means *comfortable* and that he's not expecting me to come back in a lace teddy and garter belt.

I left my overnight bag in Dean's room, so I quickly dash up the stairs to the third floor—I still can't believe this place has three fucking floors—and change into cotton boxers and a tank top. When I return to the living room, I find Dean sprawled on the couch with the remote in hand. He's shirtless. Shocking. But his low-slung trousers show off the sexy vee of his hips, and my tongue tingles with the urge to lick all that delicious man flesh.

I moisten my suddenly dry lips and walk toward him. "What are we watching?"

"See for yourself." He clicks the remote, and I gasp when the opening credits of *Solange* flash on the largest screen I've ever seen outside a movie theater.

"How is this on?" I exclaim.

"I called ahead before we left Briar and asked the concierge to track down season two for us."

I'm dumbfounded. After I'd randomly stumbled on this show while surfing YouTube, I paid a girl in my dorm to download all the episodes and burn them for me. *Solange* is huge in France, but nobody here has heard of it, which means it's nearly impossible to find online, and ordering the DVDs off Amazon is pointless because they only work on European players.

"You made one phone call and got your hands on an obscure

French soap opera?" I stare at him. "Fuck. The Life of Dean is truly glorious."

"Told ya." Stretching out on his back, he raises one hand and beckons me.

I waste no time snuggling up beside him and resting my head on his shoulder. His bare chest is warm and sturdy, and he smells heavenly. I don't bother asking what kind of aftershave he uses, because it's probably something I've never heard of that costs a thousand bucks a drop.

We lie there for a while watching the show, which now features a whole slew of new characters who are causing trouble for Solange.

"You know," Dean muses, "if Marc had half a brain, he'd dump Christine and hook up with Monique."

"I like Christine," I protest. "She's sweet."

"She's conning him, babe. Nobody is that sweet all the time."

"*I* am."

Dean's snort vibrates against my cheek. "Yeah right. You're maybe twenty percent sweet. Tops."

I pretend to be hurt. "Do you really think that?" I ask in a small voice.

He strokes a soothing hand down my spine. "Nah," he says gruffly. "Don't worry. You're one hundred percent sweet."

"Ha. I wasn't worried in the slightest. Just wanted to hear you say that."

He chuckles and holds me closer. As the episode unfolds, we get more engrossed in it, falling silent to watch. Dean is absently caressing me, his long fingers grazing the side of my boob with each slow stroke of his hand. I don't think he even realizes he's doing it, but it makes me feel…fine, it's making me horny.

"I'm telling you, she's up to something." Dean's green eyes are focused on the TV, but his hand keeps stroking.

On the screen, Christine sits at a table at an outdoor bistro, whispering into her cell phone. The conversation seems pleasant enough. Then again, it's in French, so who knows.

"I bet you she's hiring a contract killer." Dean's thumbnail grazes my nipple.

I'm now thoroughly distracted.

He's still talking away.

"We need to find a version of this show with English subtitles."

His thumb moves away from my nipple, then eases toward it again.

"I get you're trying to learn the language, babe, but it's driving me nuts not knowing what's going on—"

"Dean."

"Mmm?"

"Stop doing that."

"Stop doing what?"

"Touching my boob."

"Oh. Was I doing that?"

I prop myself up on my elbow so I can see his face. His impish expression tells me he wasn't as oblivious as I thought.

"You knew exactly what you were doing," I chide. "And now you need to stop doing it."

His tongue comes out to lick his lips. "Why? Is it getting you all worked up?"

"Yes."

He responds with a deep chuckle, then rolls us over so we're lying on our sides facing each other. He cups my left breast and squeezes gently. This time when his fingertips find my nipple, it's with absolute purpose. He rubs the rapidly hardening bud. Then he releases my breast and slides his hand inside my boxers.

I cast an alarmed glance in Beau's direction. He's not snoring anymore, but his eyes are still closed.

"Beau's sitting right there," I hiss at Dean.

"He's asleep." His fingers tease the waistband of my panties, then dip beneath it. When his thumb presses on my clit, I have to bite my lip so I don't moan.

"Dean," I murmur nervously.

"Allie," he murmurs back.

The pad of his thumb gently circles my clit, sending a hot shiver racing up my spine. He rubs and teases until I'm swollen, aching, and my hips involuntarily hitch forward, seeking deeper contact. He chuckles again.

"Dean…" It's a warning.

"Allie." It's a taunt.

His hand moves lower, the calloused palm scraping my pussy on its descent. One talented finger slips inside me. A cross between a breath, a sigh, and a groan escapes my lips, but it's instantly cut off when Dean presses his lips to mine.

I kiss him back hungrily, helpless to resist him. Dean Di Laurentis is in my blood now. I didn't expect the intense sexual chemistry between us, but it's here, and it's addictive and I don't know how I can ever give it up. He grinds the heel of his hand against my clit, and the delicious pressure has my thighs clenching together. Pleasure gathers between my legs, making my entire body tremble.

I'm far too aware of the sounds we're making. Our heavy breathing. The wet glide of his finger moving inside me. I pray to God that Beau isn't a light sleeper.

"I always know when you're getting close," Dean whispers.

"How?" The methodical thrust of his finger is distracting. I start to squirm, my inner muscles bearing down on him as the pleasure intensifies and dances along my heated flesh.

"Your cheeks turn bright red, and your eyes…they glaze over." His warm mouth skates over my jaw before traveling down my neck. "Your pulse throbs…right here"—he licks the center of my throat—"and your pussy squeezes me so fucking tight, like it's trying to trap my finger inside of it."

My breaths go shallow. My mind is foggy. His deep voice and magical hand are all I'm able to focus on, but when he curls his finger and starts moving it faster, my brain shuts down completely.

"That's it," Dean says hoarsely. "Come for me, baby."

I close my eyes and let the sensations take over, gasping softly as the pressure finally releases and I float away on a cloud of bliss. Sighing, I rest my cheek against his pecs while lingering flutters of pleasure sweep through my body.

"You guys know I'm awake, right?"

Beau's wry voice triggers a rush of horror mingled with the burn of embarrassment. I bury my face against Dean's chest, too mortified to look over at the armchair.

"And now I'm hard as a rock," Beau adds in a jaunty voice. "So I'm just gonna go ahead and ask—any chance of a threesome?"

My head lifts in indignation, but I can't help but laugh when I see the intrigued gleam in Dean's eyes.

"Don't even think about it," I order, jabbing my finger into his chest. I sit up to fix Beau with the same stern look. "Erase that idea from your pretty head, Maxwell. Because it's not happening."

His smile is downright saucy. "Tonight, or ever?"

"Ever."

"Give me one good reason why not," Beau challenges.

"Because a) I don't want to, and b) picture this: It's ten years from now. I'm a Hollywood A-lister, a three-time Academy Award winner, the most sought-after actress ever to grace the silver screen... and then the latest issue of *People* magazine hits the stands. And you know what the headline reads?" I move my hand through the air as if I'm spelling out the headline. "'Celebrity Debauchery Exposed. Allie Hayes, College Threesome Queen.'"

Beau spells out his own headline. "'Super Bowl Champ Beau Maxwell Quoted as Saying "Best Night of My Life."'"

I sigh and turn to Dean, who's clearly trying not to laugh. "And *now* it's time for bed. Say good night to your friend Beau, sweetie."

"Good night, Beau," Dean says obediently.

CHAPTER 24

ALLIE

DEAN AND I ARRIVE BACK AT CAMPUS AT NOON THE NEXT DAY.
Since the team bus leaves at one o'clock for their game in Burlington,
he should be hightailing it out of the parking lot if he wants to go
home and change first. But he stays rooted in the driver's seat.

"What's wrong?" I can't decipher his expression.

"Can I see you tonight?" His voice is husky, and there's an
inexplicable chord of...something...in it.

"I have rehearsal, so it depends on when Steven lets us out. Call
me when you're back from Vermont and we'll see where I'm at?"

He nods. Still doesn't move.

"Do you mind helping me with my suitcase?"

Another nod.

I fight a pang of uneasiness as we get out of the car. There's no one
in the parking lot to see us unload my bag, but that isn't what's making
me apprehensive. It's the intensity Dean is radiating. It's like he wants
to say something but doesn't know how to broach the subject.

"Everything okay?" I ask lightly.

Those green eyes sweep over me so intently that I feel self-
conscious. I know my hair is a wavy mess, and I'm pretty sure there's
a tiny zit forming on my chin. I hope that's not what he's staring at.

"All good, baby doll," he finally says, snapping out of whatever deep thoughts he'd been having. "C'mere and give me a good-luck kiss. We desperately need to win this game today."

My gaze flits around the lot. A slight frown touches Dean's lips, and seeing it triggers a flash of guilt. We just spent three days together. We fooled around in front of Beau, for crying out loud, and I'm afraid to kiss him in an empty parking lot?

I bridge the distance and lean on my tiptoes to brush my lips over his. "Good luck," I whisper. Then I slip him a little tongue and smile when his breath catches.

He groans softly. "Tease."

My smile widens as I take a step back. "Thanks for the ride. And the night out."

"And the dirty, dirty sex," he reminds me.

"One dirty would've sufficed." Except nope, I'm wrong. What we did this weekend requires *at least* two dirties. Four would probably be the right amount.

"You sure you can manage that thing?" he asks as I roll my overstuffed suitcase toward the path.

"I'm fine. It has wheels."

"What about the stairs?"

"It's fine," I insist. "Go, Dean, otherwise you'll miss your bus."

Just as I give him a gentle shove to spur his sexy ass into gear, a familiar voice echoes behind us.

"Hey, Allie."

My hand freezes against Dean's chest. I quickly let it drop to my side, then turn around to greet the approaching figure. It's Jim Paulson, one of Sean's frat brothers. My nerves flutter in my belly as I wonder how much he heard. And saw...

Shit. Did he see me kiss Dean?

"Hi," I say, forcing a smile. "How was your Thanksgiving?"

"It was all right." Jim's gaze flicks toward Dean. "Hey, man."

"Hey," Dean says tightly.

"Where are you guys coming from?" His unmistakably suspicious gaze lands on my suitcase.

"New York," I answer casually. "Dean's from Manhattan and I'm from Brooklyn, so we carpooled. Go, environment!" I pretend to wave a little flag, but Jim doesn't even crack a smile.

"Cool." He continues to study me. "Uh, so yeah…nice seeing you."

His parting smile is friendly enough, but as I watch him walk away, I can't control the ball of dread that lodges in my throat. Fuck. I have a very, very bad feeling about this encounter. There's no doubt in my mind that Jim will tell Sean about it. A part of me doesn't care, because Sean's not my boyfriend anymore.

Even so, the anxiety eddying in my stomach refuses to go away, and I know I'm going to be worrying about this all fricking day. Waiting for the other shoe to drop.

THE SHOE DROPS AT ONE IN THE MORNING. IT DROPS HARD. NO, IT drops *loudly*. As in, I'm rudely awakened from a deep sleep to noisy pounding on the door.

I sit up and frantically look around, because it takes my not-yet-alert brain a few seconds to comprehend what's going on. Once it registers that the sounds are coming from the front door, I fly out of my bedroom and stagger into the common area. Two shadowy figures stumble out of Hannah's room at the same time. My sleepy roommate and her boyfriend halt abruptly when they spot me.

Bang.

Bang bang bang.

"What the hell?" Garrett sounds groggy as he turns his head toward the noise.

My pulse speeds up when I hear Sean's voice.

"Allie!" he shouts from behind the door. "I know you're in there! Let me in, goddamn it!"

Just like that, Garrett is wide-awake and marching to the door.

I squeak in alarm, but he doesn't open it—he simply pounds his fist against it a couple times. "Shut the hell up, asshole. You're going to wake up everyone on the floor."

"Like I give a shit!" comes Sean's furious reply. "I need to talk to Allie."

"Then pick up the phone and call her like a normal, *sane* person," Garrett snaps. "And do it tomorrow morning. Allie's asleep."

Hannah moves beside me and rests a hand on my arm. My skin is ice-cold and I know she feels it, because she gives a soft, comforting stroke. "Garrett will get rid of him," she whispers.

But she's underestimated Sean's stubbornness. "She's not asleep," he snaps back. "I know my girlfriend—"

Ex-girlfriend! I almost yell.

"—and she's standing right behind the fucking door. I know she is." The pounding picks up again. *Bang. Bang bang bang.* "Allie! Open the door! We need to talk!"

I flinch. Hannah wraps one arm around my shoulders.

"Bang on this door one more time and I'm calling the fucking cops," Garrett hisses out.

Bang bang bang.

My throat squeezes shut. Goddamn it. He won't go away. I know he won't, and I'm suddenly overcome with visions of campus security and a police brigade swarming Bristol House like a SWAT team taking out a bank robber. Which wouldn't just be mortifying but completely disruptive. From that point on, everyone in this dorm will think of me as the chick with the insane ex-boyfriend.

"Let him in," I say weakly.

Garrett whirls around, his gray eyes blazing. "No fucking way, Allie. He's drunk."

"I know, but he'll calm down once he's inside." My shoulders droop unhappily. "He'll stay out there all night, Garrett. Just let him in and I'll talk him down. I can handle this, I promise."

Hannah's boyfriend remains skeptical. I don't blame him. Sean is absolutely acting like a crazy person right now. But I spent four years with the guy, and I know he's all bark and no bite. He would never hurt me in the physical sense.

Garrett points a finger at me. "If he tries anything, I'll beat the shit out of him."

I nod.

Cursing under his breath, he flicks the lock and eases the door open. I half expect Sean to barrel inside and do a somersault before popping to his feet, like an army commando on a mission. But he enters with slow, labored steps that match his ragged breathing. His brown eyes instantly seek me out.

"We need to talk," he mutters.

Garrett has glued himself to Sean's side. Hannah has glued herself to mine.

I gulp nervously, easing myself out of my best friend's grip. "Can you guys give us a minute?"

"Absolutely not." Garrett's expression is awash with disbelief.

"Please. It's okay. We're just going to talk." I shoot Sean a pointed look. "Right?"

His jaw tightens, but he nods. "Right. Just wanna talk."

Several seconds drag by. Then Garrett swears again and scowls at Sean. "Don't do anything stupid, man. You so much as look at her the wrong way and the only thing you'll be talking to is my fist."

Sean's head dips in another nod. Hannah's boyfriend has about five inches and fifty pounds on him, and it's obvious Sean takes the threat seriously.

Hannah squeezes my arm. "We'll be in my room. Shout if you need us."

I don't think it'll reach that point. Sean seems to have calmed down, his breathing steady, his gaze no longer burning with malice. The moment Hannah's door closes, he sinks onto the couch and makes a low, agonized noise.

"Dean Di Laurentis?" he moans, and the hurt and betrayal

flashing in his eyes cuts into me like a dull blade. "Are you kidding me, Allie?"

My pulse races as I step closer. I don't sit beside him. I stand in front of him, knees locked, arms crossed tight to my chest, because my whole body is shaking so hard it's the only way to stop from swaying on my feet. I don't know what to say, so I say nothing.

"Are you together?" His voice suddenly drips with icy revulsion.

I swallow, unable to form any words. Why does he still have this kind of power over me? He always knows exactly which buttons to push, exactly how much disgust and disapproval to inject into his tone in order to make me feel guilty, to make me feel awkward, to make me feel awful.

"Are you?" he demands.

I force my vocal cords to cooperate. "Yes and no. We're not a couple. We're..."

"Sleeping together," Sean finishes tersely.

I nod, which brings another flash to his eyes.

"So he's just your fuck buddy, is that it?" A hiss escapes his mouth. "You don't have fuck buddies! You're not like that."

My skin tightens with offense. "Like what?"

"The kind of girl who sleeps around. We waited *four months* before we slept together for the first time. Since when do you hop into bed with someone after a few days? Or was it hours? How fast did you jump on Di Laurentis's dick?"

I wince as if he's struck me. I can tell he's drunk because of his ruddy cheeks and hazy eyes, but he's not slurring his words, and each one fires out like a bullet, hitting its mark and reigniting the discomfort I've always felt toward casual sex.

"And of all the guys you could've chosen, you chose *him*? Do you realize how many bitches he's stuck his dick in? He fucking lives in the campus health center, with all the STD meds he has to take!"

I stiffen. "Stop it. You're acting like a total ass right now."

But Sean's not even close to being done. "Did you screw him when we were together?" he demands.

My jaw drops. "*No*. Of course not."

"And I'm just supposed to take your word for it?" He bolts to his feet. I take an instinctive step back, but he doesn't advance on me. He starts pacing the hardwood floor instead, raking his hands through his hair like he's trying to tear it out from the roots. "So now I fucking need to get tested? Is that it? I need an *STD test* because my girlfriend cheated on me with a dirty fucker like Di Laurentis?"

Anger rises in my throat. "I didn't cheat on you," I bite out. "And you're being ridiculous right now! You don't have an STD—"

"But *you* might," he cuts in, and then he starts to laugh, low and harsh. "You're sleeping with a slut. *You're* a slut."

I recoil at the cruel indictment, but somehow I manage to keep my breathing under control. Somehow I manage not to lunge at him and smack him in the face. "I'm not a slut," I say coldly. "And I didn't cheat on you. And now it's time for you to go."

"You know what? I'm *glad* you dumped me. I want nothing to do with you." His voice rises, and I cringe because I know Hannah and Garrett must hear him even with her door closed. "I was a fucking *idiot* for trying to win you back! Why the *fuck* would I want to get back together with a disease-ridden whore—"

"*That's enough!*"

Garrett's booming proclamation comes too little, too late. Sean's last remark has already done its intended damage. I stumble backward as if he'd just slapped me. God, he might as well have. My cheeks are burning. My bottom lip quivers wildly, and I have to dig my teeth into it to make it stop. I have to fight the strangled sob that's desperately trying to rip out of my throat.

I'm vaguely aware of Garrett grabbing my ex-boyfriend by the collar. Hauling him to the door. Hissing out a threat. But my face is on fire and my vision is fuzzy, making it difficult to focus on what's going on.

I jerk when I feel a pair of soft arms wrap around me. It's Hannah, hugging me tight. My head drops against her shoulder and I blink away the tears threatening to surface.

"Are you okay?" she asks urgently.

"No." My response is muffled against her sleeve.

"Garrett went downstairs with him. He's going to call a taxi and wait with Sean to make sure that fucker gets in the cab." She rubs both hands between my shoulder blades. "Allie. Talk to me. I need to know that you're all right, sweetie."

For some reason, the sympathy in her voice blows apart the last thread of my control. The tears spill over and stream down my cheeks. A sob flies out as I shudder in her embrace. How could he have said all those awful, hurtful things? We were together for years. He *loved* me. He *knows* me. He knows I'm not a…I choke on another sob…a *disease-ridden whore*.

As shame floods my body, I push away from Hannah and hurry to my bedroom. I hear her footsteps behind me, reaching my door just as I collapse on my bed. I curl up and swipe at my tears with the sleeve of my T-shirt, but they keep falling faster, stinging my eyelids and sliding into my mouth.

"Allie," Hannah says softly.

I ignore her, gulping through the sobs as I stick out a hand and fumble on the nightstand. I need… God, I need *Dean*. I need him to wrap his strong arms around me and give me that speech again, the one about erasing *slut* from my vocabulary and not letting small-minded people convince me I've done anything wrong.

My fingers collide with my phone and I moan when I discover it's dead.

"Allie." Hannah sounds exceedingly worried. "Talk to me."

I inhale a wobbly breath. "Can you do something for me?"

"Anything," she says instantly. "Just tell me what you need."

"Can you…" I speak through the tight lump in my throat. "Can you call Dean and ask him to come over?"

I don't check her face to gauge her reaction. I don't need to, because I hear the bewilderment loud and clear in her voice.

"Dean?" She pauses. "Dean Di Laurentis?"

"Yes." I curl up again, tucking my head against the pillow.

"You want me to call Dean."

"Yes."

"Dean Di Laurentis?"

"*Yes.*" I lick my dry lips, which are salty from my tears. Tears that won't fucking stop falling. "Please...just call him. I..." I feel my entire face collapsing again. "I need him."

CHAPTER 25

DEAN

"WHERE IS SHE?" I MUSCLE MY WAY PAST GARRETT BEFORE HE CAN even fully open the door. My gaze darts around the common room, but Allie isn't in here. Wellsy is, and she immediately shoots to her feet when she sees me.

"She's in her room—"

I charge forward, only to be intercepted by the petite brunette. "Hold on a second," Hannah orders, planting her palm against my chest. "You're not seeing her until you tell me what the *hell* is going on."

"You tell me," I snap impatiently. "You're the one who called me at 1:00 a.m. and told me to come over because Allie needs me. What happened?"

"Sean showed up," Garrett says grimly. "Drunk and pounding on the door and demanding to talk to her. I let him in—"

"You let him in?" I roar.

"She told me to," he mutters. "Said she could handle him."

Hannah speaks up angrily. "You should've heard the way he was shouting her. Calling her a slut and saying she has STDs—"

What the *fuck*?

Fury sizzles up my spine, ripped from my throat in the form of a menacing growl. "Get out of my way," I tell Hannah.

"Dean," she protests as I sprint toward the short hallway. "What are you even doing here—"

The thump of my footsteps drowns out the rest of that sentence. I burst into Allie's bedroom, then skid to a stop when I find her curled up on the bed. She lifts her head at my entrance, and the desolate look in her big blue eyes shreds my heart to pieces.

"Baby," I say softly.

A startled gasp sounds from the door. Gritting my teeth, I spin on my heel and proceed to slam the door in Hannah's and Garrett's astonished faces. They don't exist to me right now. Only Allie does, and I'm on the bed before she can blink, drawing her into my arms and cocooning her in them. She buries her face against my chest, and I can feel her trembling.

"What happened?"

"Sean was here." The answer is muffled against my hoodie.

"I know, G told me. But *why* was he here?" A curse slips out when I remember our run-in with Paulson this morning. "His frat brother… Paulson told him he saw us together?"

Her nod bumps her head on my collarbone.

"Asshole," I mutter. Then I take a breath and smooth my hand over her silky hair. "I take it Sean was pissed?"

"He…" Her voice cracks. "He called me a disease-ridden whore."

Red-hot fury slams into me like a cross-check to the chest. It takes every ounce of strength to push it away, to banish it from my body. I want to kill the bastard for saying that to her.

"You…are not"—I take another breath—"a disease-ridden whore. Do you hear me, baby? You are *not* that. Ever. I don't know why that son of a bitch would even—"

"Because of you," she whispers.

My hands clench into fists against her shoulders. "What?"

"He thinks you're riddled with STDs because you…have an active sex life—"

"I'm clean," I interrupt. My voice is low, rippling with anxiety.

Fuck, I really hope she believes me right now. "I've never had unprotected sex in my life, Allie. I got tested before the season started, but I can do it again if you—" I stop. Fuck that. I'll do it even if she doesn't ask me to, just to squash any seed of doubt that piece of shit Sean might have planted in her head.

"I trust you, Dean. I know you're safe, okay? It wasn't the disease part that upset me. It was the other part. The way he looked at me…" Her small body shudders. "He was so disgusted. It's like in that moment, he truly saw me as a whore and he hated me for it."

The fissure in my heart cracks wide open, sending jagged shards to my gut. Sean should be thanking his lucky stars he's not here right now. I want to wrap my fingers around his throat and squeeze the life out of him.

"Baby…" I swallow my rage. "Baby, look at me."

She slowly raises her eyes to mine.

"I don't give a shit what Sean says or what he thinks—you didn't do a goddamn thing to deserve his verbal attack, you got it? You're not a whore. You're…" *Perfect*, I almost say, but I don't get the chance, because she's trembling again.

"Then why do I feel like one?" She blinks rapidly, as if she's trying not to cry. "God. I hate this. I told you, I'm not cut out for casual sex."

My palms grow damp. I don't want her to continue. I'm too terrified of what she's going to say.

"I'm not sure I can do this anymore."

Fuck.

"It's too confusing. Sleeping with you when we're not actually together—"

"We're together," I bite out.

She startles. "What?"

It feels like someone jammed a handful of gravel in my throat. I gulp through it. "We're together," I repeat.

She looks baffled. "We… Why?"

"Because we are." A nonsensical response, but it's all I've got. I don't want this to end. I can't explain why, but I just know I don't want this to fucking end.

"You want…" The groove in her forehead deepens. "You want to be with me?"

My heartbeat grows erratic. I haven't had a conversation like this with a girl in years. Not since Miranda. But Allie isn't Miranda. Allie is… She's… Fuck, I can't make sense of my jumbled thoughts. Except for one. The bone-deep certainty that I *can't* let this end.

"Dean?"

I tighten my hold on her, burying my face in the crook of her neck. "I want to be with you," I mumble. "So that means we're fucking together, okay?"

Shaky laughter tickles my cheek. "You're freaking me out right now."

"I'm freaking myself out." Groaning, I lift my head and cup her delicate chin with both hands. "Why did you ask Wellsy to call me?"

Allie falters. "Because…" She bites her lip. "Because I wanted you to tell me that Sean is wrong. Because I needed…" She stumbles again, as if she's as freaked out by this as I am. Her uncertainty only makes me more certain.

I rub my thumb along the seam of her lips, soothing the tiny indentation she made with her teeth. "You want it too. To be with me?"

She's quiet for so long that I'm nervous again. Then she nods.

"Tell me why," I say gruffly. "I need to know it's not just because casual sex makes you feel slutty. That it's not just because you're insecure about everything Sean said."

Allie slowly runs one hand over my cheek. "It's not." Her fingertips scrape the bristles of stubble on my jaw. "I want to be with you because it feels right."

The tension in my chest dissipates, replaced by a strange rush of warmth I couldn't explain if I tried. We don't speak after that. Which is equally strange, this long inexplicable silence that doesn't need to be filled. I release her only so I can peel my sweater off, kick away my jeans. I reach out and click the bedside lamp.

Darkness falls over us. Allie gets under the covers. Without a word, she shifts over so there's room for me.

I slide in behind her, curling one arm around her slender body and drawing her closer. She makes a contented noise and snuggles her ass to my groin, her back to my chest. Her hair tickles my chin. I fall asleep to the sound of her soft breathing and the steady beating of her heart beneath my palm.

HANNAH AND GARRETT ARE IN THE SMALL KITCHENETTE WHEN I emerge from Allie's room the next morning. They're holding the most ridiculous pink mugs—Wellsy's has *ALLIE'S BFF!* scrawled on the front in a purple script font. Garrett's says *HAN-HAN'S BFF!*

I smother a laugh. Why do I get the feeling the custom mugs were Allie's doing?

Since I expected a cross-examination, I'm not surprised when they attack the moment they notice me.

"What kind of game are you playing with my best friend?"

"I *specifically* told you to keep your dick away from her, man."

I follow the aroma of freshly brewed coffee to the narrow counter. It's not even nine o'clock. I'm not awake enough to have this conversation yet.

Unfortunately, my pointed effort to ignore them has no effect. They keep firing questions at me as I pour myself some coffee.

"How long has this been going on?"

"Why didn't you fucking tell me?"

"Why didn't she tell me?"

"This is going to ruin our whole group dynamic, you know."

"You think so?" Hannah's attention is on Garrett now. "If it's just a fling, it probably won't change anything."

"Your girl doesn't do flings, babe. She's a nester."

It's the same observation I'd made about Allie on the drive to

New York, but hearing Garrett dissect the sexual habits of the girl I'm dating raises my hackles.

The girl I'm dating. Jesus. Never thought I'd be saying *that*. But it's the way it is, and I've decided to roll with it.

"Hey, I have an idea." I lean against the counter and stare at them over the rim of my mug. "How 'bout you guys mind your own business?"

Wellsy's jaw drops.

Garrett's eyebrows soar.

A choked laugh comes from the hallway. A moment later, Allie saunters into the main room. "Morning," she says casually.

There's a beat. "Morning," Hannah answers.

Allie approaches the counter and picks up the coffeepot. When she leans on her tiptoes to grab a mug from the top cupboard, I can't help but give her jutting ass a little smack.

Hannah glares at me.

Garrett shakes his head.

"What?" My expression is innocent.

Allie sips her coffee, then wraps both hands around the mug and addresses the room. "Okay. Real talk, guys." She glances at Hannah. "Dean and I are together. There. It's out in the open. You may now commence with the questions."

Hannah's mouth stays closed. For someone who'd had questions galore only moments ago, her silence is surprising. Worrying. Her troubled green eyes tell me she's not happy with this new arrangement.

"No? Nothing you want me to say?" Allie lifts the mug to her lips. "All righty then."

I hide a smile and turn to Garrett. "Hunter and I have an hour of ice time today. Coach signed off on it. You want to come?"

He rubs a hand over his jaw, scratching the dark stubble there. "You still giving Davenport pointers? Working one-on-one?"

I nod. "He's eager, works hard. But I think some tips from another forward will do him some good."

Garrett nods back. "Sure, I'll tag along. Wouldn't mind working with him on penalty killing. He made too many mistakes during that Burlington power play yesterday."

"At least we won the damn game."

"True. Our record still blows, though."

"It's a fucking bummer, man. My Hurricanes have a better record, and they're frickin' middle-schoolers."

"*Your* Hurricanes?" He grins. "Dude, admit it. You're in love with those kidlets."

"Fuck off. I just have fun coaching—"

"You both need to go!" Wellsy announces, a mix of annoyance and exasperation on her face.

Garrett is visibly hurt. "You're kicking me out?"

"I'm sorry, babe. I love you with all my heart, but it's time for some girl talk, and last I checked, you don't have a vagina. Therefore, you need to go." She scowls at me. "You too, Dean."

I know better than to argue with Hannah Wells when she's set her mind to something. She wants us gone, then gone we shall be.

I drain the rest of my coffee, place the empty cup in the sink, and glance at Allie. "I'll call you later?"

"Yep." She walks up and gives me a chaste kiss on the cheek, but there's no way I'm leaving without something a little more substantial. Capturing her chin in my hand, I tip her head back and press my mouth to hers. The kiss I give her is deep and hungry, involving a helluva lot of tongue and lasting long enough to make Hannah squawk.

"Okay, enough!" she orders.

As Allie and I break apart, I toss a grin in Wellsy's direction. "Oh, relax, baby doll. It's just a little French kissing between me and my girl. Nobody died."

Hannah's mouth falls open. Then she points to the door and growls, "*Out.*"

ALLIE

"His girl?" Hannah says the moment Dean and Garrett are out the door. "Explain yourself, Allison. I mean it. Explain. Yourself."

I swallow some more caffeine. I need to jump-start my brain if we're going to have this conversation right now. Though honestly, I'm not sure I *can* explain myself. I can't make heads or tails of this Dean thing either.

I guess I'm his girl?

Which means he's my guy?

Because we're a couple now?

Bottom line: I did not expect last night to end the way it did. After the way Sean completely lost it and treated me like a clump of dog shit under his shoe, I should've been ready to swear off all men, and somehow I wound up with a boyfriend. Life is fascinating sometimes.

"When did this happen?" Hannah's voice softens as she searches my face. "And why didn't you tell me?"

I shrug awkwardly. "I was embarrassed."

"Why would you be embarrassed?"

Sighing, I carry my coffee cup to the sofa and sink down on it. I tuck my legs under me and wait for Hannah to join me. "Because… because it's *Dean*. Dean Di Laurentis, the biggest player we know." I feel bad saying it, but I've always been honest with Hannah. "He's annoying and ridiculous and totally not my type."

Or at least that's what I used to believe, before I got to know him. Sure, he's still annoying and ridiculous more often than not, but there's so much more to Dean than I ever could've imagined.

Hannah purses her lips. "All right. Start from the beginning. When did this happen?"

"When do you think?" I say wryly. "The night I stayed over at their house."

Her face pales. "Oh God. So this is my fault? *I* did this to you?"

I burst out laughing. "No, I did it to myself. I got drunk and wound up in his bed. It's all on me."

"And now you guys are together?" She looks flabbergasted. "How is that even possible? You said so yourself—he's the biggest player we know. Why would you ever agree to date him?"

"Because I like him," I say simply.

"Are you sure we're not dealing with a rebound situation here?"

I shrug. "It might have started as one. I can't deny that Dean's attention made me feel good. It was...different from Sean's attention. Sean always needed me but in ways that I could never satisfy. Nothing I did was good enough for him. I was always making him angry and disappointing him, and a part of me knew we weren't right for each other, but...I like being in a relationship." Those last words hang between us like a giant anvil. I don't even have to look at Hannah to anticipate her next question.

"You sure you aren't rushing into a relationship because you *need* to be in one?" Her skepticism is digging a hole into what felt right last night, what even felt right this morning.

Stricken, I look at her. "I don't know. I tried to tell Dean no. After the first night we had sex"—mind-blowing, unforgettable, can't-stop-thinking-about-it sex—"he kept calling and texting begging for round two and I kept putting him off until it seemed stupid. I wanted him and he wanted me, so why not?"

"But you couldn't keep it just sex?"

I groan. "I tried, I really did, but I'm not wired that way, Han-Han. And I don't know how it happened, but I started enjoying more than just his magical dick." She snickers, but I keep going. "He's good to me. He's a great listener. He's fun to be around. The sex is off-the-charts amazing."

Wait, did I just put sex *fourth* on that list? Apparently so. But that's because...well, because sex isn't the first thing I think of anymore when I think of Dean. We've come a long way from just being two sweaty bodies on an orgasm quest. We've watched a French soap opera where, between us, we only understand every third word. We've danced together. We've hung out. He met my high school friend. He met my *dad*—

"And he's the first person you want to talk to when you're upset," Hannah adds shrewdly.

I press my lips together. Even if I wanted to, I couldn't deny what happened last night. My first instinct was to get Dean's arms around me, as if he was the only person who could make it all better. And he did. He soothed my hurt pride, my wounded feelings, and held me all night long. I wouldn't have slept a minute last night if he hadn't come over.

"Are you worried he's going to hurt me?" I ask with a sigh.

Hannah rubs the rim of her coffee cup a few times before answering. "No. I think I may need to worry about Dean. He's never rushed to anyone's side before. I'm not saying he's selfish. He's a good friend. But I know Garrett would call Logan before he'd call Dean."

"I don't know why," I say irritably. "Dean would give anyone the shirt off his back. No questions asked."

"Logan's reliable."

"And Dean isn't? Just because he's a little sex-obsessed doesn't make him unreliable!" A few lukewarm drops of coffee spill out as I slam the cup on the table.

Hannah bursts out laughing, her unwelcome sounds following me into the kitchen where I grab a few paper towels to clean up my mess.

"What's so funny?" I demand, tossing the damp towels in the trash.

"You and your needless defense of Dean." She rises from the sofa and joins me in the kitchen, giving my shoulder a small squeeze. "Look, if you want to be with Dean, then be with Dean. I'm just worried because you don't sleep with guys just for funsies. I'm not saying that sleeping with him right after breaking up with Sean is wrong or dishonorable in any way. It's just not *you*."

I sag against the counter. "I know it's not me. I keep telling myself that, but…I really like being with him, damn it."

"Are you in love with him?"

"No. I don't have that squishy feeling when it comes to him. Not like I had with…" I trail off. I was going to say *not like I had with Sean*, but I can't remember the last time I felt soft and warm toward Sean. The only feelings I remember having are ones of restraint, irritation, impatience, and, last night, hurt.

Hannah shoves a new cup of coffee in my hand. "Stop overthinking it and just see where it goes."

CHAPTER 26

ALLIE

Over the next week, I take Hannah's advice and try to turn off my brain. Dean and I start going out together as a couple. Nothing explicit is said. We don't wear little badges, but our interactions make it obvious.

When we're out, he's always touching me, but not in a way that makes me feel like he's trying to mark his territory or show off. He's just super physical. If I'm near him, his hand is somewhere on my body. Usually his palm is glued to the top of my ass, but sometimes he brushes my hair back or dangles his fingers over my shoulder. He kisses my temple and cheek. Not once do I feel like he's holding me back.

Of all of our friends, Garrett is the most concerned. Hannah wants me to be happy, and as long as I'm smiling, she's smiling. Garrett, on the other hand, waffles between worry and wary acceptance. He's convinced that Dean is going to break my heart, which will therefore create a rift between his girlfriend and one of his best friends.

I've tried to reassure him that I'm all grown up and can handle any heartbreak that comes my way, but then the conversation winds its way back to Sean, who I just want to forget. Dean makes that pretty easy.

Any time he's not in class or on the ice, he's with me. Sometimes he's reading a book while I rehearse my lines; sometimes he helps me out by reading a part with me. His high-pitched fake female voice has me dying with laughter so it usually takes a few tries to get through an entire scene, and by the time we're done he's horny. From my laughter, he says. Although I get the impression that I could do just about anything and Dean would be ready to go.

The most important thing is that we're happy—way happier than I've felt in a long time. Which is fucking mind-boggling. If someone had told me six weeks ago that Dean Di Laurentis and I would not only be dating but *happily* dating? I would've laughed my ass off.

"What do you have going on after rehearsal tonight?" Dean asks from the bed. He's lying against the pillows, hair tousled, looking like the sex god that he is. I refocus my eyes back to the mirror and away from him so I don't accidentally stab myself with the mascara wand.

"Nothing. I'll probably just grab dinner in one of the meal halls. Why? What are you up to?"

"I've got an errand to run and then I rented some ice time for the Hurricanes."

My stomach falls a little. Not see him tonight? I force myself not to show any disappointment. Just because we're together doesn't mean we need to be joined at the hip.

"Want to meet for dinner after?" he adds.

My heart flips over. "Sure."

"Cool. Can you come to the arena? There's this restaurant nearby that I think you'd like. It's an Italian place, but it's got all this fun old-time movie memorabilia." His hand wanders underneath the blankets, which are pulled down to his waist.

I poke myself in the eye. "Would you stop touching yourself?" I drop the mascara tube on the table and pick up a tissue to wipe the smear of black I just made at the inside corner of my eyelid because I can't keep my fricking eyes off Dean.

"What's wrong, baby? You jealous? I was thinking of how hot you look." He rolls to his side. "You make a little circle with your mouth when you put your eye makeup on. It's basically begging me to stick my dick in there."

Nope, there's nothing warm and squishy about my relationship with this guy. I shoot him a disbelieving glance. "We just got done having morning sex," I remind him. I apply two quick swipes of the mascara before Dean's hand can do more damage under the bedsheets.

"That was thirty minutes ago. Since then, you've showered, waved your tits and bare ass in front of me getting dressed, and then made little blow job circles with your mouth. So yeah, I'm horny again. Sue me."

I throw my coat on and lean a knee on the mattress to kiss him goodbye. "You'll have to jerk off then because I have class and I don't want to be late."

He curls up and kisses my neck first, then my lips. "I'm going to rub one off now so that I can last longer tonight."

Damn it. Now *I'm* horny.

DEAN IS ON THE ICE WHEN I ARRIVE AT THE SMALL ARENA ACROSS from Hastings Elementary. I always thought coaches sat on the sidelines and barked out orders, but he's in the middle of the rink, his attention fixed on one slight figure wearing pink skates. *Pink?* I thought the Hurricanes were a boys' league.

"You're getting too high. Stay low so your weight is better distributed." He crouches low enough that his own head is barely higher than the miniature player and his butt is skimming the ice.

I watch in amazement as he actually skates a few yards before stretching out a leg and spinning around. His smoothness on the ice is pretty amazing.

"Come on. Give it another try."

The skater wobbles forward.

"Remember, when you're perfectly straight, you're actually standing on the inner and outer edge of your blade. The middle of the blade is scooped out." Dean makes an upside down *U* shape with his finger. "You want to use your edges to keep your legs from spreading too far out. It feels weird at first, but I promise you'll get the hang of it."

One pink skate pushes forward tentatively, followed by the opposite one, and the whole motion is repeated again until the figure glides past the crouching Dean.

"Is this okay?" a little girl's voice calls out. "Am I doing it right?"

"You sure are." He watches her intently as she floats along the ice. "You're a natural, Koty."

"Who's Koty?" she asks.

"You're Koty. Or wait, maybe…Dakota-y? Everyone needs a nickname."

"What's yours?" Dakota puts her tiny fists on her slender hips.

"Awesome. I'm Awesome." He winks at her and then pulls her hands into his, and the two of them skate together. Or I should say Dean skates backward and Dakota clings to him. Her eyes are fixed on his face, two adoring spots savoring his every movement.

Despite the chilly air in the arena, I'm completely warm. Dean's patience toward this young girl is making my ovaries explode. This is a side of him I've never seen before, never thought I even cared about.

Sweetness unfurls inside of me, filling in the cracks and holes I didn't realize existed, taking me completely by surprise.

"Are you in love with him?"

"No. I don't have that squishy feeling…"

I think back to my conversation with Hannah, and…fuck. What am I feeling then? How is it that everything he does makes me smile? Why was he the first one I turned to when I was desperately upset? Why—

An ear-piercing whistle cuts off my silly thoughts, and I'm

grateful for the interruption. The sound of what seems like a hundred sticks pounding against the ice fills the arena. I notice a line of pint-size hockey players on the other end of the rink.

Dean gestures for them to skate forward and they all race to do his bidding, sending up a wall of shaved ice when they stop at the center line.

"While Dakota practices her skating, I want you to break into two groups. The first group will carry the puck, head up from the blue line and back again. The second group stands in the middle of the ice. No reaching or trying to steal or checking. Just stand there. Once the first group returns to the blue line, switch. Most important part of this drill is keeping your head up."

Dean arranges the boys who serve as the obstacles at varying points along the ice and then remains in the middle of the action as the team splits into two and starts racing up and down the ice, swerving neatly to avoid their teammates.

"He's doing a great job with them," a deep male voice tells me. I turn to find an older man joining me on the bleachers.

"Dean?" I ask. The man nods. "Yeah, he looks like he's enjoying himself."

"He is. I'm Doug Ellis."

We shake hands. "Allie Hayes. Friend of Dean's. He was bragging about how well the Hurricanes are doing this year. Better than his team."

Ellis chuckles wryly. "Briar's not going to get another Frozen Four appearance this year, which is too bad. How's Dean taking it?"

"All right, I guess. He wants to win, but…I don't think hockey is his life. He plans to go to law school next year." Dean hasn't spoken of the pros at all, not the way Garrett does. From what I can tell, he loves the game but the game doesn't define him, which I appreciate. Sometimes Garrett's hockey talk gets really tiresome. I'm not sure how Hannah handles it, but I guess when you're in love you overlook things like that.

Beside me, Ellis sighs. "Seems like a damned shame, this law school thing. He's got teacher written all over him."

We watch the players run their drill while Dean takes the time to speak to a few of the skaters who aren't as fast or as smooth as their teammates. He doesn't raise his voice, but the kids listen intently. He pats them on the head or back before he lets them go.

"Do you have a kid out there?" I dip my head toward the ice.

"Not anymore. I have a son who played on the Hurricanes, but he's in high school now. One of the other PE teachers offered to take over for me after Wyatt moved on, but I wouldn't give up this coaching post for anything. Kids at this age are special. They're hungry to learn, still think an authority figure is there to help them, not hold them back, and just the threat of discipline works as effectively as the actual act of punishment."

"It's all downhill from there, I take it?"

"You have no idea." He shakes his head in mock dismay. "The older they get, the more they think they know. Dean, though, he's got the touch. I've had older kids hang around just to listen to him talk to the Hurricanes. And it isn't just the boys that are drawn to him." Ellis points to Dakota. "That little girl looks at him like he hung the moon, and she looked that way even before he gave her the pink skates. He's patient and speaks to the kids like they're important. You don't see that in a lot of college students. Hell, you don't see that kind of behavior in most adults." Ellis shrugs. "If Dean took an interest in coaching, he'd be great at it, but I guess spending your days with middle-schoolers isn't a glamorous job like being a lawyer."

"Dean didn't pick law because it's glamorous," I object, feeling the need to defend him again.

"Then you should talk to him about teaching, or coaching, anything that lets him work with kids. He's made for it." Ellis starts to get up, but I stop him.

"Why are you telling me this?"

"Because you also look at him like he hung the moon. And I get the sense he feels the same about you." Ellis tips his head and then he's gone, skating over to join Dean and the boys on the ice.

DEAN

"WHAT WERE YOU AND DOUG LOOKING ALL SERIOUS ABOUT?" I tease, linking my fingers through Allie's as we cross the parking lot toward my car. I click the key fob. "Please don't tell me he was hitting on you."

She blanches. "Oh, God no. In front of children? That would be so inappropriate."

I can't help but laugh. For someone who's such a dirty girl in bed, her obsession with propriety and labels is kinda ridiculous. "So what did he want?"

We slide into the car. Allie still hasn't answered the question, which brings a frown to my lips. Okay, now I'm starting to think she lied to me and Coach Ellis *was* hitting on her. But she opens her mouth and startles me by saying, "He thinks you should be a teacher."

My eyebrows fly up. "He said that?"

She nods. "A teacher, or a coach, or anything that lets you work with kids. Those were his words. Personally, I think you should consider being a Phys Ed teacher. Then you get to blow a whistle and wear those tiny gym shorts. Your ass would look great in them." A slight smile tugs at the corners of her mouth. "Anyway, I guess Ellis saw your 'something.'"

"My something?"

"That's what happened to me when I was twelve," she explains. "I went on my first casting call and the casting director told me she saw 'something' in me. It's what convinced me to keep auditioning and pursue acting as a career."

I scoff. "Yeah, but you were talented to begin with, babe. All I did today was give a kid a skating lesson and run some hockey drills with the boys."

Which was a lot of fun, I can't deny that. But the idea of making a career out of running around a gymnasium and blowing a whistle at little kids is…crazy. It's crazy, right?

"I don't know…" Allie says teasingly. "Maybe dodgeball games are your destiny. Or coaching, at least. You'd be amazing at that. You love working with those boys."

True. But…oh, for chrissake, why is this even a topic of discussion? I'm headed to law school next fall.

I start the car and reverse out of the parking space, changing the subject before Allie can tease me again. "How'd rehearsal go?"

"Good, actually. Mallory memorized the final act, so Steven is happy. But I'm still a tad worried."

"How come?"

"We're taking a three-week hiatus for the holidays. What if she falls into an eggnog coma and forgets all her lines?"

I chuckle. "I'm sure it'll be okay. When is opening night?"

"First week of February." She pauses. "By then I'll probably know if I got that Fox pilot too."

There's no enthusiasm in her voice, and I glance over with a frown. She told me she'd sent an audition tape to the producers in LA, but other than that, she hasn't mentioned the role, and I don't think she's even called her agent for an update.

But she ought to be clamoring for an update, right? I don't know much about show biz, but a Fox pilot feels like a pretty big deal to me.

"Do you *want* the part?" I ask slowly.

Her hesitation is more telling than anything else she could've said.

I press my foot on the brakes as we near a red light. "Talk to me, babe. What's bugging you about this project?"

Allie shrugs. "I'm just not in love with the role. And…well, lately I've been thinking I might want to stay away from comedies and find more dramatic roles. Or maybe stage work. Maybe in New York."

The confession startles me, but when I stop to think about it, it becomes obvious where it stems from. "You want to stay close to your dad."

She turns to me with sad blue eyes. "That's definitely part of it. He's getting worse, and I'm not crazy about the idea of living on the opposite end of the country from him. What if something happens and he needs me? I'd have to sign a contract. I can't exactly walk up to the producers and say 'Sorry, gotta go to New York for a few weeks. Shoot around me.'"

"What about hiring a nurse?" I suggest.

"God no. He'd never be cool with that. I actually brought up the idea last year. It wasn't something he needed at the time—we were just discussing options for the future—but he freaked the fuck out. He said he could take care of himself, thank you very much."

I fight a smile, because I can almost hear Joe Hayes's crotchety voice in my head uttering those words.

She bites her lip. "It's true—right now he can take care of himself. But the numbness in his legs is so much worse than it was last year. So is his vision. He's using the cane for now, but what if eventually he needs a wheelchair? What if we're looking at paralysis? Blindness? If that happens, he *will* need someone. Maybe not round-the-clock care, but I don't like the idea of him being all alone in Brooklyn."

I reach over the center console to squeeze her hand. It's cold. Trembling. She's scared, I realize. Scared of losing her father, the way she'd already lost her mother. I'm not sure what to say to make her feel better, because truth is, she has every right to be scared.

Both my parents are healthy and active, so I don't spend much time worrying they might die. When I'm with them, I don't see a thundercloud of doom hovering above their heads.

But Mr. Hayes is suffering from a disease that's slowly eating away at his nervous system. He's dealt with it for years, while his daughter stood on the sidelines watching it progress, helpless to stop it.

Jesus. I'm suddenly floored by her strength. I hadn't understood, not until this very moment, how difficult this must be for Allie.

"Let's not talk about this anymore. I'm bumming myself out." Her voice wobbles before steadying. "Tell me more about this restaurant you're taking me to."

AFTER DINNER, WE DRIVE TO MY HOUSE. LAST NIGHT I STAYED with Allie in the dorms, so tonight it's her turn to sleep over. We've got a nice, fair arrangement going, except for the times when Allie plays the vagina card, in which case the arrangement becomes *do what your girlfriend wants.*

My girlfriend. Fuck me. It still boggles my mind. I ain't complaining, though. Allie and I have a blast together. We also have wild, sweaty sex on the regular. So I'm trying to focus on that and not read too much into the rest of it.

Too bad my friends can't do the same. Garrett is convinced I'll do something to screw up the relationship and that it'll end in a massive fireball that blows up in all our faces. Sometimes I wish he gave me more credit.

Says the man who almost drove someone to suicide.

The painful memory grips my heart, conjuring up the image of Miranda, and her tears, and the harrowing late-night phone calls where she threatened to kill herself and accused me of ruining her life.

Christ. I feel sick every time I allow myself to think about it, so I shove the unwelcome reminders aside. She never accepted my friend request, I realize. I guess that's not much of a surprise.

Allie and I walk into the cramped front hall of the townhouse, which smells almost as good as the restaurant we just came from. Tucker must be home.

"Tuck? Where you at?"

"Kitchen" is his faint reply.

I shrug out of my coat and toss it on one of the hooks in the wall. Allie does the same before bending over to unzip her leather boots. I smack her ass, then grin when she scowls at me. "Whatcha making?" I call out to Tucker.

"Soup," he calls back. "And baking some bread."

I sigh. "Sometimes I worry about him," I tell Allie. "The more domestic he gets, the bigger the risk of his penis falling off."

She tsks in disapproval. "Sexist bastard."

"I think you mean *sexy* bastard," I say helpfully.

"No, I got it right the first time."

We move toward the living room just as the front door swings open behind us. I turn around, and I literally have one second to react before a blond tornado flies toward me and launches herself at me.

"*Surprise!*" the tornado shouts, flinging both arms around my neck. "Guess who's spending the weekend!"

I'm so dazed and taken aback that I return the hug on instinct. From the corner of my eye, I see Allie's mouth twist in a deep frown. Shit. I know the conclusion she's jumping to right now, and I need to squash it, pronto.

When Allie clears her throat purposefully, the intruder swivels her head and says, "Oh. Hi. And you are?"

"Dean's girlfriend," Allie replies tightly. "Who are *you*?"

Rather than respond, Summer whirls toward me again. "You have a *girlfriend*? What the hell, Dicky! Why am I always the last one to know these things?"

Allie makes a noise. I think it might be a growl. "Did you just call my boyfriend *Dicky*?"

"Yeah, so what?" Summer challenges.

I quickly intervene before a catfight breaks out. I mean, catfights in general are hot as fuck, but not when I'm related to one of the pussycats. "Summer, this is Allie. Allie, Summer." I sigh. "My little sister."

CHAPTER 27

ALLIE

I'M ANNOYED WITH MYSELF FOR NOT REALIZING IT SOONER. OF course this stunning, vibrant girl is Dean's sister. Now that my claws have retracted, I can clearly see the resemblance.

Summer's hair is the same shade of blond, her eyes the same vivid green. She's a lot shorter than Dean, but far taller than I am. At least five nine, if I had to guess.

"What are you doing here?" Dean directs the demand at his sister, who isn't put off in the slightest.

"I told you I was coming to visit, remember?"

"No, you told me you *wanted* to visit." He makes an aggravated noise. "You can't just show up at people's houses without giving them any warning, Summer. What if I wasn't home?"

"But you were." She beams. "And now I'm here. See? The universe always gets shit right."

He arches a brow. "And did the universe happen to mention that I have an away game tomorrow? And that the bus leaves at eight in the morning? And that I probably won't get back until midnight?"

Disappointment fills Summer's eyes. "Fuck. And I'm leaving early on Sunday morning." She goes quiet for a moment, and then her expression brightens. "That's fine. It just means we need to do all our catching up tonight. Where should I put my bag?"

I press my knuckles to my mouth to smother a laugh. I get the feeling there's nothing on God's green planet that can bring Summer Di Laurentis down. She seems like the kind of chick who falls asleep wearing a smile.

Dean speaks in a strained voice, as if he views his sister's surprise visit as a major inconvenience. "I kinda had plans tonight, boogers."

Boogers?

"Plans change," she says flippantly. "And your plans now include me." Her green eyes flick in my direction. "You're cool with me hanging out with you and Dicky tonight, right, Girlfriend?"

The laugh I was trying to hold in pops out. Actually, it's more of a howl, because oh my God, why does she call him *Dicky*?

"I don't mind at all," I assure her. I meet Dean's irritated gaze and add, "Are you going to explain the nickname, or should I create my own backstory for it?"

Summer grins at me. "It's one of my least interesting anecdotes, actually. I couldn't pronounce his name when I was little. And our older brother Nick I called Nicky, so I just replaced the first letter and voilà—Dicky." She winks conspiratorially. "He hates it."

I don't blame him. I can see a minx like Summer having way too much fun tormenting her big brother with an embarrassing nickname like that.

"So what are we doing tonight?" Summer asks eagerly. She tosses her long blond hair over one shoulder and does a little twirl. Sweet Jesus. This girl is far too energetic. "Is there a club anywhere around here? A bar? I have my fake ID with me, so—"

"Then you'd better hand it over," Dean interrupts. "Because there's no way I'm aiding and abetting a minor."

His sister snorts. "Don't give me that shit. You were getting drunk when you were thirteen."

"I was very mature for my age."

"You're not mature for your age *now*."

"At least I didn't get kicked out of Brown for setting togas on fire."

"I didn't get kicked out of Brown, and I did *not* set anything on fire."

"How would I know? I have no idea what you even did to get kicked out, because nobody in the family will fucking tell me."

"I didn't get kicked out!"

My head is spinning from moving back and forth between them. Is this what all siblings are like? If so, I feel fortunate that I'm an only child. All this bickering seems like it would be exhausting.

"And if you quit yelling at me," Summer is grumbling, "then maybe we can sit down like adults and I'll tell you why I'm on probation." She waves a manicured hand. "But let's save that for later. I'm in the mood for a party. You think one of the frats is hosting one tonight? Wait, what am I saying? Of course there'll be a party on Greek Row. It's the only way those pervos ever get laid, right?"

I choke on another laugh.

Dean is more on edge than I've ever seen him, his fists balled against his sides as if he's trying not to throttle his sister. "We're not going to a party tonight. I already told you, I've gotta be up early to meet the bus. Which means we're staying in. A nice, quiet night in," he says firmly.

Of course, he says this right as the front door opens again and four hockey players trudge inside. Or maybe three players and a civilian, because while I know Logan, Fitzy, and Hollis, I don't recognize the fourth guy. He has dark spiky hair and looks too small to be a hockey player.

"Hey." Logan nods in greeting and shrugs out of his jacket. The hallway isn't big enough to accommodate so many people, and I find myself being squashed up against the wall as the guys push their way inside.

"This is my sister," Dean says in a resigned tone that makes me hide a smile.

The guys nod and say hello, but they're in a big hurry to get to the living room. Logan glances at us over his shoulder. "Morris got his hands on a demo version of the latest *Mob Boss*. Hasn't even hit the market yet. We'll probably be up late."

Beside me, Summer breaks out in a broad smile.

"Don't make it too late. Bus leaves at eight tomorrow," Dean reminds his roommate.

Logan shrugs. "I'll sleep on the bus." Then he disappears into the living room.

Summer is practically vibrating with excitement now. She sidles close to me and hisses, "Who was *that*?"

I wrinkle my forehead. "You mean Logan? He lives here. But don't get any ideas. He has a girlfriend."

"No, not him." Her hand flutters dismissively. "The big guy with the tats. I didn't catch his name."

"Oh. Fitzy. Colin Fitzgerald," I clarify. "One of your brother's teammates."

Summer's green eyes twinkle. She flips her hair again and announces, "I want him."

"Summer!" Dean says in exasperation while I desperately try not to laugh.

"What? I'm just being honest." His sister blinks innocently. "Be honest or be a jerk—that's what you taught me when I was twelve, remember? After I stole your favorite shirt and then accidentally dropped it in the sewer?"

"How do you *accidentally* drop a shirt in the sewer?" I blurt out.

"I wasn't *wearing* it. It fell out of my backpack." She smirks at Dean. "And then I lied about what happened and you gave me a speech about honesty, remember? Well, congratulations, Dicky. I'm super duper honest now." She points her finger at the living room doorway. "That was the hottest piece of man meat I have *ever* seen. And I want him."

"I'm going to murder you in your sleep one day," Dean tells his sister. "Swear to God."

Her smile is the epitome of sweetness. "Aw, Dicky, you would never, ever do that. Wanna know why?"

"Why?" he grumbles.

"Because you love me."

Honestly? I think I love her too.

DEAN

I AM TERRIFIED OF WHAT I'LL FIND WHEN I GET HOME TONIGHT. I'LL only be gone for sixteen hours, but Summer Heyward-Di Laurentis is capable of doing earthquake-level damage in sixteen minutes.

When she was thirteen, Nick and I were home alone with her. We turned our backs for twenty minutes, tops, and when we walked into the living room, the liquor cabinet was overturned, broken glass was everywhere, and Summer grinned at us and said, "Oops."

She said she'd wanted a taste of alcohol to see what all the fuss was about. Destroying thousands of dollars' worth of liquor in the process.

Granted, she's twenty now. But do I trust her? Absolutely not. I'm just hoping Allie can find a way to control her. And yes, I recruited my girlfriend into babysitting my sister today. No way was I letting Summer loose on campus without a chaperone.

During the five-hour bus ride to Scranton, Allie sends me updates about their day, along with running commentary about how great my sister is and OMGs! every time Summer reveals an embarrassing detail from my childhood.

Allie: Having breakfast at the diner.

Allie: OMG—your first word was "booby"? Why does this not surprise me??

Allie: Taking S to the salon. She wants a mani.

Allie: You're scared of tattoo needles?? S just told me you almost got a tat when you were 18 but had to leave b/c you were scared. Bwahahahahaha.

I fucking hate my sister.

My phone stays in the visiting team's locker room during the game, and not even O'Shea's cold glares and snarled criticism can bring me down today, because we skate off the ice after third period with an actual W under our belts.

My good mood follows me out of the arena and onto the bus, and I settle in for the long ride, relieved by the latest batch of messages I find.

Allie: Driving to Boston for lunch. S wants to do some shopping.

Allie: Awesome lunch. Heading home now.

Allie: Ooh it's snowing! S and I are taking a walk.

Allie: Home. Chilling and girl talk. Tell Tuck his tomato soup is da bomb.

Allie: Saw on twitter you won the game! FUCK YEAH!

Allie: Movie marathon. Putting phone on silent. See you when you get back.

The last message came in around eight o'clock. Good. I hope that means Allie and Summer are tucked under a blanket in the living room watching a movie and not out causing trouble.

Huh. And Allie was right. It *is* snowing. Once the bus crosses the state line into Massachusetts, there are suddenly white flakes dancing outside my window. I love winter, so I wholly approve of the sight.

It's close to midnight when we arrive at our own arena. I ride home in the Beemer with Tuck, while Garrett and Logan head for the dorms to spend the night with their girlfriends.

Ten minutes later, I pull into our driveway. Not a single light flickers in any of the windows, but I catch flashes from the television flickering behind the living room curtains.

The front hall is pitch-black when we step inside. I walk ahead of Tucker, kicking off my shoes as I fumble for the light switch.

I don't get the chance to flick it, because a bloodcurdling shriek suddenly slices through the silence.

Before I can react, I'm showered from head to toe with what feels like a tidal wave of lukewarm liquid. Another scream shatters my eardrums, and I'm still struggling to figure out what the fuck is going on when something hard connects with my left temple.

Crack.

Pain swims in my head, and I hit the floor like a sack of potatoes.

CHAPTER 28

DEAN

Fact #1: the Hastings police department has about eight officers on staff.

Fact #2: I think every single one of them is at my fucking house right now.

"Do you want to press charges?" The officer in charge hovers over Allie like a protective bear, a sneer on his face as he glares accusingly in my direction.

From my perch on the bottom step of the staircase, I glare right back at him. The EMT who's examining my temple makes a reprimanding sound when I swivel my head in the opposite direction, but I ignore him. Because what's happening right now is goddamn ludicrous.

"If anyone should be pressing charges, it's me," I say in disbelief.

The cop holds up a hand to silence me. "We're speaking to Miss Hayes, sir."

Oh yes. Miss Hayes. The crazy maniac who happens to be my girlfriend. The kung-fu master who knocked me out with a Wayne Gretzky paperweight.

But hey, at least the lights are on. This way, everyone and their fucking mothers can witness my disgrace.

"You're speaking to the wrong person," I mutter through clenched teeth. "I'm the one who was attacked."

One of the female deputies narrows her eyes at me. "From what we can see, sir, the young ladies are the victims here." She waves her hand at the floor. "We walked in to find you lying in a pool of blood—"

"It was soup! Tomato soup!"

"—and shouting obscenities at Miss Hayes and Miss Di Laurentis."

"Because they *knocked me out*."

"Clearly they felt you were a threat if they took measures to incapacitate you," another officer says coolly. He purses his lips, and the sexual predator mustache he's rocking bushes up.

Oh my fucking God. I'm going to strangle them. The moment these cops leave, I'm going to fucking *strangle* them.

"Sir, we're conducting an interview," the lead officer snaps. "Please refrain from speaking unless addressed."

Tucker, who's leaning against the wall a few feet away, looks like he's about to pee his pants laughing. His laughter is of the silent variety, vibrating in his broad shoulders and staining his cheeks bright red.

At least Allie has the decency to look sheepish. Summer just looks bored.

"I overreacted," Allie confesses.

"Talk us through what happened," the lady cop urges gently.

I grind my molars as Allie takes a breath. Meanwhile, the paramedic at my side is groping the back of my head like he's trying to get me off.

"I just finished heating up a bowl of soup in the kitchen. Well, it wasn't too hot, because I prefer my soup to be lukewarm, otherwise it burns the roof of my mouth and I hate it when that happens." She sighs. "Sorry, irrelevant. Anyway, I was on my way to the living room. All the lights were off because we were watching a movie. I heard footsteps outside the front door and suddenly someone just walked in like they live here—"

"I *do* live here," I growl.

Allie avoids my furious gaze. "I thought it was an intruder."

"An intruder with a key to the house?" I say sarcastically.

The cops glare at me again. I close my mouth.

"I threw the bowl at his head and grabbed the first weapon I could find." She points to the Gretzky paperweight we use to hold down the mail on the hall table so it doesn't fly away whenever someone opens the front door. Now it's on the hardwood floor next to a massive puddle of tomato soup. I'm surprised the cops didn't put little evidence flags around it.

"It wasn't Dean's fault," Allie insists. "Seriously, it's all on me. I freaked out for no reason." She finally looks over at me. "See? This is why I don't like horror movies! You watch *one* scary movie when you're a kid and suddenly everyone who comes to your door is a serial killer."

"Are you kidding me right now? You'll watch a horror movie with my *sister* but not me? *We* have to watch the *cancer* movie?"

"Dicky," Summer chides. "You're being grumpy."

I glare at my sister with enough force to make her wince. "Not one word out of you," I snap. "And don't think I didn't feel you kick me right before I passed out. Who does that, Summer? Who kicks a man when he's down?"

From the corner of my eye, I see Tucker sink to the floor. He buries his face in his hands, shaking with laughter.

The EMT blocks my line of sight by squatting in front of me. "I need to examine you for a concussion."

Oh, for fuck's sake.

He whips out a penlight and blinds me with it. Allie appears behind him, worry etched into her forehead. "Oh no. Does he have a concussion?" She kneels down and touches my arm. "Do we need to call your coach?"

Her question captures the attention of the cop in charge. "Your coach? Shit. You're one of Jensen's boys?"

I give an irritable nod. I still want to throw down with these assholes for treating me like a suspect instead of the victim.

"What's your name again?"

"Dean Di Laurentis."

"Oh yeah, I recognize you now." He sounds excited. "That was some Frozen Four win last season, kid. You played a good game."

Mustache Cop strides up. "The team's not looking too good these days. What's going on over there?"

"But that Davenport kid is *fast*," another cop raves. "Any chance Jensen will put him on Graham's line?"

For the next ten minutes, the cops badger me about the team and our chances for another national title while the paramedic forces me to endure his unnecessary concussion protocol until finally determining I don't need to go to the ER. He gathers up his supplies, and then he and the cops file out of the house. The moment they're gone, I shoot to my feet.

My wet socks squish uncomfortably with each step. My entire torso is stained red, and tomato soup drips from my hair as I advance on the girls. Well, namely Allie, the person who'd wielded the weapon that knocked me out.

"I'm taking a shower," I announce. "And when I get out, you and I are going to have a little talk about how fucking crazy you are."

Her cheeks redden. "I'm sorry, okay? I already admitted I overreacted."

"You think?" I hop on one foot, then the other, to peel off my disgusting socks. "I'm serious. I'm not done being angry at you, so you better be waiting for me in my room when I'm out of the shower."

"What are you going to do, spank me?"

I growl. "Don't fucking tempt me, babe."

"Gross," Summer pipes up. "Please don't discuss your BDSM sex games in front of your sister."

I point my finger at her. "Not. Another. Word." I glance at Tucker, the traitor who was getting so much joy out of my misery.

"Please escort Summer to Garrett's room and figure out a way to lock her inside it."

Tuck snickers. But he reaches out his hand to her. "Come on, little sis, let's leave the poor man alone. He's already taken enough of a beating tonight."

ALLIE

I'M NOT TOO PROUD TO ADMIT WHEN I'VE SCREWED UP.

Tonight? I screwed up royally. Not only did I attack my boyfriend with a paperweight, I then proceeded to call the police, because for a second there I was genuinely worried I might have killed him.

I feel awful. Awful enough that I'm willing to let Dean yell at me for as long as he wants, which is why I'm sitting at the edge of his bed just like he'd ordered.

"Look at that—she listens," Dean mocks as he enters the bedroom.

He drops his towel and walks toward the dresser. As he puts on a pair of black boxer briefs, I dutifully wait for a lecture that doesn't come.

"I thought you were going to yell at me," I remind him.

He rubs the side of his head, groaning softly. "I changed my mind. My head is killing me."

Alarm shoots through me. "That's not good. Should we go to the emergency room?"

"Nah. I'm fine, Allie-Cat." Guilt continues to twist in my stomach as I watch him rub his temple. "I haven't been hit that hard in years and I play *hockey*," he grumbles. "You're freakishly strong, you know that?"

"I know." I offer a sheepish look. "I told you, my dad made sure I knew self-defense."

"Well, kudos to your dad for making sure you could protect yourself. Followed by a 'fuck you' to your dad for turning you into a deadly weapon." He groans again. "Jesus. I can't believe you got the drop on me like that. You're lucky I love you, babe. If any other girl had done this to me—"

"You love me?" I blurt out.

Dean halts midsentence. For a second, he looks genuinely confused, as if he doesn't know what I'm talking about. As if he doesn't realize what he'd said.

But I heard it. Loud and clear. My heart skips a beat. He just told me he loves me.

"You just said it," I tell him, fighting the huge smile that's threatening to surface.

"I..." He clears his throat. "Well, damn. I guess I did."

"Did you mean it?" When he nods, my lips start twitching uncontrollably. God, I want to smile so fucking bad right now. "I want to hear it again," I beg.

He scrubs his fist over his chin, looking adorably uncomfortable. "Aw shit, babe. Don't make me say it again. It's bad enough that I said it *first*. That's never happened to me before."

The smile breaks free. It stretches my face from ear to ear. I fly off the bed and into his arms, too giddy to kiss him like a grown-up. My kisses are sloppy and overly eager and Dean is laughing like crazy as I maul him with my mouth.

I abruptly pull back. "Are you sure your head doesn't hurt too badly?"

"It's fine," he insists, and a deep rumble of delight leaves his throat when I smack some more kisses all over his face.

"Okay, good, because I think we should have sex now." I push him toward the bed and reach for his waistband.

He's highly amused. "We should? And why's that?"

"Because you told me you love me, and I love you too, and you *know* how turned on I get by all this emotional stuff." I'm already ripping my shirt off. "You have no idea how wet I am right now, sweetie."

The humor in his eyes is replaced with smoky desire. "Show me," he orders.

I ease my yoga pants off my hips. Undies too. I kick them away and move closer. Then I take Dean's hand and bring it between my legs. He instantly curls it over me, and I cover his knuckles with my palm, grinding both our hands against my damp core.

Dean groans, and this time not in pain. Or maybe it's a different kind of pain. His erection tents in his boxer briefs, a hard, long ridge of arousal that I'm dying to feel inside me.

"Allie…" His voice is husky.

"Mmm?" I rock my hips against our hands.

"I love you."

Those three syllables send a jolt of heat to my core. I moan. So does he. I know he felt the way my thighs clenched and the rush of moisture that must have coated his palm.

"Jesus," he chokes out. "This love thing really does make you wet."

"Told you." I give him another shove and he hits the mattress, falling back on his elbows. "I'm going to be coming all over you. Like, exploding ovaries and multiple orgasms kind of coming."

Dean reaches into a drawer for a condom, and I'm on top of him before he even has his dick out. "Love you," he whispers, then presses his mouth to mine.

The kiss is sweet and gentle, sending flutters of pleasure through my body. His hand trembles as he puts the condom on, and our mouths are still locked when he rolls me over and pushes just the tip of his cock inside me.

I wrap my arms around his shoulders and cant my hips, trying to draw him in deeper. It works. With a soft groan, he slips in another inch, then another one, until finally he's all the way in, stretching me, filling me.

Our eyes lock in a hazy stare as he starts to move. I feel so fucking full. It's incredible. Dean pushes a strand of hair off my forehead and strokes my cheek, making love to me in a lazy, blissful tempo that has my toes curling.

"Love you," he says again, and damned if my entire body doesn't sing with joy.

I hold him tighter against me, welcoming each slow thrust. He slides his hands under my ass and lifts me up so his pubic bone presses into my clit every time he drives deep. It brings stars to my eyes. Makes me gasp and moan and writhe until my whole world centers on Dean. When my orgasm ripples through me, I have the words "I love you" on my lips.

His green eyes burn with emotion. He lets out a husky groan and sags on top of me, thrusting deep one last time. Then he says, "I love you too" as he trembles with release.

CHAPTER 29

ALLIE

THE REST OF DECEMBER FLIES BY. BEFORE I KNOW IT, THE HOLIDAYS are upon us, and I'm rewarded with three weeks of downtime, family time, and stuffing-my-face-full-of-holiday-treats time.

I'm spending the break with my dad, but I'll be in Connecticut with Dean for the first two days. His family is heading to St. Bart's for a couple of weeks, so this is my only chance to see him until he gets back, at which point he'll join me in New York for our last three days of freedom.

Dean had asked me to go to the island with him, but as much as I hate turning down a free trip to paradise, I'd rather be in Brooklyn. Who knows where I'll end up after I graduate—I need to take advantage of every second I have with my dad.

Still, I can't say I'm not bummed when I have to leave Connecticut. Although Dean had told me his parents were cool, laid-back peeps, a part of me had doubted it. I mean, they're filthy-rich lawyers who own *three* houses. Hell, maybe more than three. Dean doesn't have a bragging bone in his body, so for all I know, his family has a house in every country on the globe.

You'd never know it just by looking at them, though. Dean's mom wore jeans and a flannel shirt the whole time I was in Greenwich, confessing to me that her favorite thing about having time off is ditching the business attire she wears to the firm. Her name is Lori, and apparently she kept her maiden name and practices law as Lori Heyward.

Dean's dad, Peter, is equally easygoing. He did some paperwork in his office every morning, but for the most part, he spent all his time with his kids, going skiing with Summer, playing two-on-one hockey with his sons on the outdoor rink behind their mansion. Yep, they have their own skating rink.

Dean's brother, Nick, is one of the nicest men I've ever met. He brought his new girlfriend, a lawyer at another firm, and though she was uptight at first, she was sweet once I got to know her.

And Summer… Well, she's just Summer. No filters, larger than life, contagious laughter. Sometimes I think I love Dean's sister more than I love him.

As sad as I am to say goodbye to the Heyward-Di Laurentises, I'm excited to see my dad. I decide to splurge and take a cab from Greenwich to Brooklyn, and it's late afternoon when I roll my huge suitcase into the front entryway and call out for my father.

I find him in the living room, wearing sweats and reading a book called *The Physics of Hockey*. He greets me with an indulgent smile, then fusses and gripes as I kiss his cheek and hammer him with questions about how he's feeling. He finally cuts me off to ask about my visit to Connecticut. When I reveal what an amazing time it was, he looks slightly disappointed, which makes me frown.

We speak on the phone a couple times a week, so he's already aware I'm dating Dean, but he's been surprisingly tight-lipped about it. After I told him, he simply grunted and hasn't commented on the relationship since.

He comments now.

"He's not long-term, AJ," Dad says with a tired sigh. "I hope you know that."

The blunt words sting. I mean, it's not like Dean and I are

planning to mail out save the dates next week, but I don't envision us breaking up anytime soon. We're twenty-two. We're in love. Going forward might be tough, what with me in LA or New York, and Dean in Cambridge for the next three years, but I'm certain we can make it work if we try hard at it. And once Dean finishes law school, he'll be able to practice law wherever he wants. Wherever *I* am. We haven't discussed it, but Dean hasn't given me any indication he wants to break up after graduation.

"He could be," I say quietly. "Long-term, I mean."

Dad gives an adamant shake of his head. "He's not." His voice loses some of its hard edges. "Do you want to know the most important thing I learned after eighteen years with your mom?"

I sit on the couch beside him and wait for him to continue.

"Relationships are a fucking pain in the ass sometimes."

I have to laugh. "Mom told me the same thing." The thought of the last conversation I had with my mother brings an ache to my heart. "She told me you guys had problems at one point in your marriage," I confess. I've never discussed this with him before. Mom had been open about their struggles, though. Not in detail, but she did make sure I knew how hard they'd worked on their marriage.

"We did," he confirms in a pained voice. "It was the traveling. Eva gave up modeling after you were born, so she was always at home. And I was always on the road." He gives me a fierce look. "I never touched another woman, AJ. That's not what our issues were about."

"I know."

"It was goddamn hard. The long separations. The brief phone calls. I'd come home and we'd feel like strangers, have to get to know each other all over again. It took a lot of effort to work through that." Agony flashes in his eyes. "Then she got sick, and it got even harder."

A lump forms in my throat. I was twelve when she was diagnosed with lung cancer. I remember begging to go with them whenever Dad drove her to chemo. They never let me, and on the days where the side effects were too debilitating, when her skin was grayer than ash and she was vomiting so violently she'd cracked a rib, they would send me to my aunt in Queens. They hadn't wanted me to see her like that. But I saw enough.

"Dean…" My father clears his throat, shifting the subject again. "I know men like him. They aren't equipped to handle the big stuff. The life-changing setbacks. The game-changers. If you—God forbid—got sick? Or injured? Or if a recession descends on this country and bankrupts your man's empire?" A disdainful note bites into his tone. "He'd fall apart like a cheap tent."

"That's not true," I protest. "Dean is a good man. And he's good to me. Good *for* me."

"You're fooling yourself, AJ. Yes, he's good to you—*now*. He lives a perfect life. He pays other people to clean up his messes. And as long as everything keeps going his way, he'll be the best thing that ever happened to you. But if shit goes south? He'll be gone. He won't stand by you, because that would entail stepping out of his perfect bubble, letting the ugly stuff in. That boy doesn't do ugly."

"You're wrong," I whisper.

He curses. "Christ, it makes me sick to say this to you, sweetheart. You think I like seeing that hurt look on your face? Rips me apart, AJ. But I want you to be prepared for when it happens." Dad lets out a resigned breath. "Mark my words. You won't be able to count on him. Better wrap your head around that now, before it's too late."

I DON'T ALLOW MY FATHER'S WARNING—AND HIS COMPLETELY unjustified opinion of Dean—to ruin the holiday for us. I get it. He's worried. He doesn't want me to suffer another broken heart. And I can't even get pissed about the blunt way he'd presented his case, because blunt is my dad's middle name.

But he's wrong. Dean *would* be there for me if I needed him. He already has, rushing to my dorm the night Sean's verbal attack ripped me to shreds. So I'm choosing not to second-guess the relationship

I'm receiving so much joy from and forcing myself to enjoy the rest of the break.

I spend Christmas Eve, which also happens to be my birthday, at home with my dad. We watch *It's a Wonderful Life*, as we always do, and I bawl my eyes out, as I always do. Then we drink hot chocolate and he gives me the same present he always does—three hundred bucks, with a scribbled note telling me to buy myself something pretty. Dad sucks at gift giving. I don't care, because I already got the only gift I wanted: my father, as healthy as he can be at the moment, alive and here with me.

A few days later, Dean is back from St. Bart's, looking tanned and relaxed as he picks me up at the brownstone. I'm surprised he chose to drive, since it would've been easier for me to hop the train and meet him in the city, but when I question him, he just grins and says, "We're not going to Manhattan. I have a birthday surprise for you."

"You already gave me a birthday surprise," I remind him. He totally had too—a call from St. Bart's and the hottest phone sex I've ever had in my life. I made so much noise when I was coming I had to thank my lucky stars that my dad is a heavy sleeper.

"This one is even better," Dean promises, and then he plants a quick kiss on my lips and pulls away from the curb. "I missed you."

I can't fight a goofy smile. "I missed *you*."

Winking, he reaches for my hand and places it directly on his crotch. Which is sporting a noticeable semi. "Little Dean missed you too."

"I can see that."

I rub the growing bulge, and he groans. "Keep doing that and I'll shoot in my pants," he warns.

My smile widens. "Is that a challenge?"

I drag down his zipper and slide my hand inside, curling my fingers around his hard, pulsing shaft. Jeez, he wasn't kidding. Less than a minute of stroking, and he groans again, clutching the steering wheel in a death grip as he chokes out one word. "*Coming*."

I don't let him ruin his pants, because they're probably more expensive than my college tuition. Instead, I lower my head and swallow up his release, moaning as his salty, masculine flavor coats my tongue.

"Sweet Jesus," he mumbles, then reaches out to tenderly stroke my cheek. "I fucking love you, baby."

"Nah, you just love road head."

"You." He stubbornly shakes his head. "I love *you*."

Damned if my heart doesn't soar. I settle back in my seat, gazing out the window as we cross the bridge toward New Jersey. I don't know where the heck he's taking me, but I'm happy to let him. I'd follow Dean Di Laurentis to the ends of the earth. To the bowels of a volcano, if he asked me to be the Meg Ryan to his Tom Hanks. To fucking Mordor, if he asked me to be the Sam to his Frodo. To—

"We're here," he announces.

I'm jolted out of the most ridiculous train of thought I've ever ridden. Dean parks the BMW in front of a small building in what seems to be an industrial area in Newark. I peer through the windshield to read the sign. Then I gasp.

My head whirls toward him. He's grinning.

"Oh my God. Really?!"

"Yup." He hops out of the car and rounds the front bumper to open my door. I take the hand he holds out, and I'm practically skipping all the way to the double glass doors. Excitement bubbles inside me. My chest feels hot and gooey, and the thick layer of emotion clinging to my throat makes it difficult to get a single word out.

I look around the front lobby of the dance studio, then meet Dean's twinkling eyes. "I thought you said you didn't want to salsa dance. And Dean Di Laurentis only does what he wants, remember?"

He shrugs. "I am doing what I want."

My eyebrows knit together as I wait for him to clarify.

"I'm making you happy."

Squish. That's the noise my heart makes. Because it's so fucking full of love it can no longer contain it all.

DEAN

REAL LIFE IS BECKONING. I WANT TO SHOO IT AWAY AND TELL IT to bother me later, but that's not the way the world works. As much as I loved lying on the beach with my folks, and catching up with my siblings, and putting a smile on my girlfriend's face by surprising her with dance lessons, it's time to snap out of holiday mode and into life mode.

My first week back at campus is busier than ever, as hockey practice, classes, and coaching the Hurricanes eat up most of my time. Luckily, Allie is busy with rehearsals again, so she doesn't complain that our sex life is pretty much a series of quickies this week.

On Saturday, the team loses another home game. Nobody is even saying the word *playoffs* anymore, because we all know it ain't happening. Despite that, I keep working one-on-one with Hunter. No matter what happens this season (spoiler alert: nothing will happen), Hunter will still be playing for Briar next year and hopefully serving as a team leader for the others.

Coach O'Shea, who's been shockingly pleasant lately, signs off on an hour of extra ice time for us on Sunday night, which Hunter and I make good use of. The solo session goes well, and I drive home from the arena in a good mood. Since I don't have an early practice tomorrow, Allie's spending the night and I can't wait to fuck my girlfriend. *Really* fuck her. I'm talking three straight hours of balls-deep heaven instead of the hurried trips to the bone zone we've been taking all week.

My head is down as I wander into the kitchen. I'm so focused on the task of checking if Allie texted that it takes a second to register that my roommates are sitting around the table. Even Tucker, who's been AWOL since the new semester started. I don't even bother teasing him about it anymore. It's obvious he has a girlfriend. Or maybe a boyfriend? Fuck, he's so secretive these days that nothing would surprise me.

"What's up?" I ask absently.

Nobody says a word.

I tuck my phone in my pocket and glance around the table. Their stricken expressions make my heart beat faster.

The moisture I glimpse in Logan's eyes makes it stop beating altogether.

"What's going on?" I demand.

The eerie silence drags on. Logan scrubs his fist over his eyes.

Fucking hell. Now I'm worried. No, now I'm *scared*.

"Seriously, if someone doesn't tell me what's going on right this fucking second—"

"Coach called," Garrett interrupts. His voice is low. Somber.

I wait for him to continue. My hands feel like two blocks of ice. And now they're starting to shake.

"He just got off the phone with Patrick Deluca, and, uh…"

Okay, this is moving in a direction I didn't expect. Pat Deluca is the coach of the football team. What the hell would he have to say to Coach Jensen?

Garrett sees my confusion and keeps talking. "I guess Deluca called him because he knows we're friends with Beau—"

Beau? "This is about Maxwell?" I cut in. "What about him?"

Logan averts his gaze.

So does Tucker.

The only one with the balls to meet my eyes is Garrett, who exhales in a slow, unsteady rush before speaking.

"He…ah…died."

CHAPTER 30

DEAN

MY BROTHER AND I TRAVELED AROUND EUROPE THE SUMMER AFTER I graduated high school. France, Italy, Spain, and we finished the trip in Germany and Austria. The latter is home to a massive ice cave that Nick insisted on seeing. I'll admit, it was pretty fucking cool. The tour only lets you walk the first mile or so, which is covered in ice. Beyond that, the interlocking chambers and endless passageways were formed of limestone. Nick and I weren't interested in one measly mile, so badasses that we are, we broke the rules and snuck away from the tour group.

We got lost. Hopelessly fucking lost, and to this day I still remember the suffocating feeling that came over me. The echo of our voices bouncing off the impossibly high walls. The cold breeze blowing through the cave. The footsteps of the tour guide who came to our rescue—we could hear those footsteps, clear as day, but it was impossible to figure out which direction they were coming from. The echoes fucked with our ears.

That's how I feel now. I hear Garrett talking, but I can't see him and I can't be sure of what he's saying. His voice is an echo. Bouncing off the walls and off my ears and just kinda...swirling around aimlessly.

My brain still can't comprehend the first thing he said.

Beau died.

As in, he's dead?

Beau is dead?

Beau Maxwell?

My friend Beau Maxwell?

"...on impact."

My head snaps up. It's like Garrett's words are spitballs that he's firing at the wall, and the last two finally stick.

"What?" I ask stupidly.

His gray eyes are lined with sadness. "I said he died on impact. He didn't suffer."

I blink. Repeatedly. "Can you tell it to me again? What happened, I mean."

He curses. "Goddamn it, why?"

Because I didn't hear a word you said! I almost roar. I take a breath and say, "Because I need to hear it again."

Garrett nods, albeit reluctantly. "Okay."

I stagger to the counter and open the top cupboard. Good. There's a bottle of Jack in it. I twist off the cap and take a deep swig, then join my roommates at the table. I sit next to Tuck, and the Jack Daniel's gets passed around as Garrett starts talking again.

It's not a very long story.

But it's a gut-wrenching one.

Beau flew to Wisconsin this weekend for his grandmother's birthday. I already knew this—he called me before he left. We made plans to grab beers on Tuesday night.

Last night, the Maxwells celebrated Grandma's ninetieth at a restaurant in her small town. The roads were icy. They took two cars—Beau was with his dad. His dad was driving.

Joanna told Coach Deluca that dinner was a ton of fun.

On the drive back, Beau's father swerved to avoid hitting a deer that darted out in front of their car.

The car hit a patch of black ice. It flew off the road, flipping over twice.

Then it slammed into a tree.

Beau's neck snapped on impact.

His father didn't have a scratch on 'im.

I swallow another mouthful of whiskey. It burns my throat and sets my insides on fire. My eyes are on fire too. They're hot and stinging, and when Garrett finishes speaking, I scrape my chair back and pick up the bottle.

"Going upstairs," I mumble.

"Dean—" It's Tucker, his voice rippling with sorrow.

Tuck barely knew Beau. Neither did Garrett, aside from chilling with him at parties. Logan was close to him, I guess. I know he went over to Beau's place to hang out. But me...I was one of Maxwell's best friends. He was one of *mine*.

Somehow, I make it up the stairs without falling over. My hand shakes so badly I nearly drop the whiskey bottle half a dozen times before I stumble into my room. I collapse on the bed and tip the bottle, pouring a stream of amber liquid into my mouth. It splashes my neck and soaks into the collar of my shirt. I don't care. I just drink more.

So I guess Beau's dead.

He was twenty-three.

I drink more. And some more. And then some more, until my vision is nothing but a fuzzy gray haze.

I'm wasted now. No, I'm beyond wasted. My brain don't work so good anymore. Hands? Working? Fuggedaboutit. I try to set the bottle on the nightstand and it crashes to the floor. For some reason, that makes me laugh.

I think time passes. Or maybe it doesn't. Maybe it's standing fucking still because Beau Maxwell's neck snapped like a twig and now he's dead. Dead. Dunzo. Dun-zo.

"Dean...?"

A voice whispers my name from far, far away. Jeez. Maybe I'm in the cave again. Maybe I never left it. How fucked up would that be? If I died in some cave in Austria but didn't know it? If the life I've been leading ever since that Europe trip is really a figment of my imagination and my dead body is actually decomposing in an ice cave right now?

"That's fucking trippy," I slur.

"Dean." Warm hands cup my cheeks. There's a soft curse. "Jesus. You're drunk out of your mind."

I'm bouncing. No, the mattress is. It's shaking because someone is climbing on the bed with me, and my stomach starts to feel queasy. Nausea sticks to my throat. I swallow. I breathe deeply. I can smell the whiskey, but there's another fragrance in the room too. Allie's mysterious scent.

"Baby." I feel my head moving. She's tugging it into her lap, threading her fingers through my damp hair. I'm sweating bullets. Why is it so hot in here? "Logan just told me what happened. I..." Her hand trembles in my hair. "I'm so sorry, sweetie."

"Broke...his neck." My voice sounds far away, too. It doesn't even sound like my voice, actually. Jesus, I'm so drunk. Disgustingly, pathetically, lost-in-oblivion drunk.

"I know," Allie whispers. "And I'm so, so sorry. I know you're hurting right now. I..." She strokes my hot forehead. "I'm here, okay? I'm here and I'm not going anywhere."

I draw a ragged breath. "Babe," I mumble.

"What is it?"

"I'm gonna..." I lift my head, but the simple act of doing so incites the very thing I was trying to warn her about.

The nausea spirals to the surface and I throw up on my girlfriend's lap.

ALLIE

THE MEMORIAL SERVICE FOR BEAU IS HELD IN THE FOOTBALL stadium. The entire team is there, along with the coaching staff, his friends, his family, hundreds of alumni, and thousands of people who probably never even met him.

One notable absence?

Dean.

Before I left the house, he was upstairs in his room, wearing a black suit and a somber expression. He told me to go on ahead with Hannah and Garrett and he'd meet me at the memorial.

When I get back to the house, he's still in his room, still wearing the black suit and the somber expression. Except now he's clutching a vodka bottle and his cheeks are flushed.

He's drunk.

He's been drunk every day this week. Well, either that or high. Two nights ago, I watched him smoke four joints, one after the other, before passing out on the living room couch. Logan had to haul him over his shoulder and carry him upstairs, and the two of us stood in the doorway, looking at Dean passed out and spread-eagled on the bed. "People grieve in different ways," Logan mumbled.

I get that. Believe me, I get it. When I lost my mom, I went through the various stages of grief. Denial and depression mostly, until eventually I learned to accept that she was really gone. It took a while to reach that acceptance, but I got there. Dean will get there too. I know he will. But it's been painful—no, *unbearable*—to watch him turn to alcohol and weed this week when he could've been turning to me.

"Couldn't do it," he mutters when he sees me in the doorway. He'd taken off his jacket and tie, and the collar of his white dress shirt is askew. His blond hair is mussed up, as if he's been running his fingers through it repeatedly.

I enter the room with timid strides, still wearing the simple, high-necked black dress I chose for the memorial.

"Just couldn't stomach it, baby." It's a whisper. Ringing with misery. "I kept picturing his parents...and Joanna...seeing their faces..." Dean sets the vodka bottle on the dresser and slowly sinks to the edge of the bed.

Taking a breath, I sit beside him and rest my head on his shoulder. "She sang."

"What?"

"Joanna," I say quietly. "There was a stage set up with a piano. She sang 'Let It Be.' It was beautiful. And sad." I blink through an onslaught of tears. "It was sad and beautiful."

Dean makes a choked noise.

I stroke his cheek with the pads of my fingers. His skin is hot, but he doesn't seem as inebriated as he was last night. He leans into my touch, his unsteady breaths puffing against my hand. "I couldn't do it," he says again.

"I know. It's okay, sweetie."

Is it, though? He should've been there, damn it. Beau's *family* was there. If they were able to "stomach it," then so should Dean.

The harsh recrimination sparks a flutter of guilt. Who am I to decide what someone should or shouldn't do? People skip funerals and memorials all the time, for all sorts of reasons. Maybe they want to grieve for their loved ones in private. Maybe it's too hard for them. Maybe they just don't believe in funerals. It's not my place to judge, and I force myself to remember that as I gently run my palm over Dean's cheek.

"I can't believe Beau is dead," Dean says dully.

I'm momentarily startled because this is the first time he's said Beau's name since it happened. I'm even more startled when I tip my head and glimpse the unshed tears in Dean's eyes. He blinks, and a couple drops spill over, sliding down to where my fingers are stroking his jaw.

His tears trigger mine, in the way yawns are said to be contagious. Suddenly we're both crying, Dean burying his face against my breasts as his whole body shudders in silent sobs. I don't know who kisses who first. Or who undresses who. But the need for each other is undeniable. We wind up tangled together on the bed, naked, gasping, sticking our tongues in each other's throats and frantically touching each other's bodies. Megan told me some crazy statistic once about how eighty percent of people who were interviewed for a grief survey admitted to having sex right before, during, or directly after a funeral.

I guess it makes sense if you think about it. Celebrating life in the face of death. Needing someone to hold on to, a tangible connection to another living, breathing person.

We release simultaneous groans when he slides inside me. No condom, but we haven't been using them since the new semester started. We both got tested before the break, and I was already on the pill.

I welcome his thick, pulsing cock into my body, arching my hips to meet his desperate thrusts. The orgasm that sweeps through me stuns me with its force. I didn't think it was possible to feel this kind of pleasure, raw, all-consuming, when I'm so overcome with sadness.

Dean makes a deep, tortured noise as he comes, trembling violently as he pulses and spills inside me. His breathing low and shallow, he collapses on top of me, then shifts us over so my sweaty back is plastered to his sweaty chest. I feel moisture on the back of my neck. Not perspiration, but tears. All the tears he would've been trying to hold in if he'd gone to Beau's memorial.

I roll toward him, wrapping my arms around his broad shoulders as he cries for the friend he lost. I don't know how long we stay in that position, but eventually Dean goes still and falls asleep with his cheek pressed up against mine. For the first time in seven days, I feel a tiny flicker of hope. Hope that the emotional release he'd just experienced will ease some of his grief, lead him closer to the road of acceptance.

The worst thing about hope, though?

More often than not, it leads to disappointment.

CHAPTER 31

ALLIE

OVER THE NEXT TWO WEEKS, ALL I CAN DO IS STAND IDLY BY AND watch Dean spiral. He has a new routine. He wakes up in the morning. He goes to class. He goes to practice. Then he comes home and drinks or smokes himself into a stupor.

Amazingly enough, he still finishes his course readings and turns in assignments. When I sneak a peek at one of the papers he's written, I discover that it's *good*. It's like he handed the reins over to the intelligent brain he doesn't like people knowing about and is now operating on autopilot. He's doing it on the ice too. Just letting his strong, athletic body and his years of training take over and do the job for him. His heart—hell, his *consciousness*, I'm starting to think—doesn't play a role.

Neither does his libido. That's gone too. Well, no, not quite. It rears up at a certain threshold of his fucked-up-ness, somewhere between buzzed and unconscious. But I turn him down every time, because the guy who's flashing me those cocky grins? Who's whispering dirty things in my ear and whose skillful hands are attempting to work under my shirt or into my pants? It's not my boyfriend.

My boyfriend doesn't want to fuck me only when he's drunk, and my boyfriend's carefree grins aren't drug- or alcohol-induced.

Dean Di Laurentis fucks because he loves to fuck, and he smiles because he goddamn loves to smile.

This drunk, stoned Dean is an interloper. He doesn't even care when I tell him I'm not in the mood, because he isn't in the mood either—the substances surging through his blood are just making his body think he is.

He's grieving. I repeat these words to myself a hundred times a day. I remind myself that Beau Maxwell is dead and that Dean misses him desperately. I chide myself for getting angry over the fact that he's handling Beau's death in a different way than I would.

But…damn it, I don't know how to handle the way he's handling it. What am I supposed to do, take him to rehab? He's not an alcoholic. He's not a drug addict. And the worst part is, the booze and weed have no effect on his academic or hockey life. He just rolls out of bed in the morning and skates like a champion or aces a test.

There's one thing missing from his routine, however—the Hurricanes. After the news of Beau's death broke out, time kind of stood still for a week. Dean and Logan were excused from hockey practice because they were close with Beau, and Dean bailed on the middle-school practices too. I thought it was a temporary hiatus. Grief leave, if you will. But now three weeks have passed and Dean still refuses to go back. I urged him to reconsider, but all that got me was an emphatic *no*. He flat-out said he doesn't want to work with the kids anymore.

I suspect it's because working with them brings him joy. And right now, he doesn't want to feel joy. He doesn't want to feel anything.

Me, I'm feeling plenty of things. Sorrow. Frustration. Anger, which then leads to guilt, because he lost his best friend, for fuck's sake. I'm not allowed to be angry with him.

Today, I'm feeling determined. I've decided that Dean can't wallow in grief forever. At some point, he'll find a way to pull out of this tailspin he's caught in, and when that happens, I don't want him looking around and discovering that he lost something important to him.

The Hurricanes are important to him.

I park Dean's car in front of the arena and kill the engine. He was already on his fourth beer when I left the house, where I've been staying ever since Beau died. I told him I needed to borrow his car so I could buy tampons. Life hack: If you don't want someone asking you questions, say the word *tampon* and the conversation ends.

I enter the small building and walk down the hall, past the vending machines and toward the double doors leading to the rink. A chill hits my face as I push through the doors. On the ice, the boys are in the middle of a fast-paced drill that involves skating super fast and then stopping super hard. I don't really get it, but sure.

Turning my head, I catch sight of a lone figure in the bleachers. Dakota. Her face lights up when she spots me. I wave at her, then hold up one finger to indicate I'll be a minute.

I approach the low wall near the home team bench just as Doug Ellis skates up. "Allie. Hi." He peers at the entrance. "Dean with you?"

I shake my head, and he looks disappointed. So do the boys, who clearly recognize me from the handful of times I met Dean here so we could go for dinner. I think they associate my face with the assistant coach they'd idolized.

Ellis tells the kids they have five minutes of free skate, then turns to me and listens without comment as I apologize for Dean's absence and assure him that Dean will be coming back soon. "He's going through a rough patch right now," I say quietly.

Ellis nods. "He told me about his buddy. It was all over the local papers too. The football quarterback, huh?"

I nod back. "Beau Maxwell. He..." I picture Beau's sparkling blue eyes and rogue grin, and my heart clenches. "He was a really great guy." I swallow a lump of sadness. "He and Dean were close, and...yeah...it's been hard. But Dean wanted me to tell you he'll be back to work with the kids very soon."

"No he didn't," Ellis says.

I avoid his shrewd gaze.

"He didn't send you here to talk to me, honey. And he didn't say he was coming back." Ellis shrugs. "But you want him to."

My throat closes up. "Yes, I want him to." I gulp again. "I wanted to make sure you'll still have him if—*when* the time comes."

"Of course I will." He nods toward the ice. "Question is, will *they*? Kids don't take well to being abandoned."

"But they're also quicker to forgive," I point out.

Although maybe not all of them. When I join Dakota on the bleachers a few minutes later, it's evident that forgiveness is the last thing on her mind.

"Dean doesn't like me anymore," she tells me in a flat voice. "And I don't like *him*."

I stifle a sigh. "That's not true, sweetie. You both like each other just fine."

"We do *not*. If he likes me, then why isn't he teaching me skating anymore? And he doesn't help Robbie anymore too! He hasn't been here in *years*."

Three weeks. But I guess to a ten-year-old that might feel like an eternity.

"Is he mad because I didn't want to wear the boy skates?" Her bottom lip quivers. "My mom said it was rude for me to make him buy me girl skates. Is that why he hates me? Because he paid money for girl skates?"

And then she starts to cry.

Oh God. I don't know what to do in this situation. I'm not related to her. Am I allowed to hug her? Will I get in trouble if I do?

Fuck it. I don't care if it's inappropriate. Dakota is bawling in earnest now, and she needs comfort.

I wrap one arm around her and hug her tightly. And then, as my heart throbs uncontrollably, I spend the next twenty minutes reassuring a sad little girl that my boyfriend doesn't hate her.

My father's gruff voice plays on a loop in my head during the drive back to Dean's house.

I know men like him. They aren't equipped to handle the big stuff. The life-changing setbacks. The game-changers.

He'd fall apart like a cheap tent.

I'm terrified that my dad is right. But he can't be. Dean is just in pain. He's mourning the loss of a friend.

He lives a perfect life.

He pays other people to clean up his messes.

A chill flies up my spine as something occurs to me. Fuck. Is that what I'm doing right now? Cleaning up Dean's mess by trying to ensure that his position at the middle school is secure? By begging a ten-year-old to forgive him for deserting her?

God, I'm so tired. These past three weeks, I've been focused solely on Dean. Trying to make him feel better, trying to get him through this. I'm slacking on my schoolwork. I show up to rehearsals bleary-eyed and exhausted because I spend all my time tending to my drunken boyfriend. Dress rehearsals start tomorrow, damn it. Opening night is in five days. I should be concentrating on the performance, but I can barely remember what this goddamn play is about.

My frustration only intensifies when I walk through the door fifteen minutes later and am greeted by a blast of deafening music—Nirvana's "Drain You" is blaring through the house. Wonderful.

I find Dean on the living room couch, holding a beer bottle in one hand and air-drumming with the other. He's shirtless, but not even the sight of his spectacular chest can soothe my jagged nerves.

"Dean!" I shout over the music.

He pays me no attention.

I grab the remote from the coffee table and stop the music. Silence falls over the room, and his blond head jerks over in surprise. "Hey, babe. I didn't see you there."

"Hey."

I sit on the edge of the couch and gently pry the bottle out of his hand. To my surprise, he doesn't protest. And I think he's more buzzed than drunk right now, because he doesn't slur his words when he says, "You got rehearsal tonight?"

I shake my head. "No, but dress rehearsals start tomorrow."

"Shit. Already?"

"Opening night is on Friday," I remind him.

"Oh. Right."

He acts as if he'd known that, but I'm pretty sure my play hasn't crossed his mind in weeks. He hasn't shown any interest in what I'm doing. In what *anyone* is doing. It's like he's frozen in place, stuck in that harrowing moment when he found out Beau was dead.

Everyone else is continuing to live their lives. Including Beau's family. Joanna is still performing on Broadway. We've been emailing since the memorial, and she told me both her parents went back to work last week.

Dean is the only one refusing to move forward.

"Baby…" My throat squeezes, worry and fear forming a knot in my windpipe. "You'll be there on opening night, right?"

His green eyes flare. "Why would you even ask me that?"

Because you weren't there for Beau's memorial.

I bite back the accusation and draw a deep breath. "I'm just making sure, that's all."

"Of course I'll be there." For the first time in weeks, I glimpse genuine emotion in his eyes. Honest-to-god warmth. "Where else would I be?"

HE'S NOT HERE.

Widow opens to a packed auditorium and closes to a standing ovation. The tears swimming in my eyes when Mallory and I take our bows have nothing to do with the overwhelming response we received from the audience.

The spotlight makes it difficult to see a single face beyond the first three rows, but the second row is all I need to see, because that's where my friends are sitting. Well, standing, because they're on their feet applauding along with everyone else.

Hannah. Garrett. Megan. Stella. Justin. Grace. Logan.

Hysterical laughter threatens to spill out as I scan the familiar faces and experience a *Wizard of Oz* moment. And *you* were there and *you* were there and *you* were there—and you know who *wasn't* fucking there? The man I love. The man who promised he'd be here.

Backstage, I dutifully accept hugs and accolades from everyone who was involved in the production. Steven. The student producers. Our faculty adviser. The art students who created the sets. The lighting crew. The senior who played my dead husband lifts me off my feet and spins me around. Mallory hugs me tight enough to steal the breath from my lungs, then spends five minutes apologizing profusely for being such a flake at the beginning of the project.

I barely hear a word she says. Tears stain my cheeks, but I think everyone assumes they're happy tears.

Everyone assumes wrong.

There's an after-party for the cast, crew, and friends at Steven's off-campus apartment tonight, and I assure my director that I'll be there. But I won't. At least, not right away. I have somewhere else I need to be first, and when Hannah texts to find out if we're meeting outside the auditorium or in the parking lot, I'm already behind the wheel of Dean's BMW, my shaky foot pressing down on the gas pedal.

When I pull up in front of the house, I'm startled by the amount of vehicles parked on the street. And there are four unfamiliar cars in the driveway, so I'm forced to park on the curb.

I hear the music before I even reach the front door, which is unlocked. Anger floods my stomach, bubbling and simmering and reaching a boil when I enter the living room.

It's full of monsters—man monsters, with a few petite women in the mix. Because of their sheer size, I determine that the guys lounging on the couch and armchairs and leaning against the wall must be football players. The girls, who knows. But I'm gratified to see they're draped over the football dudes and not my boyfriend. Dean is alone, sprawled in an armchair with his eyes closed.

As if he senses my presence, his eyelids pop open, and his face lights up when he spots me in the doorway. His happiness is short-lived, though. I'm still in the gingham housedress that my character wore tonight. I've still got my stage makeup on. My hair is still pulled back in a harried, messy bun. I'm not Allie right now. I'm Jeannette. And Dean's eyes widen in panic when he realizes what that signifies.

"Allie." His voice is drowned out by the music.

I take one last look at the party going on in the living room, then spin on my heel and hurry toward the staircase.

The tears well up again, and my throat is so tight I can scarcely breathe. *This* is why he couldn't be bothered to show up for opening night? Because he was partying with a bunch of football players?

I burst into his room and race to the dresser, yanking open the top drawer where I've been keeping the clothes I brought over from the dorm. I usurped half of Dean's closet too, and that's my next stop—pulling clothes off hangers and tossing them in my suitcase.

"Aw baby, don't do that." Dean appears in the doorway.

I ignore him and continue packing.

"Allie, please." He comes up behind me, and I swallow a sob when his strong arms encircle me. For one brief moment, I allow myself to sag against him. To lean into his warm, sturdy chest and feel his stubble scrape my skin as he rubs his cheek over mine. "I'm sorry, baby. I fucked up. I totally forgot your play was tonight."

I reminded you ten times! I want to shout.

"I promise I'll be there for tomorrow's performance." His hands run up and down my waist, caress my stomach, skim my ass. "You said there's three shows, right?"

My voice comes out terse. "Yes. But don't bother coming tomorrow night. I don't want you there."

He nuzzles my shoulder with his chin. "Don't say that. I know you're pissed, but I'll make it up to you. I *will* be there tomorrow."

"I wanted you there *tonight*, Dean." I still can't bring myself to turn around and look at him. And I don't know why I'm letting him rub up against me like this. Come to think of it, why *is* he rubbing against me? I can feel his erection, harder than stone, digging into my ass. How is he turned on right now?

The bizarre response of his body is what prompts me to spin around. Frowning, I carefully study his face, cataloging every detail. He's not drunk, I realize. His cheeks are flushed, but his eyes are too bright. Which means he's not stoned either, because his eyes usually get fuzzy after he's smoked weed. Right now they're shining. Sparkling with pleasure and happiness that he absolutely should *not* be feeling, not when I'm standing here in tears.

I inhale slowly. "What are you on?"

He looks confused by the question.

"What are you on, Dean?" I snap. "What did you take?"

He blinks, then says, "Oh. Just some molly."

For *fuck's* sake.

Without another word, I shove past him and zip up my suitcase.

"Where are you going?" He sounds hurt.

"Bristol," I spit out. "I'm not staying here anymore."

"Why?"

"*Why?* You blew off my opening night to throw a party and do drugs! You're hopped up on MDMA, rubbing your dick all over me when I'm fucking crying! And you're seriously asking me why I'm leaving?"

His eyes cloud over. "I didn't throw a party. Ollie and Rodriguez called, asked if I wanted to chill, reminisce about Beau. So, what, I'm supposed to say no to that?"

My jaw drops. "Don't you *dare* use Beau as an excuse for getting high!"

He flinches, but when he speaks again, his tone is defensive. "Big deal, babe. I took some molly. It's not like I do it on a regular basis. Last time was more than a year ago."

"That's not the point!" I'm struggling to breathe again. There's no use in arguing with him right now. He can't hear me, not when he's on drugs. I exhale, and the air seeps out in a weak puff. "My dad was right. I can't count on you at all."

"Are you fucking kidding me? I've been there for you from the start!" he growls. "My best friend fucking *died*, Allie. So gee, I'm sorry if I've been a tad distracted lately. I've had a lot on my mind."

His sarcasm isn't appreciated. "Distracted? You haven't been distracted. You've been drunk! And now you're goddamn high!" Resentment burns a path up my throat and pricks at my eyes. "Guess what, Dean? People die! It wrecks me that Beau is gone. It. Fucking. Wrecks. Me. But you can't just drink all the pain away."

His face turns red.

"I get it. The Life of Dean is all sunshine and roses." It's my turn to dish out the sarcasm. "But real life isn't like that. In real life, bad things happen, and you need to deal with them."

I pick up my suitcase and march to the door. I stop abruptly, spinning toward him again. I'm so mad and hurt I can't think straight.

"Life isn't perfect, Dean, and you need to grow the fuck up and accept that. I've been trying to help you, but you won't let me. I've spent almost a month watching you drink yourself stupid. Watching you push everyone away, watching you disappoint everyone around you."

He still doesn't say a word, and that makes me angrier.

"I went to Coach Ellis on your behalf!" I shout. "I convinced him to give you another shot when you decide to come back to coach the team." The tears fall faster, soaking my cheeks. "I sat with Dakota while she cried her eyes out! She thinks you *hate* her because she didn't want to wear goddamn boy skates!" I gasp for air. "Well, I'm not holding your hand anymore or cleaning up your messes. I'm done, Dean."

His breath sucks in. Finally, something I say gets his attention. "You're not done."

"Yes, I am." My hand is quaking so wildly I almost drop the suitcase on my foot. "Do you think you're the only one who's lost someone? I watched my mother die of *cancer*. I literally watched her wither away and die."

"Allie—"

"You need to find a way to deal with your grief. But I can't be there anymore to help you. I'm not going to stand by and watch you stick your head in a bottle because you're too afraid to face the pain. I'm *done*."

I storm out of the bedroom, leaving him staring after me in shock.

CHAPTER 32

DEAN

I'm awakened by a loud, agonized groan. Christ, it sounds like someone is dying, and it takes a minute to comprehend that the tortured noise had come from me. I'm groaning, because my head hurts. No, my eye hurts. Why does my eye hurt?

I sit up and gingerly touch my face. My left eye is swollen shut. And my mouth is drier than the Sahara. Shit. I'm so goddamn thirsty. And weary—just the act of lifting my hand to my face has drained me of energy.

The molly, I realize. Last time I took some, it also left me feeling drained and achy the next morning.

I slide out of bed and discover I fell asleep fully clothed. Staggering to the closet, I open the door and study the mirror behind it. Sweet Jesus. My eye is purple bordering on black, and as I study my reflection, all the events of last night come crashing back.

Missing Allie's play.

Allie dumping me.

Garrett coming home and yelling at me. What was he yelling about… I strain to remember. Right, about missing Allie's play. Oh, and because I'd invited half the football team over to the house and they…yup, a few of the linebackers were snorting coke in the kitchen. Fuck. That's when Garrett pulled me aside and started railing into me. I must have said something he didn't like, because… well, black eye.

I turn away from the mirror and sink on the edge of the bed, conducting a mental tally of what I'm dealing with right now.

I have a black eye.

I have an angry roommate who gave me the black eye.

I have an ex-girlfriend.

And I made a little girl cry.

I sat with Dakota while she cried her eyes out! She thinks you hate *her because she didn't want to wear goddamn boy skates!*

Allie's angry words blare like a trumpet in my head, making my temples throb and my stomach churn. I barely make it to the bathroom in time, gagging on the bile in my throat before I even reach the toilet. I drape myself over the porcelain bowl and dry heave for what feels like hours. I didn't eat anything last night, so there's nothing to throw up, but my stomach keeps twisting and clenching and I can't stop heaving.

When the nausea finally settles, I brush my teeth at the sink, then drop to the tiled floor and sit there for a while, thinking about what I've done. What I've lost.

Allie.

Beau.

Goddamn Beau. Why the fuck did he have to go and die?

The thought is so absurd it triggers a wave of laughter. Loud and uncontrollable, until my eyes are watering and I'm hiccupping.

There's a knock on the door. "Dean…you in there?"

I cringe at the sound of Garrett's voice. He doesn't sound pissed, though. Just tired.

When I open the door, I find a pair of serious gray eyes peering back at me. "You okay?" Garrett says gruffly.

I laugh again. "Not in the slightest."

Guilt passes through his expression. "I'm sorry about the shiner."

He curses. "But goddamn it, man, you had it coming. You should see the mess those guys left. The house is trashed."

I drag a weak hand over my scalp. "I'll clean it. And don't worry about the shiner. I deserved it. I'm surprised Allie didn't give me a matching one."

Just saying her name is brutal. It feels like someone cut my chest open with a skate and is stabbing the blade into my heart, slicing it to ribbons.

I can't imagine how she'll ever forgive me. I wasn't there for her opening night. Hell, I wasn't there for her even before that. For three weeks I've been walking around in a fog, doing my damnedest to try to forget that Beau is dead. Whenever he crossed my thoughts, I'd crack open another beer or roll another joint, because it was the fastest, easiest way to shut down my brain.

Allie's dad had said he didn't trust me to take care of her. And he was right. I can't even take care of myself, apparently.

"Wellsy is pissed at you," Garrett says.

"I'm pissed at myself." I groan, still thinking about the sheer magnitude of my screw-up. "I…" My throat hurts. "I miss Maxwell."

Garrett murmurs, "I know."

"It wrecks me to think I won't ever see him again."

"I know."

There's a beat, and then Garrett surprises me by hauling me in for a hug. Not a macho side hug or quick chest bump, but a real hug, with both his arms around me, gripping me tight.

I hug him back. "I'm sorry, man. About the house. The drinking. Just everything."

"I know," he says for the third time.

A door creaks open. "Is this a private homoerotic moment? Or can anyone join in?"

I laugh weakly as Logan lumbers toward us. Garrett releases me, and Logan takes his place. His hug is briefer, but no less comforting.

Logan slaps my back and says, "You up for practice today?" His gaze carefully studies my left eye.

"I don't have much of a choice," I answer with a sigh. "I'll just go in and let Coach decide if he wants me on the ice. With this shiner, he'll probably banish me to the weight room."

I wish I didn't have to go, though. All I want to do this morning is drive to Bristol House and see Allie. Throw myself at her feet and beg her to take me back.

"We'll tell him we were acting out a scene from *Fight Club*," Garrett jokes before his expression goes serious again. "He doesn't have to know what really went down. The party…the drugs…"

I nod gratefully. "Thanks."

And other than my eye, there's really no other sign that anything untoward happened last night. The good thing about my partying— not that anything in my life can be described as *good* right now—is that I possess the scary ability to bounce back fairly quickly, almost like nothing happened. I drink like a fish? No hangover. I smoke weed? My head is clearer than the blue skies the next day. Today, I'm a bit slower to move, but that's because of the crushing weight pressing down on my heart.

I pushed away the most important person in my life last night. It floors me how, in three short months, that's what Allie Hayes has become. She's everything to me.

Tucker has breakfast waiting for us downstairs. We eat, then book it to the arena, where Garrett swipes his ID at the door and leads the way to the locker room.

The four of us halt the second we enter the room. Coach Jensen and O'Shea are congregated in the corner of the room, chatting with a lanky, bespectacled man who's wearing a blazer and carrying a briefcase. A few of our teammates are loitering around, but nobody says a word. Hollis nods at us. Fitzy does a double take when he notices my shiner.

"Morning, Coach," Garrett calls out warily. "What's going on?"

"Drug testing" is the terse reply.

My heart drops. *Splat*. It just hits the floor. The nausea? Well, that rises. Soars up to my throat and clamps it shut.

My gaze shifts to O'Shea. He gazes back, utterly expressionless, but I get the sickening feeling that he's responsible for this. Random drug testing isn't a once-in-a-blue-moon occurrence—it happens all the time in college sports. But our season is almost over. Hell, our season is in the toilet, with zero chance of going to the playoffs. There's no reason to spring a spot drug test on us.

My queasiness gets worse and worse as other players file into the room. I can feel O'Shea's dark eyes boring into me, but my gaze stays glued to my boots. I'm in a state of panic, living out my very own *Tell-Tale Heart*, except instead of hearing a dead man's heartbeat under the floorboards, I'm excruciatingly aware of the blood in my veins. The steady flow of it, surging, pulsing, tainted with the molly I took last night.

As my pulse drums in my ears, I draw in a shaky breath, exhale slowly, and make my way over to Coach Jensen.

"Coach…can I speak to you in private?" I mutter, and just like that, he gets the *look*. The one that tells me he knows exactly what I'm going to say and that he'd rather slit his own wrists than hear me say it.

"Sure," he answers after a long, strained beat.

He leads me to his office. We don't sit. I don't speak.

He waits, but I can't bring myself to voice the confession. Christ. I'm so disgusted with myself right now. So fucking ashamed.

Coach sighs. "You're gonna make me ask you, is that it? Fine, I'll ask." He pauses. "What's going to happen when you piss in that cup, Dean?"

The shame builds inside me until I can practically taste it when I gulp.

"What are the results going to show?" he pushes, his expression unbearably resigned. "Marijuana? Cocaine?"

"MDMA," I mumble.

He closes his eyes briefly. Then he opens them. "All right. Thanks for letting me know."

I leave his office feeling like a man on death row.

Two days later, I get kicked off the team.

CHAPTER 33

ALLIE

Three days after I stormed out of Dean's house insisting I'm done, I meet him at the Coffee Hut on campus. Every girl in the room turns to admire him when he walks through the door. I do too, because…God, he looks like the Dean I fell in love with. Green eyes dancing playfully as he orders a coffee at the counter, blond hair smoothed away from his chiseled face, cargo pants clinging to his perfect ass.

All I have to do is look at his face to know he hasn't been drinking today. Maybe not for a few days, actually. Hannah told me last night that Dean failed a drug test and was kicked off the team. I can't deny my heart broke when I heard that, because I know how important hockey is to him, but the news hadn't surprised me either. You can't drink excessively and take drugs without facing the consequences. At the rate he was going, the partying was bound to catch up to him.

Surprisingly, he doesn't seem upset when I raise the subject, which is the first thing we tackle after he slides into the seat across from me. He simply shrugs. "I had it coming." With a pained expression, he adds, "But I didn't come here to talk about the team. I wanted to apologize to you."

I nod. It's what I figured when I got his text invitation, but holy déjà vu because this is the second time in three months I've been in this position. Last time it was Sean and me. Sitting in this very coffeehouse, having this very same conversation. But this time, the ache in my heart is a million times worse, because I'm still in love with Dean. Hopelessly, desperately in love with him.

"I'm so sorry, baby. I fucked up." His long, graceful fingers encircle his coffee cup. "I didn't handle Beau's death too well. To be honest, I'm not sure I'm handling it now, but hey, at least I'm sober."

I nod again.

"I'm sorry I missed your play. And I'm so fucking sorry I put you in the position where you had to make excuses for me. With Coach Ellis and"—his voice cracks—"Dakota. I plan on apologizing to them too and begging their forgiveness. But I wanted to see you first."

I know he had. He's been calling and texting for three days, but I hadn't agreed to meet him until now. My emotions were too raw.

Dean gulps his coffee. When he speaks again, his voice is thick with shame. "Can you find it in your heart to forgive me?"

My heart? God, my heart is ravaged right now. It feels like it just weathered a hurricane. Hurricane Dean. I still can't erase Friday night from my mind. Standing onstage and looking into the crowd and not seeing Dean. Coming home to find him high as a kite.

Can I forgive him, though?

Fuck, of course I can. I don't hold grudges. Life's too short for that.

"Of course I can forgive you." I don't miss the spark of hope in his eyes, and it kills me to extinguish it. "But this isn't about forgiveness."

"What's it about, then?"

"You tell me. Did you ask me here to get back together?"

He nods slowly. His entire face softens. "I love you," he says hoarsely. "I don't want to be apart from you."

Pain spirals inside me. I don't want to be apart from him either. But…I think I need to be.

"I…can't be with you," I whisper.

He makes an anguished sound.

"At least, not right now." I grip my foam coffee cup in both hands, desperately needing the warmth it's radiating. "I've never been alone, Dean. Ever. It's always been one relationship after the other with me. I'm not sure I even know how to be alone, and I think this might be a good time to figure it out. You said so yourself—you're still dealing with your loss. You still have other people you need to make amends with. So while you're dealing with your stuff, I can deal with mine."

His jaw tightens. I expect him to argue. I wait for him to argue. Because this is Dean Heyward-Di Laurentis, the man who always gets what he wants. The man who pushes and pushes until he does. But he surprises me. "How long?" he asks gruffly.

I bite my lip. "I don't know. A few weeks? A month? I don't have a timeline. I just know I need to be on my own right now. No boyfriend. Just me."

He looks sad. "Okay."

I can see the questions in his eyes. *Is this just a break or are we really over? Did I ruin this for us? Do you still love me?* But he doesn't voice them. He nods and murmurs, "Take as much time as you need, baby."

DEAN

I EXPECTED ALLIE TO SAY ONE OF TWO THINGS: *I'M DONE WITH YOU, Dean* or *I forgive you, Dean.* I expected a breakup or a tearful reunion, not this gut-wrenching state of limbo.

It's fine, though. Just a minor setback, right? If she needs to be alone right now, then I'll leave her alone. But I was encouraged by the fact that she let me kiss her before we parted ways at the Coffee Hut. And when I tucked a strand of hair behind her ear, she leaned into my touch and rubbed her cheek against my fingers.

She still loves me. I hold that comforting certainty close to my heart over the next few days. I need the reminder that someone still loves me as I go on an apology spree that leaves me drained. I'm armed with a *Kill Bill* list of people—well, people to apologize to, not murder with samurai swords. I wrote the names down on an actual piece of paper, because I couldn't keep track of all of them in my head.

The first few names are easy to check off the list.

Hannah is still pissed at me for hurting her best friend, but I win her forgiveness by spending an entire hour reciting everything I love about Allie and everything I'm going to do if—no, when, damn it—*when* she's ready to see me again. Hannah is mollified.

WELLSY ✔

Next, I apologize to my teammates for letting them down. Technically, I didn't get kicked off the team—I'm suspended until next season. But I'm graduating in the spring, so there is no next season.

The guys are surprisingly cool with the screwup that took me out of hockey commission. Honestly, I think they've given up on the season. Garrett assures me the guys are still bringing it hard on the ice, but I think everyone is ready to wash their hands of this disastrous year and start fresh in the fall. Hunter, especially. He's the one I apologize to the most, promising I'll make it up to him for bailing on our private sessions.

THE TEAM ✔

But that's not my only team, and my heart is heavy as I drive to the arena in Hastings. Again, I'm taken by surprise, because it takes very little effort to make amends with Coach Ellis. Before I can deliver the long speech I prepared, he claps me on the shoulder and says, "Save it for the boys. Good to have you back."

COACH ELLIS ✔

The boys? Also easy to win over. This time I manage to get halfway through my prepared speech, which includes a promise to take them all out for pizza. When I try to keep going after that, Robbie interrupts me by shouting, "Dude, you had us at pizza!"

THE HURRICANES ✔

I stay to help out with practice. My heart is no longer heavy. It's soaring, because Allie was right—I *love* this. Skating with the kids, giving them tips about how to position their bodies, when to take their shot. After the final whistle blows, I help Ellis put away the equipment and we spend ten minutes discussing options I never even realized were available to me.

My anxiety resurfaces when I climb the bleachers.

Dakota has her pink notebook in her lap, pencil poised on a blank page. She tenses when I sit beside her. She doesn't say hello, and I clearly see the hurt flickering in her huge blue eyes.

"So what did the evil Mrs. Klein assign for us today?" I ask gruffly.

She ignores me.

"If you're supposed to write a paragraph about your hero, I'm sure I don't qualify. But if it's a description of the person you hate the most? I bet you can write ten pages on me, easy."

She giggles, then covers her mouth in horror, as if she's trying to shove the high-pitched sound back inside.

"Dakota," I sigh.

She finally looks at me. Fiercely. "I'm mad at you."

"I know you are, kid." I swallow a lump of shame. I'm such an asshole. I bailed on our skating lessons, didn't come by to explain. I just disappeared from her life.

Dakota and Robbie are being raised by a single mother. Dakota talks about her often, and she admitted that her dad walked out the door one day and never came back. It makes me sick to my stomach that I might have brought back those painful memories for her.

"My friend died—" I stop abruptly, because I can't think about Beau without feeling a shooting pain in my heart. Fuck, I miss that big oaf. I miss talking to him, just shooting the shit with him. Who else can I discuss *Twilight* with and not feel judged?

"I didn't handle it very well," I tell Dakota. "I've never lost anyone before. Well, Gramps Kendrick, but he died when I was five. Maybe I was more resilient as a kid?"

She's watching me warily.

"I'm sorry, Koty. I'm really fu—fudging sorry for disappearing without a word. I give you permission to punch me in the face as hard as you can. But quick, do it now, when Coach Ellis isn't looking."

She giggles again. Then, proving that kids really are more resilient, she reaches over and pats my arm. "Stop being such a girl, Dean. I like you again."

I choke down a laugh. "You do?"

"Uh-huh." She blows a bubble with her gum, then points to her notebook. "I have to write one page about my favorite movie and why I like it."

"Gotcha. What's your favorite movie?"

"*The Princess Diaries.*"

Of course it is.

"Okay then." I crack my knuckles as if I'm preparing to throw down. "Let's do this thing."

DAKOTA ✔

I call Joanna Maxwell when I get home, luckily catching her on her dinner break at the theater. I apologize for not coming to the memorial. She forgives me. We talk about Beau for almost an hour before she reluctantly says she has to rehearse. We promise to keep in touch, and there's a dull ache in my heart as I hang up. I'm not breaking that promise, though. Beau was important to me. Joanna is his big sister. I'm keeping in fucking touch.

JOANNA ✔

I have one more phone call to make, and I'm not looking forward to it. A few days ago, I asked Fitzy to track down Miranda O'Shea for me. Fitz illegally gets his hands on video games all the time without buying them, so I figured he might have the skills to track down a phone number. Turns out I was right. I have no idea how he did it, and I don't plan on asking because I'd rather not go to jail.

I dial the number, then wait. I haven't seen or spoken to Miranda in years. I don't have feelings for her anymore, but hoo boy, there's definitely unresolved shit between us. And there was one thing I never got to say to her. I hope to change that today.

If she picks up the damn phone. It rings and rings, and I'm about to disconnect when a harried voice comes over the line.

"Hello?"

I take a breath. "Miranda?"

"Yes. Who's this?"

"It's…ah, Dean." I pause. "Dean Di Laurentis."

Shocked silence fills the line.

"I know I'm calling you out of the blue—"

"How did you get my number?" she interrupts, but her voice is soft, not angry. "My dad?"

"No. A friend of mine tracked it down."

There's an awkward pause on both our ends.

"I won't keep you long," I tell her. "I just had something to say to you. Something I never got to say back then because your dad pulled you out of school." I exhale in a rush. "I'm sorry."

She exhales too, sharply.

"I'm sorry for everything that went down between us," I continue. "For the part I played in your…uh…"

"Breakdown?" she finishes wryly. "It wasn't your fault, Dean. I was dealing with depression long before we went out."

"I know. But…we had sex…and afterward…" Jesus, this is uncomfortable. And this whole conversation feels…clinical. Like we're strangers discussing someone else's sex life instead of our own.

"We had sex because I seduced you when you were drunk." She sounds deeply ashamed. "And then I tried to guilt you into staying together when I knew you weren't happy with me. You have no idea how guilty I felt about it afterward. I wanted to call you, but I was too embarrassed. And my dad told me he'd ship me to Siberia if I ever spoke to you again. So I said nothing. I figured you'd forget about me eventually." There's a pause. "Obviously you didn't."

"No, I didn't."

Another pause.

"Anyway." I clear my throat. "That's all I wanted to say. I'm sorry if I did or said anything to contribute to what you were going through or to exacerbate it. I never meant to hurt you."

"I never meant to hurt you either."

I gulp. "So…you're doing okay now? Graduating from Duke this spring, huh?"

"Yes!" Excitement echoes over the line. "And I got into med school!"

The news startles me, because she always talked about wanting to be a social worker, not a doctor. I guess people change, though. God knows I have. We spend a few brief minutes catching up, and I'm relieved when the call ends. Miranda was an important chapter in my life, but it feels good to close it.

MIRANDA O'SHEA ✔

I didn't bother adding Miranda's father to my list. No amount of apologizing will make that bastard like me, and truth be told, I don't owe him any more apologies. The only crime I'm guilty of is breaking up with his daughter. I didn't deserve to be punched in the face and treated like dirt for it.

Frank can work through his issues on his own.

I'm working through mine.

ANOTHER WEEK PASSES. ALLIE IS STILL DOING ALLIE. I'M STILL doing me. We've texted a few times, just brief *How ya doing*s and not much else. I'm dying to see her. Hold her. Kiss her. Make love to her. But I promised to be patient, so I keep my distance.

I do, however, poke Hannah for information every chance I get. I know that Allie aced her screenwriting course. I know she got her nails done at the salon in town. Bright green, Wellsy had revealed, and it made me smile.

The next time I pester her for an update, Hannah reveals that Allie flew to LA. My heart immediately drops, because I think she left for good, but Hannah is quick to reassure me. Turns out the people at Fox wanted Allie to come in and read for them in person. They'd loved her audition tape but wanted to test her chemistry with the two actresses she'd be working with.

My heart damn near explodes with pride when I hear that, and I send her a congratulatory text. I don't hear back from her until several hours later. She says she's about to board the flight home and that we'll talk soon.

I board my own flight on Saturday morning out of Logan Airport. I'm making a quick trip to New York, because there's one final item I need to cross off my list.

CHAPTER 34

ALLIE

"You can't turn down the part." Hannah looks outraged that I could even suggest such a blasphemous course of action.

"Why not?"

"Because it's a lead role on a sitcom! What if the show's a huge hit? You could win an *Emmy*!"

I shrug and sip my coffee. I know I'm talking crazy right now. Believe me, Ira already dished out his own dose of disbelief earlier, begging me to accept the job. But when it comes to my career, I always go with my gut, and my gut is telling me this is not the role for me.

"I haven't made my final decision yet," I tell Hannah. "They gave me until Wednesday." It's Saturday night. That means four whole days to think it over.

My gut insists there's nothing to think about.

I'm tempted to call Dean and ask for his advice, but I force myself not to. I'm so used to running my decisions by my boyfriend. I did it with Fletch, Sean, Dean. But nobody else can make this decision for me. It's all on me.

Honestly, I've enjoyed being on my own these past couple weeks. It's nice to just think about myself for once. But I miss Dean. I really, really do. I know he's doing well, because I've been harassing Hannah for status reports. She said he's working with the Hurricanes again. He's gone out to Malone's with the guys a few times, but only had a few beers, as far as Hannah knows.

There aren't any pictures of him on Instagram or Facebook making out with other girls, but a part of me still worries about it. Dean is the most sexual guy I've ever met. I'm praying he's jerking off a lot, because I don't know what I'll do if I find out he slept with someone else. I didn't bring up the subject at the coffeehouse because I just assumed he'd keep his pants zipped while I took this time to clear my head.

That was selfish of me, maybe. But I love him, and if I hear that some chick tried to put her hands on him, I'll beat her senseless. He's *mine.* And I'm finally ready to claim him. The time apart succeeded in centering me, but now it's time to get my man back.

The only problem? Dean is in New York visiting his parents for the night. Hannah mentioned it earlier, which triggered a flash of concern, because it's weird that he would fly to Manhattan for only one night.

My ringing phone interrupts our coffee chat, and I'm even more concerned when I see my dad's number.

A second later, his voice rumbles over the line. "I don't want you to worry" is how he starts, and oh my God, who *says* that? Now I'm worried!

I slam my mug on the kitchenette table and stumble to my feet. Hannah eyes me in alarm.

"What's wrong?" I demand. "What happened? Are you okay?"

"I just told you not to worry, didn't I?" God, sometimes I really want to kill my father. "I took a little spill this afternoon, that's all. Thought I might have broken my arm, so I called an ambulance."

Fear pummels into me. "Oh my gosh. Are you all right?"

"I'm *fine*," he says firmly. "It's just a sprained wrist. No broken bones, I promise." A sarcastic note creeps in. "I can ask the hospital to send you copies of my X-rays, if you'd like."

I clench my teeth. "Don't be a jerk, Daddy."

He sighs heavily in my ear. "I'm sorry. I just knew you'd overreact when I told you. I promise you, sweetheart, I'm fine. My wrist is a little sore, but I have my pain meds."

"How did you get home from the hospital?"

"Taxi. And now I'm lying on the couch watching the Hawkeyes game."

I inhale a slow, calming breath. "Okay. Don't walk around. Don't try to lift anything heavy. Please, Dad, just take it easy for a couple days."

"I will. Love you, AJ."

"Love you too." I hang up and turn to Hannah, who instantly asks, "Is your dad okay?"

I nod. "So he says." But Dad was a hockey player. Hockey players *always* say they're okay, even when they're bleeding from their ears and spitting their broken teeth at your feet.

I take another deep breath. Then I pull up Dean's number and press Send.

DEAN

JOE HAYES ANSWERS THE DOOR WITH THE BIGGEST, MEANEST scowl I've ever seen on another human male.

"You've got to be kidding me! She sent you over to check on me?"

I gently touch his shoulder to move him out of the way. God knows he won't be inviting me in. "Yup," I confirm. Then I walk inside and look around.

Fortunately, nothing seems amiss. I glance at the stairs—Allie told me over the phone that Joe had taken a "spill." There's no blood on the hardwood, no broken floorboards. That's good. And he's not sporting any bruises or visible injuries. He's using the cane, but he looks steadier on his feet than the last time I saw him.

"Please don't tell me you got on a plane and flew all the way here just to give me the onceover," he mutters.

"No. I was already in the city visiting my folks and brother."

Mr. Hayes settles on the sofa and proceeds to ignore me.

I take off my jacket and drape it over the back of the armchair. Then I sit down.

He balks. "What are you doing?"

"Getting comfortable." I raise a brow. "Didn't I mention? I'm spending the night."

"Like hell you are!"

His outrage makes me chuckle. "Come on, sir. I thought we already established that arguing with your daughter is pointless. She asked me to stay the night and keep an eye on you, so that's what I'm doing." Because I will do anything that woman asks. I'd sell my soul to the devil himself if Allie told me to do it.

"I don't like this," Mr. Hayes grumbles.

"I don't care," I say cheerfully.

And that's how I wind up watching college football with Joe Hayes for the next hour. It's almost nine o'clock now, and my stomach is grumbling. I hadn't eaten dinner, and Mr. Hayes doesn't object when I order a pizza. "Sausage and bacon okay?" I ask him as I place the order.

He grunts. I guess that means yes.

Another hour passes. We don't talk. We scarf down pizza, drink beer, and switch from football to hockey. The Bruins are playing tonight. Every time we shout at the screen or cheer for a goal, we glance at each other warily afterward, as if remembering who we're with.

Between the second and third period I put down my beer and say, "I love your daughter, sir."

And he says, "I know you do, pretty boy."

I don't know if that's acceptance, or if it's a "yeah, you love her, but I still hate you." I decide to treat it as the former.

Around eleven, I help him up the stairs and wait outside his bedroom door, listening to him wander around and change for bed. Then I knock. "You all right in there?" I call out.

"I'm fucking fine. Go to bed."

Chuckling to myself, I duck into Allie's childhood room, where Joe said I could crash tonight. First thing I notice? The scent. Holy shit, it's the *scent*. The mysterious fragrance that's always surrounding Allie and that I can never place.

I wander over to her dresser and pick up a small vial of perfume. Or at least I think it's perfume. The label is pale-blue and reads *Allie* in a pretty script font. What the fuck?

"Eva had it made for her."

I jump in surprise, turning to find Mr. Hayes standing in the doorway wearing nothing but plaid boxers. I can't help but gape at his chest. Dude's in his late forties and suffering from MS, and he's rocking a *six-pack*. I'm impressed. I guess that explains how he landed Allie's smokin' hot model mom. Shit, and it suddenly occurs to me that if this is how Allie's dad looks now, she's got expectations. I'm going to have to look forward to working out for the rest of my life.

At my blank look, he gestures to the perfume bottle in my hand. "My wife…AJ's mom…she had a friend in France, this fruity-tooty fashion designer she worked with once. He knew a perfumer— Is that what you call 'em? Perfumers?"

"I have no idea, sir."

"Anyway, Eva's friend gave her perfume one year, a scent made especially for Eva. AJ was green with envy, so for her twelfth birthday, Eva told her she was getting a special perfume for her too. My wife was sick at that point, real sick, so she was doing everything she could to make AJ happy. She asked AJ what scent she wanted, and AJ says"—he snorts in amusement—"strawberries and roses."

I laugh too, because now it makes total sense why I could never figure it out. Roses and strawberries. Two completely different fragrances, yet somehow, when combined, they work. They're *Allie*.

"She got six vials made. I think AJ might be down to three? I'm not sure. She's very stingy with that shit. Doesn't want it to run out, I guess."

"So Allie has a French perfume that was created just for her? That's kinda badass."

He shrugs. "Eva spent a lot of time in France. Spoke French fluently too. She always wanted AJ to learn it, but AJ wasn't interested."

My heart squeezes. "She's interested in it now."

He looks surprised. "Yeah?"

I nod. "She's trying to teach it to herself by watching a French soap opera."

Mr. Hayes grins.

"I've watched two seasons with her." I sigh ruefully. "It ain't half bad."

That gets me a full-blown laugh. It comes from deep in his throat, lighting up his blue eyes. "You ain't half bad either, pretty boy," he says, and then he walks out of the room.

ALLIE

I'M WAITING FOR DEAN IN HIS ROOM WHEN HE WALKS IN ON Sunday night. I would've picked him up from the airport, but he left his car in the short-term parking, so he drove back from Boston himself.

His green eyes soften when he sees me. "Hi."

"Hi." I hastily stand up, but neither of us makes a move toward each other. We're standing five feet apart.

The distance is unbearable.

With a strangled noise, I throw myself in his arms and he catches me easily, his big hands settling around my waist and pulling me close. I bury my face against his chest and whisper, "Thank you for checking on him."

"You're welcome." I feel his fingers thread through my hair. He tips my head back, forcing me to look at him. "He's fine, babe. I promise. I think he just called the ambulance as a precaution. His wrist is a little sore, but that's it. He's totally, completely fine."

I'd already heard all this over the phone, from both him and my father. But the reassurance and certainty in Dean's eyes is what I needed to see. I hug him tighter as relief pours through me

His lips brush my temple. Then he inhales deeply, as if he's smelling my hair. "I missed you," he murmurs.

"I missed you too." Swallowing, I ease out of the hug and meet his gaze. "I don't need any more alone time."

A slow smile curves his lips. "Thank fuck." He flops on the edge of the bed and tugs me into his lap. "I've been going crazy without you these past few weeks."

"I know. But the time apart was good for me. I needed to take a look at my life, and to take a look at *myself*, just me, and not the me that's always in a relationship. I needed to know I could be alone."

"And can you?"

"Yes." I scrape my fingers over the dark-blond stubble on his movie-star jaw. "But I don't want to be alone. I want to be with you."

He kisses me. Soft and sweet, no tongue. Just his lips brushing mine, over and over again until I'm whimpering for more. Just when I part my lips to invite his tongue, he pulls away.

"Wellsy said you're thinking of turning down the Fox pilot." There's a chiding note in his voice.

"Argh. Why is everyone giving me shit about this?" I sigh. "I haven't made my decision yet."

"But you're planning on turning it down."

I hesitate. Then nod.

It's his turn to sigh. "I know why you're doing it, babe, and I'm sorry, but I can't let you."

I blink and I'm off his lap, my butt hitting the mattress. Dean walks over to where he dropped his coat. He reaches inside one of the pockets and his hand emerges with an envelope.

Oh no. Stupid aliens are déjà vu'ing my brain again.

He slaps the envelope in my hand and says, "Open it."

I open it without a word, and yep, I find the same fucking thing that Sean tried to give me. Confirmation numbers for two flights to Los Angeles. For crying out loud. Do all guys share one brain or something? Like a collective consciousness that causes them to make the same bone-headed moves?

"You're not coming to LA with me," I inform Dean.

He looks startled.

"I'm not turning down the part because I don't want be away from you. I'm—"

"The ticket isn't for me."

"—turning it down because—" I stop. "Wait, what?"

"It's not for me," he explains. "It's for your dad. I know you don't want to be away from *him*. So I figured instead of you giving up your dream to stay on the East Coast with him, you keep the dream and he comes to the West Coast with you." Dean shrugs. "I already ran it by him and he's on board. He said he'll start looking for a place to rent once you give him the word."

I'm...shocked. I can't help but remember the day at the coffee-house with Sean when he insisted on coming with me. And now here's Dean, insisting on me going without him.

My dad was wrong. And right. He was right *and* wrong. Dean fell apart, yes. But maybe he needed to fall apart in order to learn that life isn't perfect, that bad things *do* happen and you can't stop living when they do.

Smiling, I hand the envelope back to him. "I'm turning down the project."

He looks annoyed. "Allie-Cat—"

"Not because of my dad," I cut in, "although I'm glad to know he's willing to relocate if I do end up working in LA. I'm turning it down because the project isn't right for me. I don't connect with the role. And the contract requires me to commit to seven seasons if the show takes off. I'm not signing away seven years of my life to play a part I can't stand."

"Oh. Well, fuck. I guess I should've asked you before I bought these nonrefundable tickets, huh?"

"You think?"

Chuckling, he yanks me back in his lap, and I wrap my legs around his hips and my arms around his neck. I try to kiss him, but he speaks before my lips can connect with his.

"I made some decisions too."

I raise my eyebrows. "Oh really? Like what?" When his cheeks turn pink, I pounce immediately. "Holy shit, are you blushing? Okay, now I'm *really* curious. What's going on?"

"I'm, ah…gonna be a gym teacher."

My jaw falls open. "Seriously?"

He looks embarrassed. "I spoke to Coach Ellis about my options. Turns out private schools play it fast and loose with the requirements you need to teach there. I don't need a degree in education, but it helps. And when I was in New York, I hopped on the phone with the admissions officers at NYU and Columbia. Both told me the same thing—I can upgrade my degree. It's just an extra year of classes, kinesiology, health and wellness, that kind of stuff. But I'd be able to teach at the same time, depending on the school that hires me." He shifts awkwardly. "I did something crappy."

"Uh-oh. What did you do?"

"I used the Di Laurentis name with those admissions officers."

I fight a laugh. "Oh, sweetie, that's okay. It's for the greater good, right?" Because Dean working with kids is *good*, damn it. He could really make a difference. He could help those kids build confidence, become better athletes, better people.

"And then I spoke to the new hockey coach at my prep school and asked him to let me know if there are any openings in the private school sector, either for a PE teacher or a coach." He sounds excited now. "There's an opening for both at a school in Manhattan, grades one to eight. The job would start in the fall. Phys. Ed classes for all grades, and coaching the girls' hockey team."

"Girls?" I grin. "That should be fun."

"I think I might interview for it."

"Damn right you will. If this is what you want to do with your life, then it's what you need to do." I pause as something occurs to me. "Wait. Does that mean you're not going to law school? Did you tell your parents?"

"Yes and yes. That's why I went to New York this weekend. I sat down with my dad and we talked for hours. Did the same thing with Nick later, before you called me to check on your dad. They were both really supportive."

I'm not surprised. Dean's family is awesome. "I'm proud of you," I announce.

"I'm proud of me too." He nuzzles my cheek before planting kisses along my jaw. Then he sucks on my neck and pleasure ignites between my legs.

Oh sweet Moses. It's been way too long since we had sex. Almost a month. Or maybe more than a month? God, I can't remember. The feel of his warm, wet lips traveling along my throat is turning me on beyond belief.

"Dean," I murmur.

"Mmm?"

"I love you."

"I love you too." He licks the shell of my ear.

"But I don't want you right now."

His head jerks up, his expression beyond insulted. "Can you repeat that please?"

"I don't want you." I flash an impish grin. "I want Little Dean."

My boyfriend throws his head back and laughs. Then he unzips his pants and gives me exactly what I want.

CHAPTER 35

DEAN

GRADUATION IS LOOMING. I'M KINDA INDIFFERENT TO IT, IF I'M being honest, but whatever, I'll wear that cap and gown and throw my diploma up in the air, because I know it'll make my parents happy. Me, I'm just happy in general, because I'm in love with the greatest girl in the world, and the greatest girl in the world is in love with me.

And even though the team didn't make it to the playoffs, that doesn't mean there isn't any news on the hockey front. My man Logan was signed by the Providence Bruins, the farm team for the Boston Bruins, which means in a year or two? He might actually get called up to play for the pros. As for Garrett, his agent is working hard behind the scenes. Apparently several teams have shown interest in G, and I'm crossing my fingers that he ends up somewhere good.

I already know where I'm ending up—Manhattan. Last week, I interviewed for the teaching position at Parklane Academy. Yesterday morning, the headmaster called to tell me I got the job. It's a two-year contract, the second year conditional upon whether I upgrade my degree.

And I guess my sister is onto something about her universe

theory, because an hour after my call with Parklane Academy? Allie's agent phoned with news that made her shriek so loud that Garrett heard her all the way from his shower and flew into my room buck-naked, armed with a hockey stick.

Once we assured him everything was okay—and commented on how pretty his dick looked—Allie revealed she'd been offered a role on a cable show being developed by hotshot director Brett Carson, who she did a play with last summer. No audition necessary—Carson liked working with her so much that he offered her the role outright. The best part? The show is being filmed in New York City.

Allie says she still wants to do theater too, when the show is on hiatus or if it bombs, which I don't think it will. But the most important thing to her is that she wasn't cast as the ditzy airhead. This new role is serious and "meaty," as she likes to say, and I know she's looking forward to the challenge.

"What if I have to show my boobs?"

Her wry voice jolts me from my thoughts. We're walking hand in hand on the path leading away from the drama building, where her monologue class just let out. There's still a chill in the air, but everything is starting to look green again, and the snow has melted away, leaving a layer of slush on the cobblestone path.

"Did Ira say that?"

"No, but this is HBO. Chances are, they'll ask me to do nudity. At least a topless scene."

"Would you be okay with that?" I ask carefully.

She shrugs. "As long as it's not gratuitous, then sure, I'd consider it." There's a pause. "Would *you* be okay with it?"

I cast her a devilish grin. "Babe, your tits are fan-fucking-tastic. I'd never deprive the world of them."

"Be serious. Would you mind?"

I consider it, then shake my head. "I'm cool with it. It's part of your job, and if you're comfortable flashing some skin, then so am I."

She leans in and smacks her lips against my cheek. "You're awesome. You know that?"

"Of course I do. I hear it at least ten times a day."

Her answering laugh is cut short when a familiar figure steps into view. My shoulders go rigid as Allie's ex-boyfriend slowly approaches us.

Sean stares at our joined hands. I don't need to look at Allie's face to know what she's feeling right now. I can tell by the way her fingers tighten around mine that she's not happy to see him. That she hasn't forgotten all the callous shit he said to her after Thanksgiving.

"Hey, Allie." Sean looks miserable, but I don't have an ounce of sympathy for him. "I thought about calling you."

"Don't," I say brusquely. "You need to forget her number."

Allie gives me a reassuring squeeze. "We already said everything we needed to say," she tells her ex. Her tone is soft but firm.

Sean clears his throat. "I owe you an apology."

"Yep, and you've just made it and I accept. But we're not friends and we won't be." She moves forward. I'm reluctant to do the same. I'm aching to punch that bastard in the face, but Allie is pulling me away from him, her fingers laced tightly through mine. "He's not important," she murmurs to me.

She's right. He isn't.

We've barely taken five steps before I spot another familiar face. This one belongs to a hot blond who smiles and waves as she passes us. "Looking good, Di Laurentis."

I don't return the compliment, because I like having balls and Allie will rip them off if I flirt with Michelle. Besides, I don't *want* to flirt. Allie's killed that desire. She's the only one I want to flirt with. Plus I like having my balls attached to my body.

So I just say "Nice to see you" and continue along.

"I guess this is the day of the exes, huh?" Allie says dryly.

I roll my eyes. "Michelle's not an ex."

"Right. She's just someone you had a threesome with."

"*Almost* had a threesome with. You cockblocked me, remember?"

"Yep." She looks pleased with herself, and I pretend to pout. "Ha. Don't act like I ruined your *one* chance for a threesome. I'm sure that wasn't your first rodeo."

I offer a little shrug.

"Fucking hell. How many threesomes *have* you had?"

This time I wink. "A few. You?"

"Tons."

I stiffen. "Names and dates," I growl. "I need to make a new *Kill Bill* list."

Allie bursts out laughing. "Relax. You were there for all of them."

A frown touches my lips. Uh, I think I'd remember being in a threesome with—

"You, me, and Winston," she says happily.

I groan in exasperation. "That doesn't count."

"Sure it does. DP was involved."

Hell yeah it was.

AN HOUR LATER, WE'RE BACK AT MY PLACE. IT'S ALLIE'S TURN TO pick a movie, which means I have time to take a shower, because it always takes her a ridiculously long time to decide what she wants to watch. I wander into the living room ten minutes later to find her snuggled under an afghan, fiddling on her phone.

Her mouth falls open when she sees me. "Oh my God, Dean. Why are you naked?"

"I don't like shirts."

"What about pants?" she squawks. "Got something against those too?"

I cross the room and drop my naked ass on the couch, then grab the edge of the blanket and throw it over my lower body. Allie watches me in amusement.

"What?" I say defensively.

"I've never met anyone who's so anti-clothes. It's *so* weird."

I take her hand and bring it under the blanket. Placing it directly on my semi-hard dick. "Weird, or awesome?"

She rubs her thumb around the head of my cock, then sighs. "Awesome," she amends.

"So what'd you pick?" I gesture to the TV screen, all the while enjoying the slow, lazy strokes beneath the blanket.

"Oh, you'll like this one!" Her hand stills as she turns to beam at me. "It won an Oscar."

A groan slips out. "No, baby doll. *No.* I refuse to watch another one of your Oscar winners."

She clicks the remote with her free hand and my eyes widen in delight.

"*The Exorcist*?" I blurt out. "The fucking *Exorcist*?" The hand job I'm getting doesn't even register anymore. I'm too pumped that she chose a horror movie, and Little Dean is paying the price for my nonsexual-based happiness.

"See what a good girlfriend I am? I'm all about the compromises." She grins. "This relationship rocks."

"Damn right it does." I kiss her cheek, then suck in a breath when something occurs to me.

"What is it?" she says in concern.

I turn to her with even wider eyes. "Babe...are we boring?"

Allie hoots. "Did you really just ask that?"

"Yes, I fucking asked that." I wave a hand around the room. "Look at us. It's Friday night and we're on the living room couch, talking about how great our relationship is. That's the most boring thing we can be doing." I sigh loudly. "Is this our life now? Doomed to stay in and cuddle every night? Is the excitement over?"

"The excitement isn't over," she assures me.

"Are you sure? Because it kinda feels like—"

"Hey." Tucker's voice cuts me off, and we both look up to see him standing in the doorway.

"Hey." I wrinkle my brow. "I thought you were hanging out with Hollis tonight."

"Plans changed." He enters the room, taking in the sight of us under the blanket. "G and Logan around?"

I shake my head. "At the dorms."

"Shit." He drops his hand to his side. His strained expression is alarming. So is the way he keeps shifting his feet, like he can't find the right position he wants to be in.

"Everything okay?" Allie asks lightly.

Tucker hesitates. "I… Fuck, I was hoping the others would be home so I could tell everyone at once."

"Tell us what?" My uneasiness grows.

"I…uh…" He stops, closes his mouth. Opens his mouth. Stops again. Then he lets out a breath that sounds like it's sucked right out of his soul. "I'm having a baby."

Silence crashes over the room.

From the corner of my eye, I see the wide O of Allie's mouth. Her shock is as palpable as mine.

Like an idiot, I stare at Tucker's abdomen for a good ten seconds, before remembering that we don't live in a world where Arnold Schwarzenegger can carry a child.

"You're having a *baby*?" My mind continues to spin like a carousel, making it hard to speak without stuttering. "With…with *who*?"

Tucker meets my confused eyes and says, "Sabrina James."

And beside me, Allie starts to laugh.

I swivel my head toward her, but her laughter keeps sputtering out, low and wheezy, until finally she catches her breath and gives me a wry look. "The excitement is over, huh?"

Well, fuck me.

Keep reading to discover Elle Kennedy's bestselling book *The Goal*, the addictive love story of Sabrina James and John Tucker.

OCTOBER
SABRINA

"Crap. Crap. Crap. Craaaaap. Where are my keys?"

The clock in the narrow hallway tells me I have fifty-two minutes to make a sixty-eight-minute drive if I want to get to the party on time.

I check my purse again, but the keys aren't there. I run through the various locations. Dresser? No. Bathroom? Was just there. Kitchen? Maybe—

I'm about to pivot when I hear a jingle of metal behind me.

"You looking for these?"

Contempt lodges in my throat as I turn around and step into a living room so small that the five pieces of dated furniture—two tables, one love seat, one sofa, and one chair—are squashed together like sardines in a can. The lump of flesh on the couch waves my keys in the air. At my sigh of irritation, he grins and shoves them under his sweatpants-covered ass.

"Come and get 'em."

I drag a frustrated hand down my flat-ironed hair before stalking over to my stepfather. "Give me my keys," I demand.

Ray leers in return. "Da-amn, you look hot tonight. You've turned into a real babe, Rina. You and me should get it on."

I ignore the meaty hand that's falling to his crotch. I've never known a man so desperate to touch his own junk. He makes Homer Simpson look like a gentleman.

"You and I don't exist to each other. So don't look at me, and *don't* call me Rina." Ray's the only person who ever calls me that, and I fucking hate it. "Now give me my keys."

"I told you—come and get 'em."

With gritted teeth, I shove my hand under his ass and root around for my keys. Ray grunts and squirms like the disgusting piece of shit he is until my hand connects with metal.

I drag the keys free and spin back to the doorway.

"What's the big deal?" he mocks after me. "It's not like we're related."

I stop and use thirty seconds of my precious time to stare at him in disbelief. "You're my stepfather. You married my mother. And"—I swallow a rush of bile—"and you're sleeping with Nana now. So, no, it's not about whether you and I are related. It's because you're the grossest person on the planet and you belong in prison."

His hazel eyes darken. "Watch your mouth, missy, or one of these days you'll come home and the doors will be locked."

Whatever. "I pay for a third of the rent here," I remind him.

"Well, maybe you'll be in charge of more."

He turns back to the television, and I spend another valuable thirty seconds fantasizing about bashing his head in with my purse. Worth it.

In the kitchen, Nana is sitting at the table, smoking a cigarette and reading an issue of *People*. "Did you see this?" she exclaims. "Kim K is nude again."

"Goodie for her." I grab my jacket off the back of the chair and head for the kitchen door.

I've found that it's safer to leave the house through the back. There are usually street punks congregating on the stoops of the narrow townhouses on our less-than-affluent street in this less-than-affluent part of Southie. Besides, our carport is behind the house.

"Heard Rachel Berkovich got knocked up," Nana remarks. "She should've aborted it, but I guess it's against their religion."

I clench my teeth again and turn to face my grandmother. As usual, she's wearing a ratty robe and fuzzy pink slippers, but her dyed-blond hair is teased to perfection and her face is fully made up even though she rarely goes out.

"She's Jewish, Nana. I don't think it's against her religion, but even if it is, that's her choice."

"Probably wants those extra food stamps," Nana concludes, blowing a long stream of smoke in my direction. Shit. I hope I don't smell like an ashtray by the time I get to Hastings.

"I'm guessing that isn't the reason Rachel's keeping the baby." One hand on the door, I shift restlessly, waiting for an opening to tell Nana goodbye.

"Your mama thought about aborting you."

And there it is. "Okay, that's enough," I mutter. "I'm going to Hastings. I'll be back tonight."

Her head jerks up from the magazine and her eyes narrow as she takes in my black knit skirt, black short-sleeved sweater with a scoop neck, and three-inch heels. I can see the words forming in her mind before they even leave her mouth.

"You're looking uppity. Going off to that fancy college of yours? You got classes on Saturday night?"

"It's a cocktail party," I answer grudgingly.

"Ooh, cocktail, schmocktail. Hope your lips don't get chapped kissing all the ass down there."

"Yeah, thanks, Nana." I wrench open the back door, forcing myself to add, "Love you."

"Love you too, baby girl."

She does love me, but sometimes that love is so tainted, I don't know if it's hurting me or helping me.

I don't make the drive to the small town of Hastings in fifty-two minutes *or* sixty-eight minutes. Instead, it takes me an entire hour and a half because the roads are so damn bad. Another five minutes pass before I can find a parking space, and by the time I reach Professor Gibson's house, I'm tenser than a piano wire—and feeling about as fragile.

"Hi, Mr. Gibson. I'm so sorry I'm late," I tell the bespectacled man at the door.

Professor Gibson's husband gives me a soft smile. "Don't worry about it, Sabrina. The weather is terrible. Let me take your coat." He holds out a hand and waits patiently while I struggle out of my wool jacket.

Professor Gibson arrives as her husband is hanging my cheap coat among all the expensive ones in the closet. It looks as out of place as I do. I shove aside the feelings of inadequacy and summon up a bright smile.

"Sabrina!" Professor Gibson calls out gaily. Her commanding presence jerks me to attention. "I'm so glad you arrived in one piece. Is it snowing yet?"

"No, just rain."

She grimaces and takes my arm. "Even worse. I hope you don't plan on driving back to the city tonight. The roads will be one sheet of ice."

Since I have to work in the morning, I'll be making that trek regardless of the road conditions, but I don't want Prof to worry, so I smile reassuringly. "I'll be fine. Is she still here?"

The professor squeezes my forearm. "She is, and she's dying to meet you."

Awesome. I take my first full breath since I got here and allow myself to be led across the room toward a short, gray-haired woman dressed in a boxy pastel suitcoat over a pair of black pants. The outfit is rather blah, but the diamonds sparkling in her ears are larger than my thumb. Also? She seems too genial for a professor of the law. I always envisioned them as dour, serious creatures. Like me.

"Amelia, let me introduce you to Sabrina James. She's the student I've been telling you about. At the top of her class, holds down two jobs, and managed a 177 on her LSATs." Professor Gibson turns to me. "Sabrina, Amelia Fromm, constitutional scholar extraordinaire."

"So nice to meet you," I say, holding out my hand and praying to God it feels dry and not damp. I practiced shaking my own hand for an hour leading up to this.

Amelia grips me lightly before stepping back. "Italian mother, Jewish grandfather, hence the odd combination of names. James is Scottish—is that where your family is from?" Her bright eyes sweep over me, and I resist the urge to fidget with my cheap Target clothing

"I couldn't say, ma'am." My family comes from the gutter. Scotland seems far too nice and regal to be our homeland.

She waves a hand. "It's not important. I dabble in genealogy on the side. So, you've applied to Harvard? That's what Kelly has told me."

Kelly? Do I know a Kelly?

"She means me, dear," Professor Gibson says with a gentle laugh.

I blush. "Yes, sorry. I think of you as Prof."

"So formal, Kelly!" Professor Fromm accuses. "Sabrina, where else have you applied?"

"Boston College, Suffolk, and Yale, but Harvard is my dream."

Amelia raises an eyebrow at my list of tier two and three Boston schools.

Professor Gibson jumps to my defense. "She wants to stay close to home. And obviously she belongs at someplace better than Yale."

The two professors share a contemptuous sniff. Prof was a Harvard grad, and apparently once a Harvard grad, always an anti-Yale person.

"From all that Kelly has shared, it sounds like Harvard would be honored to have you."

"It would be my honor to be a Harvard student, ma'am."

"Acceptance letters are being mailed out soon." Her eyes twinkle with mischief. "I'll be sure to put in a good word."

Amelia bestows another smile, and I nearly faint in happy relief. I wasn't just blowing smoke up her ass. Harvard really is my dream.

"Thank you," I manage to croak out.

Professor Gibson points me toward the food. "Why don't you get something to eat? Amelia, I want to talk to you about that position paper I heard was coming out of Brown. Did you have a chance to look at it?"

The two turn away, diving deep into a discussion about intersectionality of Black feminism and race theory, a topic that Professor Gibson is an expert in.

I wander over to the refreshment table, which is draped in white and loaded with cheese, crackers, and fruit. Two of my closest friends—Hope Matthews and Carin Thompson—are already standing there. They're the two most beautiful, smartest angels in the world.

I rush over to them and nearly collapse in their arms.

"So? How'd it go?" Hope asks impatiently.

"Good, I think. She said that it sounded like Harvard would be honored to have me and that the first wave of acceptance letters is going out soon."

I grab a plate and start loading it up, wishing the pieces of cheese were bigger. I'm so hungry I could eat an entire block. All day I'd been sick with anticipation because of this meeting, and now that it's over, I want to fall face-first into the food table.

"Oh, you are so in," declares Carin.

The three of us are advisees of Professor Gibson, who's a big believer in helping young women along. There are other networking organizations on campus, but her influence is solely geared toward the advancement of women, and I couldn't be more grateful.

Tonight's cocktail party is designed for her students to meet with faculty members of the most competitive graduate programs in the nation. Hope is angling for a place at Harvard Med while Carin is headed for MIT.

Yep, it's a sea of estrogen inside Professor Gibson's house. Other than her husband, only a couple of other men are present. I'm really going to miss this place after I graduate. It's been a home away from home.

"Fingers crossed," I say in response to Carin. "If I don't get into Harvard, then it's BC or Suffolk." Which would be fine, but Harvard virtually guarantees me a shot at the job I want after graduation—a position at one of the nation's top law firms, or what everyone calls BigLaw.

"You'll get in," Hope says confidently. "And hopefully once you get that acceptance letter, you'll stop killing yourself, because Lord, B, you look tense."

I roll my head around my neck stiffly. Yeah, I *am* tense. "I know. My schedule is brutal these days. I went to bed at two this morning because the girl who was supposed to close at Boots & Chutes bugged out and left me to close, and then I was up at four to sort mail. I got home around noon, crashed, and almost overslept."

"You're still working both jobs?" Carin flips her red hair out of her face. "You said you were going to quit the waitressing gig."

"I can't yet. Professor Gibson said that they don't want us working our first year of law school. The only way I can swing that is to have enough for food and rent saved up before September."

Carin makes a sympathetic noise. "I hear you. My parents are taking out a loan so big, I might be able to afford a small country with it."

"I wish you'd move in with us," Hope says plaintively.

"Really? I had no idea," I joke. "You've only said it twice a day since the semester started."

She wrinkles her cute nose at me. "You'd *love* this place my dad rented for us. It's got floor-to-ceiling windows and it's right on the subway line. Public transportation." She waggles her eyebrows enticingly.

"It's too expensive, H."

"You know I'd cover the difference—or my parents would," she corrects herself. The girl's family has more money than an oil tycoon, but you'd never know it from talking to her. Hope's as down to earth as they come.

"I know," I say between gulping down bites of mini sausages. "But I'd feel guilty and then guilt would turn into resentment and then we wouldn't be friends anymore and not being your friend would suck."

She shakes her head at me. "If, at some point, your stubborn pride allows you to ask for help, I'm here."

"*We're* here," Carin interjects.

"See?" I wave my fork between the two of them. "This is why I can't live with you guys. You mean too much to me. Besides, this is working for me. I've got nearly ten months to save up before classes start next fall. I've got this."

"At least come for a drink with us after this thing is over," Carin begs.

"I have to drive home." I make a face. "I'm scheduled to go in and sort packages tomorrow."

"On a Sunday?" Hope demands.

"Time and a half. I couldn't turn it down. Actually, I should probably take off soon." I lay my plate on the table and try to catch a glimpse of what's going on beyond the huge bay window. All I see is darkness and streaks of rain on the glass. "Sooner I'm on the road, the better."

"Not in this weather you're not." Professor Gibson appears at my elbow with a glass of wine. "The weather advisory is for sheets of glass—temperature's dropping and the rain is turning into ice."

One look at my adviser's face and I know I have to concede. So I do, but with great reluctance.

"All right," I say, "but I do this under protest. And you." I tip my fork in Carin's direction. "You better have ice cream in the freezer in case I have to crash with you, otherwise I'm going to be really mad."

All three of them laugh. Professor Gibson wanders off, leaving us to network as best as three college seniors can. After an hour of mingling, Hope, Carin, and I grab our coats.

"Where are we going?" I ask the girls.

"D'Andre is at Malone's and I said I'd meet him there," Hope tells me. "It's like a two-minute drive, so we should be fine."

"Really? Malone's? That's a hockey bar," I whine. "What's D'Andre doing there?"

"Drinking and waiting for me. Besides, you need to get laid and athletes are your favorite type."

Carin snorts. "Her only type."

"Hey, I have a very good reason for preferring athletes," I argue.

"I know. We've heard it." She rolls her eyes. "If you want a stats question answered, go to the math geeks. If you want a physical need met, go to an athlete. Bodies are the tools of an elite athlete. They take care of it, know how to push its limits, yada yada." Carin makes a yapping gesture with her left hand.

I flick up my middle finger.

"But sex with someone you like is so much better." This comes from Hope, who's been with D'Andre, her football player boyfriend, since freshman year.

"I like them," I protest. "…In bed."

We share a giggle over that, until Carin brings up a guy who brought down the average.

"Do you remember Ten-Second Greg, though?"

I shudder. "First, thank you very little for bringing that bad memory up, and second, I'm not saying there aren't duds. Just that the odds are better with an athlete."

"And the hockey players are duds?" Carin asks.

I shrug. "I wouldn't know. I didn't ax them from my list of potentials because of their performance in the sack, but because they're hyper-privileged jerks who get special favors from the profs."

"Sabrina, girl, you got to let that go," Hope urges.

"Nope. Hockey players don't make the cut."

"God, but look at what you're missing out on." Carin licks her lips with exaggerated lasciviousness. "That one guy on the team with the beard? I want to know what that feels like. Beards are on my bucket list."

"Go on, then. My boycott against hockey players just means more for you."

"I'm on board with this, but…" She smirks. "Need I remind you that you hooked up with the man-slut Di Laurentis?"

Ugh. That's a reminder I *never* need to hear.

"First, I was totally drunk," I grumble. "Second, that was sophomore year. And third, he's the reason I've sworn off hockey players."

Even though Briar University has a championship-winning football team, it's known as a hockey college. The guys who wear skates are treated like gods. Case in point: Dean Heyward-Di Laurentis. He's a poli-sci major like me, so we've had several classes together, including statistics in our sophomore year. That course was hard as fuck. Everyone struggled.

Everyone but Dean, who was screwing the TA.

And—shocker!—she gave him an A, which he absolutely did *not* deserve. I know this for a fact, because we were paired together for the final assignment, and I saw the garbage he turned in.

When I found out he aced it, I wanted to chop his dick off. It was so unfair. I worked my butt off in that course. Hell, I work my butt off for everything. My every accomplishment is stained with my blood, sweat, and tears. Meanwhile, some asshole gets the world handed to him on a platter? Fuck. That.

"She's getting mad again," Hope stage-whispers to Carin.

"She's thinking about how Di Laurentis got an A in that one class," Carin shout-whispers back. "She really does need to get laid. How long has it been?"

I start to flip her off again when it occurs to me that I can't remember my last hookup.

"There was, um, Meyer? The lacrosse guy. That was in September. And after that was Beau…" I brighten up. "Ha! See? It's only been a little over a month. Hardly a national emergency."

"Girl, someone with your schedule isn't allowed to go a *month* without sex," Hope counters. "You're a walking ball of stress, which means you need a good dicking at least…daily," she decides.

"Every other day," Carin argues. "Give her lady garden some time to rest."

Hope nods. "Fine. But no rest for the pussy tonight—"

I snort in laughter.

"You hear that, B? You've been fed, you had an afternoon nap, and now you need some sexy times," Carin declares.

"But Malone's?" I repeat warily. "We just established that the place is crawling with hockey players."

"Not exclusively. I bet Beau is there. Want me to ask D'Andre?" Hope holds up her phone, but I shake my head.

"Beau's too much of a time commitment. Like he wanted to talk during sex. I want to do the deed and leave."

"Oooh, talking! Scary."

"Shut it."

"Make me." Hope tosses her head, her long braids smacking against my coat, and then exits Professor Gibson's house.

Carin shrugs and follows her, and after a second of hesitation, I do too. Our coats are drenched by the time we reach Hope's car, but we have our hoods on, so our hair survives the downpour.

I'm really not in the mood to chat up any guys tonight, but I can't deny that my friends are right. I've been plagued with tension for weeks, and these past few days I've definitely been feeling the…

itch. The kind of itch that can only be scratched with a hard, ripped body and a hopefully above average-sized cock.

Except I'm extremely selective about who I hook up with, and just as I'd feared, Malone's is thick with hockey players when the girls and I stride inside five minutes later.

But hey, if that's the hand I've been dealt, then I guess there's no harm in playing it and seeing what happens.

Still, I have zero expectations as I follow my friends to the bar counter.

ACKNOWLEDGMENTS

I've been dying to tackle Dean's book since I first introduced him as Garrett's roommate in *The Deal*. I couldn't frickin' wait, because I just KNEW he was going to be so much fun to write—and he did not let me down. I had a blast with this story, and I'm so thrilled you guys took the time to read it!

Note: I fudged the timing in regards to the hockey team's holiday schedule. Most Division I teams play through December and January, but I wanted Dean to have a longer stretch of time off, so I cheated with the timing of it. But I loved every second that Dean and Allie spent together in New York. So...I regret nothing! Nothing, I tell ya!

As always, I want to thank my early readers/cheerleaders/besties for helping me whip this book into shape: Viv, Jen, Sarina, Katy, Monica, Nicole, and Sophie. I love you guys.

On the business end, I couldn't survive without Nic and Natasha (friends and assistants extraordinaire!), Gwen (don't ever leave me!), Sharon (we still need to plan the wedding), and the person who keeps me sane: Nina Bocci.

To everyone at Bloom Books, for their enthusiasm and love for this series: my editor, Christa Désir, and the rest of the team: Pam, Molly, and Katie.

Kimberly Brower, for some pretty kickass agenting.

To all the bloggers and reviewers who helped with cover reveals, posted reviews, and pretty much talked up the series to anyone who would listen—you are rock stars. Rock. Stars.

And to all my readers—you have no idea how honored I am that you continue to support/love/gush over this series. You guys are awesomesauce to the degree of amazeballs!

ABOUT THE AUTHOR

A *New York Times*, *USA Today*, and *Wall Street Journal* bestselling author, Elle Kennedy grew up in the suburbs of Toronto, Ontario, and holds a BA in English from York University. From an early age, she knew she wanted to be a writer and actively began pursuing that dream when she was a teenager. She loves strong heroines and sexy alpha heroes and just enough heat and danger to keep things interesting!

Elle loves to hear from her readers. Visit her website ellekennedy .com or sign up for her newsletter to receive updates about upcoming books and exclusive excerpts. You can also find her on Facebook or follow her on Twitter (@ElleKennedy).

THE MISTAKE

He's a player in more ways than one...

College junior John Logan can get any girl he wants. For this hockey star, life is a parade of parties and hookups, but behind his killer grins and easygoing charm, he hides growing despair about the dead-end road he'll be forced to walk after graduation. A sexy encounter with freshman Grace Ivers is just the distraction he needs, but when a thoughtless mistake pushes her away, Logan plans to spend his final year proving to her that he's worth a second chance.

Now he's going to need to up his game...

After a less-than-stellar freshman year, Grace is back at Briar University, older, wiser, and so over the arrogant hockey player she nearly handed her V card to. She's not a charity case, and she's not the quiet butterfly she was when they first hooked up. If Logan expects her to roll over and beg like all his other puck bunnies, he can think again. He wants her back? He'll have to work for it. This time around, she'll be the one in the driver's seat...and she plans on driving him wild.

THE GOAL

She's good at achieving her goals...

College senior Sabrina James has her whole future planned out: graduate from college, kick butt in law school, and land a high-paying job at a cutthroat firm. Her path to escaping her shameful past certainly doesn't include a gorgeous hockey player who believes in love at first sight. One night of sizzling heat and surprising tenderness is all she's willing to give John Tucker, but sometimes, one night is all it takes for your entire life to change.

But the game just got a whole lot more complicated

Tucker believes being a team player is as important as being the star. On the ice, he's fine staying out of the spotlight, but when it comes to becoming a daddy at the age of twenty-two, he refuses to be a benchwarmer. It doesn't hurt that the soon-to-be mother of his child is beautiful, whip-smart, and keeps him on his toes. The problem is, Sabrina's heart is locked up tight, and the fiery brunette is too stubborn to accept his help. If he wants a life with the woman of his dreams, he'll have to convince her that some goals can only be made with an assist.

THE LEGACY

**Four stories. Four couples. Three years
of real life after graduation...**

A wedding.

A proposal.

An elopement.

And a surprise pregnancy.

Life after college for Garrett and Hannah, Logan and Grace, Dean
and Allie, and Tucker and Sabrina isn't quite what they imagined it
would be. Sure, they have each other, but they also have real-life
problems that four years at Briar U didn't exactly prepare them for.
And it turns out, for these four couples, love is the easy part. Growing
up is a whole lot harder.

Catch up with your favorite Off-Campus characters as they navigate
the changes that come with growing up and discover that big
decisions can have big consequences...and if they're lucky, big
rewards.